NONE
LEFT
TO TELL

NOELLE W. IHLI

Published 2024 by Dynamite Books

ISBN: 979-8-9878455-8-5

This book is a work of fiction. References to real historical events, people, or places are intended to provide a sense of authenticity and are used fictitiously. All other names, characters, and places are products of the author's imagination.

First printing, October 2024.

Dynamite Books, LLC

ADVANCE PRAISE FOR
NONE LEFT TO TELL

For Saleta and Kahpeputz.
You have not been forgotten.

Here 120 men, women, and children were massacred in cold blood early in September.
They were from Arkansas.

–Inscription by US Cavalry, marking a mass grave at Mountain Meadows, Utah

AUTHOR'S NOTE

This was not an easy book to write.

The story that follows is fiction; however, it is tightly based on real events that took place in Southern Utah. What happened during that five-day attack in September outside Cedar City was one of the deadliest massacres on US soil prior to September 11th, 2001. Despite this fact, most people are not familiar with the story.

Those who know it are typically the descendants of the ones who perpetuated and hid this heinous crime.

That's the reason I know this story.

And that's the reason I'm telling it now.

— Noelle W. Ihli

CONTENT ADVISORY

This book contains some graphic descriptions of violence, including violence against children; the death of a child; and a non-graphic scene involving the death of an animal. It also includes outdated and racially insensitive phrases and words about Native people, endemic to the time period.

NOTE ON HISTORICITY

This novel is firmly rooted in real events. I relied heavily on research from historians including Juanita Brooks (author of *The Mountain Meadows Massacre*), Will Bagley (author of *Blood of the Prophets*), and Barbara Jones Brown and Richard E. Turley, Jr. (authors of *Vengeance Is Mine*). That said, I have taken some liberties for the sake of clarity, pacing, and coherence. For instance, some character and location names have been changed or consolidated (there were a *lot* of people named Joseph in this particular story). I've also condensed the chronology of events in some places to maintain pacing and narrative. While all quotations used in this book are drawn from real historical documents, I have condensed and edited some for brevity and to enhance readability for a contemporary audience. Any deviations made from real names, events, or quotations were made with careful consideration and the goal of preserving their original spirit and intent.

— Noelle W. Ihli

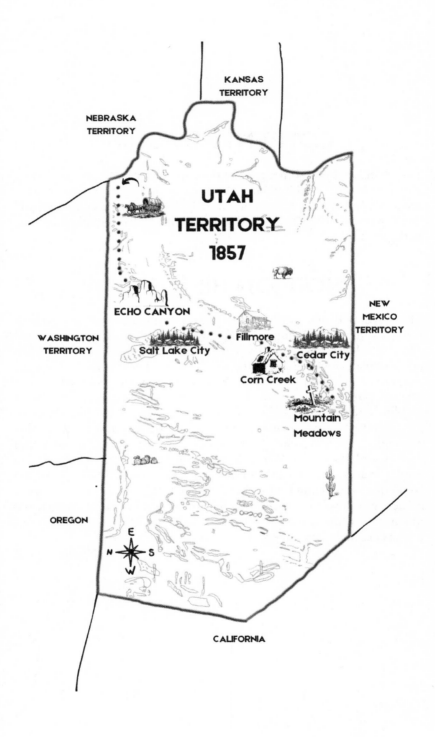

CHARACTER LIST

ARKANSANS
Katrina and Peter Huff
Children: Mary (17 years old), William (9 years old), James (14 years old), Nancy (6 years old)

Louisa and Urial Huff (Brother of Peter Huff)
Children: Triphena (1 year old)

UTAHANS
Lucy and Vick Robison
Children: Proctor (14 years old), Almon (10 years old), Albert (8 years old), Adelia (4 years old)

Chief Kanosh
Wives: Kahpeputz (Sally), Inola, Numa, Povi
Children: Awan (17 years old)

*Map by Brett Mitchell Kent

NANCY HUFF

The sky, then weeds and dirt, spun in front of my face.

All I could see through the brush in the Meadow were bodies falling down and red, so much red.

All I could hear was crying and screaming and lots of booms.

"Mama!" I screamed, but my voice got lost in a hundred others.

She was already pulling me down to the ground, scrambling into the sagebrush. The branches scratched my arms, and the sharp smell bit my nose.

"Don't look," Mama whisper-cried, turning her head to me, her voice so upset it frightened me even more. There were tears on her cheeks. Her brown eyes were wider than I'd ever seen. "Stay quiet, baby. Follow me."

Then Mama started crawling on her hands and knees, belly low to the ground.

I wanted to ask where we were going, but I was too scared to do anything but crawl after her through the grass and around trees.

We were headed toward the front of the group. It was the last place we'd seen Aunt Louisa and Mary.

I tried not to think about James and William and Uncle Uri.

Any second, I just knew that one of the evil men was going to leap on top of us and bash our heads with a club, too.

When we got to a thicket of brush so dense we had to part the weeds to look, Mama peeked out. She didn't stop me when I did the same.

The red-stained Meadow turned blurry in front of my eyes, and my body felt floaty and heavy at the same time.

No, no, no.

That was when I finally saw Mary and Aunt Louisa.

They were holding onto each other, trying to run this way, then that. Mary's braids had come undone, and they whipped across her face.

A man with a big rock in his hand ran straight for them, showing his teeth like he wanted to bite them.

I knew I was screaming again, knew Mary was screaming too from the way her mouth moved, but I couldn't hear any of it anymore, just my heavy breaths and heartbeats in my ears.

Mama was shaking. I was shaking.

There was nowhere to look that wasn't bad, so I closed my eyes.

SIX WEEKS EARLIER

1. KATRINA HUFF

CORN CREEK, UTAH
AUGUST 1857
60 DAYS TO CALIFORNIA

Whoever said that little girls are made of sugar and spice and everything nice never met girls.

Not mine, anyway.

Over the past four months, they'd turned fully feral.

Six-year-old Nancy had been dragging a dead snake through the wagon ruts for the last three miles, insisting her daddy would earn a good price for the "rattler" when we traded for supplies next. I couldn't argue that the demand for rattlesnake tails—and their supposed medicinal properties—was surprisingly high. But Nancy's seventeen-year-old sister Mary knew full well it was a gopher snake.

If I had to guess, this was Mary's way of keeping her brothers away for the afternoon. Both of my snips-and-snails-and-puppy-dogs'-tails boys were terrified of anything that slithered.

I sighed and slowed my pace to avoid the worst of the dust our wagon wheels churned up a few yards ahead. I could only imagine how tightly my mother would have clutched her pearls to see my girls wearing nothing but loose-fitting nightshirts and dust-caked bloomers, their hair in raggedy braids, playing with a dead snake. When we'd left Arkansas in the spring, I would have joined her in giving the girls a lecture about *young ladies* and *unseemly behavior*.

Even my mother would have taken off her corset by now, though.

Over the past four months, we had walked nearly a thousand miles.

Peter and I had forced our four children to drink the putrid, grassy contents of a heifer's stomach when we ran out of water outside Nebraska Territory.

I'd seen one of our family's wagons and two of our oxen burn when a prairie fire swept across the sunbaked grass, racing us to the rocky pass.

And I'd watched the Haydons, our neighbors back in Arkansas, lose two of their children when a wagon tipped, crushing the boys.

There would be time to tame my children again when we reached our destination in California.

For now, I focused on the fact that Mary's cough—the one that sometimes turned the sleeve of her dress red when she covered her mouth—was getting better day by day in the arid desert. Just like we'd hoped. Most of the members of our sprawling wagon train had packed their bags with dreams of fertile soil and orchards that gave twice what they did in Arkansas. But Peter and I had been content with our modest peach harvest and our cocoon of family who visited for Sunday dinner every week. That was until the rattle in Mary's lungs got so bad she could barely get out of bed. Dr. Jarrel finally put it like this: *The tuberculosis loves the humidity. It isn't going anywhere unless you leave it behind. And you'd better do it soon.*

"Ba da, da, dah, and joy be to you all!" Nancy's strong, clear baby voice rose above the sound of the lumbering wagon. She flicked the bedraggled snake side to side with each word.

I smiled in spite of the sweat dripping down my back and the ache in my feet. It was the song her father, Peter, sang while he unyoked the oxen at night, insisting it calmed the animals. That line was Nancy's favorite, and the lyrics tumbled out of her mouth at random most days.

At least she hadn't pestered me to ride in the wagon today. I hated to tell her no when she asked, but forcing the exhausted oxen to pull any extra weight was out of the question. The animals had started the trip fat and sassy, but were shriveling into lean, weary versions of their former selves; a mirror image of the land around us as it withered. The dry, sagebrush-choked Utah Territory we had now reached seemed to get hotter by the day. There was hardly any grass. And the last so-called creek we'd crossed had been so dried up, it was mostly mud.

"Mary, can you see Uncle Uri and Aunt Louisa's wagon?" I called, squinting through the dry silt suspended in air. "Are you doing all right in this dust?" We'd spread out farther than usual today, to avoid the worst of the dust. It had driven Louisa to wrap her eighteen-month-old baby in blankets from head to toe, despite the heat.

Mary flashed me a smile. "I'm all right, Mama. Just a few little coughs." Then she turned her head and pointed at the back of our wagon. "I can hardly see anything ahead. James probably can, though." James was my fourteen-year-old son.

Mary wrinkled up her nose and laughed. "Did I tell you? Baby Triphena said 'papa' this morning. But she was looking at James when she did it. Not Uncle Uri."

I smiled. "I bet Uri lost his mind." Peter's brother was the proudest papa I'd ever seen. I was thrilled when he and Louisa decided to come along to California. They were one more bit of home to hold onto. I still told myself maybe my parents would make the journey when the railroad finally spanned east to west.

James held the reins in the driver's seat in the wagon ahead. He always drove the oxen when Peter was helping the cattle hands wrangle the steers. I should have been the one driving, but I still balked at the idea of sitting on that tiny wooden bench above the enormous four-legged creatures who had the power to tip us if they wanted.

Bang.

A gunshot cracked in the distance and I jumped.

I should have been used to the sound by now, but my insides seized up anyway. I scolded myself for startling over nothing.

"It's okay, Mama!" Nancy called to me, dragging the snake past a cow pie in her path.

Even the milk cow, lumbering behind the wagon, barely flinched. She'd been as nervous as I was at the start of the journey, bawling all day and tugging at her rope. Now she just sighed.

We're safe.

We're together.

We're nearly there.

I'd been repeating those sentences to myself since we left Arkansas for California.

I hated nearly everything about the trail west.

7

But as long as those three things stayed true, I could last one more day.

2. KATRINA HUFF

CORN CREEK, UTAH

AUGUST 1857

60 DAYS TO CALIFORNIA

Like most of the women in our wagon train, I'd had soft hands and a soft bed all my life.

Marrying my Peter was the first wild thing I'd ever done.

This arduous journey was the second.

I'd grown up practicing the piano, reading poetry, and learning to manage a home. He'd grown up with his hands in the dirt, tending to peach trees in his family's small orchard near the tupelo gum swamps—and selling them at a roadside stand on the main road through Benton. I loved peaches, and I loved Peter from the first day I saw him sitting there surrounded by all that ripe fruit with his dark, curly hair and baby-blue eyes. When he asked if I'd like to walk with him through the orchard that evening, I said yes.

I'd been saying yes to him ever since, even when it meant walking halfway across the country in the dirt.

Part of me envied him and the children for how easily they'd shed their skin and become wild here. A bigger part of me just wanted to cook a meal over a real stove and sleep in a real bed again. Every day on the trail to California felt like holding my breath. But every day, I watched Mary breathe a little easier. Even with all the dust. It was just enough to keep me moving.

I watched as Mary whispered something to Nancy and waggled her fingers at the poor snake. Nancy squealed in delight—then suddenly shrieked.

Like a ghost materializing through the dust, nine-year-old William brushed past me and dashed toward his sisters. Then he yanked on one of Mary's braids before darting just out of her reach. "Better watch out, or the Mormons will get ya both!"

Before I could open my mouth to scold him, Mary had snatched the dead snake out of Nancy's hands and lobbed it after her brother as hard as she could throw. "You leave us alone, William Huff, or the next one will be in your bedroll!"

The snake hit William squarely in the chest. He howled and thrust out his hands, pitching the poor dead creature into the sagebrush, where it disappeared.

Nancy stopped walking. "My rattler! Mary, my rattler!"

"It's all right. It had a small tail anyway," Mary soothed, glaring at William.

I sighed. "William Thomas Huff, leave your sisters alone. I won't have that kind of talk about the Mormons, either."

He pushed out his lower lip. "But Uncle Uri said—"

"I don't care what Uncle Uri said," I insisted, rolling my eyes.

The farther we moved into Utah Territory, the more Peter's brother Uri had been filling the children's heads with stories about Mormons. I'd heard some of the rumors back in Arkansas. A dozen wives to each man, a militia that planned to overthrow the government and place their prophet—Brigham Young—as king of the entire country. There was even talk about human sacrifices in their temples. I suspected that some of the rumors were meant to keep children from wandering too far from their wagons. For instance, the stories about Mormons kidnapping young women in order to hypnotize them into becoming polygamous wives.

Mary took Nancy's hand and gave William a withering look as she fell back to walk alongside me. I stifled a laugh. With the girls' dust-caked hair and clothes, they practically faded into our surroundings. The only color they had to set them apart was their wide blue eyes. If Mormons *were* roving around looking for young women to kidnap, my children would be passed over if only for how well they blended in with the earth itself.

"Listen to your father—and Captain Alexander. *Not* Uncle Uri," I insisted.

According to Captain Alexander, who had led another wagon train through Utah just a few years earlier, the Mormons were friendly people and eager to trade. It was part of the reason we'd taken the Overland Trail this way. With nearly one hundred and forty travelers in our group, two hundred and fifty head of cattle, and wagons loaded for a new life in California, all of us valued safety over speed. The local Indians had been some trouble, but everyone traveling west knew to expect that. We'd already had three cattle raids so far since crossing into the territory. The cattle hands we'd hired to defend the animals did their best, but our herd was so big that we were still vulnerable to careful thieves at night.

A breeze cleared the dust for a few moments to show the molten horizon, where the earth sizzled in the heat. My shoulders hunched in relief when I saw that the dots I'd caught sight of earlier had taken shape into horses, cattle, and the first wagons circling up near the shimmer of a stream—Corn Creek. With fifteen more minutes of walking, we'd be there. But now that I could see the creek more clearly, it was smaller than I'd hoped. And I knew that by the time the cattle finished tromping around, it'd be mostly mud.

My neck itched at the idea of fresh water and a bath. Even little Nancy, who could hardly ever be bothered to bathe anymore, had started asking when she'd be able to swim again. The lakes and ponds we'd taken for granted in Arkansas, then Kansas, had long since disappeared. The water we gathered came from muddy ponds and the occasional shallow river now.

I tried to pick out my Peter's lanky shape and dark curls before the breeze and the wagon wheels kicked the relentless dust skyward again. He'd ridden ahead with the cattle hands hours ago. Once the steers had smelled water, there was no holding them back. Weary as they were from the drought and poor forage, they'd flared their nostrils at the scent of water then lifted their tails like calves and ran.

"Just a little farther," I called to the children, wondering how many times I'd repeated those exact words. Even Bright and Belle, our little red oxen, seemed to understand me from the way the wagon wheels rolled a little faster.

Two more months until we reached California.

Sixty more days of *one more mile*, feral children, and the cursed dust.

I followed Bright and Belle's cue and picked up my pace, eager to see Peter again—and eager to find the end of another endless day. I'd tucked away my parents' efforts to raise a woman of society just like the first editions of *Jane Eyre* and *Wuthering Heights* I'd wrapped in quilts and brought along. Beautiful, but frivolous compared to our spare wagon axles, food, and clothing.

I could recite poetry by Emerson. I could turn fabric into a quilt with my confident stitches. I could teach my girls the proper way to set a table. But there were no tables to be set anymore. No spare fabric for quilting. And all the Emerson in the world couldn't fix a broken wagon axle or deliver a calf.

When I said this in tears to Peter one night, a week into the trek, he fixed me with a look so serious I was afraid I'd convinced him. Instead, he said, "If I wanted somebody who could deliver a calf, I would have married one of the cattle hands."

When I refused to laugh, he pulled me to him and kissed me, tasting like leather and sweat. "What was the line from that poem—the one about the honey you recited on our wedding night? I need that a whole lot more than I need a wagon axle right now."

I finally softened, leaning closer to his ear to whisper, "Come nigh to me limber-hipp'd man. Stand at my side till I lean as high as I can upon you. Fill me with albescent honey …"

I let that memory carry me twenty more minutes until the wind lifted the swirling brown clouds in a gust that sent the girls—and William, who was walking a few paces behind his sisters—laughing as it made their loose shirts billow. Mary's cough drew my ear like it always did, but the sound was dry. Nothing like the terrifying wet rattle from before.

When the dust settled, I could finally see the circling wagons, riders, and cattle right in front of us.

A smile softened the set of my jaw.

We'd made it one more day.

We're safe.

We're together.

We're nearly there.

My eyes found Peter just as the wind set the dust back down.

Then the smile died on my lips.

He stood over one of the steers. The black-and-white animal was sprawled on its side, unmoving.

Peter's rifle lay on the ground, at his feet. I darted my eyes to the blood pooling from a bullet hole in the steer's stomach.

At first, I thought maybe he'd shot it for meat, but that didn't make sense either. Butchering a steer would take time we didn't have. There were nearly two hundred head of cattle that needed grass and more water—and we wouldn't find much of that for another hundred miles when we reached Mountain Meadows.

When my eyes locked on Peter again, I saw what I'd missed at first glance. There was a stricken look on his face—and a bit of red dripping through the curls at his neck.

I picked up my skirt and ran past the wagon, where James had pulled the oxen to a stop.

"What happened? Are you all right?" I couldn't get the words out fast enough.

Peter shook his head, still staring at the dead steer. His hand went to his neck. "I'm okay. I didn't expect him to charge. Caught me with his horn." He kept his eyes locked on the animal. "Poor forage and bad grass is making them crazy."

My heart stayed in my throat until I got close enough to verify for myself that Peter truly was all right, and grateful to see it was just a nasty scratch across his neck. Just a little blood.

"Daddy? Daddy, I had a good little rattler earlier, but William made me lose it," Nancy called from behind us.

I turned to tell Mary to take Nancy and William to collect sagebrush, so we could start a fire.

Before the last word left my mouth, Peter dropped to his knees.

3. KATRINA HUFF

CORN CREEK, UTAH

AUGUST 1857

59 DAYS TO CALIFORNIA

Within an hour, the wound on Peter's neck went from a scrape to a weeping ulcer.

His neck swelled up like the throat pouch of a toad.

After another hour, the fever and chills took hold.

Then the vomiting.

Then the stillness.

His breathing became so shallow, I kept my ear against his chest all night, to feel for the rise and fall.

None of it made sense. He'd been fine one moment, suffering the next.

My throat constricted in what felt like an inkling toward panic, but I couldn't fall apart. He was sick, but he'd get better. He *had* to get better. That was all there was to it.

We're safe.

We're together.

We're nearly there.

The words galloped faster with each passing hour, a prayer that lasted all night. While the children slept at the front of the wagon, I crouched beside Peter in the back with a wet cloth for his forehead. Every so often, I dipped my fingers in the sticky salve Uri's wife Louisa had given me and applied another layer to Peter's injury. His skin was so hot to the touch, the ointment melted in drips that ran down his shirt and under the collar.

When I ran out of words, I whispered the lyrics to the song he sang to the cattle each night. The one Nancy loved. The tune was

15

sweet and simple, an old Irish melody that reminded me of "Auld Lang Syne." The words always brought a lump to my throat. And tonight, they closed it altogether.

Of all the comrades that e'er I had
They are sorry for my going away
And all the sweethearts that e'er I had
They would wish me one more day to stay

But since it falls unto my lot
That I should rise and you should not
I'll gently rise and I'll softly call
Good night and joy be with you all.

* * *

At the crack of dawn, the Paiute Indians at Corn Creek demanded we break camp and leave. Their chief, a man named Kanosh, rode out to deliver the message himself. They'd been polite when we made camp. But that was before our herds of cattle had overwhelmed Corn Creek, churning the water into mud as the animals frantically ate up the precious grass.

The captain of our wagon train, Alexander Fancher, didn't argue with the Paiutes. We were in their territory for the next two hundred miles. We didn't need any trouble.

Three more of our steers had died overnight, bloating up so quickly that they almost looked like their former fat selves. There wasn't time to butcher any of them.

I stayed in the wagon bed beside Peter while James drove the oxen. I no longer cared how much I asked of Bright and Belle in carrying our extra weight.

When Peter woke up after barely a mile, he cried out so loudly that James pulled back on the reins.

"Mama?" James called. So many questions in that one word. Questions I felt creeping around the outskirts of my mind, too, but refused to entertain.

"It's all right," I told James in the strongest voice I could, even though Peter's breath came in shallow bursts and he arched up like he was trying to escape his own body. His neck had swollen to twice its usual size now, mottled red and purple. It hurt just to look at his stretched skin, so hot and tight.

I let my hand drift up to my own neck, startled to find the collar of my dress wet with tears.

"Stay with me," I begged him in a whisper. Then I lay my head back gently against his chest, not wanting to add any extra pressure at all. I closed my eyes, willing him to be well again.

"Your body to me is sweet, clean, loving, strong,

"Your eyes are more to me than poems,

"Your lips do better than play music,

"The lines of your cheeks, the lashes of your eyes, are eloquent to me." I choked on the last sentence, but Peter's breathing had turned shallow and calm again.

"Mama, is Papa any better?" James called every mile or so from the front of the wagon. Mary and Nancy echoed him from the back.

"He might be," was the best I could manage, less of a lie and more of a refusal to let myself believe anything else.

We circled the wagons as soon as Corn Creek was out of sight. I knew Captain Alexander was stopping because of Peter. I also knew that, no matter what happened, we couldn't stop for long. Not for the sake of one family.

Uri set out to find a doctor in Fillmore—less than half an hour's ride. James rode with him on our sweet-tempered sorrel mare.

While they were gone, Peter asked for whiskey in a raspy voice, even though he couldn't swallow much more than a drop at a time. Mary, Louisa, and I took turns sitting next to him, dipping a cloth into the bottle to dribble a little into his mouth every time he cried.

At first, I wouldn't let Nancy in the wagon, worried the sight of Peter's neck would be too much for her. But she put up such a fuss, I finally let her nestle beside him. "I need to sing to him, Mama. It'll help."

"Ba da, da, da," she whispered, again and again. "And joy be to you all."

The sound of it made me choke up, and so I went to the back of the wagon, standing with eyes on the horizon watching for James and Uri until the sun dipped low.

I'd sent them with enough money for ten doctors. So why weren't they back yet?

When daylight slipped past the hills to the west, I finally made out the silhouette of two horses, riding fast toward our camp.

Nancy and William ran out to meet them, waving their hands as if they might miss our sprawling wagon party.

My breath hitched when I saw James's face, bracing and dazed, like he'd been kicked in the stomach.

"Damned Mormons," was all Uri would say at first.

My stomach lurched. "What happened?"

James's eyes were wide as he slipped from the saddle. "They pointed their guns at us, Mama."

When Uri finally calmed down enough to tell me what happened, he said they'd been stopped by a group of Mormon riders in uniform —a raggedy militia—at a long border of rocks stacked chest-high outside Fillmore.

"Plenty of Indians in these parts," one of the uniformed riders had said ominously. "You should go back to your wagons."

"Ain't that the gun?" another man had piped up before Uri could answer, indicating the pistol at his side.

"The gun?" Uri had asked in confusion.

"The one you used to kill Brother Parley P. Pratt back in Arkansas," a third man spat.

When Uri had tried to tell him he didn't know who Parley P. Pratt was, that he just needed a doctor and medicine, the riders raised their weapons.

"Move along, gentiles," James said another man had warned.

And then Uri told me that when he and James rode farther south in search of another town, the uniforms followed close behind.

Gentiles. I blinked in horrified confusion. What did that mean? Back in Arkansas, I'd only ever heard that word used in Bible verses. "Jews and gentiles" and the like.

"Here, it means anybody who's not Mormon," Uri explained, tight-lipped. "We're the gentiles. Dirty outsiders."

Uri and James were told there was no doctor. There was no medicine. Not in Fillmore. Not in Meadow. Not in any of the cities or forts in Southern Utah. Not at any price. Not for "gentiles."

* * *

When the tremors that racked Peter's body let him go in one last violent shudder, I dared to hope he would come back to me.

But when I lifted my head from his chest and looked into his glassy eyes and gaping mouth, the hope withered.

"Kit," was all he said, half-groan, half-gasp.

"I'm here," I told him, trying not to let my tears fall onto his skin.

The wagon jostled a little, and Uri came to crouch beside me.

He lay a hand on my arm.

"No, no, no." I watched for Peter's chest to rise again. My eyes blurred, but I refused to blink in case I missed it. But his chest stayed perfectly still.

"Peter? Peter, come back to me," I begged.

"No such thing as an easy death, Kit," Uri choked out.

He said it like he was revealing some truth about the world. Like death was just one more thing I'd been sheltered from back in Arkansas.

But he was wrong. I already knew death didn't take anyone gently by the hand.

It ripped from the roots.

Even my grandmother, who died in her sleep at seventy-five, didn't pass easily. We all insisted she did. Everyone talked about peace and dignity and the blessing of dying in your bed. But I'd been the one to find her, tangled in the quilt that morning, after clutching her chest so hard she'd ripped the pearl buttons off her nightgown and broken the skin with her seashell-smooth nails.

My grandmother's passing, and the other handful of losses we'd had on the trail, lapped at my feet like the Mississippi in winter: icy and sharp, but bearable once you warmed yourself by a fire.

Peter's death was different. His death swallowed me whole, like the swamps at the border of the peach orchard we'd left behind in Arkansas. The place we'd told the children never to play, with warnings of quicksand, gators, and snakes as thick as your thigh.

Uri and some of the other men began digging a grave to bury Peter an hour later, three feet down in the hard earth, already scorching with the first rays of daylight beating on the desert floor. James and William helped, even though Uri kept trying to guide them back to the scant shade of the circled wagons, where Mary and I sat with Peter's quilt-wrapped body.

Nancy refused to be comforted—or watch. I could still hear my youngest daughter's cries coming from within the sagebrush a short distance from camp.

With each strike of the shovels, my heart shuddered and I gripped the quilt edge a little harder.

When the men finished digging, sweat—or tears—dripping down their faces, the grave looked so shallow that Mary cried, "But Mama, the coyotes will get him."

There wasn't time for anything deeper, though. We had to keep moving. Captain Alexander warned that there wouldn't be any more grass for the cattle for another hundred miles.

Two more oxen had died early that morning, bloating up so quickly that Captain Alexander warned us not to eat the meat.

The steers were going mad. Maybe from bad forage on the drought-choked plains. Maybe from the water at Corn Creek.

It was impossible to say.

All I knew was that everything in Utah Territory, it seemed, was mad.

4. KAHPEPUTZ (SALLY)

CORN CREEK, UTAH

AUGUST 1857

"Just *go*, Sally. You know the way. *Bake bread*," Numa told me, pointing at the well-worn trail that led to the white Mormons' settlement in Fillmore.

I glanced east, where the sun hadn't yet appeared over the distant mountain peaks. The morning air was already buzzing with cicadas and scorching hot. Then I looked back at Numa, confused.

I'd only been to Lucy Robison's house once, having just arrived at the Paiute tribe in Corn Creek. I was pretty sure I remembered the way. But I was shocked that Numa and Povi, Kanosh's third and second wives who had been put in charge of watching me for the day, didn't insist on coming along.

If they were going to let me walk to Fillmore alone, I wasn't about to complain, though.

I took a step away from the wickiup, where Povi was gathering everything they'd need to butcher two of the four dead steers the wagon train had left behind. Kanosh—my new husband—had forced the group to move on earlier that morning.

"Heavenly Father, thank you for this bounty," Povi murmured, bowing her head but keeping her eyes open.

"Amen," Numa added happily.

I stayed silent and kept my gaze toward the mountains. All of the Paiute Indians at Corn Creek—including Chief Kanosh—were Mormon. They'd been converted by missionaries over the past three years. I was Mormon too, technically, anyway. I wasn't Paiute, though. I was Bannock. Not that anybody had asked. Not that I would answer.

21

I looked around, but Kanosh's first wife, Inola, was nowhere to be seen. Of the three wives—four, now that I was here—she was the most diligent in Kanosh's orders to keep me in sight.

They all thought I might run, if given the chance.

Still, I suspected that they knew, deep down, that I had nowhere to go.

Povi looked at me and smirked, studying my ridiculous outfit. The one Chief Kanosh still insisted I wear around the Paiute camp.

The only thing I liked about the ugly dress was that it had strange, large pockets on the sides that hid the little yucca-spine horses I'd had for as long as I could remember. One horse was mine. One had once belonged to a little boy named Tyee. I couldn't remember who made the horses for us—someone among my Bannock birth tribe—but I liked to think it was my mother.

I was proud that I'd managed to hide them all these years, tucked away and unseen, like every other tender part of me I'd pushed down deep.

I ran one finger along the rabbit-skin mane of the horse in my left pocket, then the right, feeling instantly calmer.

Povi was staring at me when I met her eyes again. "Brigham's strange little doll," she clucked for the hundredth time since I'd arrived five weeks earlier.

I held my tongue and kept my face blank, pretending not to understand.

Numa snickered. "Not much of a doll with that scarred face," she murmured, and the two women laughed out loud. "Should we let her change into moccasins, at least? Those ridiculous shoes are going to fall apart on the walk to Fillmore."

Povi put down the knife she'd been sharpening and studied my feet in amusement. "I guess so. Kanosh will be angry if she ruins them."

I clenched my jaw but took my hands out of my pockets and gratefully accepted the moccasins Numa handed me. I hated my new husband almost as much as I hated the pinchy shoes and scratchy black crinoline dress he insisted I wear instead of the softer, simpler dresses the Paiute women wore.

Even Brigham Young's wife Clara, who I'd attended as a servant since I was eight, hadn't made me wear these clothes in the Beehive House except on special occasions, like a baptism. However, Clara had dressed me up like a doll the day Brother Brigham sent me to the Paiute camp to marry their chief, Kanosh.

Kanosh loved how I looked in the high-necked, long-sleeved, lace-collared dress. It was the dress I'd been wearing when he first laid eyes on me in Brigham Young's meeting room, where he gathered up the local chiefs once a month.

Kanosh also loved that the other women called me "Brigham's little doll," thinking they meant it as a compliment.

"Brother Brigham could barely stand to let her go," my new husband crowed to anyone nearby whenever he saw me wearing the dress and shoes. "Sally was like a daughter to him."

I couldn't tell if he believed his own words. But I knew for certain that nobody else did.

Brown on the outside, white on the inside, Numa and Povi said, not even bothering to lower their voices when I passed by.

I kicked at a rock and intentionally scuffed the side of one shoe as I took it off. Like Kanosh himself, the shoes were unyielding, unsightly, and unpleasant to touch. I wanted to fling both away from me, as far as I could. I gladly replaced them with the pair of soft, worn moccasins Numa had given me.

When I put them on, my feet relaxed and my heart caught.

They felt like home, but this wasn't home.

"When you get to Fillmore, tell Lucy Robison that two of the dead steers are hers. We have no melons, no corn to spare. *Two steers,*" Numa told me, nearly shouting the last part.

"You know she doesn't understand you," Povi grumbled.

I kept my face blank, happy to prove her point.

The Paiutes assumed I spoke only English after having lived in Brigham Young's household since I was a child. On the other hand, the Youngs had always assumed I spoke only "Indian."

They were wrong.

Not that I'd ever felt the need to correct anyone.

I'd lived with the Youngs for nine long years. Long enough to learn English. Long enough to scrub plenty of pine floors in what was called "The Beehive House," a mansion made up of endless hallways and rooms. Long enough to master the preparation of buttermilk donuts, a delicacy served once a year on Brother Brigham's birthday. Long enough to wash endless trousers and petticoats.

23

It turned out that even prophets produced their share of dirty laundry.

Sally was what the Youngs always called me, a little louder than necessary. It was the name they'd given me. One they could pronounce. *Sally Indian. Sally, here,* they'd say. Then they'd gesture wildly, repeating the same words over and over until I nodded and did whatever they asked.

Brother Brigham's youngest wife Clara—I'd been gifted to her as a servant—never once asked about my native tongue, my childhood among my people far away from Utah, my family. Those were the only things I really *wanted* to talk about but wasn't allowed to, so what was the point?

I pretended I'd forgotten about my life before I came to the Young household.

I never did though, even when I put on the stiff shoes and itchy cotton dress, a far cry from my soft deerskin shift and moccasins I'd worn among the Bannock. Even when I was baptized as a Mormon at age ten, as "Sally Indian."

But today, in the Paiute village, I was desperate for a few hours on my own, even if it meant pretending to have a sudden breakthrough in understanding the Paiute dialect.

"Yes," I said to Numa, nodding my head vigorously and smiling. "Two steers."

Numa and Povi looked at each other in surprise.

"Clever little doll," Numa said, mimicking my pretend smile. "Off you go, then."

* * *

I'd only been walking for half an hour when I caught sight of the wagons, circled up. There were so many of them, with so many head of cattle, that I knew it was the same wagon train that Kanosh had forced to leave Corn Creek in a rush earlier that morning.

The ones who'd left the dead steers behind.

My heart beat faster, and I slowed my walk. It was strange that they'd made camp again such a short distance away from Corn Creek. Were they angry that Kanosh had insisted they leave? Would they think I was here to steal their cattle?

I might have spent most of my childhood cleaning floors in Brigham Young's mansion, but I knew that when it came to people like me, the men in the wagon trains liked to shoot first, ask questions later.

I hesitated for a few seconds then started walking again, deciding to cut around the trail of worn wagon ruts and skirt through some scrub oak to stay out of sight.

That was when I heard the crying.

Not soft, quiet, careful tears—like the ones I'd long since learned to cry—but snuffling, loud, hiccupping sobs.

I took a step closer and peered through the brush.

There, sitting in the dust, was a little girl with dark, curly hair. She knelt with her head in her hands, beneath the shade of a dead tree.

I hesitated again, tempted to tiptoe back through the overgrowth and give the crier a wide berth.

I needed to get to Lucy Robison's house in Fillmore to bake bread. The Paiutes needed the food. There wasn't time to stop.

"Joy be to you all," the little girl wailed, half-song half-cry, and my heart thumped so hard against my ribcage that I couldn't help but move toward the sound.

I remembered crying like that once, just once. When Tyee died.

It had earned me a bloody face and a beating.

For a moment, I felt those old sobs bubble up from the place I'd locked them away. I carefully pushed them down with a practiced resolve and walked a few more feet, staying silent like the doll I was supposed to be.

The little girl whimpered again, and I turned around.

Then, against my better judgment, I moved back toward her.

I studied her face in the seconds before she saw me. It was red, and her eyes were puffy from crying. When I parted the sagebrush, she scrambled to her feet but didn't run away.

For a few seconds, we stared at each other curiously. And for a moment, it was like I was looking at a mirror of myself. A sad, skinny girl with dark hair and red-rimmed eyes, tears rolling down her cheeks.

"Oh," the little girl said after a few seconds had passed, her brows knitting together in confusion and voice thick with tears as she took in my brown skin paired with my crinoline dress. Then, she added,

"My papa is dead." Her bottom lip trembled when she said it, like she was about to cry all over again. "They dug a hole for him."

I nodded to show I understood. So this was why the wagons had stopped again so soon.

"I didn't want them to put him in that hole with the dirt and bugs, so I ran away," she said, the last part of the sentence coming out as a shaky sob.

"I'm sorry," I told her quietly, even though I'd promised myself to speak as little English as possible. What good would it do me?

Her big brown eyes widened at my words, and her eyes went back to my ridiculous dress. "Are you a princess?" she asked shyly, wiping her tears and standing up from where she'd been sitting in the dirt. She took a few steps toward me. "Uncle Uri told me that the Indians—"

"No," I said gently, wishing I'd answered differently the second I saw her face fall. I wasn't the daughter of a chief. And even if I were, the word "princess" didn't make sense in my world.

"What's your name?" she asked.

"Sally," I responded automatically.

"I'm Nancy," she said, wiping her nose with one sleeve. She glanced back in the direction of the wagon train, and her lip began to quiver again. "I want my papa ..."

"Here," I said. And before I could think better of it, I reached into my left pocket and pulled out one of the yucca horses.

Tyee's horse.

Her eyes went impossibly wide when she saw it. She blinked, and more tears slipped down her dusty cheeks. "Is that for me? I love horses. We have two."

She took the horse in her little hand and gently stroked the rabbit-skin mane the way I'd done for the past nine years.

"That always makes me feel better, too," I told her. "The boy who made that horse died a long time ago, but the dead are never really gone." I touched my hand to the place where I felt the lonely ache in my own chest, only half-believing the words I spoke. "Your papa is still with you."

She nodded like she was willing to rest on those words for a moment, wiped at her eyes, and touched the horse's mane again with a fingertip wet with tears.

"Go back to your mama," I said, feeling my throat close around the words.

And then, before my own tears could breach the part of my chest where I'd walled them off, I turned and walked away.

5. LUCY ROBISON

FILLMORE, UTAH

AUGUST 1857

I eyed the rising sun through the window, wondering what was taking the Indian women so long this morning. Today was the fifteenth, which meant some of the Paiutes from Corn Creek would be coming by to bake bread in exchange for corn, melons, and moccasins. Usually, they were here at sunup on baking days. Shrugging, I turned back to the pile of trousers on the kitchen table. There was plenty of work to do otherwise.

"The girls are lucky they get to wear skirts," Proctor grumbled from where he stood across the room, loud enough for me to hear.

"You'll count your blessings, Proctor Robison," I told him, but when I looked up his brown eyes were playful.

"Just look, Mama." He pointed back to the kitchen table, where I'd lined up his younger brothers' trousers. "They could stand up all by themselves."

I snorted. He was right. The rough cotton on the boys' trousers was so stiff, the pants didn't even need a pair of legs to prop them up.

I meant to patch the knees before the other children came home from swimming at the pond. They each had one pair of school trousers, and if I didn't take care of the holes before the little brick schoolhouse opened up next week, they'd be sent home with a note.

"Go on and water the apple trees with your daddy," I told him, wiping my forehead. I'd started the clay oven heating an hour ago, feeding the stacked firewood into its greedy belly, and already it was hotter inside the house than out. "Yours are the only trousers without holes in the knees anyway." I swatted him on the behind with a piece of kindling. "Thanks to those new long legs of yours."

He beamed. At fourteen, he was already an inch taller than his father, Vick. I knew he was proud of it.

One of our horses whinnied outside, a sure sign somebody was finally coming down the dirt lane. I wiped my hands on my dress and looked out the window. "Looks like we're baking bread after all."

I'd come to look forward to this time with the Paiute women each month, even though we usually spent the hours in silence. Most of the Paiutes at Corn Creek had been baptized Mormon in the spring, when Apostle George A. Smith visited Fillmore. Those once-wild people were one of us now, and the idea that I was baking bread with descendants of the ancient Lamanites made goosebumps pop up on my arms.

The Lamanites in the pages of the Book of Mormon were wicked, cursed with a dark skin so the Nephites—or white folk—knew to stay away. But Heavenly Father promised that in the last days—right now—they'd turn righteous and become our allies. It was a miracle to live to see it happening.

Proctor lingered in the doorway, and I gently swatted him again. "Waiting for somebody?"

I'd seen the way his eyes went wide at the sight of Chief Kanosh's new wife Sally last month. She was only a few years older than him, and with her brown doe eyes, high cheeks and long black hair, I could see why she'd caught Kanosh's attention—and Proctor's.

Proctor's cheeks turned red and he shook his head. "No, Mama."

A shadow moved across the open front door.

"Hello, Sally," I called and raised an eyebrow at Proctor. The slip of a girl smiled but didn't come inside, wearing the same bulky crinoline dress she had last time I saw her.

Proctor ducked his head and hurried past her.

I strained to see beyond her, out into the yard. Usually at least three of the Indian women came to bake bread, but today it was only Sally. And she was empty-handed.

Seeing me glance at her hands, Sally whispered, "Melons gone." Then she quickly raised her hand and pointed at the milk cow tied up outside. "But steers."

It took a moment for me to find my tongue. I didn't realize she spoke English.

"Steers?" I asked, not sure what she meant. The Paiutes had some horses, but not steers.

"Dead steers. We take the meat. You take two skins?" she said hopefully.

After a little more back and forth, I learned that the gentiles who had passed through Corn Creek had left four steer carcasses untouched that morning when they broke camp in a hurry. Two were ours for the taking, in exchange for the bread this month.

I nodded at Sally to show I understood, still shocked by the fact that she could speak a bit of English. She was making a generous offer. Leather fetched a good price in Salt Lake. "I'll send Proctor for the skins. He's strong as an ox. And growing faster than I can keep up with." I chuckled and pointed at the pile of clothing waiting to be mended on the table. "All my boys could use a second pair of trousers."

Even with dust devils on the horizon promising a wind storm, Proctor had saddled his fast blue mare and was off to skin the steers before Sally and I moved into the kitchen to start kneading dough.

We baked ten loaves that day, all in all. We didn't talk any more while we worked. Sally had gone silent again, but from the way she followed my directions, I could tell she understood what I was saying well enough.

When she left that afternoon, I sat on the porch of our fine three-room house, putting up with the dust if it meant getting a breeze. I expected the younger children to come skipping home at any moment, smelling of muddy pond water. Then Vick soon after, covered in dust after spending the day in our apple orchard.

I sat on the rocker to patch the first pair of trousers, wanting to soak up the silence but needing to keep my hands busy.

I dropped the needle in surprise when I heard the blue mare's high-pitched whinny after only a few minutes.

Proctor must have made quick work of the steers.

There he was, nearly home, a mountain of skins that was nearly as tall as my boy himself draped in front of and behind the saddle.

Before I could lift a hand to greet him, though, he slumped against the mare's neck, doubling over at the stomach.

I set the trousers down, thinking the pile of skins had gotten away from him. "Proctor, you need help?"

31

He didn't answer. Just let go of the skins he'd worked so hard to scrape, letting them slip from the horse's back.

"Proctor!" I ran from the porch, too late to catch my boy before he tumbled off the horse like a rag doll, landing on top of the hides.

The blue mare just stood there, looking at me like she was worried, too.

When I got closer, I realized that my boy's whole face was red and swollen.

I thought maybe he'd been sunburnt.

Until I saw his eye. It was so puffed up he could barely open it.

6. LUCY ROBISON

FILLMORE, UTAH

AUGUST 1857

"Come on back to me," I whispered to Proctor in the dark, quiet bedroom that smelled like sick.

His hand gripped mine back, so that meant he could still hear me.

The house didn't feel calm anymore. More like it was holding its breath with me while I crouched by my firstborn son's bedside.

The sky had gone coal-black hours ago. After much urging, I had finally convinced the younger children to go to bed. Vick had yet to return with the help I prayed would save my child.

I closed my eyes and bowed my head in prayer for the hundredth time, but the only word that came now was *please.*

All I could see, even behind my eyelids, was Proctor's poor misshapen face. I tried to hold the hot tears back so hard, they burned me up from the inside out.

He didn't even look like my boy anymore. Over the past few hours, his head had swollen so badly, I barely recognized him. Even his lips and throat had bloated so much he could barely swallow the spoonfuls of broth I offered, that instead dribbled down his chin.

I dipped a fresh cloth in water and laid it on his feverish head. Then I dabbed some arnica oil on the cracked skin around his eye. I couldn't help thinking that the oozing, puffy skin looked like a split melon in the darkness.

The thought made me sick.

Earlier, once I'd managed to get him cleaned up and in bed, Proctor told me the trouble with his eye had started right after he got to Corn Creek. He'd settled down to separate the hide from the first steer carcass, hurrying to get out of the swirling dust. The flies had settled in, too.

When he'd swiped at one of the insects that landed on his head, a drop of steer blood got into his eye. He blinked it away and kept going, but after a few minutes, his eye started itching like the devil.

He'd said he set down the knife, washed his face and hands in Corn Creek, then went back to his work. Before he'd finished skinning the first steer, his head started to spin. By the time he finished with the last, he could barely see straight.

It was a miracle he'd made it home at all.

When Vick had gotten home from watering the apple orchard, pulling barrels back and forth from the muddy pond where the children swam, he'd become as panicked as me and hurried after Bishop Brunson, who was also our doctor.

I'd always taken comfort in the idea that the leader of our church in Fillmore was a proper physician. With the power of God *and* medicine in his hands, I felt safe from all kinds of harm.

The last time I saw him, standing on our porch, was the exception. He'd stopped by unexpectedly after supper on Sunday to speak with Vick and me. The reason for his visit was to encourage Vick to submit his name for approval to take a second wife.

It wasn't the first time he'd hinted at it. Just last Sunday, during service, Bishop Brunson had read a letter from the pulpit sent from the prophet himself. The words he spoke were addressed to the women of the congregation, who were usually the sticking point in adding another wife.

"Sisters, you must round up your shoulders and fulfill the law of God in every respect. I have found that there is no end to the everlasting whining of the women in this territory. But if the women of Utah continue to turn from the principle of Plural Marriage and despise the order of heaven, I will pray that the curse of the Almighty may be close to their heels."

That was the first time he'd asked me and Vick outright. I'd sent the bishop on his way with a firm, "We'll pray about it."

The words he'd read in church rang in my ears now as I heard the sound of the front door opening, then boots tromping down the hall.

Vick and Bishop Brunson.

Thank you, Heavenly Father.

But then a prickle of fear wormed its way into my heart. I hadn't prayed about Bishop Brunson's requests. A lie and a sin, all by itself. Was this the curse of the Almighty for my wickedness in wanting Vick for myself?

I'm sorry, Heavenly Father, I begged.

A few minutes later, Bishop Brunson sat on the edge of Proctor's bed and began his examination.

"Might ... just ... be ... the ... heat," Proctor said while the bishop prodded his swollen face. My boy's raspy voice sounded so hopeful, it cut me up.

Bishop Brunson patted his hand. "Might be, son," he said softly. Proctor's whole head had swollen so big that all I could recognize was his dark brown hair, sticking up in a cowlick.

When Bishop Brunson finished his examination, he ushered me and my husband out of the room and closed the door, putting us on the other side, his mouth turned down at the corners. "Can't do much for him, Sister Robison, Vick. I'm so sorry."

I stared at him, trying to make sense of it. "Can't do much?" I repeated. "But what's wrong with him?"

Bishop Brunson shook his head and set his mouth. "Poison. I'm sure of it."

Poison? The word made me shiver in spite of the sweat dripping down my back. "I don't understand," I said. *We'll take another wife,* I wanted to scream, knowing it wouldn't help.

I'd already failed that test of faith.

"Has to be. Nothing else spreads this quick. This violent," Bishop Brunson said softly, so the other children couldn't hear if they were listening at the door of the second bedroom.

The dark hallway swam in front of my eyes. "How?" I barely got the word out.

"Must've gotten in through his eye. He said he felt just fine until he started skinning those steers and wiped his face."

"Was it ... the Paiutes?" I asked, choking on my own words. I hated to ask, especially when we had a tenuous peace with the Indians—allies, I'd thought earlier this very day. The Paiutes were Latter-day Saints, like me. They were our friends. But Sally was the one who'd told me and Proctor about the dead steers. Had she—

"No ... the gentiles," Bishop Brunson said, his voice both soft and angry. "A couple of rough-looking men came riding out to

Fillmore, begging around for medicine and supplies after they broke camp at Corn Creek. When we turned them away, they were pretty upset. Must've doubled back and laid poison on the steers they lost."

The gentiles.

Of course.

Until that moment, my body had been drenched in guilt and fear, like a cloth dunked in water. But Bishop Brunson's words wrung me out.

The gentiles had done this to my boy.

I latched onto that thought like a steel trap.

While I knelt by my son's bedside, praying and soothing him, my gut churned sick with horror and rage.

The gentiles had done this.

The gentiles, who'd taken so much already.

They'd driven me and Vick from our land in upstate New York.

They'd burned our temple to the ground.

They'd tarred and feathered our leaders and apostles.

They'd killed our prophet, Joseph Smith.

They'd chased us out of their cities like dogs, hoping to see us freeze and die in the swamps outside Missouri and Illinois.

When we hadn't died—not all of us, anyway—the Missouri governor ordered that we be "exterminated or driven from the state." Like insects.

Then they'd pushed us nearly a thousand miles west, to Utah Territory. It was land nobody else wanted, and for good reason. It was mostly dust and locusts.

Still, they'd followed us here—under the protection of the United States government no less. Then President James Buchanan had ordered Brigham Young—our prophet, also the governor and "Indian Agent" of Utah—to make sure the travelers going west on the Overland Trail had safe passage. The grass was *theirs*. Not *ours*. Not the Indians'. Didn't matter that we had no grass to spare with a drought choking us all in dust.

And now, Bishop Brunson said the U.S. Army was coming to replace Brigham Young as governor. An *army*! And all because the people of Utah answered to God first, not man. Not even when that man was the president of the United States.

They took and they took and they took.

And now they were going to take my boy.

* * *

After Bishop Brunson had examined Proctor, he and Vick rode out to Corn Creek with two of our neighbors. They planned to burn what was left of the steers and warn the Paiutes.

But when they returned home hours later, Vick said that by the time they got to the village at Corn Creek, a few Indians were already sick with the same swollen faces and fever.

As dawn broke, Bishop Brunson and Vick laid their hands on Proctor's feverish head to give him a blessing and try to drive the poison out of his body.

"Proctor Hancock Robison," Vick began. "By the power of the Melchizedek Priesthood, I give you a blessing of comfort."

I held back a sob. Comfort? The power both men held in their hands—the holy priesthood—was the power of God. Unlike the dead religions of Catholicism and Protestantism, you didn't have to be a priest to hold it. Just a righteous, worthy Latter-day Saint man. That priesthood gave Vick and Bishop Brunson the right to bring my boy back from the dead, like Lazarus.

But only if it was God's will.

And only if my faithfulness demanded it.

My stomach heaved as Bishop Brunson ended the blessing with, "Thy will be done."

A prideful, desperate voice in my belly screamed for him to take the words back. To demand he call Proctor back from the brink of death, but I choked the sinful thoughts down with my own "Amen."

Proctor was tough and hardy like my other boys. Maybe all he needed was his father's blessing of comfort.

I held in the tears until both men were out of the room. I would accept God's will when it was done, and not before.

I begged Him to spare Proctor as the first trickles of gray light hit the window. I begged Him to forgive me. "No weapon that is formed against thee shall prosper," I whispered when my boy cried out.

By mid-morning, Proctor Hancock Robison was dead.

7. LUCY ROBISON

FILLMORE, UTAH

AUGUST 1857

The next day, we buried Proctor at the edge of our apple orchard, along the strip of land between our house and the Johnsons, right by the wide maze of skinny trees.

Vick and I had planted the Winesap trees four years ago, back when Fillmore was still just a dusty fort and our house was the only shingled rooftop for miles. I didn't believe the seedlings would ever grow. How could anything grow here? It never rained. But, like the rest of Utah Territory, we made our own rain—dragging bucket after backbreaking bucket from anywhere we could find water.

I still missed the lush green of Upstate New York, where Vick and I grew up. I missed the rivers and lakes. I missed the warm days and cool nights of summer—instead of the scorching Utah heat that refused to let go until mid-September, even at night. And I missed the comfortable home we'd left behind—or rather, been forced to abandon.

O ye of little faith.

"They'll survive. The roots will go deeper in time," Vick had said gently, as if reading my mind, when the seedlings were planted.

I knew my husband wasn't just talking about the trees. Though he'd never heard me complain, he could read me as well as any book. I would've repacked our belongings and let the apple orchard we'd planted and home we'd built crumble to dust if it weren't for the testimony of the restored gospel of Jesus Christ that burned in my heart.

Vick's prophecy had been right, though. Over the past four years, the roots of the apple orchard *had* gone deep. And now, as we lowered Proctor's pine casket into the ground beside the first rows, the spindly seedlings were nearly ripe with their second harvest.

I stared at those bright green leaves and pale reddish-yellow fruit, stark against the sunbaked earth we'd constantly turned over with manure to replenish the soil and endless buckets full of water taken from the nearby pond year after year.

"It's a good spot for him," Vick murmured, catching my eye. But when he smiled, it barely reached his eyes. A real smile crinkled up his weathered face so the pale green iris on his left side and the dark, murky green iris on his right looked almost the same color.

Proctor had curled himself tight into a ball during his last moments, and that was how we laid him to rest in the wooden box. I couldn't stand to look at him like that. Like he was still bracing from the pain, waiting for death to come.

At first, I'd tucked the quilt from his bed across his shoulders. But before the coffin was lowered into the earth, Bishop Brunson told me to pull it out for those in need.

Our neighbors, the Johnsons, had a sick baby and two skinny toddlers. We'd just learned that the husband and wife slept dressed in their winter clothes at night while the children shared one threadbare quilt. Our quilt would do more for them than it would for Proctor.

It tore me in half, but the bishop was right. My final wish to bring comfort to my boy was a selfish indulgence when others had so little. I reminded myself that Proctor didn't need it. That body in the coffin wasn't *him*.

Not anymore. He was with God.

* * *

Apostle George A. Smith traveled all the way from Cedar City to deliver a sermon the day of Proctor's funeral.

He'd been the one to send us off from Salt Lake to Fillmore four years earlier, to settle the area. To make the desert blossom like a rose, like the prophet Brigham Young had promised. Back then, he'd given both me and Vick a blessing, smiling as he sent us more than a hundred miles away into the wilderness.

Now, at Proctor's funeral, Apostle Smith sat stone-faced behind Bishop Brunson. He stared steadily through the window of the little adobe meetinghouse, like he was looking at something far beyond us.

Bishop Brunson spoke at the pulpit first. He began by quoting from the Book of Mormon, a holy text that had been delivered to Joseph Smith by an angel. He read the words of the prophet Alma. "He breaketh the bands of death, that the grave shall have no victory and the sting of death should be swallowed up in the hopes of glory."

The truth of those words burned in my heart even while grief, guilt, and rage closed my throat, threatening to starve the flames.

My grief didn't want words like *shall* and *should be.*

Not when the sting of death was so sharp right now.

I couldn't stop picturing my industrious boy as he knelt next to those dead steers, rolling up his sleeves and wiping death into his eye.

All for new trousers he'd never wear.

All because I'd asked him to go.

It was too much to bear. I swallowed down the emotions coiling in my throat, strangling faith into bitterness.

Beside me, Vick reached for my hand. Proctor's siblings, ten-year-old Almon, four-year-old Adelia, and eight-year-old Albert sat beside their father on the pew, red-rimmed eyes fixed on Bishop Brunson like he offered them a ladle of water in the desert.

Apostle Smith rose to speak next. His suit, covered in a fine layer of dust, looked as if he had just unsaddled his horse. His mouth stayed fixed in a hard line while he moved past Bishop Brunson to stand at the pulpit.

"Brothers and sisters, there is indeed cause to mourn." His voice was a low rumble at first, like thunder in the distance. Then, a little louder with each word. "But as the Lord says in the book of Matthew, 'Think not that I am come to send peace on earth. I came not to send peace, but a sword.'"

Vick's hand tightened ever so slightly over mine. I leaned forward, eager to replace my grief with fresh anger.

The peaceful sadness that had blanketed the meetinghouse shifted and prickled with an electric charge.

Apostle Smith drew himself taller at the pulpit, placing both of his dinner-plate-sized hands down in front of him on the podium. "The gentiles have tarred and feathered our people. Beaten and exterminated us. Driven us from our homelands back east."

My heart beat faster. *Yes.*

41

"In Provo, Brother Jameson still carries a few ounces of lead in his body from the Haun's Mill Massacre in Missouri." His voice rumbled louder. "In Parowan, Sister Penter raises four children alone, without her husband and two sons who died of cholera in Winter Quarters in Nebraska."

He slammed his hands on the pulpit again. "In Salt Lake City, Sister Pratt—widow of our beloved Apostle Parley P. Pratt—grieves her dead husband while newspapers across the country rejoice in what they deem the death of another 'damned Mormon'."

I squeezed Vick's hand harder, feeling the injustice beat in my chest like a drum.

"Does the government of the United States come to our aid?" He worked his jaw and stared down into the pews. "Have they *ever* come to our aid?"

Murmurs of "no" rippled through the pews. I added my voice, feeling anger warm my cheeks. The government of the United States had turned a blind eye to our mistreatment again and again, suspicious of our strange beliefs and customs—especially polygamy.

Apostle Smith waited until the room was silent again. "By now you know that President James Buchanan has sent troops marching toward us to replace our beloved Brigham Young as governor and Indian Agent of Utah Territory. Even while they demand that he protect the gentile wagon trains who poison the trail in their wake."

Apostle Smith cast his eyes over the silent congregation. "God will protect his people, and he will fight their battles in this war. But if he wants a little help, he will find us ready. Trust in God," he boomed. "But keep your gun powder dry. In the name of Jesus Christ, Amen."

We all knew better than to shout *hallelujah* like the Evangelicals. But the force of our "Amen," crackling through the meetinghouse like a volley of gunshots, meant the same thing.

EXCERPT FROM A SERMON DELIVERED IN SALT LAKE

BRIGHAM YOUNG

AUGUST 1855

In regard to those who have persecuted this people, I intend to meet them on their own grounds. We could take the same law they have taken, in other words, mob rule. And if any miserable scoundrels come here, cut their throats.

— Scribe's Note: All the people said, Amen.

EXCERPT FROM A LETTER TO CHURCH LEADERS IN PHILADELPHIA

BRIGHAM YOUNG

AUGUST 1857

For years, I have been holding the Indians back from attacking the wagon trains that roll through our territory, but Cousin Laman is at large.

If President Buchanan does not respect our wishes, travel will be stopped across the continent. The deserts of Utah will become a battleground for freedom. It's either peace and our rights—or the knife and the tomahawk. Let Uncle Sam choose.

8. KAHPEPUTZ (SALLY)

CORN CREEK, UTAH

AUGUST 1857

I took as long as possible pulling up my bulky dress, watching as the yellow rivulets of urine trickled toward a tiny brown grasshopper in the sand beneath my feet.

When the liquid reached him, he hopped skyward, leaving me behind.

I felt a pang of jealousy as I shuffled back through the sagebrush toward Inola, calculating how soon I could reasonably ask to pee again. Unlike Numa and Povi, this was one of the few times Inola let me out of her sight. As Kanosh's first wife, she seemed to take her responsibility to make sure I didn't run away a little more seriously.

Even today, when the entire village was a hive of despair and black smoke.

It felt like years had passed between yesterday—baking bread with Lucy Robison—and today.

Inola frowned when I reemerged from the sagebrush but didn't say anything about how long I'd taken to relieve myself. Maybe she was secretly glad to walk me out here and escape the thick of the chaos, too.

Word had spread fast that three Paiutes had died after eating the bad steer meat.

The same meat that Numa and Povi had been so excited to harvest, they'd let me walk to Lucy's house to bake bread alone.

"Come on, let's go," she said, gesturing toward camp to make sure I understood her.

I followed.

In my mind's eye, I could still see the sprawling gentile wagon train I'd passed when I walked to Fillmore.

And the little girl I'd found in the scrub oak, crying for her dead papa like her heart would break.

I thought I might regret giving her Tyee's horse after keeping it so long. But to my surprise, I only felt glad. Tyee had been a kind boy. He would have given the little girl his horse, too.

When I'd returned to the Paiute camp later that evening, arms full of bread, I'd told myself I would try harder to fit in. I'd start speaking more. After all, if I was going to spend the rest of my life here among the Paiutes, I might as well make an effort.

That was when I'd heard more wailing. This time, coming from the Paiute camp.

As the evening wore on, the sounds of suffering had swelled to a boil.

Death came quickly for its victims—less than a day—but not quick enough to be merciful. Dozens more Paiutes got sick, their stomachs bloated, eyes yellow, while fever and chills shook their bodies.

At first, I'd worried that Lucy Robison and the Mormons in Fillmore would blame me. After all, I was a newcomer and I'd barely met the white woman who opened her home to the Paiutes to help bake bread once a month. I was the one who had pointed her son directly to the steer carcasses, thinking she would be grateful.

Off that boy flew, smiling for what would be the last time, while I kneaded dough into loaves with his mother.

That's what I got for opening my mouth.

But as oily, dark smoke from what remained of the steer carcasses plumed skyward, nobody mentioned me.

"Hurry up," Inola muttered, breaking into my thoughts. She pointed at my feet, covered again in my husband-approved shoes, an irritated expression on her face. "Maybe you can't walk any faster," she grumbled.

I gave her a blank look, and she rolled her eyes. Apparently giving up on being understood, she slowed her steps to match mine and studied me instead. "What useless shoes," she said under her breath. "And that dress ... Kanosh is a fool."

On these two points, Inola and I agreed. I hid my smile, knowing she was unlikely to appreciate it. The first time Kanosh had tried to crawl into my bedroll in the wickiup I shared with his three other wives, I'd screamed as if a rattlesnake had attempted to join me under the blankets. I couldn't help it.

Inola had hushed me, then beckoned to Kanosh to join her instead. *"Give her some time to adjust. She's only seventeen,"* she'd murmured to him. *"And she hardly knows you."*

I'd heard Numa and Povi laughing about it together the following day. *"Such a pretty little doll, but he can't even play with her,"* Povi said.

Despite my fears, Kanosh hadn't touched me again since that night. But from the way I caught him looking now and then, I suspected it was only a matter of time.

When Inola stopped walking at the edge of the Paiute camp, I stopped walking, too. We stood side by side as the wind picked up, rattling the dried-up leaves and stalks in what remained of the parched corn and melon fields.

This is your home now, I told myself firmly.

It was the same thing I'd thought when I was eight and stood quivering, looking up at Brigham Young's enormous house.

I'd been wrong then, and I was wrong now.

I had no home. No people.

After the first Paiute died from the poisoned meat, the grieving wife had sheared off her long hair. Then the village women—including me—slashed our arms and legs with arrowheads and sharp rocks, sending our own blood back to the earth in a rusty river that pulled our grief to the surface.

When a new mother and her child died next, we did it all over again.

By the end of the following day, some of the Paiute women were weak from loss of blood.

I chose a dull rock to slash shallow lines across my skin. I mourned the ones who had died, but I was Bannock, not Paiute, and I didn't know those people.

Not really. Not after six weeks.

Their dead were not my dead.

The best I could do was pretend I had room in my heart for their grief.

There was none, though. My heart was already so heavy from missing my family and people and home it might as well have been a stone hung around my neck.

I thought of the words I'd told the little girl from the wagon train: *You're not alone. The dead are never really gone.* Where had those words come from? The Youngs? My old tribe? I wanted to believe them, but all I felt was empty as I grasped for memories of my mother, my father, Tyee. But when I tried to hold onto them, wrap myself up in their comfort, they felt thin around the edges. Like an old blanket, faded and full of holes against the cold.

I *was* alone.

Inola sighed and muttered what sounded like a prayer.

I stared straight ahead, pushing the sounds of suffering down to the bottomless place I'd stored my own pain, imagining that the sound of wailing from the wickiups was the wind.

9. KAHPEPUTZ (SALLY)

CORN CREEK, UTAH

AUGUST 1857

After long talks in the big wickiup at the center of the village, Chief Kanosh, and the other men decided to ride north toward Salt Lake to Brigham Young's house.

The prophet would decide what to do about the dead Paiutes and, of course, Proctor Robison.

Something had to be done. All the death seemed to point back to the gentile wagon train.

I had heard growing murmurs that the gentile wagon train had spread poison across the steer carcasses they left behind at Corn Creek. But Kanosh, like the rest of the Indian chiefs in Utah Territory, had learned not to take matters into his own hands when it came to white settlers.

As the riders prepared to leave, I thought of the little girl I'd met. If poison had been set intentionally, she certainly hadn't been the one to do it. But what about her papa? There was a world of difference between a grown coyote and a pup.

I pushed the memory of her sad brown eyes away.

"Maybe they'll return Brother Brigham's little doll to him when they go," Kanosh's second wife, Numa, muttered to the third—Povi —who cut her eyes toward me. She was at least a head shorter than me, but her long hair was streaked with gray and wrinkles lined her eyes. All three of Kanosh's other wives were old enough to be my mother. And Kanosh was old enough to be my grandfather.

"She's not even *pretending* to mourn the dead," Povi said indignantly to Numa, not bothering to lower her voice.

I ignored them and thrust my hands deep into my pockets to find my tulle horse while I stared into the fire, listening to the sound of hoofbeats as the first riders disappeared.

Kanosh and the elders would probably be gone for a few days, given the distance to Salt Lake. Which meant the women wouldn't try to hide their disdain for me. But at least Kanosh wouldn't make his way into my bedroll.

* * *

That night, when I entered the wickiup, I found my bedroll moved to the farthest side of the large branch and brush structure. The tule-stalk broom, usually tucked into the corner, lay on top of the bedroll. Someone had sprinkled dirt, hair, and a few dead insects across it, too.

Inola sighed and snatched up the broom, then moved my bedroll back beside the other wives' while I watched in silence. "I don't like her either, but there's no sense making this day worse for anyone," she snapped at Numa and Povi.

I lay down on the bedroll but kept my eyes open until the sound of steady breathing filled the wickiup. In the distance, some of the mourners were still wailing in the night, soft keening sounds from outside the wickiups that had lost a beloved family member.

A tangle of silvery hair still stuck to the bedroll in front of my eyes, and I couldn't help thinking of the strange, mouse-colored wreath on the door of Brigham Young's meeting room. It looked like it was made of delicate feathers artfully woven together into flowers and bows. I'd only learned that the wreath was made of human hair when—without warning—Clara had plucked a few strands from my scalp after my baptism. She tied them into the delicate wreath, pointed at her own hair, then back at the wreath, smiling with all her teeth out. I smiled too, wishing I could pluck the hairs right back.

They didn't belong there.

And neither did I.

None of Brother Brigham's many wives were invited to attend his meetings in the room behind the hair wreath. No women. The one exception was when Brigham hosted the local Indian chiefs. Then, I was invited inside to serve fresh biscuits and jam to the half-dozen guests who had traveled from across the territory.

I always did my best to disappear into the corner once the serving was done. The meetings lasted a long time, while the Mormon leaders and chiefs held heated discussions through an interpreter about land, cattle, and water, but mostly about the U.S. government and rotten President James Buchanan.

James Buchanan was coming for Indian and Mormon alike. The government had already chased the Mormons out of New York, Illinois, and Missouri the same way they'd been chasing Indians off their land to make way for wagon trains to trespass.

But enough was enough.

From what I pieced together, the American government wanted to replace Brigham Young as our state governor because the Mormons in Utah listened to him more than anyone else. Including the federal officials who kept showing up in Utah Territory—then storming back to Washington in a huff.

No other governor had twenty-seven wives. Or spoke directly to God. Brother Brigham was a prophet first. His roles as a governor and Indian Agent came second.

James Buchanan didn't like that one bit. But Brother Brigham said that the president was in for a surprise if he tried to unseat him.

"It is not in the power of the United States to destroy us," he boomed, gesturing around the table at the chiefs the last time I served biscuits and jam. The meetings in the hair-wreath room tended to shift into sermons quickly, with Brother Brigham standing at the head of the table. *"And if they send an army against us, we have every constitutional and legal right to send them to hell."*

I noticed that when he said *we,* he made fierce eye contact with each of the chiefs.

One day, I made the mistake of keeping my eyes open during the closing prayer at a meeting with the chiefs. In doing so, I caught the eye of Chief Kanosh, who was the only brown man I'd ever seen with a mustache. It curled above his weathered upper lip like the tail of a small animal. I couldn't stop staring.

He winked at me and smiled, which made his mustache twitch.

A few days later, Clara told me I would need to pack my things—consisting of two scratchy dresses, one pair of hard shoes, and a small, shiny brooch the Youngs gave me as a goodbye gift along with a pat on the shoulder.

I would be joining the Paiutes near Corn Creek—as Kanosh's fourth wife. Four didn't seem like very many compared to Brother Brigham's twenty-seven. But I didn't want to be anybody's wife.

The day I arrived at the village near Corn Creek, Kanosh paraded me through the wickiups. He told the elders and his three other wives that Brigham Young was a powerful ally against the U.S. government, which posed a threat to Paiute and Mormon alike. According to Kanosh, the prophet had parted with his beloved Sally as a gesture of goodwill. He told the others I was like a daughter to Brigham. His treasured possession.

The scars on my cheeks and my shabby clothing told a different story—one that Kanosh's three other wives were quick to notice. I could see the disdain and judgment in their eyes from the first moment. Of course, they said nothing.

And neither did I.

We all knew I was a trade. Not a treasure.

Still, Kanosh had promised to build me a cabin instead of the shared wickiup, to show Brigham next time he rode out to Corn Creek. So that the prophet could see he cared for me above all else. The other wives rolled their eyes when he looked away.

I smiled vacantly as if I didn't understand a word he said.

10. KAHPEPUTZ (SALLY)

CORN CREEK, UTAH

AUGUST 1857

Since the first week I'd arrived, Awan—Inola and Kanosh's only son —had accompanied me to fetch water at Corn Creek each day.

At eighteen, Awan was just a little older than me. I figured he was basically my brother—and my stepson? With his quiet voice, serious coal-dark eyes, and long brown hair that perpetually fell across his face like a horse's forelock, I liked him immediately.

From the careful way he eyed me behind that floppy lock of hair, I understood that the other wives had passed him the task of preventing me from running away. But even so, gathering water with Awan had become my favorite part of the day.

He led the mule that toted the pitch baskets, just like every other day. I dipped them into the shallow water of Corn Creek until they were full enough for our needs but not so heavy that the mule couldn't carry them. While I worked, Sweet Pea the mule snatched bits of dry grass along the bank.

The morning after the final deaths in the village, Awan and I set out as usual.

When I finished filling the first pitch basket, I cupped my hands and raised a tentative mouthful of water to my chapped lips. After the agony I'd seen in camp, I hadn't taken a sip of water or a mouthful of meat since the sickness broke out. Some of the Paiutes insisted that the gentiles had poisoned the steer meat. Others said they'd poisoned the creek itself. But I couldn't last much longer without water.

As I raised the water to my mouth, Awan suddenly darted forward. "No, stupid! You'll die too."

At first, I thought he was talking to me. Without thinking, I scrambled to my feet and shrieked, tipping the pitch basket in the process. The water spilled into the muck at our feet.

When I turned to face Awan, he wasn't looking in my direction, though. He'd grabbed Sweet Pea's rope and was pulling the mule away from a dried patch of forage growing near the creek shore.

Awan gave me a strange look then turned back to the mule.

One of the dusky purple flowers stuck out between Sweet Pea's velvet lips. Awan swatted it away, startling the poor thing, who let out an indignant bray and stomped her foot. "Do you want to end up like them?" he asked her, pointing at the black patches of charred earth near the muddy banks a few yards away, where the men had burned the stripped steer carcasses.

"Like them?" My surprise pushed the words past my lips before I could stop myself.

The look on his face made me clamp my mouth shut so hard I bit my tongue. It was the first time I'd spoken to him.

"You understood what I said." It wasn't a question.

My hands suddenly felt shaky, and I set down the basket I was trying to refill so I didn't drop it again.

Awan pushed aside his hair and studied me intently. "You're Paiute? My mother told me you were Ute."

Anger flared in my chest, and I took the bait. "I am *not* a Ute," I said hotly, my native tongue surprising but sweet in my mouth, like the clover honey I hadn't tasted since I was a little girl. *Ute* was a curse word I'd learned almost as soon as I could speak. The Utes traded slaves. They were the reason I'd ended up at Brigham Young's house in the first place. "I'm not Paiute, either."

My native Bannock wasn't the same as the Paiute dialect Awan spoke, but similar enough that I knew he'd understand me.

Awan shrugged and motioned to the pitch basket, spinning in an eddy an arm's length away. "You can drink the water. It's fine. That plant is the problem."

He pointed at the dried-up sweet peas that the mule had just tried to eat.

When I looked closer, I realized that some of the leaves and purple flowers tangled among the dead sweet pea vines were shaped differently.

"Locoweed," he said. "Livestock eat it when forage is low."

I stared at him in confusion. There was hardly more than a mouthful on the banks of the creek. "The gentile steers died from eating that plant?"

He shook his head. "It takes a lot more than a bite. Those steers had probably been eating it for weeks in the desert. There's no grass. We haven't had rain all summer."

I nodded. The drought was relentless. The cornstalks clinging to life in Kanosh's fields were withered and sickly, half as tall as they should have been. There were no more melons. Hardly any rabbits or deer that hadn't fled into the mountains.

"My mother warned the other women not to harvest the meat," Awan continued. "The steers were way too sleek to be starved, and they bloated up too quickly. Their muscles were full of locoweed. The same thing happened a few years ago when another group of gentiles passed through. Not this bad, though." He pushed his hair behind one ear and gestured at the sunbaked earth surrounding us. The sparse, trampled grass flanking Corn Creek was the only bright green in sight. "The other women didn't listen to my mother. There's no game to hunt. All that meat was hard to pass up."

"Does your father know about the locoweed?" I asked.

Awan shook his head. "He doesn't care. The wagon trains have been bringing us death for years," he said softly. He moved his gaze away from the blackened ground, to the horizon. "But not anymore. The war has begun." He drew in a long breath and stood taller. "My father says that James Buchanan's troops are already gathering at the mouth of Echo Canyon up north, outside Salt Lake. The Americans hate the Mormons the same way the Americans hate us."

I frowned. "What will Kanosh do?"

Awan picked up the pitch basket in silence and filled it with water from the lazy current at our feet. When he met my gaze, his eyes were unreadable. "Whatever Brigham Young says. The Mormons are our allies. We will fight with them in this war."

"And the gentile wagon train?" I asked, still confused. "They aren't troops. They're families with women and children." I pictured the little girl, Nancy, crying and singing to herself on the desert floor.

Awan shook his head. "They *are* troops. James Buchanan sends them here, more every year, and tells Brigham Young to protect them. You've seen their guns. They kill our game, take our grass for their cattle, and kill our people if we fight back. We starve while they go West in search of gold."

I picked up the other basket and dipped it into the muddy water. My stomach tightened uneasily. Maybe he was right. What did I know about such things?

The memories of my childhood among the Bannock were fuzzy at the edges, but our standard of living had been comfortable back then. I remembered the tang of berries, honey, and plenty of roasted meat. Dancing and firelight.

I'd always imagined the rosy oasis of my childhood home was still intact somewhere to the north—just without me in it. But maybe, after a decade, my childhood home looked like the village at Corn Creek: hardscrabble, dust-glazed, and sinewy, like the steers that had collapsed near the creek.

And that broke my heart.

* * *

When Awan walked me to the creek the next day, he asked my name.

My real name.

I didn't answer at first.

The other Paiutes just called me Sally, same as the white Mormons, drawing out the *ll*s in the English name like the letters were stuck to their teeth in an unpleasant way. Sometimes, they called me other names. Words they thought I couldn't understand. In addition to their favorite taunt of "Brigham's little doll," "Hawk Girl" was another popular insult.

It was just another way of calling me a Ute. The notorious Ute chief, the "Hawk of the Mountains," had terrorized the Bannock and Paiutes, stealing horses, women, and children to sell to anyone who would buy them.

After a long pause, I told Awan my real name. My Bannock name. The one my mother had given me. Kahpeputz. *Walks without sound.* I couldn't remember if that was the meaning of my name, or if my mother had simply murmured those two phrases together again and again while I dashed around with Tyee. But over the years, I'd decided the meaning fit.

I'd repeated that name to remind myself silently so many times while I made meals in Brigham Young's home, tended children, scrubbed trousers, milked cows, braided hair, and ironed dresses. I felt no guilt over this small deception, having learned from a young age the difference between self-preservation and sin.

Sin was the man who had plucked me from the riverbank while I played with my best friend Tyee, walking our little yucca horses along the riverbank. He'd sprung from behind a rock so quickly, I didn't have time to scream before his knife pressed tight against Tyee's throat. *"I'll cut him up,"* the man said, his eyes and teeth popping white and wild in his face. *"Unless you stay quiet."*

He cut us up anyway, once we were far enough from the village that nobody could hear us scream. Each night, he slashed our faces with a sharp knife, then poured hot ash across the wounds. He threatened that if we ran away, he would do much worse.

When we arrived at the fort in the Salt Lake Valley, he asked fifteen dollars for me, and ten dollars for Tyee.

When he got no offers, he told the Mormons in Salt Lake that he'd be happy to kill us both instead. We were worthless to him alive, if we couldn't be traded.

A few days later, still without an offer, he pulled the knife across Tyee's neck from ear to ear.

The same would've happened to me, if it hadn't been for the Mormon man who offered his rifle in exchange for my life. It wasn't exactly the trade my captor wanted, but it was better than leaving with only fresh blood on his knife.

The Mormon man gifted me to his sister Clara Young, one of Brother Brigham's many wives.

When I told Awan my real name, "Kahpeputz," he repeated it like an oath, and I knew the word was safe in his mouth.

Hearing him say it felt like we were sharing a secret.

From then on, whenever we were alone at the creek, that was the name he called me.

PROCLAMATION

BRIGHAM YOUNG

AUGUST 1857

TO THE CITIZENS OF UTAH:

We are invaded by a hostile force, who intend our overthrow and destruction. For the last twenty-five years, we have trusted officials of the United States Government, from constables and justices, to judges, governors, and President, only to be scorned, held in derision, insulted, and betrayed.

Our houses have been plundered and then burned. Our people have been butchered, and our families driven from their homes to find shelter in the barren wasteland among hostile savages who, like us, have been denied the embrace of civilization.

Our duty to our families requires us not to tamely submit to be driven and slain without an attempt to preserve ourselves.

I hereby declare martial law.

— Brigham Young

TO THE OFFICER COMMANDING THE FORCES NOW INVADING UTAH TERRITORY:

I, Brigham Young, am still the governor and superintendent of Indian Affairs for the Territory.

By virtue of the authority vested in me, I forbid armed forces of any kind and under any pretense from entering this territory without express permission.

I make this declaration of martial law for the safety of my people —and the safety of westward travelers. As Indian Agent and governor I have long used my power to offer such travelers safe passage through Utah Territory.

I fear that your actions against myself and the people of Utah have already quickened the blood of the Indians in this territory.

The caravans travel west at their peril.

— Brigham Young

11. KATRINA HUFF

TEN MILES OUTSIDE OF MOUNTAIN MEADOWS, UTAH
SEPTEMBER 1857
50 DAYS TO CALIFORNIA

Our wagon train inched forward through the desert like a long snake of wood and canvas.

When Captain Alexander promised we were nearly at the lush meadow where we could rest our oxen, horses, and cattle, where the children could swim, Nancy clapped her hands.

I kept my eyes on the horizon.

The four-part phrase that had kept my spirits buoyed up before— *We're safe. We're together. We're nearly there*—had dwindled to three.

We're nearly there.
We're nearly there.
We're nearly there.

If the days on the trail were difficult before, they were impossible now. My mind felt numb and my heart raw, still reeling from the loss of my Peter. It broke a little more with each step under the merciless sun, farther and farther away from where we left my husband's body.

I knew my children needed me. Their hearts were broken, too. But all I could give them was one more mile, hour after hour, day after day. Somehow, by the time we reached California, I promised myself that I'd pull the pieces of my own shattered heart back together and be the mother they needed.

If my own mother were here, I just knew she would have gathered us all like a hen with chicks, clucking over our dirty hair and clothing, drawing us tighter and tighter until we felt bound together again.

My grief for Peter crashed against the grief for the family I'd left back in Arkansas until I could barely feel anything else. I had no comfort to give myself or anyone else yet. So for now, the best I could do was put one foot in front of the other.

Fourteen-year-old James, still coaxing Belle and Bright along from the driver's seat of the wagon, had turned into a man overnight. His bright blue eyes were steely and determined. Like it was up to him now to drag us all to California.

"Keep to the left, Bright! Steady now," he called out, his voice filled with an authority that both comforted and saddened me.

Mary had changed, too. And not just because I'd hardly heard her cough. She'd taken care of little Nancy like a second mother the whole trip, but now she was the one who lifted my youngest into the wagon when she got too tired. Nancy cried whenever she walked beside me and saw my pained expression. But she smiled when she held Mary's hand.

It filled me with love and crushed me each time I heard Mary's gentle voice behind me. "Look at the prickly pear flowers, Nancy. Don't they look good enough to eat?" Or, "I bet Uncle Uri will get a rabbit in his traps tonight, don't you think? Sissy Lou could make a stew."

William, silent and solemn, stayed next to me like a guard, his hand occasionally brushing mine. For once, I wished he'd tease his sisters like he used to.

Uri and Louisa, along with baby Triphena, had become the bright spot in our day when we finally circled the wagons each night. We'd made our meals separately before, but now we sat around the same fire. Most nights, Uri strummed a melancholy tune on his guitar while Louisa and the children hummed along and tried to make little Triphena smile until she fell asleep.

I joined them, too, always at the edge of camp in case I needed to slip away and cry.

I wanted to be stronger. To put on a smile and help my children look forward to the new life we'd have in California. The peaches we'd grow. The calves we'd see born in the sunny pasture. The way our hearts would burst when Nana and Papa were finally able to visit —and maybe even stay with us.

If I'd been the one to die, Peter would have been strong enough to hold onto that vision. I felt sure of it.

Instead, I paced forward, my mind curling around a piece of poetry from Whitman. The darkest words I knew. When my grandmother died, I'd found a tearstained book open on my mother's bed and committed the lines to memory.

Despairing cries float ceaselessly toward me, day and night,
The sad voice of Death—the call of my nearest lover ...
The Sea I am quickly to sail, come tell me,
Come tell me where I am speeding—tell me my destination.

Part of me had given up hope that California or Mountain Meadows were real places. From the way Captain Alexander described the idyllic resting place, it sounded like heaven.

I'd started to imagine Peter there, waiting for us.

Alexander said there would be a real river in the Meadow, just a few feet deep, but so wide it wouldn't be dry. Blackberry brambles thick with fruit. Grass so lush the oxen would be able to eat their fill and put on the weight they'd lost on the trail. The forage had gotten better as the nights turned cooler and sparse grass began to reappear, but we were still in desperate need of a resting place. A chance to smoke and dry meat, dig roots, and dry berries to replenish our supplies.

The Mormons still refused to trade with us. *Move along, gentiles.*

I no longer tried to hush Uri when he rambled on about the Mormons and Brigham Young in front of the children. If anything, the talk took my mind off the hole in my chest for a few precious moments.

"Know why they ran the Mormons out of Illinois and Missouri? Chased them here to Utah Territory?" he asked one night around the dying fire. Nancy and baby Triphena had fallen asleep an hour earlier. I'd been about to slip away, too, but now I perked up my ears. I'd wondered about this myself. I knew their people had suffered, because Peter always said he felt sorry for them.

James and Mary shook their heads, eager to hear. Louisa sighed like she'd heard this a hundred times but didn't object. Uri continued. "Their prophet Joseph Smith was growing an army called the Nauvoo Legion. More than two thousand men." He glanced at me, clearly expecting a reaction. "You know how many men are in the whole United States Army?"

When I didn't answer, Uri kept going. "Two thousand."

My skin prickled as I remembered the men in uniform who had stopped Uri and James from entering Fillmore.

"Joseph Smith ran for president and lost, but he said it didn't matter. He'd be king of the United States anyway. Said the Indians—Lamanites, he called them—would rise up to help his militia overthrow the government."

By now, James and Mary looked terrified.

I decided then it was time for bed. I could do that for my children, at least. "That's enough, Uri. Joseph Smith is dead."

He gave me an incredulous look, exaggerated in the shadows of the firelight. "Brigham Young isn't, though. And from what I've heard, God's telling him the same thing he told old Joe."

* * *

We tried to barter for supplies with the Mormons just before we reached Mountain Meadows, in Cedar City.

It was the last fort we'd find before we crossed the grueling Mojave desert that lay between us and California.

Alexander rode out to Cedar City with Uri that morning and returned within the hour, their horses lathered in sweat from a dead run. There were no supplies to be had. And we needed to break camp and make a last push toward the Meadow immediately. If we camped near the city tonight, we were putting ourselves in danger.

Louisa refused to tell me what had happened at first—or even walk by her own wagon, she was so upset with Uri.

"He volunteered to go with Alexander, just so he could jab at the Mormons," she fumed, shifting baby Triphena on her shoulder and adjusting the little girl's bonnet. The dust had, mercifully, given way to rocky ground near Cedar City.

When Louisa finally calmed down, she told me that both Alexander and Uri had nearly been arrested in Cedar City by the town marshal on the charge of "foul language."

I hadn't been expecting this. For all Uri's conspiracy theories about the Mormons, I'd never heard him take the Lord's name in vain. Peter had, at one point, started calling him "Sheriff Huff" for how much he policed the cattle hands' language. Always barking at them to mind their mouths and manners in the presence of women and children.

"Uri? Foul language?" I asked, surprised to hear the laugh that burst out of my mouth so loud that Mary and Nancy—and the oxen —turned their heads to look at me.

Louisa shook her head and tucked a loose strand of blonde hair back into her braid. "Uri and Alexander went straight to the miller to ask about trading for flour. They'd barely gotten there when the militia rode up." She met my eyes. "They wanted an entire cow for a few bushels of grain."

My laughter abruptly dried up. It was a ridiculous offer. A joke. "We'd have no cattle left to drive, let alone feed if we made that trade."

She nodded. "Uri said something along the lines of, 'By God, be reasonable.' That was when the militia called in the town marshal, charging him with 'foul language.'"

She leaned next to my ear, so the children wouldn't overhear what she was about to say next. Her voice dropped to a whisper. "Then Uri *did* lose his temper. He told them he knew exactly why they were so set on hoarding all their grain. And that he hoped the U.S. Army would throw Brigham Young in jail for treason and drive the Mormons into the mountains like animals, where they belonged."

I gasped. Even for Uri, this was bad. "What did Alexander do?" I breathed.

Her cheeks flushed red. "Tore into him as soon as the words were out of Uri's mouth, but the damage was done." She fussed with baby Triphena's bonnet again, even though the little girl was shaded from the sun well enough. Then she added, "Uri thinks the Mormons are behind all the cattle raids."

I looked over at her, skeptical again. "How could it be the Mormons? The cattle hands said the raiders wore loincloths. Like Indians."

Louisa stopped worrying Triphena's bonnet. It had been white when we began the trek, but was now a pale brown. "I know. But Uri swore he recognized our brands on some of the cattle he saw in passing when the Mormons rode them out of town. Maybe he's wrong but ... I don't know."

I shook my head. "Maybe the Paiutes traded the cattle to the Mormons."

"Maybe ..." She drew in a breath. "But Uri said the Mormons seemed to know all about the raids we've had and the cattle we'd lost."

"What do you mean?" I asked.

"When Uri told the Mormons he wouldn't pay a whole cow for a bushel of wheat, one of the men joked that maybe half a cow *was* a fair price. Since we'd already paid so handsomely in cattle. Then they all laughed."

12. LUCY ROBISON

FILLMORE, UTAH
SEPTEMBER 1857 CHAPTER 12

The first week of school turned the mornings quiet again.

The silence made the hole in my chest ache more than the bustle, so I threw myself into my daily work like a house on fire.

Four-year-old Adelia was my only shadow while I helped Vick with the first-fruits' apple harvest each morning. Our harvest was nothing compared to the bushels we'd pulled from the sturdy branches back in New York. But it was something. There would be Winesap preserves and fresh fruit to share with our neighbors. And money for new trousers, too.

At first glance, everyone else in Fillmore went about life as usual, too. We went to church, cooked our meals, washed our clothes, and harvested our crops.

But beneath the surface, we were coals hiding live embers, ready to burst into flame the second they were stirred up again. At Brigham Young's order, we had tucked our belongings—and some of our harvest—into wagons ready to flee into the mountains at a moment's notice.

"Be always watchful," we whispered to each other.

"The Army might be here any day," the older children murmured solemnly as they lay their boots by their beds each night.

"Keep your gunpowder dry," we bid our neighbors farewell when we crossed paths.

Talk of war was on everyone's lips. Utah was under siege. Any day, the United States' Army might breach the standoff with our militia in Salt Lake and finish what they'd started back in New York, Illinois, and Missouri.

They called us traitors for our allegiance to God and our prophet before country. They called us "depraved" for how we chose to worship and marry. And they were terrified of the fact that we had a militia—the Nauvoo Legion—to defend ourselves.

Everyone said that fighting hadn't really begun yet. For now, both sides were locked in a stalemate in Echo Canyon.

But in my mind, Proctor had been the first shot fired.

Some of the men in Fillmore had gone north to help shore up our defenses. We didn't have Army-issue guns or shiny epaulets on our uniforms, but we had God—and terror—on our side. Even the poorest among us could turn their scythes into bayonets, and plowshares into swords at a moment's notice.

We wouldn't run this time.

We'd fight.

And if we couldn't last, we'd burn our cities to the ground and scatter into the mountains, leaving a barren wasteland behind with only Indians to greet the wagon trains when they tried to come west.

"Mama, can I have an apple?" Adelia asked, blinking sleepily and rubbing her hands across her red cheeks. The summer heat hadn't loosened its grip one bit, and the air was already sweltering.

"Yes, my girl. And then it's time for a nap," I told her, smiling like I wasn't about to fall to the ground from exhaustion myself.

When she was sleeping, I stood on the porch in the shade for a few minutes to catch my breath, eyes moving to the horizon.

My heart seized when I imagined what it would look like when the soldiers came for us.

What it would feel like to set fire to my own house. And this orchard we'd worked so hard to coax into harvest. This time, by what would be my own hands.

My eyes moved to Proctor's grave at the edge of the orchard, strewn with dried yellow flowers Adelia had picked from what was left of the drought-ravaged summer forage. The soldiers would march right over it.

I closed my eyes and put my hand on my chest, searching for the passion that had started all of this.

The testimony of the restored gospel of Jesus Christ.

Tears slipped down my cheeks. That well of living water inside me never ran quite dry.

Ten years ago, when Vick and I were newlyweds in Syracuse, New York, our neighbors the Mendons insisted I borrow their copy of the *Book of Mormon*. I'd only asked about it to be polite, since they displayed the book on their kitchen table like a treasure. But the way Ruth Mendon placed it in my arms, so carefully it might have been a baby, piqued my curiosity to say the least. All books were precious, but I'd never seen someone touch a book like that.

I knew a little about the Mormons even before I read the text that Joseph Smith, the first prophet of the Latter-day Saints, claimed to have translated from gold plates an angel had directed him to find. *"I know it sounds strange, but just read the book,"* Ruth Mendon had insisted. *"You'll feel a burning in your bosom. A testimony that God called Joseph Smith as His modern prophet to give us more of His words. Because He loves us so much."*

So I'd read the book. And, to my surprise, Ruth Mendon was right. My heart burned while I read about Jesus's visit to ancient America—my America—where the people touched the scars in his hands and wept at his feet. I loved the Bible, but when I imagined Jesus it had always been in faraway lands. Reading about my Savior blessing little children in my own country brought tears to my eyes.

I didn't realize Vick was reading the *Book of Mormon* too—at night, after I went to sleep—until he confessed when he reached the last page.

I couldn't deny the truth of what I'd read. Each passage, each verse, spoke to me as if God Himself were whispering the words of faith, of hope, of wisdom. Like the Bible I'd loved since I was a girl, I felt the truth of it like sacred balm, soothing all my doubts. And if those words were true, Joseph Smith was exactly who he claimed to be, too.

In some ways, my decision to read the *Book of Mormon* was the start of my life.

But in other ways, it was the end.

Vick and I studied and prayed for a year, preparing to be baptized. I felt so much peace and joy. But, like the prophet Lehi in the Book of Mormon said, *"It must needs be that there is an opposition in all things. If not so, ... righteousness could not be brought to pass, neither wickedness, neither holiness nor misery, neither good nor bad."*

The opposition came in spades, mere months after I first saw that book on Ruth Mendon's table.

I still remembered the look on our gentile farmhand's face when he told us that a mob had tarred and feathered two Mormon men across town. Eyebrows arched halfway up his forehead like he could barely believe it—along with a barely contained smirk.

He said the word *Mormon* like a curse. He talked about how the men had been tarred and feathered like he deserved it.

He had no idea that Vick and I had committed to be baptized.

I already knew about the attack. I'd helped scrape the cooled tar from Arthur Mendon's skin that night. The endless black mess peeled off bit by bit in tiny patches, along with a layer of skin. By the time Ruth and I were finished, he looked like he had been skinned.

The farmhand went on, bragging that he would have gladly helped the mob, were it not for the demands of his work on our farm that particular day. *"We oughta do what they did in Missouri. Exterminate 'em before they have the chance to reproduce. Mormons breed like rats, and they vote like sheep. They wanna make Joe Smith king."*

Vick had squeezed my hand, warning me to be careful.

Would you like to tar and feather us too? I wanted to scream at the farmhand. *Exterminate our children?* Instead, I held my tongue and returned the squeeze of Vick's hand.

Two days later, on a freezing early morning in February, Vick and I were baptized in secret in the icy Oswego River. My skin burned with cold, but it was nothing when I thought of the skin-eating tar and ash.

A week later, a mob set fire to our home.

I never saw the men who did it. We managed to put out the flames before it took the whole house, but the result was the same as if it'd burned to the ground. We left Syracuse that same night with the Mendons, to join the prophet Joseph Smith and the Mormons in Nauvoo, Illinois.

The frenzy of violence from Syracuse had followed us to Nauvoo. Different faces, but the same jeering insults, the same hot tar, and the same death threats. They threw prophet Joseph Smith and his brother Hyrum in Carthage Jail just a year after we arrived.

An armed mob stormed the jail a few days later and murdered Joseph Smith and his brother in cold blood. The founder of our faith, the prophet, was dead.

Then, once again, the mob forced us to run from our homes and into the wilderness.

Before the mob drove us out, Brigham Young—now the second prophet of the Restoration—received a revelation from God Himself.

It was an oath to be added to the endowment ceremony. These sacred vows and blessings pointed the way to exaltation. Vick and I had received ours when we were "sealed" to each other for all time and all eternity. We'd been married for years by that point, but as Brigham Young explained, being sealed meant that our marriage and family would last beyond death. Our bond would be eternal.

The endowment had taught us the signs and tokens that God would require for entrance into heaven. They were simple handshakes, simple gestures, but each one symbolized our commitment to our faith. During the holy endowment ceremony, we'd made covenants with God directly to carry out His will as long as we lived. In return, He would bless us.

After Brigham Young's revelation, we added an oath of vengeance to our endowment vows. Because God would not be mocked. And when the time was right, we would be His hands in delivering justice.

We vowed that this would be the very last time we let a mob drive us anywhere. And we'd never forget the blood the gentiles had spilled. Not in Missouri, not in Nauvoo.

The oath we recited was as stark as the blessings we received were beautiful. *Each of you do covenant and promise to avenge the blood of the prophets upon this nation, and that you will teach the same to your children and to your children's children.*

Those words had thundered through my head while we fled for our lives across the frigid Mississippi river.

The faces on the other side of the river had all looked the same, twisted in gleeful hate to see us run. Their whoops and gunfire carried on the wind for miles. A verse from the Bible repeated in my head. *Vengeance is Mine, and recompense; Their foot shall slip in due time; For the day of their calamity is at hand.*

"Lucy? What are you doing?"

Vick's voice pulled me back to Utah, back to our orchard in Fillmore. I shook off the memories of the mob and the icy Mississippi, realizing I'd grabbed hold of the shovel on the porch and was holding it to my chest like a weapon.

I swallowed the memories but not the rage. "I just put Adelia down for a nap," I said.

Things hadn't been the same between me and Vick. Not just because of Proctor's death, but because we'd just submitted our names for approval for Vick to take another wife.

I thought Brigham Young might overlook the request, given the chaos of war.

Instead, it had been approved almost immediately.

13. KAHPEPUTZ (SALLY)

CORN CREEK, UTAH
SEPTEMBER 1857

When Kanosh returned to the Paiutes after meeting with Brigham Young, three white men accompanied him. He introduced each like his brother, standing beside him and clapping him on the back.

Major John Higbee and Major Isaac Haight, battalion leaders in the Mormon militia, wore pale blue military uniforms. The last man was Apostle George A. Smith. His name was the only one I recognized. Apostle Smith had visited the Young home in Salt Lake often. The other two men were familiar to me, but I hadn't known their names. I'd seen all three of them go into the room with the hair wreath many times. Those were meetings I couldn't sit in on.

But here, beneath the hazy sky in the Paiute village, Kanosh invited each man in front of the fire in turn. Then he translated their words for the Paiutes who had gathered to listen.

Major Higbee spoke first. His graying hair curled over his ears in twin tufts that straggled into a messy beard beneath his neck. I felt his eyes on me, and I shrank into the darkness at the edge of the fire when he said, "When the governor of Missouri ordered our extermination, we pled for mercy. They answered us with bloodshed. When we fled to Illinois and built a city from the cholera swamps, they burned our temple to the ground. So we left our homes and came far into the wilderness where we could worship God according to our own conscience."

He cleared his throat and rushed on. "Your story is our story. The Americans have driven you mercilessly from the lands of your inheritance. When you pled for mercy, the Trail of Tears was their answer. When you fled west, a tide of wagons followed on your heels."

His voice shook as he finished. "I have been driven from my home for the last time. I'm prepared to feed the gentiles the same bread they fed my people—and yours."

When Major Higbee finished speaking, he stared into the silent audience like he expected us to respond with whoops of applause. But he spoke so quickly that Kanosh was only part way through translating by the time he sat down on a rock beside the fire.

I caught Awan's eye then looked away quickly, not wanting Inola to see. If Awan's mother knew we had become friends, I was sure a different member of the tribe would be assigned to accompany me on my errands. Awan and I would never again be left alone together.

Apostle George A. Smith, a thickset man wearing an ugly brown suit, spoke next. He drew himself up to his full height, lifting his enormous hands in front of him. His voice boomed through the quiet night.

"Your day—the Day of the Lamanites—has arrived. I can see the light in your eyes ... those of you who have been baptized." He gestured to Kanosh and to the gathered crowd. "Already, you are becoming white and delightsome. The scales of darkness have fallen from your eyes as you soften your hearts and unite with us, your brethren, in building and defending the kingdom of God."

I stole a glance at Kanosh while he translated the apostle's words with animated gestures. Then I glanced around the crowd. Everyone's skin, like mine, was the color of rich, ochre clay.

I was familiar with some of the words Apostle Smith used: *Lamanites. White and delightsome.* In the early mornings at the Young household, Clara had gathered the other wives and children together, including me, to read from the Book of Mormon. One day, she read a passage about the Lamanites, an ancient warlike and wicked people who had been cursed with a "skin of blackness," so that they would not be "enticing" to the white-skinned Nephites. *"Just like Sally,"* she'd told the children, taking my hand and lifting it up, so the children could see my brown skin. *"But look,"* she said, flipping my hand so that the pale skin of my palm faced the group. *"Sally has been baptized. She has accepted the gospel of Jesus Christ. One day, Sally and her children will be as white as you."* She let go of my hand and gestured to the children, who stared at me in wonder.

I pretended not to understand, as usual. But when I drew my hand away, I kept it clenched in a tight fist on my lap while Clara told the children that the Youngs were descendants of righteous members of the ten tribes of Israel. That's why their skin was beautiful and white.

Something rebellious burned inside me whenever we read from the *Book of Mormon* after that.

Maybe it was all of my Lamanite blood.

Apostle Smith paused to let Kanosh finish translating, then raised his voice even louder. His words were like a slow roll of thunder. "As the Prophet Elisha said, 'Those who are with us are more than those who are with them.' We are your neighbors. We are your brothers. Who has clothed and fed you while the gentiles trample your grass and shoot your warriors? Who has baked bread with your women? The gathering of Israel is at hand, brother Laman. We will bring forth the kingdom of the Lord, united as one against our enemies. Be not afraid, for the Lord is with us."

His eyes flashed in the firelight. A smattering of claps sounded among the Paiutes, this time as Kanosh relayed the final words.

I bit the inside of my cheek when Major Isaac Haight, also a church leader in Cedar City, finally rose to speak. My head was already swimming with sermons.

Thankfully, he was brief. "We will fight back the American troops who intend to replace Brigham Young as leader of Utah Territory. And as long as the Americans make war with us, the wagon trains should expect to pay in cattle."

Isaac Haight lifted his hands, gesturing to the gathered crowd. "The gentiles' cattle—and any of the plunder you can take in the raid —is yours. This wagon train is very rich."

I stared at him in shock. Kanosh rushed to translate this part. The words drew murmurs from the crowd. An old man, one of the tribe's elders, stood to speak. "Brigham says we should not steal cattle and plunder. The gentiles have guns."

After Kenosha translated, Haight nodded. "Brother, this is not stealing. This is payment for all that the American government has stolen from your people. You are correct that the gentiles have many guns. But as Apostle Smith just told you, the Lord will deliver them into your hands. Even now, their wagons are arriving in the Meadow canyon."

Another murmur rippled through the crowd gathered around the fire.

An uneasy twinge in my stomach kept my mouth shut. I had no love for the white gentiles. But I'd just as soon let them slip away to wherever they were going instead of strike them down.

Because the memory of that little girl still chipped at the stone around my heart, the same way the wails from the Paiutes had.

* * *

When Haight finished speaking, Kanosh rallied the men. His eyes lingered on his son, Awan. Not quite eighteen, Awan was still a boy. Not a warrior. But with his broad shoulders and strong, lean build, he looked older.

Inola touched her hand to her chest when Kanosh approached. I shrank back into the shadows, wanting to hear but not be seen.

"Leave him with me," Inola said. "What if the American troops break through up north while you are away with the other men? Who will defend us?"

Kanosh kept his eyes on Awan, who held his gaze unblinking. Did Awan want to go with his father? The Paiutes had raided cattle before, culling them from the herd at night and disappearing with them. Nothing like this. From the number of men riding out, they planned to stampede the whole herd and take as much plunder from the gentiles as they could manage.

Don't go, Awan, I wanted to shout. The air buzzed with danger and hot tempers.

Kanosh patted his son on the shoulder, confirming what Inola wanted.

Awan would stay.

Then he brushed past him, scanning the dispersing crowd. I withdrew farther into the shadows. If I could help it, I wanted to stay out of Kanosh's sightline. Recent events had kept him away from camp—and away from me—but I didn't want to take any chances of catching his attention.

Go away, I begged silently.

And he did.

As Kanosh and the Paiutes rode away with the white men, headed south, I studied their silhouettes.

Major Higbee and Major Haight were imposing in their military jackets and pants. Apostle George A. Smith created such a bulky frame in his flapping suit that he looked less like a man and more like a mountain.

Even their horses were well-muscled and striking.

The Paiutes rode like shadows, their horses all sinew and bone.

14. KATRINA HUFF

MOUNTAIN MEADOWS, UTAH

SEPTEMBER 1857

49 DAYS TO CALIFORNIA

By the time we made camp at Mountain Meadows, the details of what happened in Cedar City with the Mormons had spread like wildfire through the wagon train.

Opinions seemed evenly split on whether Uri had been in the wrong. Half of my neighbors had "damned Mormons" on their lips. The other half muttered "damned Uri."

But on all sides, the relief at having escaped Cedar City without anybody getting thrown in jail was thick in the air. All I could do was stare at the Meadow, though.

It was as beautiful as I'd hoped. But the fact that Peter wasn't here—even though I knew he wouldn't be—hit me so hard I had to sit down in the grass for a few minutes to catch my breath.

For the first time, I allowed myself to think about what it would feel like to reach California without him. That "land of milk and honey" Peter had been talking about for more than a year prior to our journey.

No matter how heavenly California looked, it would be as lonely and desolate as this beautiful, bustling Meadow.

I forced myself to stand up and watch my children. Nancy and William were already splashing headlong into the river, laughing with some of the others. "Baby Tri!" Nancy called, "Mary, bring the baby down to the water! I see bullfrogs!"

"Go on and take her," I told Mary, putting a smile on my face that felt like stretched rawhide. "I'll get the fire going with Sissy Lou."

Louisa and I had always been close, but after Peter's death she'd become the sister I never had. The children gave her the nickname "Sissy Lou," since she was only ten years older than Mary.

Louisa gratefully handed baby Triphena, who had been fussing after the longest day of travel we'd had yet, into Mary's arms. Louisa hadn't been quite herself since Cedar City. And neither had Uri. The thought that he might be stuck in a jailhouse right now seemed to have sobered him. Or maybe it was the hide-tanning he'd gotten from Captain Alexander.

While James unyoked Belle and Bright, Louisa and I prepared a meal of soda biscuits and beans, using the last of the wheat flour. Every few minutes I glanced up to catch sight of Mary, who was looking after the younger children as they bathed in a shallow inlet a safe distance from the eager herds that splashed into the river headlong.

The sight made my heart lift a little.

Seeming to read my thoughts, Louisa took my arm. "There's still good things left, Kit. Look at them. They're okay."

My throat squeezed tight. "Thanks to you and Uri."

She gripped my arm tighter. "You know that's not true, Katrina Huff. You're their mother. You're just who they need."

I didn't answer. I was their mother, but they deserved more. If it hadn't been for Uri and Louisa, I was pretty sure I would have laid down in the dirt and died by now.

My heart sank with the truth of it.

In California, I'd find a way to rally. Until then, I'd do whatever it took to drag myself one more mile.

We're nearly there.

"Come on, help me with the biscuits," Louisa said gently. "There's no flour to make more, and I don't want to burn them."

I swallowed down the despair and followed her. Everything had tasted like dust since Peter died, but maybe that was for the best. We'd have to get by on whatever meat we could smoke and hardtack —or as little Nancy called it, "heart attack"—until we crossed the desert.

When I stood up from shaping biscuits by the fire to wipe my sticky hands on my skirt, I realized that Louisa had slipped away.

I listened for the children's voices above the quiet bustle of the circled wagons. Everyone was exhausted, and the usual muted chaos was barely a flicker tonight. Even the wagons, usually arranged in a tight circle, were sprawled across the Meadow in the grass like they were too tired to move an inch more.

There'd be time to circle them in the morning. The steep walls of the canyon that rose above the Meadow would make it difficult for anyone to raid the cattle tonight.

When I still couldn't hear the children, I left the fire licking the bottom of the cast iron to put eyes on the inlet where they'd been swimming.

I went around the back of our wagon and stopped. The children stood like statues in the shallow inlet, their faces turned westward in awe.

The last rays of daylight had turned the rippling river current orange and red. The basin's craggy peaks were like black teeth on the horizon, as if the valley were a mouth and the river its fiery tongue.

For just a moment, I forgot about the near-arrest in Cedar City and the cattle raids. The grain we couldn't mill. The unforgiving desert that lay ahead of and behind us. What had happened to my Peter.

At this moment, the Meadow really did look like heaven itself. Alexander had spoken of it often during our trek through the dust-choked desert. I'd secretly been bracing for it to be less beautiful than he'd described. Utah Territory was brimming with sage and rocks—a far cry from this little oasis. But if anything, he'd undersold it. Mountain Meadows was a lush green paradise, full of clumping aspens and tender grass that our herds greedily snatched up.

I watched as America Dunlap, a seven-year-old girl in our party, helped Nancy put her shoes back on while Mary re-braided her hair. I tried to make the peaceful memory stick in my mind for the days ahead.

"The biscuits are burning." Louisa's lilting voice came from behind me, and I shook myself from the reverie to hurry back to her. "But we won't taste that." She grinned at me, holding a small jar of peach preserves out in front of her.

My mouth fell open. I thought we'd run out of preserves a long time ago. "Are you sure? It'll be gone before you blink once Nancy sees it."

She laughed. "I'm sure. I've been saving it for this very moment."

I rubbed at my eyes before the tears could fall. She took my arm and drew me back toward the coals. "We all need a little sweetness tonight, I think."

* * *

A group of strangers traveling on foot entered the Meadow and approached our circled wagons shortly after the last rays of sunlight disappeared.

They appeared at the mouth of the canyon like ghosts, emerging from the Meadow that had gone pitch black except for a waning moon rippling on the current of the Santa Clara river.

The cattle hands along the perimeter of the herd nearly fired on them, thinking that a raid was about to begin.

Instead, a slender woman walked out from a cluster of aspens, holding a sleeping toddler. She was followed by two girls, a boy, and a man pulling a handcart. A few more adults, several children, and an old man leading a bony cow trailed a short distance behind them pulling their handcarts through the narrow mouth of the canyon, toward the river.

Captain Alexander invited them to sit by our dying fires for an hour before they moved on, slipping back into the sagebrush along the riverbank.

When Uri realized they were Mormons, he ran his hand along the pistol at his hip and left the fire. "I've had enough Mormons for the day," he muttered.

If he'd stayed a little longer, I suspected he would have changed his tune.

These weren't the Mormons we'd run across in Cedar City or Fillmore. These were outcasts. They'd been traveling with their handcarts under the cover of darkness for a month.

And like us, they were trying to get out of Utah Territory.

Even by firelight, it was easy to see that their children were starving, dull-eyed and dusty. The women—and the few men—were thin as rails. I'd thought our supplies were low, but seeing these poor souls reminded me that we had more than I thought. Even hardtack was a blessing compared to an empty stomach.

The old man who'd been leading the cow refused our offer of food—and even tried to stop his children from eating. But once the children saw the food, they devoured hardtack like wolves.

The other adults accepted our hardtack but, like the old man, refused to eat. Their eyes stayed on the children, uneasy expressions on their faces. They all wore thick rags for shoes, and dark sores dotted their arms, but their eyes were sharp and clear in the dim firelight. I stared in disbelief as all of them except the children held the untouched, crumbling biscuits gingerly in their hands. How could they keep from eating?

"There's plenty more," I told one of the women, but she just shook her head.

When the children had finished eating and dozed near the coals like pups, the old man told us why they were leaving Utah.

"My oldest son, Ephraim, was assigned as a missionary to the Paiutes in Northern Utah," he began. "Was gone just over a year. And when he came back, well ..." The old man trailed off. "He learned that his wife Caroline had been unfaithful.

"Ephraim met with the bishop and the stake president. There was a council. After some discussion, they decided that the only way to save her from damnation and keep her from becoming an angel to the devil was to spill her blood. Since she had sinned beyond the grace of God."

I held in a gasp. Louisa and I glanced at each other. Of all the rumors I'd heard about the Mormons, this one was new. More vicious.

The old man let out a long breath. "I was part of that council." He looked up sharply, and the firelight blazed in his eyes for a moment. "But I dissented. Caroline had sinned, but not out of wickedness. She was lonely, and my Charlie could be a poor company even when he was around. Surely she could repent. The blood of the Lamb would wash her clean."

I barely breathed as he paused and turned his eyes to the ground. The campfire popped, sending a spray of sparks skyward.

"They noted my dissent. But I was outvoted with a show of hands. They told Charlie ... my son ... that he was to cut Caroline's throat from ear to ear. And the next day, that poor woman willingly climbed onto Charlie's knee, her eyes on the knife he held until he drew it across her throat, spilling her blood onto the ground."

This time, I couldn't hold back the quiet gasp that escaped my throat. Mary and James, who had been sitting beside me and Louisa in silence since the refugees arrived, didn't move or say a peep. But I could see their wide eyes flashing in the dim firelight. I whispered for Mary to fetch the leftover beans we'd saved for breakfast.

The old man finished his story quietly. He'd been instructed to attend a disciplinary meeting the following evening. His lack of faith was concerning. Instead, he and another grown son and daughter and a neighbor had packed up their belongings and fled with their children in the early hours of the morning.

The story made my stomach clench. Had it really happened that way?

The desperation on the travelers' faces said it was the only reason they were here.

"We pulled these same handcarts all the way from Winter Quarters, Nebraska," the old man said, gesturing into the darkness behind him. "To come to Utah. To build the kingdom of God, heaven on earth."

One of the men standing above his sleeping children—a younger version of the old fellow—kept his head bowed as if in prayer until his father finished talking. In the silence that followed, he lifted his head and turned to Alexander. "We've had our fill of heaven," he said softly, casting his eyes in the direction of the Wasatch front. "We'll see what's waiting for us in hell, if we can manage the journey."

We offered the group sanctuary with our wagon party for the night, but they were quick to refuse.

When Alexander pressed them for a reason, the old man nodded toward a woman sitting wearing a dirty gray dress. Two thin, birdlike girls with long blonde braids huddled beside her, staring into the embers.

The woman spoke reluctantly, her voice so quiet I could barely hear her. She told us that she and her two daughters had joined this party of "apostates," or Mormon deserters, near Fillmore. She didn't offer a reason why she had deserted the Mormons, but I watched her thread her fingers through her daughters' hands.

Then she looked right at me. "They're angry with you," she said in a rush, like spilling a secret.

I blinked, but she flicked her gaze back to Alexander.

"And why is that?" Alexander prompted, his voice honey and his eyes steel.

The woman glanced at the old man, and he nodded.

"A Mormon boy ... and some Paiutes died around the same time our wagon train left Corn Creek," she said in a halting voice.

"All of them poisoned," she finished in a whisper, wringing her hands while she spoke, her eyes on the sleeping children sated from hardtack.

I exchanged glances with Mary and Louisa.

"What does that have to do with us?" Alexander pressed.

She looked away. "They said you did it."

More silence followed. Now I understood their reluctance to accept our food.

Alexander lay a hand on his son Hampton's shoulder and faced the woman. "Many of our friends and relatives in Arkansas will be following the Overland Trail through Utah in the coming weeks and months. They really think we'd put our own people in danger? We don't have any poison with us. What use would we have for it?"

The group was quiet when Mary returned with the heated beans a few minutes later.

Apparently satisfied by Alexander's response, even the adults ate this time.

"Thank you kindly," the old man said, passing the beans to the other adults first before partaking himself.

I wanted them to keep talking, tell us more of the stories I could see etched on their faces in the firelight. But as soon as they'd finished eating the beans, they woke the children and slipped away.

As I lay on my bedroll between Mary and Nancy in the wagon that night, I struggled to fall asleep knowing that the Mormon refugees had chosen to take their chances alone in the Mojave desert rather than risk staying with our wagon train.

I'd always thought safety lay in numbers. But maybe sometimes, it just made you easier to hunt.

15. KAHPEPUTZ (SALLY)

CORN CREEK, UTAH

SEPTEMBER 1857

With Kanosh and many of the men gone to raid cattle for a few days, life in the village felt different. Softer, somehow. Awan still accompanied me to draw water from the creek every morning and afternoon, but I had the feeling this arrangement would evaporate soon. Inola didn't try to shadow me anymore, and I got the sense I was no longer considered a flight risk.

I found myself walking a little slower on our trips to and from Corn Creek, letting Sweet Pea, the old brown mule, stop to snatch at a patch of dry grass whenever she wanted instead of tugging her along.

In his quiet way, Awan asked me question after question about what life in the Young household was like—and what I remembered from my time among my tribe.

I was delighted when I heard him laugh for the first time, a deep warbling chuckle.

Awan didn't pry about the scars on my face, so one day I told him about the man who had taken me and Tyee. Then I showed him the shabby yucca horse that had once had a twin.

Awan reached out a hand to touch the horse's soft mane in silence. Then revealed that his mother, Inola, and I had more in common than I realized.

"When she was six years old, her twin sister was taken in a Ute raid along with several other girls in the village," he said, explaining that the Paiute people didn't ride horses back then, making them one of the Utes' favorite targets. "Ten men from the village died that day, trying to rescue their stolen children," he finished sadly.

I swallowed back a bubble of sadness, wondering what my mother, my father, had done when they found me missing.

I thought of Tyee, lying motionless in the dirt where Batiste left his body on the shoulder of the main road in Salt Lake City where the men who refused to purchase him would see it. The angry scars on his cheeks were hidden by the blood and dust that covered his face and tangled his beautiful dark hair.

I hoped fervently that Inola's sister had been luckier than Tyee.

Clara Young once told me, as if I needed reminding, that most stolen children weren't lucky enough to find themselves in the home of a prophet with velvet couches. Most were sold to wealthy families in Mexico or even shipped across the ocean to work in the fields until their bodies gave out. Others were forced underground into the mines.

Other little girls weren't so lucky to be sold for a rifle—and then a handshake.

After Awan told me what had happened to Inola's sister and father, I began to speak to the other women in the tribe once in a while, pretending to learn the Paiute language at an impressive rate.

Over the next few days, the other women stopped bristling so much at my presence. Numa and Povi still held me at arm's length, but no more dirty brooms appeared on my bedroll in the wickiup. Nobody called me "Brigham's little doll" anymore. At least, not to my face.

Inola in particular seemed to soften toward me, asking Awan to find out whether I had a warm blanket for the winter. When I told him I did not, a downy rabbit skin covering appeared on my bedroll the following morning. I had seen one just like it on the other wives' beds. Someone had spent precious time sewing the delicate skins together.

The dusty, desert village still didn't feel like home. I suspected nothing ever would.

But it didn't feel like I was in exile anymore, either.

16. LUCY ROBISON

FILLMORE, UTAH
SEPTEMBER 1857

I was dreaming of Proctor when the knock came at the front door.

My boy and I were walking hand in hand through the apple orchard, marveling at how the roots had indeed deepened to sustain the trees in the hard-baked desert. He wore a new pair of trousers—the ones I'd promised to make him with the money from the steer hides. His eyes were bright and clear.

The soft rap from the other room startled me awake.

I blinked into the darkness and sat up, half terrified by whoever was out there at this hour of the night, and half sick with longing to return to my dream about Proctor.

Vick lay a hand on my shoulder and pulled on the stiff, dusty trousers he'd set by the bed the night before. Even in the low light, his pale green eye stood out from the murky one. When Vick and I had met as children in New York, both eyes had been pale. People always thought he'd suffered some awful injury or that he was blind out of that eye, but the truth was less interesting, and he could see just fine. Another boy had darted past him through a thicket in the forest while they were playing, sending a long, skinny branch snapping back at Vick's face. He joked that his better angels sat on the pale side, his demons on the dark.

"It's probably the Johnsons," Vick murmured after the door knock, knitting his thick eyebrows together and turning away from me.

The Johnsons' baby had gotten worse, feverish and listless. The poor child, already a skinny thing, had withered away over the past week. His eyes were huge, and his cries had stopped.

Now the family's two toddlers were sick as well.

"There's a little broth left in the larder," I said, shivering in the cold room while I pulled my dress over my shoulders.

A frigid breeze blew through the kitchen as the door creaked shut and Vick ushered a tall, thin man into the room. It wasn't the Johnsons.

My relief soured right back to concern when I recognized Bishop Brunson and the expression on his face. His mouth was a stark line in the light of the kerosene lantern he held.

When he swung the lantern toward me and saw the fear in my eyes, the set of his mouth softened. "I haven't brought my doctor's bag, Sister Robison." He shifted his eyes to Vick. "I'm here as your bishop. To speak with your husband."

A flurry of questions lodged in my throat. Was he here to talk about plural wives? Vick wasn't courting anyone yet. He'd only just gotten permission.

Was that a reason for such a late visit though? He'd never come to our house at this hour before.

Vick reached for my hand and squeezed it twice, the same signal we'd used since we were teenagers, courting in upstate New York. *Careful. Tread lightly,* I warned myself. It had started the first time I invited Vick to dinner after we'd gotten engaged. My father had some particular ideas about the man I was supposed to marry, and I'd promised him some signal he was about to step on a landmine topic.

I told Bishop Brunson goodnight and swallowed my questions. Then I returned to the bedroom, and tucked the still-warm quilt around my body.

The low baritone of Bishop Brunson's voice and the softer bass of Vick's responses whispered through the quiet house, but I couldn't make out a single word.

I stared into the blackness, wide awake and waiting for Vick to come back to the bedroom. The last time I remembered him squeezing my hand like that was in Syracuse. Right before we were driven from our home for the first time.

* * *

Bishop Brunson's visit was brief. The front door clunked shut after barely five minutes.

When Vick returned to the bedroom where I lay awake, he reached for his coat, hat, and rifle.

"Is it the war?" I asked fearfully.

He nodded but hesitated to speak, turning slightly away from me so I got his dark eye. I dug my fingers into the blanket, puzzled. Something told me Bishop Brunson wanted him to stay silent.

We'd never had secrets between us, though. It had been that way since we were children. It was one of the reasons I'd married him.

I figured the straight and narrow path to heaven wasn't so narrow a man and wife couldn't walk side by side. If we were one in the eyes of God, as a married couple, anything the Bishop told Vick was for my ears, too.

I suspected God would agree with me, even if Bishop Brunson wouldn't.

"Vickery Robison, you tell me what he said right now," I demanded.

"Things aren't going well at Echo Canyon, " Vick said solemnly, still keeping his dark eye facing me.

My pulse thudded while I waited for him to tell me what this meant. Were we supposed to light our house and orchard on fire and run, so that the troops wouldn't be able to make use of the supplies we left behind? Did we need to wake the children?

I moved to stand, but he shook his head then shifted his gaze to the children's room. When nothing stirred, he lowered his voice and continued. "Bishop Brunson says our militia is losing ground against the American Government."

Fear made goosebumps pop across my arms. "How long can we last against them?" I asked, my voice shaking.

"Bishop Brunson believes they'll back off soon, but we can't let them break through into Salt Lake. Our soldiers need reinforcements."

I suddenly understood the purpose of Bishop Brunson's visit.

He wanted my Vick to stand against the mob. This one, armed and trained to fight by the United States itself.

I shook my head. "They won't back off. Why would they back off?"

The mobs never backed off, let alone one as powerful as the U.S. Army.

Vick drew in a deep breath. "Because until they back down, it's not safe for any wagon trains to move through. Brigham Young warned President Buchanan that the Indians are pretty riled up over the fact that he's being replaced as governor ..." He paused. Then, like it was an afterthought, added, "All the government cares about is the wagon trains. And if the Indians are riled up, it's not safe for the wagons to travel through Utah."

I stared open-mouthed, letting what he'd said sink in as he kept going. "Chief Kanosh and the Paiutes have already followed the gentile wagon train south to stampede their cattle." His mouth twitched like he wasn't supposed to be telling me any of this. "And when they do, it'll be the biggest raid anyone's seen on the Overland Trail. That should change old James Buchanan's mind about pushing troops into Utah."

I nodded, not caring if the Paiutes stampeded every single one of the gentiles' steers. Took every single one of their wagons and all their supplies. I'd never laid eyes on the members of the wagon train that had poisoned my boy. But in my mind's eye, I saw them as clearly as I'd seen the seething mob in Syracuse, and again in Nauvoo. Faces twisted in hateful smiles, eager to drive us from our homes and exterminate us like rats.

The gentiles deserved everything they lost.

The day of their calamity is at hand.

Still, the satisfaction did nothing to temper the slivers of fear pricking my chest. What if all hell broke loose? What if I never saw him again? "Do you have to go north?" I asked Vick.

Vick squeezed my hand once more and leaned in to kiss me softly. "God willing, this will all be over soon."

I swallowed hard, wishing I could believe him.

A few minutes later, he saddled his favorite horse, a steady bay, and was gone.

17. KATRINA HUFF

MOUNTAIN MEADOWS, UTAH
SEPTEMBER 1857
49 DAYS TO CALIFORNIA

Dawn broke cold in the Meadow, filling the ravine with a thick mist that draped the wagons like a shroud.

I woke early, while the light was still pewter gray. My stomach felt sick and sour from what I'd heard from the Mormon refugees by the campfire the night before. Coffee would only make it worse, but the comforting trickle of bitter warmth called to me all the same. Louisa and Uri would have a pot brewing already, since baby Triphena still woke at the crack of dawn.

I tucked the quilts closer around Nancy, who hugged Mary in her sleep. A few feet away, James and William were snuggled together in their own pile.

I promised myself that today I would smile for them. Maybe even wade in the inlet of the Santa Clara river and splash like my wild children.

I'd ask James to teach me how to yoke the oxen properly—since I still couldn't do it. I resolved that I'd learn to drive the wagon with confidence while we crossed the Mojave.

Maybe today I'd braid Mary and Nancy's fresh-washed hair into new braids. Then I'd take stock of the provisions we had left and pick blackberries to dry.

Maybe the Meadow could be a place to rest and begin again.

Then I looked at my lone bedroll and missed Peter with a ferocity that closed my throat and made me hurry away from the wagon. For the briefest moment each morning, I still expected to find him next to

95

me. The remembering that followed was like another death every time.

My children needed their father. So did I.

What good was I out here without him?

I told myself, for the hundredth time, that when we reached California, I'd be the mother my children needed again. Like I had been back in Arkansas. For now, I just needed to get us there without coming apart at the seams.

We're nearly there.

I twisted the wedding band on my finger, feeling the grooves where the two loops fit together as one. Peter had worn one part of the gimmel band during our engagement—on his pinky. When we married, he gave me back the other half of the gimmel ring so that the two loops locked together on my finger.

I was supposed to bury him with his half of the gimmel ring. But I couldn't bear the thought of it being ripped from his finger when the coyotes dug into the shallow grave. So I kept it on my finger instead, twisting it round and round at night until exhaustion won over grief.

The wagon creaked a bit as I pulled on my dress and stockings then wrapped a shawl around my shoulders.

James's eyes fluttered open, and I shook my head. *Sleep,* I mouthed. *Stay.* It was too early for chores. Too early to carry on like we hadn't been driving through endless hostile territory at a dead run without supplies.

James nodded and closed his eyes.

I moved through the fog, past silent wagons hulking in the growing light. They looked as scattered and exhausted as I felt.

A stone's throw away, the soft clink of tin and the crackle of the first rekindled fires came from other early risers. Other than that, the Meadow was strangely silent. I peered in the direction of the river's soft burble, but through the mist, I couldn't see any of the cattle. As if to set my mind at ease, a deep lowing chorus came from farther up the canyon.

I found Louisa and Uri tucked around their small campfire with baby Triphena, huddled over steaming tins of weak coffee. A spit strung with a fat rabbit carcass hung across the flames. The smell made my stomach growl. A few feet away, another family—Uri and Louisa's neighbors from back in Arkansas, the Dunlaps—gathered around an identical spitfire, roasting what looked like quail.

I raised my hand in greeting. The Dunlaps' daughter, seven-year-old America, pointed excitedly at the small lumps of meat hanging from her family's spit sticks. She'd tucked herself so close to the fire that flakes of white ash dotted her dark braids.

Uri gave me a tired smile and motioned for me to sit. His beard had grown into something of a bird's nest, making him look slightly less like my Peter. Little droplets of coffee clung to the patch beneath his bottom lip. "I set a few snares last night and woke up to three cottontails. Finally some decent hunting."

I nodded my appreciation. Anything other than dried beef, hardtack, and beans was a welcome change.

Louisa shifted the baby to the ground and patted the dirt beside her. Then she leaned over to dip an empty mug into the pot on the fire. "I haven't milked the cow yet, but—"

Boom.

I flinched. The sound of a gunshot came from close by.

Boom, boom.

Two more in rapid succession. My hands curled into fists.

Then a flash of movement from the neighboring wagon drew my eye. I watched in horror as little America Dunlap—who had grinned and shown me her breakfast just a moment ago—toppled over, headfirst, into the campfire. The spit-stick broke and the flames hissed.

Boom, boom, boom.

The gunfire ripped through the quiet Meadow so unexpectedly that for a few moments, we all stayed exactly where we were. Louisa kneeling by the fire with the fresh tin of coffee. Baby Triphena wide-eyed and frozen. Me reaching toward her with outstretched fingers.

Uri was the first to react. He scrambled to his feet and snatched up the baby. Then he seized Louisa's hand, pulling her roughly to her feet and knocking the coffee into the dirt.

America Dunlap's mother frantically tried to pull her daughter's body from the fire. Louisa grabbed hold of my arm, took the baby from Uri, and we dove toward the wagon a few feet away.

Uri's rifle was propped against the nearest wheel. He lunged for it, wheeled around, and was swallowed up by the mist before Louisa or I could make a sound.

Boom, boom, boom, boom.

More shots fired. What was happening? Who was attacking us?

My children's names ripped through my mind in time with a volley of cracks that drowned out the wails: *Nancy, Mary, James, William.*

Nobody was there to protect them. Not me, and certainly not Peter.

The shots came again and again. The majority from a gully due west.

Louisa's grip on my arm tightened.

Baby Triphena screamed.

A man still wearing his nightclothes barreled out from one of the silhouetted wagons several yards away. I couldn't see his face through the mist, but his rifle looked like an extension of his body in the fog.

Boom.

He stopped running and doubled over at the stomach.

Then he dropped the rifle with a soft thud and crumpled beside it.

"Josiah!" The cry came from the dark wagon behind him. My mouth was cotton. My eyes burned. But I didn't dare blink.

Nancy, Mary, James, William.

They needed me. But what could I do?

"No," Louisa choked. "No." Wailing rose from the wagon, where Josiah's wife Matilda and their four children had been sleeping a few minutes earlier.

Josiah didn't move.

Louisa thrust the baby into my arms and tried to get to her feet. "Uri," she gasped. "There's another rifle in the wagon. I can help—"

"No, Louisa. *No.*" I tugged her roughly to follow me, then worked to wedge my body farther beneath the wagon.

I wanted to run, too. Dash the short distance to where my children lay sleeping, and tuck them under my arms like a coyote protecting her pups. At least be there with them.

They need you, my brain screamed. But even through the terror and guilt, I knew I couldn't help them by running through the bullets.

I yanked harder on the back of Louisa's dress and pulled her to me and the baby. The fabric tore in my hand with a sickening rip, but I clawed to keep hold. Triphena screamed louder, a siren in my ears.

Nancy. Mary. James. William.

Why hadn't I stayed with them a little longer?

Because you're not the mother they need, my mind roared.

Were they cowering on the wagon floor? Or were their bodies as motionless as Josiah's?

As America Dunlap's.

As their father's.

I put the awful thoughts out of my mind. The children would duck their little heads and hide. The bullets wouldn't find them. I pulled Louisa and the wailing baby tighter, praying I was right.

I thought of the rifles stockpiled in the larger supply wagons. We had plenty of weapons, but we'd never been ambushed like this. Never needed them this quickly.

Boom, boom, boom.

One of the bullets struck the dirt an arm's length from Louisa's face. She flinched and coiled against me and the baby, then went rigid.

At first, I thought the bullet had hit her. Then I followed her gaze.

A stone's throw away, in the mist giving way to the breaking dawn light, the silhouettes of several men hunched low in a tangle of sagebrush. With a deep-throated howl, they leaped from their cover and rushed toward our wagon in a dead run.

I caught a flash of a bare chest smeared with something black. Arms and legs slathered with red and white paint. Eager rifles roared to life with each step in a volley of sparks and smoke.

Indians!

Could they see us? I stifled the scream that rose alongside hot bile in my throat.

Boom, boom, boom.

The ground beneath me shook like thunder. Between gunshots, the bellows of our cattle, loud whoops, and a growing rumble of frantic hoofbeats filled the air.

The Indians were stampeding the cattle.

Louisa pulled Triphena to her. I pushed my face into the grass, willing it to swallow me up.

BOOM.

This time, the scream that followed the deafening chaos came from right in front of me. From the men just a few feet away from the wagon. I looked up in time to see the man with the red and white paint all over his body fall backward.

"Attack!" A familiar, deep voice sliced through the chaos.

Captain Alexander.

His command was followed by another volley of gunfire.

Only now, the shots came from *inside* our haphazard group of wagons, zipping through the mist to find our attackers.

My heart pounded hard, this time with desperate hope.

Alexander and some of the other men must have made it to our stockpile of guns. And not only were they still alive, but they were fighting back.

Please, I prayed. *Please, God, protect them.*

Our attackers drew back into the mist as quickly as they had appeared, retreating toward the walls of the ravine to take cover among the brush and boulders.

Within seconds, the trampled grass in front of the wagon was empty, except for several dark pools of blood.

"I have to find Uri," Louisa gasped, rolling away from my vise-tight grip and taking the baby with her.

This time I let her go because I understood. I was already scrambling out from under the wagon to run headlong back the way I'd come only a few minutes earlier.

Nancy. Mary. James. William.

Please, God.

The prayer died on my lips when I circled back past America Dunlap's body.

She lay splayed on the ground a few feet away, where her mother had been forced to leave her. One of her arms still reached into the coals of the smoldering campfire, the flesh curling red and black.

The rising bile in my throat fought harder for release, and I swallowed it back.

Another blast of gunfire sounded, farther away.

My stomach heaved.

I tore my eyes away from little America, ducked low, and ran for my wagon as fast as my legs would take me.

18. KATRINA HUFF

MOUNTAIN MEADOWS, UTAH
SEPTEMBER 1857
DAY 1 IN THE MEADOW

My children were alive.

Alive. Tears spilled down my cheeks as the word repeated in my head over and over, in time with the gunshots.

I hadn't let myself imagine them dead. But I hadn't quite let myself imagine them safe, either.

I found them just as I'd hoped, huddled together in a tangle like terrified baby birds. I pulled them to me on the wagon floor, taking in their wide eyes and shaking bodies, murmuring words of comfort I barely believed.

The gunfire had swelled to a fevered crescendo again, even more deafening than before. But now, the lion's share of the booming rifle reports were coming from our own weapons. As I peeked outside, I noticed that the fog had mostly cleared, and it was easy to see that even with our poor position in the canyon, our attackers were no match in a direct attack.

With the element of surprise gone, the Indians had been forced to retreat.

James crouched against one side of the wagon, our rifle clutched against his chest. His mouth moved fast, a silent tumble of words I couldn't hear through the gunshots, but his eyes told me everything. How brave he wanted to be for me, in conflict with how much he wanted to fling the rifle away and crumple into my arms like the child he still was.

"Mama!" Nancy screamed again and again, against my ear, the only word I could really hear through the chaos outside the wagon.

Bright and Belle, hobbled for the night a short distance from the wagon, bellowed loudly. So did the milk cow. She lowed and tossed her head, tugging at her rope repeatedly in a frantic motion that rocked the wagon frame. I was grateful for it, since it meant they were alive, too.

It took a moment for me to realize that someone had reached into the wagon itself and was hollering my name.

"Katrina!"

I turned around. It was Uri.

My delight curdled to dread as soon as my eyes locked on his arm.

His left shoulder looked like it had been shredded. Bright red blood and mangled muscle tangled with the ragged edges of his shirt that stuck in the mess of pulp. Prickles of bone fragments winked through the oozing red.

There was no question that the arm would have to be amputated —but only if we were lucky enough to get through this raid alive.

Uri's mouth was pulled in a tight, pale grimace. He shook his head and motioned me closer with his good arm, so I could hear him.

The children clung to me while I scrambled to reach him and pressed my ear against his mouth.

His breathing was labored, the smell of blood overpowering, but his voice was clear. "Alexander's been shot, too. Still a few Indians hidden along the river. We need to circle the wagons up tight, right now."

He paused to catch his breath. "Alexander has already ordered the men to start digging a trench around the wagons for cover. I need James and William to come with me and help." He gasped and stumbled backward. For a terrifying moment, I thought he'd been shot again. But then he drew himself upright, lurching toward me to finish. "Can you drive your wagon? I need you to bring it to the west edge of the Meadow, between ours and the Dunlaps. Pull it along the outside of the trench we've started, and get the oxen as close to the back of the Dunlaps' wagon as you can."

I nodded, even though I didn't know how I'd yoke the terrified oxen, let alone drive them where I wanted. Peter had always done that job. Then James.

Could I get the animals to keep calm and listen to me? Especially when I was taking them right beside America's lifeless body, and then along the river, where the shooters were hiding.

My mind screamed in protest as Uri beckoned James, and then William out of the wagon. James was fourteen. William was nine. How could I send them out into the open, to dig a trench? Closer to the guns that had turned their uncle's shoulder into snarl? But how could I keep them here, when every other family was being asked to do the same?

I nodded painfully. "Stay with them, Uri. Where are Louisa and the baby?" I couldn't stop the dangerous question from tumbling from my mouth even though I wasn't sure I wanted to know the answer. If he told me they were dead, I wouldn't be able to keep moving. And I had to keep moving. Had to protect my children. There was no more time to fall short of what they needed from me.

Uri squeezed my arm and motioned for the boys to follow him. "They're fine. With the Dunlaps. Move the wagon now, Kit," he urged me, grimacing.

I felt sick imagining the pain wracking his arm.

He went on. "Almost all the cattle are gone. The Indians drove them down through the canyon, but there's still gunfire coming from the brush. We think they're regrouping."

"Why? What else do they want from us if they've taken the cattle?" I could see the strain and suffering stitched into Uri's brow. There was no time for answers, but the questions piled up higher with each booming report. I'd never seen Indians act like this. They'd never been so bold as to stampede our whole herd. And I'd never seen Indians armed like this either.

"You know why, Kit." Uri's voice rasped harsh in my ear. "You know who gave them the guns."

My stomach coiled tight.

The damned Mormons.

Uri drew back and motioned for my boys to follow him.

They obeyed, their eyes fixed on the weeping crater of their uncle's shoulder. When Mary tried to follow too, I grabbed the sleeve of her dress. At seventeen, she was nearly grown. Alexander's nineteen-year-old son Hampton had started courting her a few weeks before Peter died. She was strong and lean, like her brothers. Her cough was so much better, I had no doubt she'd be even faster at digging than little William and John. But I already knew that if she tried to join the men, Alexander and Uri would send her back to me.

Keeping a woman safe on the frontline of the fight would be a distraction, and the men needed to focus on digging. There was no time to debate the order of things.

I held tight to Mary's waist to stop myself from grabbing hold of William and James, too.

In an instant, they were all out of sight.

Nancy buried her head in Mary's lap. Mary's hand found my clenched palm, weaving her fingers into mine. Her breath came fast and shallow. I pulled her to me, suddenly realizing that the last time I'd hugged her was before Peter died.

I'd give anything to go back to last night, to that glorious sunset, just to braid her hair.

Now there wasn't time.

I lay my other hand on Nancy's head, nearly overcome by the desire to race after Uri and hug my boys, too. Nancy let go of Mary and turned her body toward me, clinging tightly to my chest. I closed my eyes and hugged her back. I wouldn't let her down any longer.

I pressed my lips against Mary's ear and spoke with more authority than I felt. "Stay with Nancy while I move the wagon. Keep down."

Mary's wide blue eyes—Peter's wide blue eyes—fixed on mine. Full of panic, but also relief that her mother was, at last, taking charge.

I pried Nancy's fingers from the collar of my dress. One of the buttons came loose, but the clatter of it falling to the floor was lost in the gunshots.

Mary beckoned for her sister and held up the yucca horse she'd been carrying around. I wasn't sure where it had come from. Maybe Louisa had made it for her one night by the campfire. Either way, Nancy had latched onto the little thing, tucking it against her each night while she slept. The brittle horse had somehow survived the chaos in the wagon this morning. Its braided, sinew-tied front legs stretched wide, as if begging for an embrace.

The toy was just enough to send Nancy diving back toward Mary.

I let her go and crawled past my girls, over the driver's seat of the wagon, then climbed down to the wet grass.

Belle, Bright, and the milk cow stopped their bellowing momentarily and looked at me with glassy, fearful eyes.

Their shaking legs were hobbled together.

The big, gentle animals fascinated and terrified me on the best of days. Their heads were the size of boulders, and their short horns were sharp as knives.

Bright, the burly red bull with a dollop of white on his nose, let out a mournful noise between gunshots and swung his head back and forth. Each time he did that, his poor partner, Belle, nearly fell to her knees as he pulled her hobbles.

"It's all right," I murmured, hefting the heavy wooden yoke and pins into my arms.

I tried to remember what I'd seen Peter and James do when they yoked and unhobbled the animals.

My arms trembled. The yoke weighed more than little Nancy, and hefting it over the necks of the oxen was a feat all by itself.

"Mama, let me help." Mary's voice came from inside the wagon.

"No," I gasped, unwilling to bring her into the open. "Stay with Nancy."

On the advice of Captain Alexander, Peter had paid handsomely for properly trained animals for the trip. I'd grumbled at the price—until I saw nineteen-year-old Aden trying to yoke the green-broke Devon steers he'd gotten for a song. It took him nearly an hour to get the pins around the animals' necks each morning, and he'd nearly gotten himself trampled more than once when the team lunged forward as he attached the wagon chain.

Bright bellowed again and tried to bolt, this time knocking Belle cleanly off her feet and dragging her a few inches before she managed to right herself with an indignant bawl.

"Settle down," I told him firmly, trying to mimic Peter's voice.

For a second, he seemed to listen, locking his wild eyes on mine as I tentatively lifted the yoke.

A fresh report of gunshots ripped through the valley, and Bright swung his head again.

One of his horns sheared my arm, catching the edge of my sleeve and ripping the fabric.

I gasped and nearly dropped the yoke. My arms shook harder.

I couldn't do this.

Death waited at every turn.

Sing to them, Kit.

The words came in Peter's voice, along with the lyrics to the song he'd sung to the oxen so many nights while unhitching them, claiming it kept the animals docile as kittens. Though when I'd teased him for it, Peter had claimed that Captain Alexander did the same thing—though I'd never heard it.

Sing to them, Kit.

I didn't feel like singing. The song reminded me of the night he'd died, when I'd whispered those lyrics through my tears. But it was the only thing I could think of to avoid being gored. I cleared my throat and found the tune in the middle of the song.

"So fill to me the parting glass and gather as the evening falls.

And gently rise and softly call goodnight and joy be to you all."

My voice caught on the last part, and I realized I could no longer hear Nancy crying inside the wagon. She was listening to me sing her daddy's song, too.

The rifles continued booming intermittently. But Bright stopped tossing his head almost immediately when the first lyrics of the song left my mouth. He looked at me with a mournful pleading in his eyes and dropped his head.

I took a tentative step toward him with the heavy yoke and kept singing.

"But since it fell into my lot that I should rise and you should not,

I'll gently rise and softly call good night and joy be to you all."

Belle and Bright's lumbering bodies shuddered violently underneath my touch, but they kept their heads down while I slid the bow of the yoke over their hairy necks.

It was working. I just had to attach the pins to the yoke and chain it to the wagon itself. To do it, I'd have to stand right between the two oxen, hefting the heavy yoke into place on both bows.

I tentatively lay a hand on Bright's heaving neck, my eyes locked on those sharp horns cutting the air at eye level. "Of all the comrades e'er I've had, they're sorry for my going away ...

"Whoa, Bright, whoa, Belle.

"And all the sweethearts e'er I had, they'd wish me one more day to stay ...

"Whoa, Bright, whoa, Belle."

I waited for a pause in the gunshots.

Now, Kit. Keep singing.

Keeping my movements as calm and measured as I could, I stepped between the two oxen. If either of them spooked, I had nowhere to run from the dinner-plate-size hooves and hooked horns. All around me, wagons tucked into place to form a tight corral on the outside of the forming trench. At the far edge of the Meadow, there was an opening in the circle, a chink in our armor, waiting for my wagon.

The oxen's breath and their shaggy, sweaty bodies created a strange cocoon of warmth in the chilly morning.

"So fill to me the parting glass and gather as the evening falls," I sang again, repeating the only other lyrics I could remember. I fumbled with the pins and the unwieldy yoke, finally managing to lock it in place under Bright's throat. He shivered hard but didn't move, seeming to draw comfort from my presence.

Boom.

I had just tucked the second pin into place when Bright crow-hopped to the side. The edge of the yoke swung toward me, knocking me off my feet.

Boom, boom, boom.

The rifle blasts mingled with the thumping of frantic hooves all around me. I waited to feel one of them smash into my skull while I scrambled to safety.

A bolt of pain exploded in the big toe of one foot, pinning me where I'd fallen. Belle's foot. I bit back the scream, knowing it would only send the panicked oxen into even more of a frenzy.

Instead, I lifted my voice past the white-hot pain and sang the next line of the song as loudly as I could. Nancy's favorite. "And gently rise and softly call goodnight and joy be to you all."

It worked. Belle moved her foot back just enough. I rushed to stand, gritting my teeth through the hurt and managing to lock the second bow around her neck.

"Whoa," I commanded, reaching between them one last time to snatch the long wagon chain lying in the grass.

It looped into place with a satisfying *clank,* and my heart soared.

I'd done it. The wagon was ready to move. And the gunshots hadn't sounded again for a few seconds.

In the sudden silence, there was only the scrape of shovels smacking dirt and the cries of the wounded. I squatted to untie the hobbles binding the oxen's feet, then the milk cow's.

The silence stretched on. My ears rang with the ghosts of gunshots.

Had the Indians gone?

A dark pit of knowing in my stomach said they hadn't.

I spun around and limped for the wagon to pull myself into the driver's seat.

I'd never been up here by myself. It was more rickety than I remembered. And exposed. So exposed.

The milk cow tied to the other side of the wagon had worn herself out bellowing, but the frame still shook with her pulling.

If a bullet didn't find me, I felt sure I'd tumble to the ground all the same.

I grabbed hold of the reins and looked at the path ahead, through the Meadow.

The spot where my neighbors' wagons had been minutes earlier bore the marks of terrified animals and hasty drivers. The grass lay trampled and torn in haphazard tracks. A few feet away, the bodies of two men lay face-up and unmoving, side by side where they had fallen.

One had been struck in the mouth. The other, the forehead. Both were unrecognizable from the lead slugs that left gaping craters of skin and shattered bone.

I tried not to see, but the image seared itself deep in my brain.

"Get along, Belle. Get along, Bright." My voice shook so hard I could barely understand myself.

The oxen didn't move.

"Get along, Belle. Get along, Bright," I demanded.

This time, they obeyed.

19. KAHPEPUTZ (SALLY)

CORN CREEK, UTAH

SEPTEMBER 1857

Awan and I were just about to set out for Corn Creek to draw water when two riders appeared on the horizon, kicking up plumes of red dust and driving hard for the village.

My stomach tightened as they came into focus. It was two of the men who had ridden south toward the gentile wagon train with Kanosh.

The sick feeling only intensified when the riders reached camp, their faces set like stone.

They dismounted their skinny, trembling horses that dripped with lathered sweat, then strode in the direction of the clustered wickiups that housed the village elders.

Inola stepped forward to take the reins of two exhausted horses. They hung their heads, sides heaving for breath. One, a paint mare with a black patch across one eye and a white muzzle, had flecks of blood on the soft pink skin of her lips.

"Take the horses to water," Inola told me firmly. She put both horses' ropes into my hands and turned to Awan, locking eyes with her son. "You, go with the men."

As the chief's son, Awan would be admitted to the meeting with the elders where his mother would not. "Go," she murmured to him again then turned away.

Awan stood a little taller and brushed his long bangs out of his dark eyes. He didn't meet my gaze, but with the horses blocking everyone else's view, he put his hand on my back for half a second before walking away to follow the men.

What had happened in the cattle raid? The men should've been driving steers in front of them, accompanied by Kanosh and the others.

Something had gone wrong.

Warmth that was a strange blend of affection and fear spread to my toes while I watched Awan disappear into the nearest wickiup. The paint mare coughed, jolting me out of my stupor and sending flecks of spittle and blood onto my dress. Her glassy eyes told me she'd run until her legs had nearly given way. I placed my hand on the horse's neck to discover that she was shaking, too.

I forced myself to let the horses set the pace while we walked to the creek. But all I wanted to do was run so that I could find out what Awan had learned from the men who had returned.

Both horses were dull-eyed and spent, stumbling and shaking. Every few steps, I let them stop, heads hanging low. They were so tired that neither even tried to snatch a mouthful of grass. I feared that at any moment they would drop to the ground, before we reached the creek. "Just a little farther," I told them in a whisper, patting their heaving flanks. It was clear their riders had run them to their limit without stopping.

If they had been pushed to the brink of breaking, it meant something had gone very, very badly. Horses were precious in the village. I'd never seen anyone ride them to exhaustion like this.

When the horses finally smelled the muddy water of the creek, they pricked up their ears and seemed to revive. I smiled when the paint mare whinnied excitedly and tugged at her rope, trotting to reach the water in the distance.

I ran to keep up with the animals, finally letting go of the ropes to let them crash into the shallow creek and plunge their muzzles deep to drink. I tucked my feet beneath me and sat on the shore to watch them fill their bellies with water in great gulps, grateful for the brief distraction from my racing thoughts.

My stomach still churned with questions, but it was peaceful here. The tangle of brush lining the shores was tinged with green along with yellows and reds from the cooler evenings that promised fall. I saw locoweed everywhere now that I knew what I was looking at. While other foliage withered and died in the oppressive heat, the locoweed managed to cling to some kind of green.

I sat where I was on the bank, letting the horses pick through the sparse grass along the creek, but I kept a sharp eye on the locoweed to make sure neither horse got too many mouthfuls of it.

I suddenly realized that this was the first time I had been alone—truly alone—since before I could remember. The quiet was both strange and soothing. I squinted hard at the rugged mountains to my back and then at the rippling horizon in the distance, where the village lay.

You could still run, a little voice in my head prompted.

I shook my head, keeping my gaze forward, on the faint blips on the earth I knew to be wickiups. I didn't have anywhere to go. There was no map that would lead me home, if such a home still even existed. I doubted it. For all I knew, the Bannock were long gone, driven elsewhere in search of game, because of the endless stream of wagon trains.

An image of Awan's face appeared in my mind's eye, along with a rush of sadness. Inola had trusted me to walk here alone. Maybe Awan had accompanied me to the creek to draw water for the last time.

The Awan in my mind smiled sadly, and I felt my own lips turn upward slightly. I couldn't deny that a growing part of me wanted to stay among the Paiute. Would I spend the rest of my life here? Would I finally belong?

Before I could let myself think about this possibility, Awan's features shifted. Wizened skin and a handlebar mustache replaced his youthful features.

Kanosh.

It was alarming how easily I could forget I even had a husband. But memories of him skulked in the shadows of my mind, ready to leap out into reality at any moment. The sick feeling in my stomach came back with full force, and my heart thudded in my chest at the idea that Chief Kanosh would return soon.

And this time, when he came back to the wickiup at night, I doubted a scream would turn him away.

The image of his leering face slipped back into the shadows when I heard a loud groan—and a thud.

20. KATRINA HUFF

MOUNTAIN MEADOWS, UTAH
SEPTEMBER 1857
DAY 1 IN THE MEADOW

We had the Indians on the run.

As sunlight streamed into the Meadow, burning the dew from the trampled grass, we pushed our attackers into the boulders and brush flanking the river. The burbling water masked the sound of the gunmen's movements, but as best we could tell there were still maybe thirty Indians hidden from view.

We couldn't push them any farther than the river. The boulders and brush along the water's edge provided ideal hiding spots for them. Our position—out in the open, grassy bowl of the Meadow, boxed by the steep canyon walls—was poor to say the least. The second our men showed themselves from the protection of our wagons, the snipers fired.

We were now locked in a standoff.

Our men had dug an impressive trench inside the circled wagons. It was nearly twenty feet long and five feet deep, in addition to a bank of loose dirt along the rim.

I pressed my back against the dirt wall and drew in a long, deep breath. Louisa was tucked against my left side, her arm linked tight through mine. Nancy sat curled on her aunt's lap, her thumb in her mouth and her yucca horse tucked under her chin. William, his clothes caked in dust from helping dig—lay at my feet, sleeping from exhaustion. James remained with Uri at the edge of the trench.

Mary sat on my right, her blonde head heavy against my shoulder. Each time I felt her take a trembling breath, I sent up a

113

prayer of gratitude that, somehow, all four of my children were still alive.

America Dunlap, Josiah Miller, and seven others had not been so lucky.

Their bodies lay in the center of the circled wagons. There had not been time to cover or bury them. In the silence between gunshots, I heard the frenzied buzz of flies getting louder. Five men, including Uri, Captain Alexander, and America's father Lorenzo, had been injured.

The flies had found us in the trench, too, excited by the metallic odor that made my stomach heave. Louisa and I were covered in our share of it—though not from any injury, aside from my toe, which throbbed where Belle's dinner-plate hoof had crushed it.

We'd bandaged Uri's mangled shoulder the best we could, tucking the shredded muscle into the weeping cavity, and pulling out fragments of bone. The bleeding was contained, but the bullet was still lodged somewhere in his shoulder. There was little question he would lose the arm—if we were lucky enough to get an opportunity to amputate it before infection set in.

There was no water for drinking, let alone washing off the sticky blood. The water kegs on everyone's wagons were nearly empty. We'd planned to replenish them this morning, from the river. What little water remained in the kegs would need to be rationed for the worst of the wounded.

James, Uri, and the other men kept their rifles trained on the riverbank. They shot at anything that moved from around the boulders and within the brush. Every so often, I cautiously rose to stand, balancing on my good foot to peer over the ridge of loose dirt. Bright and Belle hung their heads a few feet away, hobbled once again but still yoked to the wagon. From the way their heads hung low, they had grown numb to the periodic gunfire.

If I craned my neck to see through Belle's legs, I could just catch the side of James's blond head past the wagons butting up next to ours. When James shifted, I caught a flash of red hair—Captain Alexander's son, Hampton.

I couldn't see Uri from this angle, but I was certain he was crouched on the other side of Hampton, gritting his teeth and stubbornly shooting with one arm. He'd never leave the boys. Not while he could still stand.

"They're okay," I said softly to Louisa and Mary each time I sat back down against the dirt. In the stillness between gunshots, I lay my hands on the earth and felt for the rumbling of our herd's distant stampede. It was still there, but barely. At first, the rumbling had been strong enough to send tiny bits of earth tumbling down the sides of the ditch where I huddled with the women and children. Now, it was almost undetectable. The Indians were driving the cattle and horses farther back north, the way we had come.

"Mama, I'm thirsty," Nancy said, removing her grimy thumb from her mouth just long enough to speak, then tucking it back in. Nearly seven years old now, she hadn't sucked her thumb like that in years. It had taken ages to convince her to stop. Now, I was just glad she had a little comfort.

Louisa lifted a hand to stroke her hair, then thought better of it when Nancy cringed away from the blood. "Just a little longer, sugar," she soothed, wincing when another bullet split the air. "Then we'll get cleaned up in the river and drink all we want. Did you know that Uncle Uri caught rabbits in his snare this morning? We'll make a stew."

Nancy didn't respond, but her eyes widened at the mention of a stew. Mary shivered against me in spite of the hot sun, her eyes dusty and red from crying.

William whimpered in his sleep and flopped a hand on top of my bad foot. I stifled a cry of my own. The pain, at least, distracted me from the growing thirst that burned my lips and throat.

It was hard to believe that just last night I'd fallen asleep thinking I'd wake up to a fresh start. Time to heal, before we drove our wagons across the Mojave. Now, all I wanted to do was drive Belle and Bright directly back into that blistering wasteland as fast as I could.

Nancy drooped against Louisa's chest, finally succumbing to sleep. Her dark, curly locks that were the same shade as mine and Peter's—stark in contrast to the other children's fair hair—plastered across her forehead in a sweaty tangle. A faint brownish-red smear, from Louisa's hand, had dried across one of her cheeks.

I leaned back against the mound of dirt and stared at the only thing I could see clearly from this vantage—the rocky valley wall the same color as the smudge on Nancy's cheek.

As my eyes traveled along the rim, they stopped on something. A lone horseman I didn't recognize, silhouetted by the rising sun, waited on the ridge near an outcropping of rocks and sage.

Not wanting to alarm the children, I reached for Louisa and tugged the arm of her dress. I pointed, and she followed my gaze to the rider. I felt her stiffen beside me. The ricochet of a gunshot hadn't sounded in at least five minutes, which meant that our attackers must have slunk farther into the brush near the river.

I shaded my eyes and squinted. Louisa did the same. I could barely feel the faint rumble of hooves in the distance anymore, as the cattle and horses stampeded even farther out of reach.

The rider didn't move. From his vantage, he would be able to see our wagons circled in the Meadow. He might even be able to see the bodies of our dead piled in the center of the trampled grass. He'd certainly also see the flag raised from the center of the circled wagons, near the bodies of the dead. The red, white, and blue flag with thirteen stripes and thirty-three stars hung upside down, a signal of the most dire distress.

My heart beat harder. "Who is he?" I whispered, but Louisa only shook her head.

It was impossible to tell anything much about the rider. Was he Indian or white? Mormon or gentile? Whoever he was, I wanted to scream, "Can't you see us? Look at my children. For the love of God, help us."

21. KATRINA HUFF

MOUNTAIN MEADOWS, UTAH

SEPTEMBER 1857

DAY 1 IN THE MEADOW

Minutes dragged into hours as we huddled in the trench.

The sun—and the flies—were relentless. But there was nowhere to run.

The children slept and startled awake over and over again to the sound of the droning buzz and the crack of bullets.

"Mama," Nancy croaked when she stirred. "I dreamed about the rabbit stew. Can I have some water yet?"

She slid off Louisa's lap and onto Mary's, beside me.

I leaned over and kissed the top of her dusty head and took her hand. "Not yet, baby. Hold on a little longer."

She drew in a shuddering breath like she was trying not to cry, then found the gimmel ring on my finger. "Papa gave you that ring, didn't he?"

"Yes," I murmured, swallowing back a lump in my throat.

She spun it round and round my finger as her thumb found its way back into her mouth and her breathing turned steady again. With one more sigh, she let go of my hand and lay back down across Mary's lap, her head on Louisa's.

"Mama, can I check on the boys?" Mary asked softly, her hand on Nancy's side.

I knew she wanted to lay eyes on Hampton, Uri, and James. So did I. It had been too long.

I tried not to wince as I got to my feet. "Let your sister sleep. I'll do it, Mare."

Each time I stood, I imagined a whizzing bullet splitting the skin at my forehead the moment I peered over the edge of the trench. I refused to let Mary, or anyone else take that risk if I could help it.

Bright stomped his foot and sent me a mournful look. Belle had lain down next to him to rest in the grass, pulling the heavy wooden yoke cockeyed against his neck. "Lay down, Bright," I coaxed him, but the fear in his eyes told me he'd stand until he fell.

I lowered myself a little and spotted a flash of blond hair. James. I lay my cheek flat against the dirt, hoping for a flash of red hair or a glimpse of Uri's brown trousers.

"Mrs. Huff?"

I startled and spun around, only to realize that I wasn't the Mrs. Huff being addressed. Next to me, Louisa was already scrambling to sit upright. So was Mary.

Red-haired Hampton stood on the back side of the trench—doing his best to keep Uri upright and appear unruffled. This, despite the blood from Uri's bandages seeping through the wound and onto Hampton's shirt.

"He collapsed. He won't say so, but he's hurt pretty bad." Hampton looked at Mary, then me. It was impossible to miss the clash of longing and ferocity in his eyes. He wanted to be the one with his arm around Mary in the trench. But he wouldn't lay his rifle down until he knew she was safe.

Louisa rose to a crouch, then reached for her husband. Uri muttered something under his breath but didn't brush us off as we helped him down into the trench. His eyes were glassy and bloodshot. The bandages that clung to his ruined shoulder were soaked through, buckling in where the bullet had left a crater.

Hampton reached for Mary's hand. Then he locked eyes with me. "The bullets aren't coming this way anymore. The shooters are tucked against that ridge." He nodded in the direction of the rocky slope near the river. "I'll keep James with me," he promised, then turned to leave.

"Hampton, wait," I asked. "Where is Alexander—your daddy—and your mama?" I could see Hampton's fourteen-year-old sister a little farther down the trench, trying to calm the baby of the family, Lizzie, who loudly whimpered, "Mama," every few minutes.

Hampton drew his lips together in a tight line and shook his head. "They're between the supply wagons in the middle of the field." He cast his gaze toward the center of the Meadow, where two of our largest wagons sat side by side. The upside-down flag hung limp in the windless Meadow, a few feet away. "They have a little water and fresh bandages."

I didn't press for details, knowing Alexander's injury must be severe if he wasn't with the other men. Like Uri, the only way that Alexander would lay down his rifle was if he could no longer hold it.

"Thank you, Hampton. I'll check on them."

He swallowed, then nodded before he ducked his head and hurried back along the trench, toward James.

I sank down. Silent tears cut trails down Mary's ruddy cheeks and landed on Nancy's dress. I wanted to tell her not to cry. Not to let the tears out. Not to waste the water. Instead, I gripped her hand hard and gave her something to do. In my experience, small, concrete tasks were the only thing that helped dampen the paralyzing waves of grief and fear. "Help Sissy Lou with Uri, Mary. I'll bring back bandages and water." *If there are any to be found,* I thought. "Stay with Nancy and the boys. And make sure your stubborn uncle doesn't try to pick up his rifle again."

Mary nodded and managed a smile, wiping her tears and turning her attention to Uri, who was already trying to convince Louisa that Hampton should have left him where he was.

I could feel Bright's and Belle's eyes on me as I shakily rose to my feet, placed my hands on the dirt, and lifted one knee out of the ditch. Bright had finally laid himself down next to Belle. "Hold on," I murmured to them, wishing I could pull them into the trench with us.

The two supply wagons stood in the center of the corral, a stone's throw away from the dead and the distress flag. I tried not to think about little America Dunlap. About the two men whose faces weren't even recognizable anymore.

For a few yards, I crawled through the trampled grass, making a beeline for the first wagon. I still hadn't heard another gunshot. And when I paused, I could no longer feel the distant thunder of the cattle and horses disappearing into the distance.

I suspected that the Indians hidden in the brush were waiting to flee until their companions had driven the cattle far enough that we couldn't easily recapture the herd. They would find eager buyers for the steers in Cedar City and the rest of Utah Territory. My heart sank at the thought. The cattle were our nest egg. Without Peter, I was already on shaky ground financially. I knew Uri and Louisa would help care for us. But a widow with four children was no small burden under the best of circumstances.

Small, finite tasks, I reminded myself so I wouldn't fall apart. *Get to the supply wagon. Get water. Get bandages for Uri. Get back to the children.*

Balancing on my heel to avoid putting weight on my crushed toe, I rose to a crouch and peered over my shoulder through the flattened grass. There was no sense crawling, pretending the open Meadow gave me any sort of hiding place. Just a few more feet, and I'd reach the first wagon.

Moving as fast as I could, I hobbled forward in stilting steps, forcing myself not to look in the direction of the frenzied flies feasting on the corpses to my right. The dried blood on my arms itched and burned something fierce, and the metallic smell made me sick.

A gunshot sounded behind me, but I didn't stop.

Faster, faster.

When I reached the two supply wagons a few seconds later, I gasped for breath and darted my eyes back to the ridge.

The rider I'd seen earlier was gone.

22. KATRINA HUFF

MOUNTAIN MEADOWS, UTAH

SEPTEMBER 1857

DAY 1 IN THE MEADOW

The large supply wagons sat side by side, six feet apart in the center of the trampled Meadow, surrounded by the trenches we'd dug and the tight corral of circled wagons.

As I approached, I saw bullet holes in the side of one of the water barrels. Beneath it was a mess of mud and grass. A shallow, dirty puddle remained, reflecting blue sky overhead.

Our water. Gone.

My heart sank a little lower. I put my full weight on my injured foot without thinking, sending the toe throbbing again, but the pain was nothing compared to what I saw in front of me.

Captain Alexander and some of the other wounded lay propped between the long supply wagons in the shade. I made a quick count. Five men, five women, two children. The ground beneath their bodies looked just like the muddy, trampled grass beneath the spilled water barrels. The injured lay in a mixture of the wasted water and blood from wounds that hastily applied bandages couldn't fully staunch.

I saw that someone had placed tin buckets underneath the biggest leaks in the water barrels, to catch the precious liquid. When Eliza, Alexander's wife, saw me limping toward her, she dipped a cup into one such bucket.

Eliza hunched on her knees, her dress a mottled mess of mud and blood. "Kit," she whispered. Her eyes were wide and desperate, pleading like I might have come to offer help instead of taking it. At the other end of the makeshift infirmary, two more women turned to

121

look at me. Both were re-wrapping blood-soaked bandages. One woman held a half-empty bottle of whiskey to a child I barely recognized through the crusted earth and blood on her face. The bullet had caught her in the neck, slicing through the flesh beneath her chin. The wound looked like a gaping second mouth.

Alexander blinked and fixed his eyes on me when Eliza spoke my name. His dark, deep set eyes always seemed slow and sleepy, in stark contrast to the quick mind behind them. Unlike the other wounded souls writhing in pain around him, Alexander looked almost serene—except for his labored breathing.

A bandage that didn't quite cover the jagged hole in his torso drew my gaze. The material covering the wound had a pattern to it, and it took a moment for me to realize I was looking at the skirt of a dress, soaked through and deep crimson. One end of the skirt had come unraveled, revealing bruised, swollen flesh that surely covered broken ribs. His chest rose and fell with the effort of breathing through the tightly wrapped bandage and the wound itself.

"How is Uri holding up?" he asked.

"Don't speak, just rest," Eliza commanded with a shaking voice, bringing one hand to rest on his cheek.

Alexander's neat black mustache twitched with the barest hint of a smile. "Yes, Captain Eliza."

"Uri is alive," I told them, kneeling beside Alexander. The sweet relief of taking the pressure off my crushed toes made me dizzy. "He's with Louisa and the children in the trench. Hampton and James are still standing guard," I said.

Alexander nodded but kept his lips pursed together.

"We need fresh bandages. And water," I told Eliza hesitantly, looking at the half-empty buckets. "How much is left?"

She shook her head. "There's only a little water left. Not much." She swallowed hard. Her lips were cracked and dry. I knew without a doubt she hadn't taken a sip for herself all day. "Take one of the buckets back to the trench with you," she instructed. "Give some to my girls ... and everyone. Here." She rose to a crouch and pulled strips of material from the prairie schooner. "We've run through the bandages, but there's clothing to spare."

I winced at the thought of someone's carefully packed second dress being used as a tourniquet. But for all I knew, the clothing belonged to the dead and dying. And besides, what was a dress if we didn't get out of here alive?

The thought made my stomach turn.

I took the half-full bucket and tin cup Eliza offered and held my tongue. The incessant buzzing of flies, whispered moans of pain from the wounded, and quiet pleas for water filled the silence. The gentle rush of the river, just out of our reach beyond the circled wagons, was audible amid all the misery.

My own dry throat ached to drink the cool water, but there were too many others who needed it more.

"The Indians have the cattle. The herd is long gone. So why won't they let us go? What are they waiting for? Did you get a good look at any of them?" I couldn't help myself. The fearful questions tumbled out before I could stop them. I clutched the bucket hard against my chest, terrified I would drop the precious liquid.

Alexander blinked his eyes open. The woman on the other side of Eliza, whose soft moans had been an awful melody to my questions, suddenly went silent. Eliza whirled around, clearly worried she had died. One of her arms hung limp across her chest, blown apart at the elbow.

But her face was turned toward Alexander, eyes open and mouth set in a tight line. She wasn't dead. She was listening.

When Alexander didn't respond, I pressed. "I saw two of the men. So did Uri. It was too foggy, too dark, to tell for sure, but they were half-naked, painted up." I swallowed. "Indians. But Uri still thinks the Mormons ordered the attack."

Alexander's eyes flashed. "We can't know it was the Mormons." His voice was firm as he went on. "We'll keep cool heads. We've been raided before—and not by the Mormons. It doesn't matter who the snipers are anymore. We'll fight like hell until we pick them off one by one, or until they run away after the cattle hustlers. Our men have already hit two more of the snipers hidden along the river." He blinked those hooded, dark eyes, calculating. "I believe they're planning on holding us here a little longer, until there's no hope of us recovering the cattle. A day. Two at most, to drive the steers so far back into Utah Territory that we won't try to chase them." He winced. "I'm sorry, Katrina. We'll all take care of you in California. Cattle or not."

His words filled my eyes with tears. Part despair, part rage, part desperate hope at the idea of leaving this valley of blood and fear behind to reach California. Poorer than when we'd left Arkansas, but alive. At least alive.

As long as we could just get out of here.

We're nearly there, I told myself firmly.

Even that part of my bedraggled prayer felt like it was hanging by a thread now.

I nodded. If there was anyone I trusted after Peter's death, it was Alexander. I loved Uri and Louisa, but Uri could be a hothead. Alexander was right. The *who* of this attack didn't matter right now so much as the *what.*

And the *what* was fighting like hell until they left us alone.

The squish of footsteps in the mud made all of us turn. It was one of our men—Pleasant Tackett. His eyes blazed while he stood panting down at Alexander. He glanced at me and Eliza but then said, "Last count, best I can tell, there's only a few gunmen left along the river. Should we rush them?"

Alexander grimaced and shook his head. "No. Don't leave the protection of the wagon fort. There's no telling how many men we'll lose if we force the fight out into the open. Keep shooting at anything that moves. And keep some of the men working to widen the trench."

Pleasant nodded once and crept back through the Meadow, the way he had come.

I kissed Eliza on the cheek and gently squeezed Alexander's hand. "Your girls are doing fine, they're right beside me in the trench. I'll be back," I said, hoping it was true.

* * *

Uri insisted I give most of the water to the children in the trench. He took a drink from the tin cup, then gave each child a sip.

While I was gone, Hampton's sister had brought little Lizzie over to play with my Nancy. They convinced her to share the little horse with her and baby Triphena. For an hour or so now, the two little girls seemed to forget we were crouched in a trench beneath the blistering sun, with the sound of flies in our ears and blood in our noses. Mary used the horse to play peek-a-boo with the babies, and the little girls laughed each time the horse hid beneath Mary's sleeve.

At long last, the shadows cast by the circled wagons shaded us from the heat. Bright and Belle sighed with relief, letting out a mournful bawl at intervals. I could only imagine how thirsty and exhausted they were, standing yoked with their noses up against the neighboring wagon on the outside of the trench. I wanted to let them out of their yoke so they could stretch their legs. Let them plunge into the river. But if I did that, we'd never leave this Meadow.

"Whoa there, Belle, whoa there, Bright," I called to them softly. "It's all right."

The last words caught in my throat.

Nightfall was still hours away, but the worst of the midday heat was past. Maybe by the time night fell, our men could sneak toward the snipers under the cover of darkness and end this horror. Or at least get down to the river undetected to gather a little water for the suffering humans and animals alike.

No sooner had I thought it than a gunshot split the air, followed by an anguished, earsplitting bellow from just above the trench.

The shadows shifted, and I scrambled upright, putting most of my weight on my good foot to see.

Bright struggled to stand in the yoke, pulling Belle and the wagon with him. Blood poured from his big, wooly neck, cascading onto the grass. He tripped on his hobbles and crashed down hard, right in front of me.

I gasped. He'd been struck in the throat.

"No, no, no." The tears I thought had dried up pricked at my eyes again.

His nostrils flared and his enormous, soft eyes rolled back. Below me in the trench, the children cried in terror, mingling with the soft bawling sound still coming from Bright's mouth.

Belle leaned her body as far away from him as she could, her legs shaking and her head tossing from side to side.

"Whoa, Belle," I told her, again and again until she hung her head in exhaustion.

The gunshot that hit Bright brought James and Hampton running, weaving and ducking through the cover of the big supply wagons toward us. Some of the snipers must have changed position. The brush and boulders along the riverbank offered a thousand hiding places. The shooters could be anywhere.

Stop, I wanted to scream to Hampton and James. If a sniper's bullet could hit Bright, it could hit them, too. But I kept quiet and watched as James lifted his rifle to his shoulder and fired.

The bloodcurdling scream from the brush told me he'd made his target. An exhale of relief escaped me, but the fear hung on.

Bright shuddered, and I scooted my body higher onto the trench ridge, so I could lay a trembling hand on his nose. "There, boy," I choked out quietly.

I sang until his body finally shivered into stillness and the lyrics caught in my throat.

"So fill to me the parting glass and gather as the evening falls.
And gently rise and softly call goodnight and joy be to you all.
"Since it fell into my lot that I should rise and you should not,
I'll gently rise and softly call good night and joy be to you all."

23. KAHPEPUTZ (SALLY)

CORN CREEK, UTAH

SEPTEMBER 1857

Thud.

I whipped around to see the paint mare lying on the ground a few feet away from me, her eyes glazed and her sides heaving.

"What's wrong, *tumi*?" I cried.

The mare lifted her head and made the pained groaning noise again. The skinny bay horse stared at her plaintively. Then he swung his head toward me, buckled his knees, and lay down beside the mare, breathing heavily.

"No, no, no," I wailed. What was happening? I was sure that neither horse had gotten more than a mouthful of locoweed. Awan had told me that it took weeks of eating the toxic forage to result in death. Had they eaten something else while I was daydreaming about Awan and dreading the day my life with Kanosh would begin in earnest?

I knelt in the dirt and stroked the mare's wet muzzle, now caked in dust where she lay on her side. If these two horses died under my care, I might have to run after all—whether I wanted to or not. I wasn't sure what would happen to me then, but I was terrified to find out.

Before I could lift my hand away, the mare jerked her head up and flicked it toward me. At first, I thought she was trying to bite me. I stumbled out of her reach—only to see her bite furiously at her own heaving side.

An image worried at the back of my mind as the bay horse nipped at his stomach, too.

The memory came into focus, of my mother, and tugging on the halter rope of a young foal. *"We must get her to her feet,"* my mother told me. *"Her stomach is twisted. We must help her stand, quickly."*

I stared at the two horses at my feet in horror, torn between the urge to run and the need to fix whatever emergency was unfolding in front of me. I couldn't remember how the foal's stomach had become twisted, but I remembered the glaze in her eyes—and the way she bit at her side in frustration while we tried to pull her to standing, just like these two were doing.

Unsure what else to do, I grabbed the wet, dirty rope lying at my feet and tugged, succeeding only in dragging the paint mare's head a few inches through the dust. She looked at me dully and groaned again. I pulled harder, planting my feet and shouting. "Get up, please get up!"

After a few agonizing seconds, the rope finally went slack and the horse stumbled to her feet, body swaying back and forth. Her belly looked swollen and distended. "Good girl," I told her shakily, then turning to the bay and tugging hard. It took all my effort to get him to his feet as well. I had no idea what to do once I got them standing up, but this was a start.

My heart leapt as the bay horse grunted and swayed on his feet. But then he sank back down. The paint mare knelt once again and fell onto her side, too. The task of getting both sick horses to their feet—and keeping them there—felt impossible for one person.

A hot tear of frustration trickled down my cheek, and I swiped it away. *Think,* I told myself as I stroked the mare's cheek. *Remember how to help them.*

"Please," I told the mare, then the bay. "I know it hurts. I know you feel bad inside, but please don't give up."

I swallowed hard, realizing how much I needed to hear my own words.

"Kahpe."

I whirled around to see Awan running through the brush toward me, like he'd leaped from my desperate thoughts.

"I don't know what to do—they're sick. I've been trying, but I can't get both up at the same time." My voice shook, and I couldn't stop more tears from rolling down my cheeks.

I handed Awan the bay horse's rope and kept pulling.

His eyes went wide. "You did the right thing. They must have drunk water from the creek too fast. Their stomachs are twisted. They need to walk."

We pulled hard on the horses' ropes until both animals finally stood again. They continued swaying unsteadily and biting at their flanks.

Awan nodded. "If we can keep them walking for a little while, they'll be okay."

I swallowed the lump in my throat and tugged on the mare's rope. She planted her hooves and swung her head, but finally allowed herself to be tugged along, a few steps at a time. "I'm sorry, it's my fault. I let them drink too much," I whispered to Awan after a few minutes of silence. Hot shame dripped through me as I thought, *I wasn't watching them very closely because I was daydreaming about you.*

He looked at me sideways from beneath his shaggy hair and shook his head. It fell back into his eyes. "You weren't the one who ran the horses until they were half-dead. How could you have known? I'm surprised you knew to get them to their feet."

"My mother ..." I trailed off. "I remembered something she said when I was little."

He kept his gaze on me and tugged the bay's rope. "I've heard the Bannock are excellent horse people."

His words rang true, and they brought the sting of tears back to my eyes.

There were horses everywhere in the background of my memories. I'd always been a little afraid of the enormous animals, but my mother told me I'd learn to ride one day. As a Bannock girl, I was meant to be part horse myself.

"What happened with the raid?" I asked. "Where are the cattle?"

Awan's face darkened, and he looked away. "More riders are coming. They're traveling slower. To bring the cattle back to the village. And the dead and wounded men."

I nearly stopped walking. The paint mare sensed my hesitation and buckled at the knees in an attempt to lie down again. I leaned into the rope and kept her moving. "How many?" I breathed. "What happened?"

He walked a few steps in silence then said, "Six wounded. Four dead. More, if the wounded don't survive the journey back here."

Awan shook his head in frustration. "My father wants anyone who stayed behind at Corn Creek to join him in the Meadow."

My heart sank. That meant Awan.

He continued. "My father says that the white Mormons are powerful allies. That they have power with God, with the government. That we must do whatever they say. But if they have such power, why are dead and wounded men on their way back to the village right now? How did a cattle raid go so wrong?"

I had never heard Awan speak with such anger about the Mormon leaders.

Like me—and Kanosh, and most of the other Paiutes—he'd been baptized. The white leaders said we were all Mormons. All one in Christ. But we knew a brown Mormon would never have the same power as a white one.

"Will you go with them?" I whispered, praying the answer was no.

He didn't respond at first. Just looked away. Finally he said, "When I left the elders' wickiup, my mother stopped me. She begged me not to go. She dreamt that I would die."

My breath caught in my throat. *No.* I turned so sharply that the paint mare whinnied in surprise and nearly stumbled to follow the rope in my hand. I faced Awan. "Then you can't go."

The paint mare bent her knees the moment I stopped walking. He reached for my hand to gently pull me along so the horse would follow.

When I complied, he didn't let go. Instead, he laced his fingers tight with mine.

"He's my father. He's the chief. I can't stay behind. Not when the other men are preparing to leave now."

In a few moments, the village would come into view. Then Awan would leave, and with him the only part of my life I cared about in the village. I wanted to tell him not to go. To plant my feet like the horses, lay down on my side, cry, and refuse to budge until he agreed he would not follow the men back to his father.

If things were going badly at the Meadow, there would be waiting rifles pointed in his direction. I wanted to scream that Awan should disobey his father. That Brigham Young and the rest of the white Mormons had no power except when it came to casting a spell over Kanosh.

Instead, I stayed silent and kept moving like my Bannock name, Walks Without Sound, promised. I knew I didn't have the influence to keep Awan here with me, and I was afraid that if I opened my mouth, tears would pour out instead of words.

I bit my lip and focused on keeping the mare moving, savoring the feel of Awan's hand in mine for as long as I could.

He tilted his head toward the bay, who had stopped trying to bite his flanks. "It's working. They're going to be okay."

The knot in my stomach didn't budge. I wondered, *But what about you?*

The first cone-shaped wickiups appeared as we crested the trail that led back to the village. Wisps of smoke drifted upward through the tightly woven thatch of several homes. The smell of roasted camas, along with something earthy, less appetizing, wafted through the air.

The women were cooking a last meal for the men who were preparing to leave—and making yarrow poultices for the injured coming back to camp.

I found myself gripping Awan's hand tighter. If Kanosh was asking for more men to gather at the Meadow, there was now a battle raging somewhere to the south.

A battle with the "troops" who had certainly not poisoned the water or the steers.

I thought again of the little girl I met. The one I'd given Tyee's horse.

My stomach churned, and I forced the memory away.

The sound of horses whinnying, and raised voices drifted toward us from the village. The bay and the paint pricked up their ears and walked a little faster.

My stomach clenched tighter. I gritted my teeth and put one foot in front of the other until Awan unlaced his fingers from mine and turned to look at me.

I refused to meet his eyes, still tugging the mare along toward the village.

He caught my arm, his grip gentle but firm. Then, without missing a step, he brought one hand to my chin, leaned in, and kissed me.

For one brief moment, the horses, the wickiups, and the smell of camas and yarrow disappeared, along with the sickening dread in my stomach.

It was over in an instant.

But I knew as soon as it happened that the feeling of his lips on mine would stretch the memory through the hours and days to come.

He handed me the bay's rope, held my gaze a moment longer, then loped away.

24. KAHPEPUTZ (SALLY)

CORN CREEK, UTAH

SEPTEMBER 1857

Awan had been gone for less than a day, but already his absence felt like hunger pangs, gnawing at my insides from the moment I woke up until the moment I finally fell into a fitful sleep, wrapped tight in my soft rabbit-skin blanket.

If I knew exactly where he was, I might have followed him. With most of the men gone and the women preoccupied with the news the wounded men brought back to camp, no one was watching to see whether I ran away.

And the truth was, I no longer wanted to run.

All I wanted was for Awan to come back and kiss me like he had before he left.

I knew it couldn't happen. I could only imagine how upset Kanosh—my husband—would be if he found out. I was pretty sure he wouldn't blame his son. Boys never got blamed. The chief would blame me. And I didn't want to find out what he'd do next. He couldn't find out about the kiss.

But I couldn't stop thinking about it. Also I couldn't stop worrying about Awan. All I knew was that he'd gone south with the remaining men to a place called Mountain Meadows.

Now the only thing I could do was wait. And pray.

"Sally will help me skin the rabbits," Inola said, breaking into my thoughts as we prepared the morning's breakfast.

I blinked in surprise and looked up at Numa and Povi, who also looked taken aback. For once, our snares set outside camp had been full in the morning. But skinning the rabbits was usually something Inola did with the other two wives. It took a while to scrape and tan the skins, and the women liked to talk among themselves while they did it.

I smiled. "Yes, of course." I'd been trying out the Paiute dialect more and more. It didn't feel natural exactly, but it made the other women bristle toward me less.

I felt a new kinship with Inola, whose eyes mirrored the pain I felt in her son's absence.

I told myself she couldn't know how I felt about him. I'd certainly never told her. But she seemed to sense that I cared for him, and maybe that was why she'd taken me under her wing after he left.

Everyone had a brother or a father or a son missing in camp, and there was no way to know how long the men would be gone. The heavy blanket of mourning had been replaced by a strange surge of energy as we all tried to stay busy and prepare for their return, not knowing if all of them would come back alive.

While Inola and I worked to skin the rabbits, we talked. I'd never actually skinned a rabbit before, so she showed me where to make the cuts to separate the meat from the hide without ruining it. Then how to use the brains to tan the skins.

Sitting side by side with Inola almost felt like it had with Awan when we walked to the creek. We didn't talk about the horrors we'd seen over the past week. Or the horrors that were drawing closer to camp with the injured and dead men. Instead, we spoke of small things. Ordinary things. Beautiful things.

It felt good to let my words ebb and flow in conversation again without counting them.

Inola told me about a pure-white deer she had seen five years ago, early in the morning. A young doe, with pale ears tinged pink like the soft skin around its eyes. "I think it was my sister," she said softly, looking away to scrape a rabbit hide. "She walked right up to me."

I nodded, trying not to let her see the tears brimming in my eyes that she would tell me such a thing.

* * *

I couldn't have prepared myself for what I saw when our riders reached Corn Creek that evening.

They brought with them the bodies of six men—two who had died at the Meadow, and four who were injured and had perished on the journey back to camp.

Two exhausted horses pulled a travois behind them, bearing the dead. After the long journey that exposed them to the sun, the bodies were dusty and bloated.

A slick of dark blood soaked the travois.

I tried not to wince when Inola and I approached, but the sight and the smell of death was enough to make my stomach spasm again and again. All of the men's mouths and eyes were open, except for those who had been struck in the face. They were unrecognizable.

I stared, unable to tear my eyes away. This time, I no longer felt a distant detachment from the dead Paiutes, the way I had when I'd arrived at the camp.

I had never seen someone torn up by gunfire. The way muscle and bone lay strewn apart made it hard for me to believe that something as small as a bullet had inflicted the damage. It looked instead like the jaws of some beast had ripped them to shreds.

For a moment, I imagined I was looking at Awan's body. I forced my eyes over the torn flesh and splayed limbs until I was certain he was not among the dead. Then I turned and retched again and again.

At the edge of camp, I saw a handful of cattle. Nothing like the herds that had been promised.

After a few seconds, Inola took me firmly by the hand and pulled me away from the chaos. I watched the way her eyes moved and knew she'd been looking for Awan, too. We hurried to a wickiup where other riders were depositing the wounded. We were ready with poultices of yarrow, sage, and lobelia. Numa and Povi were already cleaning wounds, alongside the other women.

"Get the tools," Inola told me, referring to the sharpened bones we'd prepared earlier.

My stomach churned. I suddenly understood what the tools would be for as I looked at the four gray-faced men whose bodies—though still clinging to life—had been ripped apart almost as severely as the dead. There were bullets still embedded in their flesh. And there would be no saving a leg or an arm that had been reduced to pulp.

The wickiup was a contrast of activity from the women bustling about, and stone-faced silence from the still-breathing bodies on the mats.

By the time we had finished cleaning the last man's wounds, the men who had escorted the injured and dead back to the village had already ridden off, headed south again.

The air was thick with drum beats and smoke as we burned the bodies of the dead, releasing their spirits while the bloody rags piled up around us and our wrappings dwindled.

My stomach sank as Inola reached for the last of the wrappings.

Without more supplies, the injured men—and any others who returned injured to camp—would die.

Inola wiped sweat from her brow. She knelt over a young man whose thigh had been blown apart to reveal a gaping wound and a red slurry of bone that carved a gash halfway down his leg.

An idea struck me with clarity through the haze of activity in the wickiup.

I spoke without thinking. "We need Lucy."

Inola fixed me with her gaze and shook her head. I knew what she was thinking. The idea that a white Mormon woman would come all the way out to Corn Creek was unlikely. It was one thing for her to trade bread for melons and moccasins. It was another to ask her to make the long trek to the village.

Still, I felt sure I could convince her to help. And of anyone in Fillmore or the surrounding cities and forts who might have supplies to spare, it was her. None of the other women had opened their homes to the Paiutes.

Besides, the Mormons' power had failed ten of our men, only four of which were still alive. Surely they could give a few supplies to help them now.

I realized that Inola still had no idea I spoke English. Nobody did, except maybe Lucy herself.

I swallowed. "I can speak to Lucy," I said. "I know some English."

We'd have to walk, which would waste precious time. Ordinarily, Inola might have taken a horse. Unlike me, she knew how to ride. But there were no horses to spare, with most of the men in the Meadow. And if we didn't get more medicine and supplies, more clean bandages, there wasn't much else we could do.

Inola studied me then slowly nodded. "You will bring her a gift," she said simply.

I nodded, then wrung out a cloth that dripped red.

25. LUCY ROBISON

FILLMORE, UTAH

SEPTEMBER 1857

Despite all of us preparing for the worst, Sister Johnson's baby got better. A smile tugged at my lips as I watched him eat another mouthful of porridge while all of us sat in the shade of the orchard, listening to the wind in the leaves and feeling grateful to be alive.

Even with all the fear, all the waiting and not knowing about how our men were faring against the U.S. Army up north, this was a good moment.

I wished Vick and Brother Johnson were here to see this small miracle.

I glanced at Proctor's gravestone—just a rough wedge of granite since there hadn't been time to carve a proper headstone before Vick left to go north—and smoothed an empty spot of quilt beside me, imagining he was here with us.

From across the blanket, Sister Johnson caught my eye and smiled wearily. We'd both been awake until the sun rose, trying to coax the baby into eating something. Anything. A dropper full of sugar mixed with cow's milk. The first of the ripe apples, pureed into a sauce. Even the last of the maple syrup I'd been saving for Almon's birthday. But no matter what we tried, it all dribbled back down the corners of his mouth.

I was sure it was the end. He'd stopped eating two days earlier. He'd stopped crying the day after that. Just a listless, wisp of a soul with eyes that barely blinked.

Your sweet baby will be with God, soon. Someday, there will be no more tears. All the words of comfort I knew I was meant to say stayed stuck in my throat. Those words hadn't taken away the raw ache that still sat fresh in the pit of my stomach. They wouldn't take away Sister Johnson's, either.

Before he'd left with Vick, Doctor Brunson had diagnosed the baby with "failure to thrive." The words had knocked round and round in my head while I cooed at the infant, telling him to stay a little longer. Begging his eyelids to keep fluttering while he slept. *Failure to thrive.* As if he should have tried just a little bit harder. As if it were his fault that his mother's milk had dried up. As if his sunken eyes and hollow cheeks could ever have been rosy in a family of six that ate just one meal a day.

Last night, Sister Johnson and I had laid our hands on the baby's head to bless him, again and again, as the hours wore on. Each time, he blinked and sighed like the weight of our hands was too heavy.

But then, just before the sun rose this morning, the baby had gone quiet, looked at me with his big brown eyes like he could see through to my soul, and finally let Sister Johnson feed him a mouthful of porridge.

"He's eating, oh my goodness he's eating," we both whispered as the sun broke over the mountains like God's angels arrived just in time to help.

Grateful tears streamed down our cheeks in endless lines, but Sister Johnson kept her mouth puckered tight like a drawstring for a few hours yet, as if knowing that it was too early to tell what the sunrise would bring. Her hair hung loose around her face, half of it pinned back in the remnants of a bun that she'd given up caring about at some point in the middle of the night.

By the time the sun cleared the mountains—and the children woke for morning chores—the baby was sitting up on his own and eating more. "Chores can wait a little this morning," I said, eyes bleary and heart full. "How about a picnic? Almon, will you fetch the rest of the Johnson children?"

Sister Johnson smiled and nodded, looking down at the baby who had fallen asleep on her lap. The children dashed down the dirt path like colts, and my heart soared even as my eyes longed to close.

When they returned, they brought a handful of bright sunflowers that four-year-old Adelia had picked for Sister Johnson. "Thank you, sweetheart," I told her, blinking back tears, impossibly thankful for tiny rays of sunshine, after so much darkness.

A warm breeze whispered through the leggy apple trees, bringing with it the smell of ripening fruit and the promise of harvest. I closed my eyes and breathed in deep, listening to the sound of the children in the orchard and feeling the sun on my face.

Lines from a hymn found their way to my lips. I'd never been able to hold a tune, but it didn't matter.

> *"Be still my soul the Lord is on thy side*
> *Bear patiently the cross of grief or pain*
> *Leave to thy God to order and provide*
> *In every change He faithful will remain*
> *Be still my soul thy best, thy heavenly friend*
> *Through thorny ways leads to a joyful end."*

As the first words of the hymn left my lips, Sister Johnson's high sweet voice joined mine, filling the orchard with our voices.

This is what the kingdom of God should feel like, I thought to myself as the chorus swelled.

* * *

Later that morning when Sister Johnson went home to tend to her own chores, I lingered in the orchard with my children. Their voices were bright again as they searched among the trees for apples that were more red than green. I stood nearby in the shade, sorting the fruit they picked into buckets by ripeness, saving the ones with blemishes for sauce and preserves.

"Adelia, don't tug on the branch like that," I called, wiping my brow. As I turned around, the rest of what I'd been about to say slipped from my mind.

Two women stood mere feet away from me.

Sally, I realized. And Kanosh's first wife, Inola. I hadn't seen them since Proctor died.

My stomach knotted up like tangled yarn pulled tight. I didn't blame Sally for what had happened to Proctor any more than I blamed the poisoned steers themselves. The Indians had suffered their share of losses. Three Paiutes had died, and more had gotten sick from eating the bad meat. But the sight of Sally walking toward me, lifting a tentative hand in greeting and flashing a hint of a smile, made me feel for a moment like that terrible day was starting over again.

I thought of Proctor smiling shyly, eager to lay eyes on the pretty Paiute girl with the faint raised scars on her cheeks. Then his sweet face, buzzing with excitement at the idea of earning money from the steer hides.

A lump burned at the back of my throat. If I knew then what I knew now, I'd still send him galloping south on the fast blue mare— but not to skin the steer hides. To raise the alarm. To send our Lamanite brothers after the gentiles' cattle *before* they could slip away to our borders, leaving a trail of poison, death, and trampled grass.

I set my lips in a hard line that I hoped looked like a smile. I couldn't turn the women away after they'd walked for so long to get here. But after such a long night with the Johnson's baby, I had nothing left to give. The idea of baking bread for hours today while making stilted conversation was unthinkable. I had been planning to steal a few minutes of rest when Adelia took her nap after we finished our chores.

I decided I would offer my visitors some of the first harvest. And then I would politely send them back on their way.

"Hello, Sally, Inola. I'm so sorry you've walked so far," I began, trying to keep the irritation out of my voice. "I won't be able to bake bread today. Our neighbors, the Johnsons …" I trailed off, unsure how much they could understand. "Their baby was sick. I was up all night."

The women nodded solemnly but did not move to leave.

"We are not here to bake bread," Sally said in a rush. The perfect words spoken in her soft voice caught me by surprise, and I stared at her in silence. From the way Inola glanced at her sideways, I got the impression she was a little taken aback herself. I had no idea Sally spoke English quite this well. The last time she'd been here, the day Proctor died, she'd stayed quiet, using gestures whenever she could to communicate.

Sally's cheeks turned crimson, and she glanced at the ground like she'd been caught doing something bad. Inola held something out to me, her dark eyes guarded but kind.

I took the offering—a pale tan pouch made of soft leather. It was small, about the size of my hand, adorned with intricate beadwork in shades of green, brown, and red. The scene showed an apple orchard that must have been ours. I looked at Inola, not understanding the gift. It was exquisite and had clearly been made just for me.

Inola squeezed Sally's arm, and the girl spoke again in that soft, fast rush of words. "We are sorry for your loss. Your son. He was a good boy."

My eyes prickled with the tears I had successfully resisted all morning. I couldn't blink them away fast enough. "Thank you," I managed. "I—I have apples for you—I'll get them now."

Inola reached for my arm and shook her head. There was pain in her eyes. I saw my own exhaustion and ragged grief reflected there. "What is it?" I asked, looking to Sally for the answer.

"Please," she whispered. "Our men will die."

The words filled me with shame. They had come all this way to give me a heartfelt token of sympathy, and I hadn't even acknowledged the Paiutes who had died from the poisoned steers at Corn Creek. "Yes," I began. "Yes, I'm so sorry for your losses, too. I —"

Sally shook her head, halting my words, and said something to Inola in Paiute. Then she closed her eyes and spoke more slowly, as if drawing the words from somewhere she had pushed down deep. "No. More men. From fighting." She turned and pointed south, toward Cedar City.

The exhaustion that weighed me down like a wet wool blanket now prickled with confusion and dread.

The fighting was to the north, with the U.S. Army. To the north ...

I drew in a sharp breath. She was talking about the cattle raid to the south, I realized. But how were there injuries bad enough that Sally and Inola were asking for my help? For just a cattle raid? I'd hardly thought about the gentiles for the past few days. The Johnsons' baby had been a distraction worthy of the anxious dread that bubbled in my stomach at all hours.

I fixed my eyes on Sally and Inola. "I'm sorry. Your men are injured badly?" I still wasn't sure what they wanted from me.

"You will help us? With medicine," Sally said. "And blessings."

I nodded, understanding what they wanted even if it didn't make sense. That I could do.

"Yes. Wait here." Without a doctor, my efforts had limitations. Especially for badly injured or dying men. But I had plenty of arnica oil for pain, ethyl alcohol to clean wounds, and bandages for wrapping. I'd been hoarding the supplies for my family and neighbors, in case we had to run for the hills as the Army approached. But, I reasoned, the Paiutes were my neighbors too. I could spare a little.

Bleary-eyed, I packed a bag, adding slippery elm salve and calendula for healing. A paltry offering compared to what Doctor Brunson could have provided, but I'd seen miracles performed with less.

Four-year-old Adelia begged to join me on the journey to Corn Creek, tears filling her eyes. She'd been clinging to my skirts since Proctor's death, and I hated to leave her behind. I didn't tell her about the Paiute men who had been injured, and I didn't want her to see any more suffering. No sense in filling her cup with more fear. "Stay with your brothers. Invite Sister Johnson and her children over for supper. I'll be a while yet."

I saddled the fast blue mare, always Proctor's favorite, for myself. Then I saddled the big, plodding gelding that Vick used for working in the fields and orchards. The gelding wasn't fast, but he was steady enough that Inola and Sally could ride him double.

If we pushed the horses, we'd reach Corn Creek in half an hour.

26. KATRINA HUFF

MOUNTAIN MEADOWS, UTAH

SEPTEMBER 1857

DAY 2 IN THE MEADOW

The shooters hidden along the river continued picking off our oxen and horses one by one while we baked beneath the hot September sun, and then froze at night.

There was no escaping the smell of death or the desperate thirst. The flies swarmed thick, descending on bodies we had piled at the far edge of the wagon fort, as far away as possible from the trench where we took cover.

Our wagon fort and trench were a strong defensive shelter, but also a cage we didn't dare move from. The second we left the circled wagons, we'd be easy targets in the open Meadow that lay between ourselves and the river. And without water, we could only hang on so long.

My heart seized when I looked up at the steep canyon walls that had felt like a refuge only days earlier. The only way in—or out—of the Meadow canyon was a strip of land beside the river that was so narrow our wagons had been forced to enter one by one.

There was no moving the fallen animals—oxen, milking cows, and horses. They stayed where they'd been shot.

In other words, we were trapped in every sense of the word.

When the breeze shifted just right, the sickly smell of death mingled with that of cooking beef and campfire smoke from somewhere downriver, where the enemy camped. No doubt, they were feasting on one of the steers they had stolen on the first day.

My stomach heaved and rumbled in response to the scent of food and carnage. The two aromas swirled in the air, and like oil and water, they combined but were unmistakably distinct.

When Belle dropped to her knees and then her side, falling against Bright's body, I tried to sing Peter's song to her, too. But my throat was so swollen with thirst I could barely speak.

Our meager supply of water was completely gone by the afternoon of the second day.

A few women tending the wounded had managed to collect some of the spillage in the muddy puddles on the ground. It was thick with silt and blood, but it was all we had. And those who drank it did so in careful, grateful sips.

We had food. Hardtack and dried beef that we collected from the circled wagons and the big supply schooners. It stuck in our throats like sand, but we ate it anyway, forcing the dry bits down even while they scratched our throats. We didn't dare light fires to boil beans. It would draw more gunshots.

Nancy and baby Triphena had even stopped playing with the yucca horse. Every so often, one of the children in the trench would start to cry, overwhelmed by the heat and the crush of bodies packed together, but by now I welcomed the sound. If they had the energy and tears to cry, it meant they were still alive. Still fighting. And if the trench was still packed with the living, it meant that the number of survivors still far outweighed the dead.

"There's probably another wagon train just a few days behind us," I told my children in a voice that was far more optimistic than what I felt. "They'll help us," I said. There were indeed other trains behind us, but it was impossible to know how far away.

Louisa smiled and nodded, but I could see the same fear in her eyes. Could we last that long? If another wagon train did arrive soon, would they meet our fate?

At Alexander's command, two of our men had snuck down to the river to retrieve water in the dead of night after the first day. They crept through the tightly circled wagons at the spot where we had piled the dead, then stole through the brush quietly and cut toward the river. It was impossible to know whether they'd even managed to fill the buckets they carried. But the sound of gunshots upriver—and the fact that they did not return—told the story of their last moments.

Uri's wound had stopped bleeding, thanks to the makeshift bandages I'd retrieved from the supply wagons. Louisa and I carefully dressed and redressed the gaping hole. It wasn't healing. But miraculously, it wasn't infected. Not yet.

"They're waiting us out," he rasped to Louisa and me while the children slept during the heat of the afternoon, dresses and torn cloth draped over their dirty faces for a bit of shade. "They have the high ground—and places to hide …" He stopped and closed his eyes. The sticky sound his throat made when he swallowed hurt my stomach. "And they have water."

He stared at Louisa. Then me. Neither of us offered an argument.

There was no sign the enemy was backing away. They had us cornered, and they knew it.

* * *

Both James and Hampton finally took refuge in the trench to sleep for a few hours that night, laying their rifles beside them in the dirt.

James rested his head in my lap, like he had when he was a little boy. Hampton curled beside Mary.

They barely moved until a shadowy figure approached the inner lip of the trench. "Hampton?"

Hampton scrambled to sitting and reached for his rifle. Mary moaned in her sleep but did not wake.

"It's okay. It's Thomas," I whispered when I recognized the tall, lanky shape.

The face looming over the edge of the trench blinked back at me, the wide whites of his eyes glinting huge in the half-moon rising overhead. Thomas was one of the Dunlap boys. His black hair looked almost neat in the darkness, tucked behind his ears. He couldn't be more than eighteen years old. Just a year younger than Hampton.

Hampton relaxed and blinked hard. James was awake now too, struggling to sit up and grab his rifle.

"Your father wanted me to fetch you," Thomas said in a whisper. My heart hammered hard. "If you'll come with me … I'm going to find help. There aren't any gunmen on the steep wall of the basin. I think we can scale it, if we move slow. Alexander says the Duke wagon train can't be more than three days behind us. If we can reach them, tell them what's happened here …"

"I'm coming too," James said quietly.

I stared at him helplessly, horrified. *No.*

Thomas shook his head. "Just Hampton. He knows the Meadow better than anybody except Alexander." His words hung in the air because we all knew why Alexander himself wasn't going.

I hated the wave of relief that prickled through me. Thomas was right. Hampton had accompanied his father along this route a few years ago, leading a different wagon train safely to California.

Hampton nodded at Thomas.

James tensed next to me but didn't try to follow when Hampton eased to standing.

"Tell her," Hampton told me. "Tell her …" He looked down at Mary, his expression full of resolute longing.

"I'll tell her," I said gently, not knowing what I would say but determined I would find the words for him.

Hampton eased himself over the dirt ridge of the trench, and the moonlight cast a pale gleam across his face. The flies, mercifully, fell silent at night, but the maddening burble of the river and the soft breeze through the grass swallowed up the sound of their footsteps after a few seconds.

The two young men were gone before I could blink.

I stayed awake until my eyelids closed on their own, waiting for the sound of gunfire from the steep ridge. But the only thing I heard was a sharp clatter of rocks that could have been a deer.

Let our enemies think it's a deer, I prayed, bracing for a fresh volley of bullets.

None came the rest of the night.

27. LUCY ROBISON

FILLMORE, UTAH
SEPTEMBER 1857

Inola, Sally, and I had barely reached the far edge of the apple orchard when the gelding carrying the two Paiute women stopped in his tracks and pricked up his ears.

I circled the blue mare to a stop and followed the horse's wide eyes.

There was another rider headed toward us, from the direction of the Johnsons' house half a mile down the dirt road.

My heart dropped. I looked at Sally and Inola, but their faces were apprehensive, too.

Could it be Brother Johnson or Vick, back from the north? I shook the thought off before I let myself hope. They'd only been gone a few days.

Whoever it was, they pushed fast and hard, driving directly toward us. It didn't take long before I could make out the shape of a black horse, hooves flying, in the cloud of dust.

It wasn't Brother Johnson or Vick. It wasn't anybody I knew. I was sure I'd never seen a horse that fine in Fillmore. He ran like a racer, with long lean legs and a coat that shimmered even in the murk of dust.

The mare shifted nervously underneath me, her eyes fixed on the rider, too. "Easy," I murmured. "Walk along now." I could ride a horse as well as Vick, but if my mare spooked, the buckskin gelding would too, and from the way Sally was clinging to Inola on the back of the horse, both women would come right off if he bolted.

I nudged the mare's flanks and moved her in front of the buckskin to meet the rider, who was nearly upon us.

He drove the horse at a gallop until he came within feet of the blue mare, who danced nervously beneath me. For a moment, I thought he was going to blaze past us and continue on his way. But at the last moment, he pulled up sharply on his horse's reins and skidded to a stop in a cloud of red dust.

The black horse squealed in protest, tossing his head and rolling his eyes, sides heaving and covered in a thick lather of sweat.

I studied the rider, who returned my stare. He, too, was covered in a coat of reddish dust from hairline to boots. His dark, sweat-stained shirt had come partially untucked from his trousers. A leather gun belt with a holstered revolver sat against one hip.

Despite his rough appearance and the caked-on dust, his neatly trimmed beard and sideburns spoke to a gentler upbringing. "Good afternoon, ma'am," he greeted me. "I'm Robert Haslam. Sorry to alarm you, riding up like this, but time is of the essence."

His name wasn't familiar to me, but his words made me bristle. *Time is of the essence.* He said it like an apology for whatever he was about to ask. Directions, perhaps? Maybe a bit of food or a place to water his poor horse? I didn't intend to send this stranger toward my house while I was away, no matter what he wanted. We had traveled out of earshot, so I couldn't hear my children on the other side of the orchard anymore, but I knew they'd meet a rider at the house if they heard hoofbeats.

I glanced sideways at Sally and Inola, who hadn't yet made a sound. Both sat rigid on their horse, eyes lowered.

The rider followed my gaze to study the Indian women. His mouth twitched ever so slightly.

"It's no trouble," I told him. "How can I help you?"

"I need a fresh horse. Fastest you've got," Haslam said.

His eyes were a piercing blue that stood out like wet, shimmering stones in his dusty face. He wasn't asking. He was demanding.

My irritation bloomed into indignation at the request. "I'm sorry, but I don't have horses to spare," I told him, tightening my grip on the reins. "If you're looking to water your own horse, there's a pond —"

He held up a hand, cutting me off. Then he pointed at the horse beneath him. "You can keep this fellow. He's worth at least twice that little thing."

The hairs on the back of my neck prickled while I watched him take in my blue mare, with her nimble, sound feet and her muscled withers. She'd sell at market for far less than the black horse, but I had every confidence she could match him stride for stride. None of that mattered, though. This was Proctor's horse. She'd always been an easy keeper. And I wasn't looking to trade.

"I can't let you take her," I told him firmly. "Now, I need to be on my way, so—"

"Let's start again." His voice had an edge of irritation to it now. "I'm Robert Haslam—Brother Haslam. I'm here on the errand of Colonel William Dame and General John D. Lee, delivering an urgent message for the Prophet."

The blue mare snorted and backed up a few feet. I realized I'd drawn back the reins and bit sharply against her mouth. Robert Haslam was digging into the dirty bag slung over one hip, beside his revolver. He extracted a leather-bound book and held it up for me to see. A folded piece of paper peeked above the pages in the middle.

I released the reins and the mare took a step closer to Haslam. He tucked the book and letter back into his bag. "It's confidential." He side-eyed Inola and Sally then fixed me with an icy stare. "The only thing you should need to know is that I am on the Lord's errand. You are a Saint, are you not, Sister ... ?"

"Robison. Sister Robison," I said, keeping my voice steady even though my hands were shaking. "Certainly, Brother Haslam. But there are wounded men in the Paiute village, and I can't ride that far on a spent horse."

He made a grunting sound, but his expression was dark and sour. "They can wait." Then, lower, under his breath he muttered, "Cowards."

An uneasy twinge in my stomach made me look away. Was he talking about the Paiutes? They were our allies. It didn't make sense.

Sally lifted her head and stared at him, not averting her eyes when he glanced at her.

"Oh, you understood me, did you?" He spat in the dust and nudged the poor black horse forward a few feet toward me. "Sister Robison, I've already stopped too long. All I can say is that if you knew the gravity of my errand, you would've handed me that little mare's reins the second I asked."

Then he watched me, waiting.

My blood ran cold with doubt and questions. I looked from Inola to Sally then back at Brother Haslam.

He cleared his throat impatiently. "Brother Farnsworth in Parowan, and Sister Thompson in Beaver were more than willing to supply me with this fresh horse, Sister Robison." His tight-lipped grimace was a poor substitute for a smile.

When I still didn't move to dismount from the blue mare, Haslam reached back into his bag. He retrieved a different scrap of paper and held it out for me to see. "If your faith isn't strong enough to comply, then read this."

I reached for the note, feeling Sally's and Inola's eyes on me.

Latter-day Saints. You shall furnish Brother Haslam with horses and provisions, as much as need be, so that he may travel with all haste, bearing a message of the most pressing and urgent nature.

It was signed with three signatures: General John D. Lee. Colonel William Dame. Major Isaac Haight.

My hands shook as I gave him back the note. Was this about the standoff at Echo Canyon in the north? Had the soldiers breached our defenses? Would we be driven into the mountains at any moment? Tarred and feathered? Killed? And what about Vick?

Haslam pulled up on the reins and took the note from me. Shame burned inside.

"I apologize," I told him softly, dismounting. "Please, take the mare."

He nodded curtly and dismounted to hand me the reins to the quivering black horse.

I couldn't help myself. "Please ... my husband is at Echo Canyon," I said softly. "Has fighting begun? Has the Army broken through our defenses?"

I couldn't help but wonder, was my Vick alive? Had the mob taken him from me, too?

Haslam stared at me in confusion for half a second, like he couldn't comprehend what I was asking. My blood ran cold.

He glanced at Sally and Inola, then sighed as he took the mare's reins from my hands.

"No, Sister Robison," he said in a low voice, looking over his shoulder at Sally and Inola. "The troops haven't broken through our defenses yet."

He lowered his voice so I could barely hear him. "The Paiutes have a gentile wagon train corralled at Mountain Meadows." He looked over his shoulder in the direction of the orchard. "The Indians, well ..." He shook his head and grunted. "All I can say is that Brother Laman's blood runs strong in that lot. It's a bloody standoff. Not that I mind. But President Young is the Indian Agent of Utah, so he needs to know what's going on down south ..."

A sweet shiver of relief eased the chokehold of panic constricting my throat. The trouble wasn't to the north—with the U.S. Army, where Vick was. It was to the south, with the gentiles.

"I understand now," I told him softly, tugging the black horse to follow me. "I apologize. Godspeed on your journey."

And godspeed to the Paiutes, I thought to myself.

* * *

As Brother Haslam galloped off on the mare, I led the spent horse back home through the orchard. Inola and Sally followed on the buckskin.

By the time I finished tending to the horse, tasking Almon and Albert with wiping him down and giving him a slow drip of mash to help him recover, it was obvious that he was badly lame-footed from his hard run.

He'd stepped on a stone that had lodged itself in the tender part of his back hoof, and each time he took a step, his limp got worse. With the stone removed, his hoof would heal, but riding him out to Corn Creek would be unwise.

Since we had only one horse now, Sally and I rode double on the plodding buckskin, leaving Inola to walk to Corn Creek on foot in the late afternoon heat. She would arrive later than us, but it was the only way to make time.

It was impossible to read the calm, veiled expression in Inola's eyes before I urged the buckskin forward to leave her trailing behind.

I felt a rush of gratitude for the Paiutes—and a dark relief that it was their men in danger, not mine.

Maybe Haslam thought the Paiutes were cowards, but he was wrong. I would do my very best to help their men who had sacrificed so our men didn't have to.

We rode at a steady—but slow—pace, the buckskin's plodding hoofbeats in our ears until the first of the domed wickiups came into view. The clustered, thatched dwellings were squat and black, silhouetted against the violet skyline.

The buckskin snorted nervously as the smell of smoke—and something worse—got stronger.

28. KAHPEPUTZ (SALLY)

CORN CREEK, UTAH

SEPTEMBER 1857

Terror prickled up my spine with each step the big horse took. I kept my fingers laced tightly around Lucy's waist, despite the discomfort I felt in touching the white woman. Pressed next to her starched dress that crinkled each time either of us shifted in the saddle, I realized how soft and sun-faded my own had become.

I couldn't stop thinking about the rider who had taken the blue mare and cost us precious time in riding back to Corn Creek. *Cowards*, he'd muttered, looking right at me and Inola. The word made me want to scream.

What had he whispered to Lucy when they exchanged horses? She clearly didn't want to give him the mare. Not at first, anyway. Her eyes looked different when she glanced at me after he rode away.

Unburdened, almost.

I wanted to insist that Inola be the one to ride with Lucy while I walked. But Lucy needed an interpreter. With the horse's bouncy trot, I didn't dare loosen my fingers enough to turn around to watch Inola's silhouette get smaller and smaller behind us.

To my relief—and dismay—the buckskin gelding seemed to have just one speed. Slow. By the time we reached Corn Creek, the sun was already behind the mountains, plunging the desert into a pale gray light.

I gathered my courage and asked the question burning in my stomach, each word clear, and in perfect English. Because I did not want to ask again.

"Why did Haslam need your horse?"

I felt Lucy stiffen, and I wondered if she could feel how fast my heart was hammering against her back. She didn't respond at first.

I stayed silent, waiting.

Without turning to look at me, she cleared her throat and nudged the buckskin to walk faster toward the village. The saddle bags filled with supplies flapped against his flanks with each step.

Her silence dragged on for one hoofbeat, two, five, eight, twelve.

Why won't you answer me? I wanted to scream. *You're supposed to be our allies. Our men are dying.*

From the way Brigham Young—and Kanosh—talked, we were literally brothers and sisters, two branches from the same tree. United in our faith and in our plight against the government and wicked, godless men that would invade our lands.

But those were just words. The truth was in Lucy Robison's hesitation.

She didn't trust me to speak openly. And she didn't care how quickly we reached Corn Creek. Not in the same way she would if it were pale-faced Mormons lying dying in the dust.

Just ahead, the glint of a small cooking fire crackled beside a wickiup. The flames whipped in the breeze, low to the ground like it was trying to hide, but spitting sparks that threatened to singe the nearby shelter. I was so consumed with the angry flames licking my heart, that I almost missed what Lucy said when she finally spoke.

"Haslam needs to talk to Brigham Young." She hesitated then added, "About your people and the cattle raid."

Your people.

My mouth went dry as I tried to make sense of her choice of words.

I knew the Paiutes were raiding the gentile's cattle—but not on a whim. They'd ridden south, escorted by white men. But from what I knew, the raid was going sideways. So much so that they had to consult the prophet.

I pictured Major Haight, Major Higbee, and Apostle George A. Smith, the uniformed and suited men who had convinced Kanosh to bring our strongest men to take part in the biggest cattle raid Utah Territory had ever seen. And then once again, to summon the rest of us. Including Awan.

Your people.

The fear and horror etched into the faces of the injured men came to my mind. The black and bloated corpses that had made their way home, tangled limbs and bloody clothing in a travois.

It was like I had stepped outside of my own body. I wanted to pummel Lucy with my hands, tear at her hair, until she cowered in front of me. To find the nearest knife and slash it across her cheeks until she begged for mercy, like the Ute slave trader had done to me and Tyee.

Instead, I scrambled off the horse and held my arms open while she handed me the bags of supplies. She smiled at me kindly, like she was willing to overlook the sour expression on my face on account of *my people's* predicament.

Did Inola know that the Mormons had thrown the Paiutes to the wolves in the Meadow?

Awan surely did by now.

I shuddered when I pictured the well-stocked, bustling wagon party. By now, more men were likely dead or injured, too. Was Awan still alive?

"Take me to your injured men," Lucy told me gently.

* * *

The smell of death greeted us at the threshold of the wickiup, eager and skulking.

All four men were still alive. Three seemed worse than this morning, their breathing labored and wounds still seeping blood beneath the bandages. Only one, the young man Inola had been tending to earlier, turned his head in my direction when I entered the tent with a white woman.

He looked between us, eyes blank and lips pursed tight.

The two Paiute women kneeling by his side murmured greetings of "Sister Robison." Most of the Paiute women recognized Lucy from baking bread in her kitchen over the years. They stood and withdrew to the far side of the wickiup, chins tucked in deference the way I'd seen the men surrounding Brother Brigham's table.

My blood boiled.

"Heal them," I told her bluntly, laying the bags of supplies at her feet.

155

To my surprise, she didn't reach for the fresh bandages or arnica oil first. She didn't even touch the bags. Instead, she looked me dead in the eyes and asked, "We should ask the Lord's help first. Where are the priesthood holders?"

For a moment, I couldn't figure out what she was saying. The priesthood holders? Those words made sense in Brigham Young's household. I was a constant witness to the laying on of hands any time a new bishop or leader was ordained. Any time a child or wife was sick. The men held the power of God in their hands to heal, to transfer anointing, even to console in times of distress.

As far as I knew, Chief Kanosh was the only man in the entire Paiute tribe who held the holy Melchizedek priesthood. Even if that weren't the case, the men were all gone.

I shook my head at Lucy. "They're not here." I kept silent on the fact that my faith in the Mormon God and his "priesthood" was running thinner by the second.

She nodded as if resigned to this idea, but she still didn't reach for the bags at her feet. Instead, she seemed to draw herself up a few inches taller. She looked at the other women, then at the injured men lying on the mats. Then she knelt next to the nearest wounded. "What is his name?" she asked.

"Helaku," I said. I no longer recognized the man, whose jaw and ear had been partially torn away by a bullet that exited near the base of his head. I only knew who he was because Inola told me. His name meant "sunny day." Sweat beaded on his forehead, and his skin was waxy and pale. The wound itself wept so much that the bandages could not contain the blood that dripped onto the mat beneath his head.

"Hell-law-kyew," Lucy tried, then reached inside her dress for a tiny glass vial. It held a golden liquid that I realized was consecrated oil, set apart for the blessing of the sick and injured. I suddenly understood what she was about to do. Lucy was going to give these men a blessing all by herself.

I watched in wary fascination as Lucy dabbed some oil on the crown of his head, closed her eyes, and drew in a deep breath then spoke. Helaku's chest rose and fell more rapidly, but he did not open his eyes.

"Hell-law-kyew, by the power of the Lord I bless you …" She trailed off and paused for a few seconds, as if unsure what to say next. Finally, she continued. "I bless you to make a full recovery. I rebuke the fever in your body and command your bones and sinews to heal. The Lord is pleased with your people. I pronounce this blessing in the name of Jesus Christ. Amen."

The words burned hot.

The anger smoldering in my chest kept me from translating the blessing for Helaku himself. It was difficult to know how much he could even hear. I had no doubt that God would understand the words she spoke in English, but would He find them as confusing as I did? If God was pleased with the Paiutes, He had a funny way of showing it.

Your people.

I went to stand beside the two Paiute women and watched while Lucy dripped oil on two other unconscious men, pronouncing more blessings of healing and comfort.

When she got to the young man, the only one of the four who was awake, she asked his name directly instead of consulting me. He turned to look at me and then fixed his eyes on her. I was about to translate her question for him when he spat, "Coyotl."

Coyote.

I exchanged glances with the two other women in the wickiup. The young man's name wasn't Coyotl. It was Keme. *Thunder.* He was Inola's brother. And he was insulting Lucy.

Neither the Bannock nor the Paiute really swore at each other. At least, not the way the children in the Young household sometimes hurled the words "bootlicker" and "backbiter" at one another when they thought their mothers weren't listening. *Coyote* was the exception. The word called to mind the crafty half-dog, half-wolf that represented everything low and conniving to us. He was a trickster, an opportunist, a coward who slunk in the shadows.

It was a term of great reproach. But Lucy didn't know that.

She was already offering the blessing on his head. "Coyotl, by the power of the Lord I bless you with faith and healing. I bless you to know that the Lord is aware of you and your people, the descendants of Laman and Lemuel, who even now are turning their hearts to the Lord to build up the kingdom of God in the last days. I bless you with a full recovery and relief from suffering. In the name of our Lord and Savior, Jesus Christ. Amen."

The bubble of laughter that rose in my throat burned all the way down when I swallowed it back. I'd never paid very much attention to Keme, or anyone else among the Paiute except for Inola and Awan. But I suddenly knew that if Keme died, I'd be devastated.

Tears pricked at my eyes. I tried without success to keep Awan's face from my mind. Surely he'd reached the Meadow by now. Would he be lying in this wickiup soon, torn apart like Keme?

Keme stayed silent until Lucy lifted her hands from his head and finally reached for her bags filled with medicines and bandages.

Outside the wickiup, night had fallen. I thought about Inola walking the path toward Corn Creek in the dark and hoped she was safe. Mountain lions came down often. They never went into camp because they didn't like the noise and the fires. But they wouldn't hesitate to stalk a woman walking by herself after dark. Neither would a late-night rider with ill intentions.

If I thought I could stay upright on the plodding buckskin by myself, I would have ridden back to find her.

Keme cleared his throat. His eyes moved between me and the other two women in the wickiup. He spoke again in Paiute, ignoring Lucy. "The Meadow to the south is filled with blood and death," he said. "If this woman had power—if any of the Mormons did—we would have been protected."

Lucy ignored him and laid out her supplies on a blanket.

I couldn't help but picture Awan's lifeless body being dragged home on a travois. I listened in horror as Keme continued, describing the way the white gentiles had circled their wagons at the beginning of the cattle raid, firing on the raiders with many long rifles and killing a number of men within minutes. This wasn't supposed to happen. It should have been easy. They'd just take the cattle. Apostle Smith said they were ours—and that God would protect us.

Keme told me that instead, the cattle raid had turned into a standoff with the wagon train trapped in the Meadow at the bottom of the canyon.

"What happened?" I breathed.

Keme shook his head and groaned painfully. "It was chaos. As we crept toward the cattle, one of our men fired his weapon … I couldn't see who in the mist. The gentiles fired back and corralled their wagons. Everything went to hell."

I swallowed hard.

"Our men are afraid," Keme told me bluntly. "Even Kanosh. But he says we must stand by Brigham. Stay with our allies and do what they want. That if we don't, they will leave us on our own when the American government breaks through their defenses in the north. They will take everything we have left."

The sound of the few steers lowing where we'd corralled them outside camp mingled with Lucy's soft humming as she replaced soiled bandages with fresh coverings. She ignored me and Keme, imagining perhaps that we were discussing something trivial, like the sound of the wind in the sage beyond the wickiup.

I was about to respond to him, but he winced in pain. At first I thought it was from something Lucy had done. But her hands weren't even touching him right then. He was remembering what he'd seen. "The Mormon leaders say we can't let the gentiles go. They think ... they think the gentiles know the Mormons are the ones behind the cattle raid." His eyes were glazed. "I didn't know there would be so many women. So many children."

My throat tightened so I could barely breathe.

"Speak more," I told him, desperate to know what was happening, unable to stop myself from thinking of the little girl.

At the sound of my voice, sharp and urgent, Lucy stopped what she was doing and looked at me with reproach. "Sally, quiet," she murmured. "We must be calm."

I wanted to slap her.

"Kanosh is furious, spitting threats on anyone who leaves the Meadow. But the men are afraid."

I balled my hands into fists. Awan was there, in that hell.

Keme's face darkened. He turned his gaze to Lucy, who had moved on to one of the unconscious men. "The Mormon leaders promised us cattle and blessings. But what will the cattle even eat? They will starve, just like us."

They will eat the locoweed, I thought numbly.

Keme closed his eyes, and seemed to be speaking to nobody in particular. "There were so many children. I did not know there would be so many children. So many children." He repeated over and over.

No matter how much I swallowed, a lump rose in my throat.

When Lucy had finished treating the last man, she stood and looked at me with uncertainty. "I need to get back to my family." She enunciated each word with care, and gathered up the remaining supplies and stuffed them into one of the bags.

I held out a hand to stop her.

"I'll come back in the morning," she began.

"Leave your medicine," I said. It wasn't a request. I was prepared to snatch the bags from her hands if she protested, regardless of the consequences. What if Awan and the other men returned injured in the middle of the night?

Lucy nodded and reluctantly let go of the bag. "Yes, of course. You know how to use them?"

I bit my cheek so hard I tasted the salty tang of blood. "Yes, we know how to use the medicine," I said, enunciating my words just like she did.

The look in her eyes softened some of the rage thrumming through my veins. "I will pray for them," she said, and from the tears in her eyes I could tell she meant it.

"Thank you," I managed, keeping my voice measured.

I couldn't upset Lucy. Not when there was a good chance we might need to beg for her assistance again. My mind went back to Inola, concerned for her picking her way through the sage by moonlight. "I will ride with you," I told her. "Until we find Inola."

* * *

Corn Creek glittered under the half-moon.

The buckskin pulled at his reins, begging to drink when he heard the burbling water.

Lucy let him dip his big muzzle into the creek for a few minutes. He drank in long swallows then snatched at a mouthful of grass and weeds growing in the muck.

It was impossible to see the noxious purple flowers of the locoweed along the overgrown shoreline. There was no real reason for me to fear Lucy's horse would take a mouthful of the plant. And even if he did, one bite wouldn't kill him. I knew from what Awan had told me that it took weeks of eating the dangerous forage for the poison to do its work.

Then an idea came to me.

Maybe I couldn't do anything about the horror in the Meadow to the south. Not one single thing.

But I could do this.

I let go of Lucy's waist and reached for the buckskin's left rein, pulling his head to the side. He snorted in confusion. "No, stupid horse. Or you'll die too," I told him angrily, repeating the same words Awan told me the day we stood on this same bank to gather water with the mule.

"Sally, no. Let him drink," Lucy reprimanded me, horrified.

"You can't let him eat the locoweed," I told her firmly, my voice breaking on the last word.

She twisted around in the saddle to look at me, her face a mix of bewilderment and annoyance. "It's all right," she finally said gently. "A little bit won't hurt him."

So she *did* know about the dangerous plant. Did she know that it was the real reason her son had died? Or was she feigning ignorance like Kanosh? Like Apostle Smith. Like Major Haight.

Fury plumed in my veins again.

"But a lot would hurt him. A lot would kill him," I pressed.

"Yes, I suppose it would," she said as if we were talking about the shape of the moon or chill in the night air. "But he has enough grass to eat at home."

"The gentile's steers didn't have grass to eat, though," I insisted, watching for her reaction. "Not with the drought."

Lucy didn't reply, but her eyes stayed locked on mine. I watched them widen as the truth tried to sink in. I knew I didn't have to say the words, *The gentiles didn't kill your son. Locoweed did.*

I could see her fight with the thought, then reject it.

"There are many women and children in the wagon train," I told her, my voice shaking. "They did nothing—"

"No." The word burst from Lucy's lips like an arrow, pointed and dangerous. As if her speaking it made it true. Then she clamped down her lips, as if to protect us both from what might follow.

She pulled the buckskin's head up and pushed him to a bouncy trot. I kept my mouth shut tight.

I didn't want to be the one in the middle. But there was no way around that now.

I held on to Lucy's waist for dear life while the buckskin ran, pretending that the tears streaming down my cheeks were drawn from the wind.

29. KATRINA HUFF

MOUNTAIN MEADOWS, UTAH

SEPTEMBER 1857

DAY 3 IN THE MEADOW

The raw need for water eclipsed everything else, except one thing.

Fear.

As the third day drew to a close, the number of gunmen tucked along the other side of the river—and the amount of gunfire—had doubled.

Just before the sun slipped behind the rim of the basin, a bullet struck three-year-old Sara Baker in the ear. She was sitting on her father's lap in the trench, just a few feet away from Mary. John Baker had just laid down his rifle for a few hours' sleep beside his wife and daughters.

It happened so fast, a burst of sound then blood, that none of us—including little Sara—reacted to at first.

The top of her ear was simply there one moment and gone the next.

Her tearless, hoarse scream echoed off the canyon walls. It lasted only a moment before a frenzy of gunfire from our side of the trench drowned it out.

Nancy, William, and baby Triphena, who had been lying listless on the ground at my feet, scrambled upright in horror. James, who sat beside me with his head on my shoulder, opened his mouth in a wide O as John Baker wrapped Sara in his arms and rushed for the wagons at the center of the field, bullets be damned.

Louisa tucked herself closer around Triphena and Uri, unable to hide the sound of her sobs.

I wanted to open my mouth and promise my children I would keep them safe. But the lie was so bald, I couldn't force it past my lips.

As the sobs in the trench turned to quiet wails, I opened and closed my mouth again.

Give us some words, Kit.

Peter's voice.

I swallowed my tears. How many times had Peter said that to me, at the end of a long day, to take his mind off the ache in his back from sorting peaches.

Give us some words.

"'The mind is its own place',"" I rasped loudly into the near-silence, ignoring how my mouth felt like sandpaper.

My cheeks burned hot. They were words I'd memorized a lifetime ago, before we started West. John Milton's *Paradise Lost*. I'd learned parts of it by heart when I was younger than Mary. The long, winding poem was so achingly beautiful, the words had swept me up and made me want to turn them over and over in my mind.

All four of my children, Louisa and Uri, and even baby Triphena looked at me, waiting for more.

I almost lay back down and pretended I hadn't spoken. What was I thinking?

But I remembered the way the poem—like all the words I loved —had transported me to another world outside my quiet bedroom. We needed another world right now. I couldn't get us out of this trench or beyond the Meadow. I couldn't stop the bullets. I couldn't do anything about the horrors surrounding us. None of us could. At least, not our bodies. This was what I had to offer. Maybe we could disappear somewhere else together. Maybe I could pull us out of this trench, if only for a moment, if only in our minds.

"'The mind is its own place, and in itself can make a heaven of hell, a hell of heaven.'" I looked my children in the eyes even though my face burned red from the audacity of what I was saying under the circumstances. Bullets whizzed and weapons clamored from the riverbank.

Still, I continued with the lines Peter loved.

"'Sweet is the breath of morn, her rising sweet,
With charm of earliest birds; pleasant the sun

When first on this delightful land he spreads
His orient beams, on herb, tree, fruit, and flower,
Glistering with dew; fragrant the fertile earth
After soft showers; and sweet the coming on
Of grateful evening mild, then silent night
With this her solemn bird and this fair moon,
And these the gems of heav'n, her starry train:
But neither breath of morn when she ascends
With charm of earliest birds, nor rising sun
On this delightful land, nor herb, fruit, flower,
Glistering with dew, nor fragrance after showers,
Nor grateful evening mild, nor silent night
With this her solemn bird, nor walk by moon,
Or glittering starlight without thee is sweet.'"

Uri had closed his eyes, but there was a smile on his lips. James sighed against me, and Nancy pulled Triphena into the shifting shade of Mary's body.

"Talk more, Mama," she said, reaching out a hand to twist the ring on my finger. Then she popped her dirty thumb into her mouth.

So I did.

* * *

Hampton and Thomas hadn't returned by the time we moved through all the words I could remember from "Nature."

Any time the sound of clattering rocks came from the far side of the valley, Mary's eyes popped open and Louisa murmured, "It must be Hampton and Thomas."

Each time, those few seconds of hope hurt more.

Uri had stopped opening his eyes at all, though the knit of his brow each time Louisa spoke told us he was still conscious. For now, at least. By the look of his red cheeks, fever meant infection was setting into the wound.

None of us had the energy to brush away the flies that tormented the living and covered the dead like crawling black dirt.

When darkness finally fell, we heard another trickle of rocks clatter in the distance.

"It's them," Louisa whispered in a rasp.

165

I kept my eyes closed, not wanting to see the hope on Mary's face. But just fifteen minutes later, a subtle commotion stirred from the center of the wagon fort.

A dark figure ducked between the supply wagons.

My heart beat so hard it felt like it might burst. Had Hampton returned? Had they found the Duke wagon train? And if so, was help on the way?

Mary struggled to her knees and moved to stand beside me, her breaths fast and shallow. I glanced back at Louisa, who cradled Uri's head on her lap. She pursed her sunburned lips and tried to smile.

We waited in silence until the dark figure reappeared at the edge of the supply wagons and darted toward our section of the trench.

Mary's fingers found mine. I blinked hard, barely able to believe what I thought I saw until the figure ducked safely into the trench next to Mary.

She flung herself into the shadowy figure's arms without a word. It was Hampton, carrying a bulging leather pouch strapped against one shoulder. My eyes prickled with fresh tears that somehow hadn't dried up. Mary's fiancé was alive. And if I wasn't mistaken, he was carrying water in that pouch.

"Let me pour a little into your bucket," he whispered, nodding to the dirty tin pail that lay on its side next to Uri.

At the sound of water pouring, all of the children were suddenly awake and alert. "Oh, oh, oh," Nancy cried, her tiny voice high and cracked. "Oh, look, Baby Tri!" The last time I'd heard her this animated was when she got her toy horse.

"Just a little bit now," Hampton whispered. "I'm sorry there's not more. My daddy—Captain Alexander—said to make sure everybody got just a sip. I'll go back for more when it's gone. There's a trickle of a stream that way." He nodded toward the other side of the canyon, where he'd disappeared with Thomas the day before.

While the children clamored to drink and Louisa helped Uri move to sitting upright, I studied the intricately stitched pouch that Hampton poured carefully, a little at a time, into the bucket.

It wasn't one of ours.

I waited to ask the questions burning behind my thirst until I'd taken a swallow of water. It was still cold and ran down my blistered throat like dew from heaven. By the time I'd had my drink and passed the filled bucket down the trench, the children were already curled together and falling asleep again. It had become the only escape from the horrors that pressed in from every side.

But at least, for the moment, we had a little water.

"Where did you get this, Hampton?" I asked him softly, running a hand over the big leather pouch.

He stared back at me, eyes huge in his pale face, but didn't answer at first. "It took me and Thomas maybe an hour to climb to the top of the basin rim," he said quietly after a moment. "Then we ran. I thought we'd made it."

I closed my eyes. Mary had traded my hand for his and leaned against him while he rested his back on the wall of the trench.

"It was slow going in the dark. We got maybe three miles. Headed along the Overland Trail the way we came, toward Cedar City, hoping we'd find the Duke train."

He drew a painful-sounding breath. "Finally, we saw campfires in the distance. Heard voices when we came around the ridge. It wasn't the Duke wagon train. But there was a whole camp. Maybe thirty people. A few cattle and lots of horses."

"White or Indian?" Uri choked out. I felt him stir behind me. Hampton glanced at him and set his mouth in a firm line.

"We couldn't see much, but we could hear some English. One of them said something about 'innocent blood.' He sounded angry."

Hampton was talking faster now, the story tumbling out of him. Already, the night felt different. Full of sparks ready to set everything ablaze, and I only prayed they would light the powder keg in our favor.

"I stayed back and kept watch while Thomas went down to the fires. We couldn't get past them, not easily anyway. We thought maybe it was another group trying to get out of Utah Territory. That maybe we could approach them."

He closed his eyes and dropped his voice. "Everything happened so fast. Someone started shouting when Thomas got close to the fire. He ... he tried to turn around and run. Then he fell. They shot him in the leg." He paused to gather his composure. "He got up and kept running toward me. Then they shot him in the back. That time, he stayed down." His voice shook. "I wanted to help him, I did. But I couldn't do anything but watch."

The swallow of water in my stomach sloshed like it might come back up. I drew in a breath. "What happened next?"

167

"I was sure they'd seen me. I ran back the way I'd come." He looked up at the night sky, blinking. "Then after just a few seconds I ran smack into a boy. A Paiute. He looked to be about me and Thomas's age."

None of us spoke. Hampton kept going. "He was holding a rifle. He looked shocked to see me. We stared at each other for a few seconds, both holding our guns. Then he fired his weapon in the air and shoved this pouch at me."

My mind went blank trying to understand what he'd just told us.

"He seemed as scared as I was, like he'd seen a ghost," Hampton choked out. "Why didn't he shoot me? He must have told the others I was dead, because nobody came after me. It doesn't make sense why he would do that."

"What did your daddy say about that, Hampton?" I asked gently.

Hampton coughed, or it might have been a groan. Then he fixed me with a look. "He just said to tell you that he knows what we have to do now. He wants one man from each household to come to the wagons in the center of the circle." He paused. "And you too, Katrina."

30. LUCY ROBISON

CORN CREEK, UTAH
SEPTEMBER 1857

Locoweed.
   Women and children.
   Locoweed.
   Women and children.
The phrases repeated in my head with each thud of the buckskin's hooves, long after Sally slid off and joined Inola along the dark trail.

Was it possible she was right about the steers? That the animals had died from grazing on the poisonous plant in the drought-stricken desert for months. That it was perhaps not poison spread by the gentiles?

No.

I rejected the idea before it had a chance to cool the simmering rage that made me hope the Paiutes would take every last steer from the gentiles who had killed my boy.

But a thought circled just beneath the surface of my mind like a snapping turtle ready to bite. *What if the gentiles* didn't *kill my boy?*

I thought of the four men whose heads I had just anointed with a blessing of comfort and healing. I thought of Robert Haslam, riding hard for Salt Lake.

The Paiutes were doing more than just raiding cattle. But to what end?

I squeezed the buckskin's flanks with my heels and pushed the horse harder. He obliged, finally willing to run if it meant getting home sooner.

Whatever was happening down south, the three men who'd signed Haslam's note must have had things under control. William

Dame wasn't just the highest-ranking military official in Utah—he was a Stake President in the church. So was Isaac Haight.

They were men of God, tasked with carrying out His will. The thought comforted me instantly.

As the buckskin ran, I thought back to Apostle Smith's fiery sermon. Even if the gentiles *hadn't* killed my boy, they still weren't innocent. They were the ones who had pushed my people here, into the desert—then followed us.

Perhaps they were earning a taste of their own medicine right now.

Even the children, though?

The thought stopped me cold.

Until tonight, I'd been imagining the gentiles in the wagon train as the ruffians who had pushed me into the freezing Mississippi river in Illinois.

I encouraged the horse to walk faster, but I couldn't help imagining a gentile mother screaming, like I had: *Would you exterminate me? My children?*

I denied the thought more forcefully. There was no use speculating. Besides, maybe Sally was wrong. She was just a girl. She spoke English and was a marvelous translator, but that didn't mean her judgment could be trusted.

I wished again that Vick was home from the north. That his strong arms would pull me close when I rushed inside the house to find the children already in their beds and a fire in the hearth.

The buckskin came to a stop so suddenly that I nearly pitched out of the saddle and over his head. He stared into the darkness while I gripped the saddle horn and searched the dark brush for a coyote skulking along, or maybe a snake lying in the still-warm dirt.

Instead, I heard the distant hoofbeats and the whinny of another approaching horse. The buckskin whinnied back, a curious greeting.

There was another horse and rider headed our way—fast.

I stiffened in the saddle, not wanting to cross paths with anyone else tonight. From where the moon hung in the sky, it had to be past midnight. The only people driving hard on horseback at this hour either wanted to hide under cover of darkness—or had no choice but to risk the dangerous riding conditions. Could it be Haslam, back already? I dismissed the idea. Nobody rode that fast in the dark.

I sat deeper in the saddle and nudged my horse forward, ready to push him into a gallop if need be.

The buckskin whinnied again, and I watched the rider—a man—pull up hard on the reins.

I couldn't stop the gasp that came from my lips. "Brother Haslam." I could barely believe what I was seeing. It was nearly one hundred and fifty miles from Fillmore to Salt Lake. A fresh horse could be pushed to cover around twenty miles at a gallop before giving out. It was a fast way to travel—and a fast way to ruin a good horse. If he'd made this journey in one night, that meant he'd traded spent horses again and again.

He cocked his head as if perplexed that I recognized him.

"It's Sister Robison," I told him. "I traded a blue roan mare with you."

He stared at me a moment longer then shook his head. "Yes, of course. It's been a very long night." The weariness in his voice told the story I suspected. If he'd left Southern Utah early this morning, he'd been riding hard for nearly twenty hours straight.

"Did your message reach President Young?" I asked, unable to stop myself. Surely, Brother Brigham would set everything right. He was the prophet. He spoke to God. If someone had made a mistake, he would intervene.

Haslam kicked his horse, a lithe gray mare who still looked fresh enough to run. "Yes, Sister Robison," he called as he moved past me. "All is well in the kingdom of God."

And then he was gone.

Tears of relief pressed at the back of my eyes.

I listened until the sound of Haslam's mount's hoofbeats disappeared, then pushed my own horse on toward home.

"All is well in the kingdom of God," I murmured to myself, mustering all the faith I had.

31. KATRINA HUFF

MOUNTAIN MEADOWS, UTAH

SEPTEMBER 1857

DAY 3 IN THE MEADOW

I barely felt the pain in my crushed toe as Hampton helped me toward the large supply wagons circled in the center of the matted grass.

Alexander has a plan, I repeated to myself. A plan for what, I didn't know yet. But with each step I took, I let myself believe that there was a way out of this nightmare.

I let the hope of it burn in my chest right until the moment I saw the faces of the men crouched around him beside the innermost wagon. The heads of household who remained from each family. The group was startlingly small.

No one looked hopeful. The opposite, in fact. The men turned to each other in disbelief and fear.

Alexander's eyes flicked to me, then Hampton. He wasted no time in repeating what he must have just told the small circle of men. "We can't win this fight."

My vision blurred as clear-eyed hope drained from me.

His voice rasped, but his eyes were set as he looked around. Alexander waited for his words to sink in while he took another sip of water from the pouch Eliza handed him.

Pleasant Tackett shook his head. "We're holding them off. We've still got ammunition. We can outlast them until the Duke wagon train gets here. They'll help us."

The other men murmured their agreement, even as they knelt in the dirt, so weak from thirst they could barely stand.

Alexander shook his head. "We have no idea where the Duke train is at. They could be delayed, they could be under attack as well." Then he turned to me. "Katrina, can the children last another day?"

In any other moment, I would have balked at the idea of speaking my mind so freely among this group of men. I was already sticking out like a sore thumb as the only woman. But I could hear Peter's voice in the back of my mind. He'd never been one to agree with a crowd. And now, it fell to me.

Give us some words, Kit.

"We'll die in the trenches," I said. "The children, first of all. They'll be dead by morning." I forced the words from my mouth. I didn't want them to be true. But they were, and I knew this was what Alexander wanted me to say. The men were willing to die of thirst while they picked off snipers and waited for help that might never arrive. But they wouldn't let that fate fall on the children.

No one spoke.

"Hampton said you had a plan?" I finally managed. I was afraid I'd misunderstood him now.

Alexander nodded. "We surrender."

This made Pleasant Tackett scowl. "What makes you think those savages will let us surrender when they can just wait a little longer for us to die of thirst, then walk over our bodies?"

Alexander fixed him with a hard look until Pleasant sighed and shook his head. Then, to my surprise, Alexander looked at me again. "Katrina, tell them what Uri said."

I balked. "What do you mean?"

"What he's been saying all along. About the Mormons."

I hesitated, unaccustomed to speaking in front of the men like this. "Uri thinks that the Mormons have the Paiutes in their pocket. That they ordered this raid and armed the Indians," I managed in a rush. "But you said that the Mormons—"

"I was wrong," Alexander said softly. "Uri was right."

The sound of a gunshot cracked in the distance, and I flinched.

Alexander shifted to one side to sit upright, wincing as he moved. Eliza tried to keep him lying down, but he shook her off and addressed the rest of the group. "Hampton and Thomas found a group of white men camped with Paiutes, not far from here." He lowered his voice. "I believe that if we raise a flag of surrender, we'll see white riders heading into camp to negotiate. *Not* Paiutes."

A collective murmur ran through the group.

"Why should the Mormons accept our surrender if they ordered the attack?" Pleasant asked.

"Because if they're still hiding under the pretense that the Paiutes planned this raid, it means they're still willing to let us pass through the Meadow—for a price," Alexander said. "But all of us have to be in agreement. If we raise the white flag, we do it together or not at all."

The buzz of cicadas swelled in the silence between gunshots.

An older man—Daniel Ulrich—spoke up. "They've already taken most of our cattle. Many of our horses and oxen are dead. What will we offer?"

Alexander drew in a deep breath. "We all have savings we've brought with us. Heirlooms we hoped would make the journey to California. We'll offer it all, if need be."

The men exchanged looks. Daniel Ulrich raked a dirty hand through his thinning hair. "If we give them our savings, all our supplies, how will we survive the journey across the desert?"

Alexander met his gaze. "There won't be any journey to survive unless we do this."

His words hung heavy in the air, thick with the inescapable stench of death that made it impossible to deny that he was right. The only thing we could hope to escape with was our lives.

Pleasant Tackett looked at the others then raised his hand. "Aye."

One by one, the others followed suit. I tried to think what Peter would do. I thought of my children pressed against the sweltering dirt in the ditch.

Then I raised my hand, too.

* * *

While the men spread the word through the trenches and the wagons, Eliza and I strung a white nightdress through the skinny trunk of a sapling that had been uprooted at some point during the past three days.

175

While we forked the branches through the white sleeves, I tried not to wonder whose nightdress I was holding. And whether that person was still alive.

There was some discussion of who would go out into the open and raise the makeshift flag. Hampton offered to do it. So did Pleasant Tackett.

"Oh, for goodness sake," Eliza said finally. "If any of you men show your faces, they'll shoot before they realize what you're holding. I'll do it."

Then she snatched the flag we'd made and moved to the edge of the inner circle of supply wagons.

I could see the strain in Alexander's expression. He wanted to stop her. Let Pleasant Tackett do it. But instead, he let her go.

I trailed Eliza to the edge of the supply wagons, my eyes moving directly to the spot in the trench where I knew my children were hiding. Where Bright and Belle's bodies lay unmoving too, still attached to the wagon that, if all went as planned, would be ransacked to give our valuables to the monsters who had ordered this attack.

When we'd set out with Captain Alexander's wagon train a thousand miles ago, I'd been frightened to think how many cattle, how many wagon tongues, how many axles we might lose along the way.

Now, I was prepared to give them all away, and gladly if we could leave this Meadow with our lives.

"Pleasant just gave the sign," Daniel Ulrich said from where he stood on the other side of Alexander, eyes scanning the outer circle of wagons.

My stomach coiled.

Within minutes, everyone in our group knew the plan: Cease fire if riders approached.

Eliza didn't look behind her as she stepped away. She shuffled past the tiny gap in the chained, circled wagons, hoisting the sapling and the white nightdress as high as she could above her head.

The hum of swarming flies rose to a fever pitch in the silence that followed, and I prayed like I'd never prayed before.

32. KATRINA HUFF

MOUNTAIN MEADOWS, UTAH
SEPTEMBER 1857
DAY 3 IN THE MEADOW

Eliza stood waving the flag back and forth out in the open for what felt like an hour.

Each time she lifted her shaking arms higher, I felt certain I would hear the crack of a rifle, then watch her topple onto her face like little America Dunlap.

Then Daniel Ulrich hissed, "Two white riders, on the other side of the river. They're crossing."

My mouth dropped open, and I whirled around to look at Alexander. "I'm going back to my children." I limped a step toward one of the spaces between the wagons.

Alexander offered me a tight-lipped shake of the head. Not quite a scowl, not quite a smile. "Stay here, Katrina. Daniel, gather the other heads of household back here. Once we reach an agreement for the surrender, we'll need everyone ready to act. Nobody speaks, except me. The Mormons can't know we suspect they ordered the attack."

He glanced at Eliza and Hampton. "Help me get my jacket back on."

I averted my eyes while he struggled to stand, brow drenched in sweat and furrowed in pain. My heart pounded like a drum in my ears as I leaned farther into the space between the wagons.

At first, all I saw was the matted grass and our unburied dead within the inner circle of supply wagons. Then my eyes landed on a narrow opening between two of the wagons in the outer circle.

I held in a gasp as two of the men unchained a pair of wagons and the first rider appeared, threading the opening.

I hadn't expected to see military men.

He was followed by a second man, both sitting atop a skinny horse. What at first glance appeared to be smart military uniforms quickly revealed themselves as shabby. Their dark blue coats were faded and frayed at the edges. The brass buttons, several of which were missing, looked dull and tarnished. As the riders drew even closer, I could see that the fabric of their coats had been patched in places with mismatched thread. Their trousers were a patchwork of mended tears, revealing a life far removed from any garrison I'd seen back in Arkansas.

I glanced at Alexander as he moved past me. Even with sweat beading from his forehead and blood seeping through his shirt, he looked far more regal than any of the so-called militia approaching on horseback. In less than a minute, they would be near enough that I could see the whites of their eyes. Both men were armed, their rifles holstered within easy reach.

When the two riders were a stone's throw away, they stopped. Alexander stepped into the open, Hampton at his side to support him. The man in the lead, a stout fellow with tawny blond hair, squinted in the sun, sending deep crow's feet across his cheeks.

He dismounted and approached Alexander on foot.

Movement along the trench drew my eye, and I caught a glimpse of several heads bobbing above the lip of the embankment, watching.

"We're grateful for your intervention." Alexander's voice rose strong and clear, above the hum of the cicada choir. "My name is Captain Alexander Fancher."

"General John D. Lee," the man replied, his voice matching Alexander's tone. "And Major Isaac Haight." He nodded to the man behind him on horseback. "It seems you've landed in the hornet's nest."

My stomach clenched as I moved my eyes between the two men facing each other in the trampled, bloody grass.

"It seems we've been kicking this nest since we crossed into Utah Territory," Alexander replied solemnly. "The fact that you're standing here tells me you have a great deal of sway with ... our neighbors." He gestured toward the river, where the first hailstorm of bullets had ripped through our camp three days earlier.

Lee kept his gaze focused on Alexander. "Our friends the Paiutes have authorized my militia to negotiate your surrender." He flicked his eyes to the tightly circled inner wagons. "It took some doing. Chief Kanosh would just as soon scalp the lot of you. The Paiute are tired of the wagons and emigrants, ruining their grazing land. The drought this summer has been the worst in years, and grass is mighty scarce. President Buchanan is sending a mob of soldiers to remove Governor Brigham Young, the only white man who's ever treated them kind. And you're the unlucky group they've decided will pay the price."

The way he said that last sentence made my stomach clench. Like he agreed with Chief Kanosh. I was glad, for the moment, that Uri was back in the trench with the children. He wouldn't have been able to hold his tongue.

"We've certainly paid. They've got our cattle," Alexander said. He stood a little taller. "But we're prepared to offer *them* more."

I couldn't help but hear the faintest emphasis on the word *them*. What Alexander was really asking was what General Lee—and the rest of his men—wanted.

"How much are your scalps worth?" Lee asked, turning his head ever so slightly so that his pale gray eyes met mine.

This time, I refused to look away. My skin crawled like ants trailing up and down my legs. *Don't trust him,* I wanted to cry. But these militiamen were the only allies we had. There was no other option.

Alexander hesitated only a moment. "In addition to the cattle we've parted with, we're prepared to offer plenty of fine furniture, clothing, and jewelry. There's gold hidden beneath every single one of the wagon bolsters. We'll gladly part with all but the tiniest bit."

Lee glanced over his shoulder at the other man, then gave a curt nod. Alexander's offer seemed to please him. Lee cleared his throat. "Your generosity will go a long way to soften the Paiutes' anger."

He lifted a hand and beckoned to the second rider. Major Haight had a dark, scraggly beard and tiny wide-set eyes that made me think of a toad. "We'll need to secure your rifles and ammunition before we can escort you through the canyon. Brother Haight—and the rest of my men—will assist you."

Alexander stepped back as if he'd been stung by a hornet. "Surely that's not necessary."

Lee's mouth made a hard line, and his brows furrowed as if he were displeased by the idea, too. "The Paiutes won't accept an armed surrender. Your rifles will be returned to you once my men have led you safely past the Meadow."

I cast a glance back at Daniel Ulrich. The anger and mistrust in his beet-red face and bulging eyes echoed the wariness in Alexander's. "What's to stop the Paiutes from attacking my wagon train again? Forgive my bluntness, but given what's happened, surely you understand that I have no confidence that this Chief Kanosh won't attack our unarmed party." He lifted a hand to indicate the destruction in the Meadow.

Lee nodded like he'd anticipated this objection. "Certainly. Every single man in your party will be accompanied by an armed military escort—whom the Paiutes trust wholeheartedly." He twisted his mouth up in concentration then added. "I suspect you have a number of injured among you. Many women and young children. We'll evacuate them each in turn. Accompanied, of course, by armed escorts of the Nauvoo Legion. As soon as possible, if you're agreeable. A short mile march will put you out of the canyon."

The Nauvoo Legion. The words made my skin prickle. I'd heard them before. Uri said that the Mormon militia had been formed by Joseph Smith back in Nauvoo, Illinois, with the intent of protecting the Mormons from persecution—and overthrowing the government to establish a theocracy. Now, the Nauvoo Legion answered to Brigham Young.

I'd been disturbed by the idea of a rogue militia. But now my mind clung to the thought, desperate for reassurance. Brigham Young was a man of God. And these militiamen answered to him. We could trust them.

So, despite knowing that General Lee would be lining his pockets with my family's treasures before the end of the day, my heart dared to hope.

We could be out of the Meadow within the hour.

We could survive on rationed beans the rest of the way to California if we had to. Scrape together whatever money we had left to buy oxen to replace Bright and Belle. Trade with Indians beyond the borders of Utah Territory. Crawl through the desert on our hands and knees if need be.

Anything but stay in this place.

Before I knew it, Alexander was holding out a hand and the blond man with pale gray eyes was grasping it, showing his teeth in a wide smile and directing the other men to arrange the logistics of the surrender.

Without waiting to look back at Alexander or the other heads of household, I limped across the Meadow to the trench, where I knew I'd find my children.

For the first time in three days, I didn't expect to feel a bullet tear through me.

33. KATRINA HUFF

MOUNTAIN MEADOWS, UTAH
SEPTEMBER 1857

DAY 3 IN THE MEADOW

A smile tugged at my lips for the first time in days as I approached the edge of the trench.

"It's done," I burst out before I could even see the tops of my children's heads. "We're leaving the Meadow."

My heart swelled when I saw their faces, bleary but bright-eyed again. The crush of dusty women and children lining the trench sat up and tilted their heads toward me, too.

"Does that mean we can stand up, Mama?" Mary asked hopefully.

"Thank God," Louisa whispered.

"It's a load of horse shit," Uri spat as Louisa and William tried to help him stand.

"Uri." I stared at him in shock. I'd heard him curse more since we'd reached the Meadow than all the years I'd known him. "Have a little gratitude."

Nancy, who had been lying in the dirt with her thumb in her mouth and her head in his lap, whimpered and reached for Mary's hand. So did Triphena, no matter how much Louisa cooed at her.

It was decided, though.

The plan was already in motion. More men in raggedy uniforms moved into the Meadow on foot, gathering our people into groups. A wagon carrying children aged four and under would lead our exodus out of the Meadow first, followed by a wagon carrying the wounded. The women and older children would follow on foot. Alexander and the rest of our men would be the last to leave the Meadow. Each man would be escorted by an armed militiaman.

"Horse shit," Uri muttered again under his breath.

I gripped his good arm as he faltered. "Shh," I hissed, leaning close to his ear. Louisa drew closer to listen, her face a mask of weary terror. "Alexander knows that. He knows we're paying off the Mormons as much as the Paiutes. It's the only way out."

Especially since you insulted them in Cedar City, I didn't dare say out loud.

I knew the blame for what had happened didn't actually rest on Uri's shoulders. But I'd be damned if I listened to him try to add more powder to this keg while the rest of us scurried around like insects trying to get out of this canyon by the skin of our teeth.

Mary, William, and James looked at me with the faintest flicker of concern but stayed where I'd instructed them to sit together along the lip of the trench. I hefted little Nancy onto Mary's lap, forcing my lips into an encouraging smile. "It's nearly over. We'll have plenty to drink once we get to the other side of the canyon." The sight of all my children sitting together like ducklings made my heart swell. "Chins up," I told them. "Just a little longer."

When Alexander asked for time to let everyone drink from the river, the militiamen had said no. That was where the Indians were hiding. Time was of the essence. They might change their minds about the terms of this surrender at any moment.

We're nearly there, I told myself over and over.

More armed militiamen wearing weathered and patched uniforms gathered in the Meadow by the minute, lingering along the banks of the river. Ready to escort us out of the canyon as soon as we were organized.

Beyond them, in the brush, skulked the Indians, who had finally shown themselves—at least, at a distance. Their bodies were painted with bold strokes of color, vibrant against the dusky red walls of the canyon.

I thought of the red-and-black painted man I'd seen in the early hours of the first attack and shuddered.

In all my time on the Overland Trail, I'd never seen war paint like that before. It covered their bodies from head to toe, even their hair.

The sight made my blood run cold. The Indians held a collection of rifles, wicked-looking knives, and clubs, as if they'd wanted to finish us off, every last one of us.

Despite myself, I felt a surge of gratitude toward the Mormons for negotiating our surrender.

"Children four and under," the toadlike man with the scraggly beard and wide set eyes bellowed. He walked the edge of the trench, pointing to a wagon that had been separated from the rest of the train, with the purpose of carrying the youngest children out of the Meadow first. The Mormon militia insisted that everyone's arms must be empty. Even the women. No children would be carried by anyone from our group.

"Bring your wounded to the second wagon," he barked again, motioning to a wagon behind the children, where most of the injured had already been gathered in order to be loaded up.

I locked eyes with Louisa, then Uri. "Come on. You have to go."

"I can walk," Uri growled, even as he leaned so heavily against Louisa that she stumbled to catch him. But when William and James flanked his side to help him up over the edge of the trench, he didn't object.

This was a surrender now, not a fight.

"Be good, Uri," I told him, leaning in to kiss his cheek. His wound had begun to bleed again, fresh red liquid dripping from the buttons on the jacket he insisted on keeping in place.

Uri grunted and looked past me at the military man approaching. "Traitors," he hissed, mouth set in a hard line. I didn't have to ask who he was talking about.

"Hush," I snapped. "Save it for later. Right now, they're our saviors."

Louisa hefted Triphena on her hip and took Uri by the arm. She glanced back at me as she shuffled away, eyes blank and wide. Her lips were so chapped and red, it looked like she was wearing rouge as she moved farther away from me.

Nancy shrank against my side as Major Haight reached us and pointed a thumb in her direction. "That one. How old is she?"

"All of my children are old enough to walk," I told him, keeping my voice sweet.

He raised an eyebrow and stopped walking. "That's not what I asked."

I hesitated. In my experience, women could tell a four-year-old from a six- nearly seven-year-old. Men rarely could. If I told him Nancy was four, she could ride in the children's wagon with baby

Triphena—who was already whimpering at the idea of being separated from Louisa. The thought was a rock in my gut.

"Ma'am?" he asked impatiently.

"She's six," I admitted finally, unwilling to let Nancy be separated from me.

Haight nodded. Then he shifted his gaze to my foot. Blood soaked through the shoe covering my crushed toe. "You're injured," he stated. "You'll slow everything down. Paiutes won't like that."

"I can walk," I told him. Then I took a few steps forward to prove it, even though my toe screamed in protest.

He frowned but shrugged. "As long as you can keep up."

But since it fell unto my lot ... That I should rise and you should not.

The lyrics to Peter's song slapped me with so much force, so sharp, so clear, that I made a little "oh" sound. But the man's back was already to me as he circled down the trench, calling out again for any more injured. For any younger children.

I shook the lyrics off, confused, wondering why it was the song that had been stuck in my head since Peter died. I could almost hear them in his voice, sung sad and mournful and sweet at the same time. A lump rose in my throat, and I knew that if he was with us now, he'd be humming the tune.

I gripped Nancy's hand harder and tried to focus. But an uneasy feeling bloomed in the pit of my stomach as the words came again.

But since it fell unto my lot ... That I should rise and you should not. This time, the lyrics came with a memory of Peter explaining the song's origin. A farewell song, penned by a Scottish prisoner on the night of his execution.

My skin prickled with goosebumps, despite the heat.

I found myself staring across the Meadow at Louisa, attempting to place baby Triphena into the wagon for the littlest children—the babies. Triphena was red-faced and screaming, trying again and again to get out of the wagon and into Louisa's arms.

A clean-shaven military man, accompanied by an older fellow with salt-and-pepper hair, was trying to calm her, but she'd have none of it.

I looked down at little Nancy and locked her hand in mine.

But since it has so ought to be ... By a time to rise and a time to fall.

Come fill to me the parting glass ... Good night and joy be with you all.

Nancy's favorite line.

Triphena's shrieks got louder. I wondered again if I should put Nancy in the wagon with her cousin and the younger children.

I gritted my teeth. We'd been through so much over the past three days. I'd been drifting in a fog of grief for longer than that. I wouldn't abandon her again if I could help it. The Mormons would be none the wiser if she walked with me.

My eyes moved to the wagon full of wounded, where Uri had settled, behind the wagon carrying the children. A cross-looking uniformed man with a balding head had climbed into the driver's seat. There was something strange about his neck. A red smear, like he'd been wounded, but too bright for blood.

I squinted at it then turned my attention to Louisa, who was still trying to convince little Triphena to stay put in the first wagon, after parting with Uri. The baby frantically held out a hand toward her mother, still making those little shrieks.

Louisa fixed me with a helpless gaze as she walked away from her daughter across the Meadow, face pinched and puckered with tears that wouldn't come after so many days baking in the sun.

Behind her, baby Triphena suddenly went quiet, eyes fixed on an unidentifiable woman being carried toward the wagon for the wounded. She'd been caught in the face by a bullet. I wouldn't have believed she was still alive if not for the way her hands clutched the top of her bloodied dress.

The cross-looking driver didn't move to help.

I motioned to Louisa then grabbed Nancy's hand and turned to Mary, James, and William. "Everyone stay together. There will be water soon. It will be all right," I promised them.

We're safe.

We're together.

We're almost there.

I forced all three phrases through my head again and again, willing them to be true. My children's heads nodded in unison. I planted a kiss on each of their dusty faces then pulled Nancy along as I stumbled through the field, behind the wagon where they'd loaded the woman without a face.

I swallowed back the tears. There would be time to weep when the danger had passed.

The clean-shaven man had climbed into the driver's seat of the children's wagon. When his eyes met mine, I saw a stricken look on his face.

I realized, with a start, that something about him reminded me of Peter.

The thought pressed at the corners of my mind, insistent, in time with the lyrics still circling round and round.

Beside me, Louisa fixed me with a look that made me wonder if I had said it out loud. When she spoke, her voice wavered with tears. "Tri wouldn't stop crying, Kit. She wants to be carried. I couldn't make her understand."

"She'll be back in your arms soon," I said, my own voice shaking. I cut my eyes back to the silver-haired man who was prepared to drive the wagon carrying the babies.

So fill to me the parting glass ... And drink a health whate'er befall. The lyrics galloped through my mind in Peter's gentle voice, stronger than ever. And I let them. Because for a moment, it felt like he was here with us in this awful Meadow.

And then, suddenly, the song went quiet.

Leave her with Triphena, Kit.

I gripped Nancy's hand so hard she made a little squeak. "Mama, ow."

I found myself shaking my head as the fear in my heart clenched its fist. *No.* Peter was gone. I was here. And I'd be damned if I let Nancy go. She would stay here, with her mother. With her aunt and siblings. Baby Triphena would ride with the man who made me think of Peter.

We're almost there.

"Last call for little children."

I shrank away from the voice. The man with the wide-set eyes was circling around.

When nobody answered him, he raised his voice and boomed, "Five minutes. Keep your hands at your sides. The wagons will lead out. Once they're on their way, you'll follow. Then your men."

I looked back at the line of men—the last group to be escorted to safety. At each man's side stood an armed, uniformed member of the Nauvoo Legion.

A few minutes later, the wagons carrying the babies and the wounded jolted, and a whoop went up from those of us on foot.

We were finally leaving the Meadow.

34. KAHPEPUTZ (SALLY)

CORN CREEK, UTAH
SEPTEMBER 1857

Awan was back.

Awan was alive.

I wanted him to wrap his arms around me. To kiss me like he had the night he left. To show me the shy smile he saved for me when he looked up through that long black hair.

There were no smiles, though. Not from Awan, not from the other men who returned with him.

Their faces were drawn, their eyes blank. They looked like ghosts of their former selves.

After a few minutes, their mothers and sisters' cries of delight went quiet. I didn't understand. Almost all of the men had returned to camp, including a stone-faced Kanosh. But not because they were injured.

The men had a few more of the gentiles' cattle with them, but nobody seemed victorious. The village hummed with an unspoken tension.

I desperately wanted to pull Awan aside and ask him to tell me everything, but there was nonstop work to be done preparing food and tending the horses that had returned dusty and shaking from a hard ride.

All day long, I took animals to water with the other women, careful not to let the horses drink too much. It wasn't until the sun began to sink in the west, and I made my final trip to the churned-up, muddy creek that Awan found me.

He wouldn't look at me at first, even when I reached out a hand to place it on his arm.

He flinched at my touch. When he finally turned to face me, there were tears brimming in his eyes.

In a voice so soft I could barely hear him, he said, "You were right. They weren't troops."

Then he told me everything.

35. KATRINA HUFF

MOUNTAIN MEADOWS, UTAH

SEPTEMBER 1857

DAY 3 IN THE MEADOW

We were moving.
    We'd have water soon.
    It was almost over.
    We're safe.
    We're together.
    We're nearly there.
    With my injured toe, Major Haight's predictions proved correct. Despite my best efforts, I was significantly slower than the other women and children. "Stay at the front with the children, so you can keep eyes on baby Tri and Uri's wagons," I told Louisa reluctantly, not wanting to create a bottleneck with so many of us moving slowly.
    I pressed Mary's hand into Sissy Lou's and squeezed my boys' hands.
    Then Nancy and I lagged to the back of the crowd. When I turned to look, I could just see the start of the long line of our men marching single-file, each one escorted by a Mormon militiaman.
    It was like a strange parade. But it didn't matter. The shooting had stopped, and we were almost out.
    I couldn't see the wagons carrying the smallest children or the wounded anymore. When I craned my neck, Nancy squeezed my hand. Then, so quietly I could hardly hear her, "I miss Papa."
    The tears I thought had dried out with the thirst prickled at my eyes again. "I do, too."
    Nancy was quiet for a few seconds. Then she added, "He'd be proud though, wouldn't he?"

"He would," I managed. "He'd be proud."

I turned to glance behind me again so she wouldn't see me cry, trying to catch a glimpse of Captain Alexander in the line of men, but it was so long that I couldn't make him out.

A quiet cheer for the Mormon militia rippled through our men. I smiled, knowing how much Uri would hate to hear it in the wagon for the injured.

And then, from the front of the line came a booming voice.

"Halt!"

My mouth went dry.

The man riding between us and the men pulled up his horse, lifting his rifle in the air.

I clutched Nancy's hand tighter. Was something wrong? Were the Paiutes going back on their word? Was there about to be a battle?

Sweat dripped faster down the back of my dress, and I darted my gaze to the canyon walls.

Not a single Paiute in sight. The Meadow was peaceful.

Then I watched in horror as every single one of the Mormon militiamen escorting our men raised his rifle.

Not pointed toward the hills, toward the sagebrush and the Paiutes by the river. But directly toward our men.

No, no, no.

The seconds dripped like molasses as the scream rose in my throat.

Pleasant Tackett, at the front of the line, was still looking straight ahead. His eyes were on the women and children in front of him, his mouth still open in the cheer he'd just joined.

Run, I wanted to shout, but there wasn't time.

The scream ripped through my throat at the same time the militiamen fired in unison, the sound of it lost in the deafening boom of gunshots.

My vision blurred at the edges.

A crimson spray erupted from the side of Pleasant Tackett's balding head as his body jerked sideways and he crumpled to the ground.

Behind him, the rest of our men—necks snapped sideways from the force of the bullets, faces half-obscured by gore and bone—crumpled in tandem like a macabre dance.

Fifty men, dead in seconds. Executed by firing squad.

My heart nearly stopped in my chest.

Pleasant Tackett was dead. Captain Alexander was dead. Daniel Ulrich was dead. Almost all of our men were dead.

No, no, no.

But there was no time to mourn, no time to process, no time to drop to my knees and retch.

Because more men, all of them painted, began swarming down from the riverbanks, knives and clubs and rifles raised over their heads.

Right toward us.

I yanked on Nancy's arm, thinking of nothing but Louisa, Mary, William, and James.

Then Peter's voice, louder than ever as my body unfroze.

Run, Kit. Run.

PART TWO

THREE YEARS AFTER THE MASSACRE

ARTICLE IN THE
LOS ANGELES STAR

LOS ANGELES, CALIFORNIA

In our last publication, we shared a rumor about the massacre of a large party of emigrants on their way to California, through Utah Territory. We were unwilling at first to credit the statement and hoped that rumor had exaggerated the facts, but the report has been confirmed, and the loss of life is even greater than at first reported.

This is the foulest massacre Indians have ever perpetrated on this route, and calls loudly for government intervention. There is no longer reason to doubt the facts—we have them from different parties, and all agree in placing the number of the dead at over one hundred souls, men, women and children.

36. KAHPEPUTZ (SALLY)

CORN CREEK, UTAH

JUNE 1860

I tried to make my footsteps move in tandem with the sound of beating drums that got softer with every step I took away from the village, toward Corn Creek.

My heavy heart refused to keep time.

Keme was dying. The last of the men who'd been injured at Mountain Meadows, finally succumbing to the crippling injuries to his stomach that had tormented him for the past three years.

I walked faster, tugging on the old mule's rope to urge her onward.

Keme's death, like every other painful reminder of what had happened at the Meadow, would reopen the wound that had been festering in the Paiute camp ever since.

And, like always, I would be punished for it. The Paiutes couldn't turn their lingering anger on Brigham Young or the Mormon leaders. That would be suicide. But they could turn it on me.

It had been years now since anyone had called me "Brigham's little doll." I was still technically Kanosh's wife. But there was no more talk of building me a special cabin. I existed among the tribe like Sweet Pea the mule. There to obey, there to work, there to kick when the mood in camp soured.

I was invisible on the best days, a scapegoat on the worst—like today.

For a brief moment in time, I'd thought the Paiutes could become my people. I loved Inola like a mother. And I loved Awan like a husband.

But neither could be true.

When Kanosh had returned with the rest of the men after what happened at Mountain Meadows, he was stone-faced and humming with indignation. "Cowards," he spat at the Paiute men—including his own son—who had abandoned the Meadow when it became clear that the white leaders intended to leave no witnesses to the failed raid left alive.

But over the year that followed, Kanosh's indignation had melted into rage—not at the Paiutes who had abandoned their allies, but at Brother Brigham and the other white leaders.

The US Army had retreated from Salt Lake one year after the massacre at the Meadow, when Brigham Young agreed to step down as governor and Indian Agent of Utah Territory, claiming he wanted to "focus his attentions on building the kingdom of God."

I suspected that the real reason had something to do with what had happened in the Meadow three years ago.

A man named Alfred Cummings replaced Brigham Young, and his administration no longer treated the Paiutes or the Blackfoot or the Bannock or any of the tribal leaders as allies in a war against the United States.

Brigham Young and the Mormons had abandoned the Paiutes.

They'd lied to us.

There had been no uprising by Mormon and Indian against the government of the United States. There was no safety from the wagon trains, which once again rolled through our land in an endless stream, pointing their guns at us any time they wanted.

There were no more meetings with the chiefs in Brother Brigham's mansion, in the room with the hair wreath.

Even the pitiful number of cattle we'd taken from the white gentiles had lasted only a few months. We'd eaten them to keep from starving during that winter.

As for the rest of the cattle and plunder? It had been taken by the Mormons in Southern Utah.

The last time the white leaders from Fillmore and Cedar City had ridden out to Corn Creek, they'd come with a warning on their lips. *Keep quiet about the Meadow. Let the dead bury the dead.*

Kanosh did exactly that, refusing to speak with the Army men who passed by Corn Creek in search of the missing wagon train.

He ignored their questions again when, nearly three years later, the Army men finally uncovered the mass graves in the Meadow.

But now it was fear, not loyalty, that earned Kanosh's silence. Every promise had been broken, and there was no end to his fury. He directed most of it at me, insisting Brother Brigham had given "Sally Indian" to him as just one more manipulation.

I couldn't say I disagreed with him.

Sally Indian. That's what most of the Paiutes called me after the massacre. Not "Brigham's little doll." Not "Sally." But "Sally Indian," stressing the last word like a taunt.

Inola joined the rest of the village in scoffing at my presence—at least outwardly. When no one was looking, she spoke to me just like she had before.

As I approached Corn Creek, I reached into the pocket of my crinoline dress. The black color had become so faded it had turned a pale brown in the sun. The stitching at the collar had come undone, along with the lace along the bottom, and there was a long rip at the hem that showed part of my stomach.

I wore it anyway, knowing better than to ask for anything else.

The pockets of the dress still held, at least. I tugged on the mule's rope with one hand and felt for the familiar shape of the little yucca horse with the other.

"I'm sorry," I whispered as I stroked the rabbit-fur mane.

I looked up to see a red-winged blackbird warbling along the wall of cattails that formed a protective wall on the far side of Corn Creek.

I glanced to my right at the dusty desert, then the left, to see if anyone was nearby. The blackbird trilled again and nibbled at the cattail. Just a song. Not a warning. So I continued toward the creek.

Upon reaching the shore, I let go of the mule's rope so she could graze while I crossed through the shallow water, to the other side of the creek.

When I was a few steps from the cattail wall, another tune rose up to greet me. Not a blackbird, but a whistle I'd learned to love over the past three years.

I returned the sound with a smile, giving myself permission to forget everything else for just a moment.

* * *

I relaxed against the warm earth with Awan's head on my bare stomach, trying to memorize the moment. The muttering sound of the reeds in the breeze, the fine red silt that met the small of my back, the faint smell of damp from the muddy banks of the creek.

"One more minute," I murmured. I'd already stayed too long, but the idea of walking back to the village was almost unbearable.

Awan had cleared this patch of ground for us earlier in the spring. Like he had for the past three years.

Now, the lush green wall of reeds and cattails woven with sweet peas surrounded us on all sides like a protective oasis. Even the mosquitos weren't bad this morning. The drought had finally ended, breaking the storm clouds open across the withered desert for once.

The drought would return. But for the past few years, our cornfields had been tall and green. The melons spread runners all across the land.

Everything was blooming.

It wouldn't last. But in my experience, beautiful things never did.

"I've already stayed too long," I said, keeping my eyes closed and weaving my fingers through Awan's hair.

I felt him sigh, his warm breath tickling my stomach, but he didn't argue. Just ran a hand along my bare thigh, circling his fingers teasingly as if he were about to begin again.

I pushed his hand away, even though it was the last thing I wanted to do. "I need to get back. Someone will come looking to find out whether I've been eaten by a puma."

Awan laughed, but we both knew what would happen to me if we got caught. And it would be much worse than being eaten by a puma.

Like many of the Paiutes in the aftermath of what happened at the Meadows, Kanosh no longer considered himself a Mormon. But that didn't mean he was above Blood Atonement if he found out his fourth wife had been sleeping with his son.

Awan sat up beside me. When I reached for my dress, he caught my arm and pulled me into one more kiss.

His lips tasted earthy and sweet, like Awan himself. "Tomorrow," he said simply. Then he pulled on his clothing and disappeared through the tall reeds, toward the paint mare he'd ridden to meet me at the creek.

Tomorrow, I thought, already wishing away the time in between now and then.

We'd parted this way nearly every day over the past three years. At the edge of the creek in spring and summer. In the underground caves he'd shown me a short distance from Corn Creek in fall and winter. What looked like an alcove in a rocky bluff was actually the opening to a short tunnel leading into a dark room big enough to stand.

Not that we'd wanted to stand.

Awan was supposed to be hunting during these times. I was supposed to be gathering water. As long as I hurried, nobody would be the wiser. The stolen time at the creek made everything else in the village bearable.

I picked up my pitch baskets and filled them with water. Then I walked back to the mule, who was feasting on the lush spring grass along the banks. "Come on, Sweet Pea," I told her, once I'd loaded the baskets, even though Inola insisted the chubby donkey didn't deserve an affectionate name. She had a habit of stubbornly planting her feet and refusing to move forward.

I'd secretly learned the trick to making her walk quickly— dangling half a cooked camas root just out of reach until we arrived at the creek. Then dangling the other half when we walked back to the village. I saved the sweet, nutty camas root from my breakfast each morning, even though it was half of what I got to eat. Sweet Pea made it easy to explain why drawing water took so long. And I loved her for it.

The mule brayed and picked up her feet. "Good girl." I held the rope with one hand and dangled the root an arm's length in front of her face. "You'll get your treat soon." I couldn't help smiling because I'd already gotten mine.

When the first wickiups came into view, I tightened my grip on the mule's rope and dropped my expression to make my face blank to anyone who would observe.

Sometimes, I wondered if Inola suspected the love I had for Awan —and him for me. When the other wives talked about who he might marry, she brushed the talk away, insisting he would marry when he was ready.

I loved her for this, but I knew Awan wouldn't be able to put off marrying forever.

He was twenty-one. Time to choose a wife and begin his own family.

Kanosh chided him about it all the time, pointing to the widow of one of the men who'd died at Mountain Meadows. She was beautiful, with amber eyes the color of honey and a birdlike frame. And she was clearly in love with Awan.

I watched her stare at him with unmasked adoration whenever he was nearby, but I couldn't do a thing about it.

In addition to the chores I'd already been assigned—like gathering water—I spent my days collecting dead sagebrush for the fires, disposing of horse dung, and cleaning dirty clothes. The chores nobody else wanted. Same as I'd done back at Brother Brigham's.

And, same as before, I'd slowly stopped speaking to anyone except Awan—and sometimes Inola, when Numa and Povi weren't nearby.

Thanks to Kanosh, I'd become a symbol of the Mormons' bad magic and our men who had died at Mountain Meadows.

My daily ridicule seemed to please Kanosh. I accepted it without complaint. Because at least it meant he hadn't tried to crawl into my bedroll again, even though I still shared a wickiup with the other wives.

The message was clear—I still belonged to him.

He'd taken away my rabbit blanket, insisting it was being wasted. A real Paiute deserved a blanket like that. Not a girl like me, brown on the outside but white on the inside.

But rabbit skin or not, ridicule or not, endless chores or not, I was happier than I'd ever been. I lay down each night covered in invisible kisses, burning with anticipation for the following day when I'd see Awan again.

I'd never belonged anywhere. But I belonged with Awan.

I belonged with his strong, lean body that had lost all of its sharp, skinny edges. I belonged with his warm brown eyes that shone like pebbles in the creek when he saw me. I belonged with his gentle hands that knew just how I wanted to be touched. His lips, which called me by my real name, *Kahpeputz,* and were softer than any rabbit blanket. His heart, which beat steadily against my ear when I lay my head on his chest.

Even though I knew that what we'd been doing couldn't last much longer, I'd decided that I was going to live in these stolen minutes as fully as I could until they ran out.

Just like the rain that would inevitably dry up.

My past was filled with darkness. My future looked just as murky.

Like Sweet Pea, all I had was the sweetness right in front of me. Close enough to touch, but just outside my grasp.

It kept me gladly putting one foot in front of the other until I could taste the one truly good thing I had left.

Tomorrow.

37. LUCY ROBISON

FILLMORE, UTAH

JUNE 1860

When I found Vick in the middle of our apple orchard, lying on his back among the last of the crumpled brown blossoms that had fallen from the trees, I thought he was dead.

I froze where I was, heart pounding, holding the bread-and-butter sandwich I'd made for him.

His eyes were closed. His mouth slack in a half-open frown.

Horror then sadness then despair ripped through me, and the only thought that took shape clearly in my head was, *It killed him.*

I wasn't sure what *it* was, exactly. All I knew was that nothing had been the same since he'd returned from the north.

Vick blinked and rose to standing. His frown didn't go away, though.

I swallowed hard, trying not to let the tears fall. He *wasn't* dead. Still, he wasn't alive, either.

Fighting had never officially broken out with the United States Army three years ago, and thank heaven for that. The Army outmatched us in weapons and numbers, but not zeal. Our men had held the line in Echo Canyon by day. By night, they set fire to the prairie grass the troops counted on to feed their animals, stampeded their oxen, lit their wagons ablaze, kept them from sleeping in surprise night disturbances, and blockaded the road in front of them with fallen logs. By October, with early snows, the soldiers had been forced to draw back.

That's when my Vick had come back to me.

I'd learned what I knew about the standoff with the troops back then from others—not Vick. While he hadn't seen direct combat, his time in Echo Canyon had changed him all the same.

He refused to talk about what he'd done and seen. And I'd stopped pressing him long ago.

The last time I'd demanded he answer my questions, it was the only time I'd ever been afraid he might hit me.

The distance between us had grown like a canyon of its own over the past three years, sending cracks through all the places I'd thought were strong.

Vick had taken a second wife the week after he returned to Fillmore—a widowed Bannock Indian woman named Kima.

Several of the men in Fillmore had gone on to take Indian women as second or third wives, after a sermon from an apostle traveling through our city proclaimed, *"It is my will that you should take unto you wives of the Lamanites, that their posterity may become white, delightsome, for even now their females are more virtuous than the gentiles."*

Though Kima spoke little English, she was as hardworking as she was kind, young, and beautiful. The children accepted her with open arms, and she them. But no amount of faith made my stomach stop clenching when Vick went into her room for the night.

There was also the fact that her deep brown skin and eyes made me think of Sally—who I hadn't seen since that night I blessed the Paiute men, and what had happened at Mountain Meadows. Word had spread like wildfire in the days and weeks following the cattle raid down south.

According to the rumors, the Paiutes hadn't just raided the cattle. They'd slaughtered every last gentile. More than a hundred men, women, and children.

At first, Apostle Smith and the other leaders had sung the Indians' praises in our sacrament meetings—along with strict instructions not to speak of the matter to gentile outsiders. But when newspapers in New York and California started printing ridiculous rumors that Mormons were involved in covering up the fate of the missing California-bound wagon train, the praise quickly dried up.

Now, nearly three years later, more rumors—that the U.S. Army had finally discovered the bodies in the Meadow—had been trickling in.

Everyone still whispered that the gentiles deserved what they got from the Indians. For poisoning the steers they left behind. For their hand in murdering Joseph Smith back in Illinois. For their wickedness.

I kept my mouth shut and did my best to carry on, but sometimes, in the back of my mind, I could still hear Sally's words.

Locoweed. Women and children.

"There you are," I told Vick brightly, pretending I hadn't been standing there like a statue behind the trees, thinking he was dead. "It's long past time for lunch. You must be starving. Kima and I made sandwiches."

Vick startled and jerked his head toward me like I'd fired a gun.

For a split second, the mask dropped and I saw the old Vick. *Oh, you are dear to me,* I thought as my eyes moved over his lean face, those peculiar eyes. One pale green, one dark green, like the beginning and end of summer. *There you are.*

I missed the Vick who used to sing hymns while he tended the orchard, coaxing the roots to go ever deeper into the dusty Utah ground. The Vick who'd slept in my bed each night, arms tucked around my waist. But just as quickly, that man retreated back to the place he'd been hiding, locked away from all of us. Even the children.

Vick turned away from me, so I could only see the murky green of his dark-colored eye.

I swallowed hard.

One more bit of goodness the gentiles had stolen before their troops retreated.

Sister Johnson said that Brother Johnson had been a different man since he returned from the north, too. I knew it before she said so, though. You could see it on his face in the guarded way he said hello and the tightness to his jaw. Like if he let it loose for even a moment, something awful would tumble out.

Vick picked up his bucket of tobacco water, meant for the aphids and whiteflies that were swarming in the orchard in late spring. "You can leave it," he said gently. "I'm not hungry yet. Might be out here a while."

I knew he'd be out here until after dark, whether he was finished treating the trees or not. The orchard seemed to be his one refuge.

It used to be me.

"The children will want to say goodnight," I replied softly. "And little Amina drew a very pretty picture."

This made him jerk his head up. "A picture of what?"

I frowned. "An apple tree ... I think it's meant for you."

Our family had grown by yet one more, shortly after Vick's marriage to Kima, when he returned in early November. Bishop Brunson brought baby Amina to my doorstep like the stork one Sunday after dinner. It was supposed to be a temporary arrangement. The little girl's mama had died during childbirth the year before, and Amina had been born with a twisted, withered arm. When the arm had to be amputated, her poor papa turned to Bishop Brunson for help. He could barely take care of the six children he already had, let alone an ailing baby. So, out of desperation, he gave Amina up.

We had the means to adopt her. So, we shuffled our beds and prepared for yet another soul to join our household. This time, my faith made room without protest. Her brown eyes reminded me of Proctor's, dark and deep. I loved her fiercely from the moment Bishop Brunson held her out toward me and Kima—and she clung to my neck first.

Vick sighed but didn't say anything else. He turned around and picked up the bucket of dark, foul-smelling tobacco water, wringing out the sponge, wiping the leaves and branches around the trunk.

Come back to me, I begged him silently. *What will it take?*

"Vick?" I prodded.

He acted like I hadn't spoken until I added, "Peach will be here tomorrow—with the rest of the Willis girls."

That drew a nod and the barest smile—and broke my heart all over again.

All summer, every Wednesday morning, sixteen-year-old Peach Willis had been making the three-mile walk to our home. We paid her a little money to tend Amina and clean house while me, Vick, Kima, and the older children spent the day at the tithing house. As Bishop Brunson's first counselor, Vick was in charge of opening up the cellar filled with ten percent of Fillmore's produce, goods, and clothing that had been donated to the Church for the benefit of the poor. It was an all-day affair, distributing the goods, throwing out anything spoiled, and organizing new donations.

Our Adelia was old enough now, and could have stayed behind to watch Amina. But we all knew there was more to the arrangement than that.

Two wives wasn't that many. Not for a family with our means, so when Bishop Brunson had prodded us to consider taking a third wife —perhaps sweet Peach Willis—we'd agreed without question. I wouldn't let my faith get away from me again.

I set the wrapped, buttered bread beside him, then turned back the way I'd come, taking the path along the far side of the orchard that would lead me past Proctor's grave.

The trees had grown and flourished so much over the past three years, I barely recognized the forest they'd become.

Some days, it felt like the thriving orchard survived on my grief alone.

38. EMMA WILLIS

FILLMORE, UTAH

JUNE 1860

When I tried to scream, the sound came out funny, like my mouth was full of cotton.

After thrashing around in bed for a few second, I realized my mouth *was* filled with cotton. I'd gotten myself so twisted up in the sweaty quilt that even my head was wrapped in the scratchy blanket.

I clawed at my face to peel the fabric away and sat up in bed gasping as quiet as I could, trying not to stir up the whole house in the dead of night.

I blinked in the dark room, trying to see whether I'd woken up my sisters in the bed next to me. If I had, they didn't show it. Peach breathed steady and soft. Violet had scooted herself nearly to the foot of the bed, scrunched in a ball.

I rolled over and put my hand under the bed to feel for the familiar, poky edges of the little horse. I had no idea where it'd come from, but it had been under there for as long as I could remember, hidden from view in the gathering dust. I didn't dare sleep with it, even though I wanted to. The black strips of sinew binding two of the legs had already started to come undone.

A familiar wave of shame washed over me as I stroked the little horse's rabbit-fur mane and tail. The nightmares were getting worse, not better. *You're a big girl now.* Mama's voice. *Not a baby who cries at night.* She was right. At nearly eight years old, I should've stopped waking up screaming in the night long ago.

But by now, my nightmares were so familiar, we'd mostly learned to sleep through them.

Everyone but me, of course.

I listened for Mama's stern, clomping footsteps, but the house stayed silent. If she was still asleep, Papa probably was too. I especially hated to wake him, on account of him needing to leave before dawn for the gristmill.

But try as I might—and I tried—I couldn't stop the screams from burning their way out of my lungs. Couldn't stop them any more than I could stop myself from vomiting the time Mama made a soup out of spoiled deer meat.

The fear had to go somewhere, I guess.

The nightmares always started with me wrapped in Mama's best quilt—the one she kept in a chest at the foot of our bed, that none of us were allowed to touch, let alone sleep with. In the dream, the fabric was soft against my face at first, warm against my body. I felt safe, tucked away.

After a while, the dream shifted. Something would splatter against my cheek. Softly at first, like a sprinkle of warm rain. *What is that?* I always asked myself in the dream, unwrapping myself from the safety of that warm cocoon to find out where the water was coming from.

That's when I realized I was in a big bed with Mama and Papa, and my sisters Peach and Violet. The bed seemed to grow around me as I sat up, until it filled the whole room.

The bed grew, and I kept finding more people tucked in with our family. All of a sudden our neighbors were there, too. Brother and Sister Robison—Amina's parents. Then, our whole congregation. Everyone tucked in together. They were all wiping their faces, like me. But it wasn't rainwater. The liquid was dark and thick, smearing into a mess.

I couldn't see the source of the dark droplets for a few seconds. Just wiped them away from my eyes, looking at my hands in confusion.

Then I thought to look up.

When I did, I could make out dark shapes hanging in the air, directly above those of us lying in bed.

Not just shapes, but bodies. Floating near the ceiling.

I realized that the dark liquid was blood.

All of us in the bed started wiping at our faces faster, clawing at the giant-sized quilt, trying to get away.

The blood dripping down on my face—all of our faces—turned into a waterfall of gore.

In the dream, I could taste that thick, dark red liquid: metallic and warm, like when I accidentally bit my tongue. It ran over my face and into the corners of my mouth, falling faster and harder.

Amina screamed next to my ear.

I screamed, too. All I wanted was Mama.

Mama, I wailed through the chaos, choking and smothering. Just her name, again and again. *Mama, Mama, Mama.*

Her hand always found mine somehow, while the blood poured down from the ceiling and I squeezed my eyes shut to avoid seeing. *"Try, baby,"* she said sternly. *"Try."*

"Try what?" I always asked, frantic to obey her. I'd do anything to get away from the blood and the bodies on the ceiling.

Instead of answering, she pressed something small and round into my hand. *"This is yours,"* she said.

It was a ring, the metal surface warm and smooth against my skin. I squeezed it tight, knowing it was somehow meant to save me.

There was an inscription on the inside of the band that I could feel when I rolled it against my fingers. Words that would stop the blood from pouring if I just tried hard enough to read them.

I never could.

Sometimes, like tonight, the dream ended right then and there, with me screaming and thrashing in my bed, sometimes waking up Peach and little Violet, and then Mama and Papa.

Other times, the dream kept going.

Those nights were the worst.

I hated falling asleep. But when the dream wouldn't end, I hated sleeping even more.

As soon as I had the ring in my hand, the bloody rain stopped and I opened my eyes, thinking it was over.

I cried, I was so glad. The bodies above me were gone. But next to me lay Mama, Papa, Peach, Violet, and the rest. Lifeless and barely more than skeletons, all covered in blood in the bed with me.

Most of the time, the dream ended there.

Sometimes I screamed so loud my throat felt raw and swollen all the next day.

I'd tried telling Mama about the dream once, tears and snot running down my cheeks while I wiped them across my face.

I thought maybe she'd ask Papa to lay his hands on my head and give me a blessing, like he'd done for Violet when she had a high fever.

She didn't call for Papa, though. She fixed me with an uneasy look and said, *"Child, those dreams are from Satan. Do not speak of them to me or anyone else."*

She said it would only give Lucifer and his angels more power over me. That talking of dark things would only make them worse. Especially with my "clever little tongue."

Once, when she didn't know I was listening, I heard her tell Papa, *"She talks like she's already grown. It's not proper, a child speaking to adults like that."*

So I kept my thoughts to myself when I could, and did what Mama said when the dreams came. Pray.

She said that whenever I needed to, I could just fold my arms and kneel by my bedside. Heavenly Father answered the prayers of all little children, since he loved them best of all. The prophet Joseph Smith had been fourteen—just a few years older than me—when God the Father and His son Jesus Christ had appeared in a vision while he prayed in the grove. God would hear my cries, too.

I told Mama that praying had worked. Heavenly Father had taken the bad dreams away.

But what really happened was I started sleeping with my head buried deep under the covers, to muffle the sound of my own screams. Peach and Violet still woke up once in a while—given that they shared a bed right next to mine. Most of the time though, their breathing stayed heavy and deep while I gasped for breath, strangling under the stuffy, scratchy blanket, sweaty and afraid, wanting Mama, and sure I could still feel the blood on my face.

Dear Heavenly Father,

Please protect me from evil. Please make the bad dreams go away. Please.

Thy will be done.

In the name of Jesus Christ, amen.

No matter how much I prayed, the dreams didn't stop. This made me despair nearly as much as the dreams themselves.

From what I'd learned about prayer in Sunday school, Heavenly Father couldn't help but answer a righteous prayer—as long as it was according to His will.

My teacher, Brother Larsen, read us a passage from the Doctrine and Covenants. "Section eighty-two, verse ten, is my favorite scripture," he'd said, looking each of us in the eyes. "It means that Heavenly Father will always bless us with the righteous desires of our hearts. He's bound to do so, by his own promise."

I looked the scripture up later and memorized it. *I, the Lord, am bound when ye do what I say; but when ye do not what I say, ye have no promise.*

If my dreams were coming from Satan, like Mama said, surely me and God agreed on wanting them to stop.

But the dreams hadn't stopped.

If anything, they'd gotten worse this summer.

Which meant, I began to suspect, that the problem wasn't God's ears.

It was me.

39. EMMA WILLIS

FILLMORE, UTAH

JULY 1860

All that summer, Mama sent me, Peach, and Violet to the Robisons' house once a week on Wednesdays.

Sixteen-year-old Peach was the only one who got paid for minding the house and caring for Amina, but she was supposed to be teaching me and Violet how to do her chores. She wasn't likely to be hired help much longer.

Mama suspected that Brother Robison planned to propose to her soon, which meant that Peach wouldn't get paid for her labor anymore. But I might, if I could learn to "put my shoulder to the wheel," like Papa always muttered. Violet was even more hopeless than I was, but to be fair, she was barely four. I was nearly eight.

I tried my best, but most of my waking hours felt fuzzy at the edges. The dreams had gotten so bad that I hardly slept at night, for fear of what I'd see. Some days, it was all I could do to keep my eyes open. But school started again next month, so there were new things to worry about. Our teacher, Sister Brady, cut a fresh willow branch each morning as a warning to lazy and forgetful children. I was well acquainted with its sting.

I was also terrified to tell Mama that Heavenly Father hadn't actually answered my prayers. What if it confirmed what I already suspected? That I was a wicked child.

Peach was as pure and good as fresh snow. Quick to act, quick to obey, with a perpetual smile on her pretty face. Even her hair seemed to comply without a fuss when she plaited it. And that was just the outside. Peach's mind was as soft and sweet as she was. And little, cherubic Violet was her spitting image with bouncy, tawny curls, bright blue eyes, and skin the color of sego lilies.

Me, on the other hand? My dark brown hair was a mess of cowlicks that never lay flat. Mama said I looked like her brother Richard, and by the tone of her voice I could tell it wasn't a compliment. Instead of a creamy white, my skin was a sallow mess of freckles, and dark circles under my eyes. And my mouth curved down in a perpetual frown, no matter my mood. *Smile,* I sometimes had to instruct myself. And that was just the *outside.* I was clumsy, slow, and forgetful, but worst of all, there was a darkness *inside* me, pressing at the edges of my mind all the time like it wanted to swallow me whole. It came out at night without fail, when my tired body finally lost the battle with sleep. Then it emerged from the shadows to run amok in my dreams.

I could tell by the way Mama and Papa looked at me that they suspected as much. When Mama was particularly flustered with my mistakes, she sometimes thundered, "The devil is surely in you, child."

She never said that to Peach or Violet.

* * *

The only one who knew that my nightmares hadn't stopped was Peach.

Soon after Violet and I started coming with her to the Robisons' house, I broke down in a puddle of tears when I tripped over a loose board on the floor and dropped a whole dustpan of debris.

"It's ok, Emmy," Violet told me, while Peach brushed the dirt off my dress and the tears from my cheeks. Amina, who never said a word, patted me with her one hand. I laced her fingers with mine and she smiled up at me.

The kindness in their eyes brought all my fears to the surface in a jumble of words that barely made sense. Eyes on the floor, I rambled on about my downturned mouth and the devil in my dreams. About the blood that dripped from the ceiling and turned Mama, Papa, Peach, Violet, and even my friends from Sunday school into dead bodies.

Peach was silent for a long time after I finished talking, while Violet kept patting the hand I'd scraped on the floor. "You just need some rest," she told me finally. "You're a good girl, Emma."

After that, Peach let me sleep for a few hours each Wednesday, curled up on the floor in the corner of the Robisons' three-bedroom house while she cleaned the house and then washed laundry outside. Both Violet and Amina could generally be coaxed into cuddling up next to me part of the time, listening to the soothing rhythm of the broom scratching back and forth while Peach swept. The air in the quiet room was still and sticky from the pressing July heat, but it felt so good to get some rest from the overwhelming tiredness that I didn't care. The dreams never came during the daytime while Peach busied herself with chores I was supposed to be learning.

Most days of the week, Brother Robison, his first wife Lucy, his second wife Kima, and their children worked in their apple orchard. But on Wednesdays, when they opened up the tithing cellar to the poor, Mama and Papa always stopped there first thing, before Papa went to work at the gristmill.

We relied on the donated food and clothing in the cellar of Bishop Brunson's house as much as anybody in Fillmore, except for maybe the Robisons. I'd heard Mama say that most of the donations in the cellar came from them.

No one wanted to say it, but the harvest would be poor in October. Again.

Elder George A. Smith visited Fillmore once a month, to check in on the gristmill and the sawmill, which both served surrounding cities with flour and lumber. And when he did, he got a report from Papa, who oversaw the whole gristmill. Each time, he came by our house and stayed for Sunday dinner.

The darkest, meanest, most selfish parts of me hated these visits. We ate small rations of beans for days in advance of his arrival, hoarding food so that we could serve him a proper dinner—which he ate with gusto. Sometimes I stared at his jowls, wobbling back and forth while he chewed on a biscuit dripping with butter that might have been mine. I had to keep my mouth clamped shut to hold back a burble of disgust.

He's an apostle of the Lord, Emma, I reprimanded myself with all the ire Mama would have used if she could read my thoughts. *It's an honor to share your table with a servant of the Almighty.* But between my grumbling stomach and my dark and willful mind, I couldn't help it.

I couldn't say exactly why, but I deeply despised him.

* * *

All of the families in Fillmore were poor. Especially the mill-working families, like mine. But compared to my family, Vick and Lucy Robison were plenty comfortable. They didn't pay much for Peach's chores—fifty cents a week, forty-five cents after tithing—but as Mama liked to say, we'd just be underfoot for free at home once we finished our own chores.

On Wednesday afternoons, Brother Robison came home a little early from his service at the tithing house—to say hello to Peach.

When Peach heard his horse's hooves clatter on the hard dirt road leading to the farm, she roused me, Amina, and Violet from sleep then set to preparing a supper of camas roots, venison from the larder, and dried beans that she'd started soaking in the morning. Violet and I helped with this part—and wolfed down a small helping of our own before Brother Robison's boots thumped toward the front door.

Peach ate her meal with Brother Robison. Vick—she was supposed to call him—while Violet and I walked home along the dusty road to start our own pot of beans boiling.

Brother Robison wasn't courting Peach officially, but he'd made his intentions clear enough. Sometimes Peach returned with a handful of wrapped horehound candy to share, or ribbons for her hair. One time, she even came home wearing a whole new dress—a hooped thing made of crinoline that Brother Robison had purchased on one of his trips to Salt Lake City. It came up to her neck in a crisp white collar and down to her ankles in an elegant, flouncing bell that made Peach look like a woman of substance and status instead of a skinny girl from Utah Territory.

Mama asked for every detail of these dinners, bursting with pride when Peach reported that Brother Robison asked about Apostle Smith's most recent visit to the gristmill. Brother Robison was the first counselor in the bishopric to Bishop Brunson now, and a longtime friend of Papa's.

Sweet Peach praised Brother Robison's spiritual knowledge, his dedication to building up Fillmore, and his affection for his dear wives Lucy and Kima.

During one of these conversations, I learned that the Robisons had spent time in Winter Quarters Nebraska before they made the journey West.

Peach herself had been born in the very same camp. This knowledge sobered me. Still, I sometimes wondered if a small, mean part of Peach watched Brother Robison chew his venison with the same disgust I watched Apostle Smith eat. If she did, she never showed it on her face.

Unlike Apostle Smith, Brother Robison had no trace of jowls. Instead, his pale face was drawn and skinny. He was only forty-five, the same age as Papa, but his thin hair and strange eyes—one pale green, the other nearly black—made him look much older than that.

* * *

I never told Peach, but after a while, Brother Robison started showing up in my dreams.

When he did, all the pale skin on his skinny face was gone, replaced with a bony skull and empty eye holes. Instead of arms, he hefted big black wings that shielded the enormous bed from the dripping blood on the ceiling.

In the dream, his dark eye was gone, replaced by a gaping black socket.

Mama, I screamed. Always Mama. But under the cover of those wings, the blood stopped raining down long enough for me to catch my breath in the nightmare. Like always, her hand clasped mine and pressed that ring into my palm. In this new version of the dream, the ring wasn't sticky and slimy with blood anymore. It was dry and smooth in my hand. I still couldn't read the inscription in the dark, but when my fingers traced the letters, I suddenly knew what it said as clearly as if I'd read it on the chalkboard in Sister Brady's classroom.

It said simply, BELOVED.

For the briefest moment, under Brother Robison's dark wings with Mama's hand and that ring pressing into mine, I felt safe and loved. Like maybe I wasn't a wicked child full of cowlicks and evil thoughts. Like maybe everything would be okay this time.

But the blood kept coming.

40. EMMA WILLIS

FILLMORE, UTAH
JULY 1860

"The answer is Jesus!" I burst out, thinking about how the answer was usually Jesus. But it earned me a withering look from our Sunday school teacher, Brother Larsen.

Amina's sister, Adelia, made a startled little O with her mouth. Same as she always did.

"Emma, the question was for *Amina,*" Brother Larsen scolded me. "She'll never learn to answer if you always speak up for her."

I refused to apologize. Everybody knew Amina didn't talk. Maybe she could, maybe she couldn't. But the fact was, she didn't. And if her own sister wouldn't stand up for her, I would. Amina's missing arm already made her stand out as different.

When Brother Larsen turned back to the Book of Mormon, I made a silly face at him, knowing Amina was watching me.

It earned me a rare smile from her—and Peach, who was righteous enough not to make faces but sweet enough to know that Brother Larsen was in the wrong for how often he tried to make Amina speak.

I loved that about her.

Everybody loved my sister Peach.

Everybody except maybe Sister Robison. When we spilled out of Sunday school, Peach and I walked Amina back to her mother like we always did, following seven-year-old Adelia.

Sister Robison already had three children of her own, but Peach told me her son Proctor had died three years earlier. And adopting little Amina seemed to fill some of that mothering hole inside of the woman that had been empty ever since.

"Hello, Peach," Sister Robison said with a pretend smile, like she always did. With her smooth, dark hair and baby face, she barely looked older than Peach, even though she'd been married to Brother Robison for twenty years.

"Hello, Sister Robison," Peach said, letting go of Amina's hand. "Your dress is just beautiful."

Sister Robison murmured her thanks, pleasant as anything, but there was no ignoring how she stiffened up whenever sweet, beautiful Peach came around.

Sister Robison smiled and tugged Adelia by the hand, but the smile never crinkled up her eyes. I'd noticed she wore the same expression when she looked at Kima.

Poor Peach smiled hard enough for all of us, but it was no use.

Brother Robison's two-toned eyes moved between me and Peach. He was looking right at us, but something told me his mind was somewhere else. He blinked, shook his head, then held out a hand for shaking like everyone did in church when you said hello.

"Nice to see you, Peach. And Emma." Brother Robison added my name like he'd wanted to end the sentence differently and changed his mind at the last second. "We'll see you on Wednesday."

Brother Robison didn't seem to notice—or care—about the daggers in Sister Robison's eyes. As long as she mustered up some kind of smile, he seemed happy enough—whether or not it was real. Brother Robison hadn't proposed to Peach yet, but we all expected it was just a matter of time.

Mama cared, though. One night, when I was lying awake in bed trying my best not to fall asleep, I heard her talking with Papa in the next room.

"It's pride, pure and simple," Mama huffed in a voice loud enough that I knew she thought all of us girls were fast asleep. "Polygamy was good enough for Adam, Enoch, Noah, Abraham, David, Solomon. I could go on. But *not* Lucy Robison? She looks at Kima like she'd just as soon strangle her. I'm sure Brother Robison would have proposed by now, if it weren't for his wife's selfishness." She tutted and set something on the floor with a soft *thud*. "I, for one, would welcome the help. She's lucky to get Peach and not Emma."

The words barely stung. Mama was right. Peach was everything I wasn't.

I strained my ears but couldn't hear Papa's reply.

Truth be told, I sometimes daydreamed that Papa would take another wife, like Brother Robison. Maybe he could find a Lamanite woman, like Kima. Unlike Sister Robison, she always smiled at me.

I loved Mama fiercely, and I believed she loved me too deep down, but sometimes I wondered what it felt like to be Peach. To be liked as much as loved.

When I was feeling extra wicked, I thought about what it might be like to be adopted, like little Amina.

Sister Robison didn't love Kima—or Peach. But she loved all her children, including that little girl who wasn't hers by blood, with a ferocity that made my stomach hurt.

With Amina's enormous blue eyes, pale skin, dark curls, and perpetual silence, she seemed just like a porcelain doll—except for her missing arm.

When I learned about Amina's mama dying and her papa not wanting her, I'd started paying extra attention to her. Though we'd never said a word to each other, she was the kind of quiet that was easy to be around. And when Peach started working for the Robisons —with me and Violet tagging along—Amina warmed up to me so quick, I wondered if she'd been hoping I'd speak to her all this time.

I told her and Violet stories while Peach cleaned house, lulling all of us to sleep out of the way behind the Robisons' woodpile and stove.

My stomach grumbled as Peach, Violet, and I walked home from church with Mama and Papa in silence. I tried to keep my mind on Jesus like I was supposed to, but my stomach was demanding. It was the first Sunday of the month, or "fast Sunday"—but it was anything but fast. Today was the day we skipped breakfast and lunch and donated a little more money to help the poor.

More and more, I wanted to ask Mama and Papa or maybe Brother Larsen why we did this. This "fasting." It was meant to remind us of the poor among us, who went without food.

We were poor, though. We were *all* poor—except the Robisons. And most days we already skipped breakfast and sometimes lunch, too, when it had been a bad year for the crops. Like this year.

I was old enough to know better, though. The less sense something made, the more faith you had to muster.

I kicked at a rock in the dirt road, and the clatter made Mama turn around to frown at me.

"Sorry." I wrapped my arms around my stomach, trying to squeeze it into thinking it was full. The one good thing about fasting was that it made your stomach so small, you felt full after eating just a little for dinner. Sometimes, I slept better those nights. And I needed sleep worse than I needed food.

My eyes stung with longing for a good rest, and I let them close for a few seconds while I walked, hoping I wouldn't kick any more rocks.

Little Violet giggled up ahead as she walked next to Peach, but Mama didn't scold her.

Please, Heavenly Father, don't let the bad dreams come tonight, I prayed in my head. I almost asked Him to soften Sister Robison's heart toward Peach while I was at it. But my selfishness won. If Brother Robison was delaying his proposal on account of Sister Robison, I'd just as soon keep my sister a little longer.

41. LUCY ROBISON

FILLMORE, UTAH

JULY 1860

My boys were picking apples in our orchard, exclaiming over the branches full of fruit the size of melons. All three of my boys. Almon, Albert, and Proctor.

"You must be proud to be their mama," the woman with the dark curls said, her voice sincere and soft.

"I am," I said, watching my boys, heart swelling up the same as it did on Sundays during the hymns.

Then a feeling rushed me, like the floor dropping out beneath my feet. Something wasn't right. At eleven and thirteen years old, Almon and Albert were nearly men, tall and lanky. Proctor looked the same as he always had. Fourteen years old.

Because he's dead, my mind whispered. *Because you never got to see him grow up. Because this is a dream.*

The awful thought tried to wake me, but the woman's voice called me back. "They're good boys," she said, reaching for my hand. "Kind boys, and handsome."

I looked at her, and she smiled. She wore a simple brown dress, high at the collar, with buttons down the front. Finer than anything my neighbors wore.

"Thank you," I said, staring at her in puzzlement. "Do I know you?" I asked, suddenly not sure.

"Of course," she said, "We're all sisters, aren't we?" Then she laughed softly, twining her fingers in mine. "Look, Lucy, there are my children."

I turned my head, peering through the sun-dappled orchard to see another group of children—two girls and two boys, sitting in the grass. They sat close to each other, heads ducked shyly.

"They're beautiful," I told her. "Your children are just lovely."

"I know now how Jesus could liken the Kingdom of God to a child," the woman whispered, eyes shining.

She said the words like a quote, so I asked, "Is that scripture?"

She shook her head. "Charles Dickens. He's one of my very favorite writers."

We sat in silence a few minutes longer, moving our gazes between my boys picking apples and her children sitting in the grass. "Are your children hungry?" I asked, suddenly ashamed I hadn't thought to ask earlier.

She nodded sadly.

Then her children began to cry softly, a mewling sound that made my stomach ache. I tried to move to go to them, but my body was immobile. Proctor heard them and turned around, shirt untucked and filled with red fruit.

"Look, my son will bring them apples right now," I insisted, desperate to stop the children's cries.

She shook her head, eyes filling with tears as the mewling sound got louder. "You know he is dead. Just like my children."

I awoke with a start to hear Amina crying beside me in bed.

"It's all right, it's all right." I pulled her to my chest and she clung to me, trembling all over. I couldn't tell whether the wetness on my cheeks was from her tears or my own.

42. KAHPEPUTZ (SALLY)

CORN CREEK, UTAH

JULY 1860

"No, no, no," I whispered, shifting my hips against the tight rock passage, trying to wriggle free.

My stomach heaved, and I swallowed back the bile.

For a moment, I thought I'd sealed myself inside the cave.

I'd been here before. Awan and I had used the lava tubes for our winter meetings when the weather got bad. But I'd forgotten how narrow some of the passages were.

I'd only meant to explore today—figure out how far the lava tube extended beneath the ground. Find a small chamber where, in a few days, I could tuck myself away with the meager stash of food I'd been hoarding in a skin pouch under a rock behind the wickiup.

But the cave was narrower than I remembered, and I must have taken the wrong tunnel. Now there was nowhere to turn around. And crawling out backwards, inch by inch, was proving impossible.

"Idiot," I whispered to myself, grunting and dragging myself a few more inches forward.

I imagined that my belly dragged along the bottom of the cave most of all. It was just my imagination. My stomach was still mostly flat, but over the past month it had puffed out just enough that I had to force myself not to constantly touch my middle.

My pregnancy was getting more difficult to hide. The billowy crinoline dress hid my rounding stomach well enough, but the morning sickness was getting hard to explain away.

With the risk of discovery mounting by the day, I couldn't stay in the village for much longer. But I also couldn't bear to leave Awan, who still insisted we'd find a way out of this mess.

So, we'd decided I would hide. Buy ourselves a little more time to come up with a plan. I thought I remembered that this particular tunnel opened up into a larger cavern, but the longer I crawled, the narrower the dark, humid space got.

I pushed my body another few inches along the floor of the tight cave and swallowed back another wave of nausea, no longer caring that my arms were getting scratched up or that my dress was going to be filthy. I didn't even care that I'd be missed in camp soon.

How long would it be before anyone noticed I was missing? Before Awan would think to look for me here?

My breath came fast and shallow as I peered into the darkness. Would he find me? I'd left the tiny yucca horse on a rock near the cave entrance, but it would be easy to miss.

"Idiot," I told myself again harshly. The words knocked back and forth in the rocky corridor, loud in my ears. Why hadn't I turned back earlier, when the cave was less narrow?

I drew in a shaky breath and lay my head on my hands.

Was I going to die in here? Was this how my story would end? Was there any other ending left to find?

I thought of the last time I'd see Awan, who still waited for me by Corn Creek each day when I went to gather water with Sweet Pea. Only now, instead of lying together on the warm grass, we would stand inside the safety of the cattail walls, whispering half-spun plans to run away, find a life together outside Corn Creek. Take our chances and hide the pregnancy a little longer.

But each time we parted ways, we were no closer to a real plan. Because every scenario ended in Kanosh finding out what had happened—and he would.

Which meant that, in all likelihood, the only way I was leaving the Paiutes' camp in the long-term was dead. But as long as there was a chance, as long as Awan loved me, I'd keep trying to find a way out.

* * *

I finally found a small pocket in the lava tube big enough for me to turn around.

An hour later, panting and exhausted, I felt a breeze on my face as I re-emerged at the mouth of the cave. I closed my eyes and took a steadying breath, willing my heart to slow its hammering. I was safe again—for now.

But when I peered out through the opening and blinked into the sun, now high in the sky, I heard an unexpected sound. Sweet Pea's honking bray.

I opened my mouth in surprise. I hadn't brought the mule with me. Not here—not when I didn't want anyone to follow me.

My heart seized up in fear, and I scrambled past the rocky lip edge and onto the dirt, trying to see the mule. Had she followed me all this way? I'd already been to the creek once this morning with her, to gather water. Maybe—

"Sally."

Not *"Sally Indian."* I heard the words at the same time I laid eyes on the mule—and the woman holding her rope.

Inola.

Sweet Pea pulled the rope tight, clearly ready to go home. When she saw me, she flicked her big ears forward and brayed again.

Inola sat in the shade of an enormous sagebrush, beside the mule. Her eyes moved to my scratched arms and legs, then to my belly, then to the hole in the earth where I'd just emerged.

There were a few times I'd caught Inola studying me in the village, her brow creased in an unreadable expression. But to my relief, she'd never said anything. Deep down, I wondered if she might have a soft spot for me, but if my pregnancy ever came to light, I knew she'd do whatever she could to protect Awan. Not me.

Inola reached for the pitch basket hanging at the mule's side and pulled out something I couldn't see. She took a step closer to me, still not saying anything. And opened her hand. In it was the yucca horse.

I reached for it, put the little horse in my dress pocket, and forced a smile as I swiped off some of the sweat and dirt on my arms. "Thank you."

I finally dared meet her eyes, and when I did, she frowned. She didn't look angry—or ashamed, or even sad.

She looked just like Awan. Determined and stubborn.

"He told you," I said, not really asking.

When she didn't respond, I looked at my feet again, studying the lacing on the worn moccasins that had finally replaced my pinched shoes when the straps broke. "Inola, I …" I trailed off, feeling tired and ashamed and so deeply sad I couldn't bear to look at her.

In another world, she would have been my mother-in-law. Not my sister-wife. Her son would have been my husband.

And my baby would have been her grandchild.

Inola nodded. "Yes. This morning. I'm sorry, Sally."

She studied me with kind eyes but didn't try to tell me that everything would be okay. Didn't try to convince me that Kanosh would somehow let this slide.

I was grateful for that.

"I came looking for you. Those caves are nowhere to hide," she added gently.

Then she drew in a breath. "I told Numa and Povi—"

She must have seen the terror on my face, because she quickly added. "I told them I'd sent you to gather prickly pear leaves."

My shoulders sank in relief. The thickets of tiny cactus leaves were difficult to harvest without earning a few spines. It was the perfect job for me. "Thank you."

"I also told them that I was coming out here to confront you."

This made me look up sharply. "To … confront me?"

She nodded and yanked on the mule's rope, pulling her toward me—and a patch of grass. "They've always thought I secretly hated you. Like they do."

I didn't understand why she was telling me this. I'd never gotten the sense that Inola hated me. Not the same way Numa and Povi did. If anything, I'd always felt like she pitied me.

Her eyes softened. "Things won't be good for you when we get back to camp." She studied my scraped legs and dirty dress.

Terror seized in my stomach. She was taking me back to camp? "I won't go—" I began.

"My brother Keme died this morning, while you were away."

My stomach seized and I leaned over, sure I was about to vomit. Keme had been clinging to life for the past month. And every time he took a turn for the worse, Kanosh fell into a sullen despair, muttering about Brigham Young—and me, his *"stupid little doll."* "I'm sorry, Inola."

I looked at her and winced, then hung my head, thinking of Keme. He was a good man.

When I moved away from the cave opening and started walking toward camp, Inola sidestepped in front of me to block my path.

She leaned in closer to examine the bruises forming on my elbows and knees. "That's not enough."

I shook my head in confusion. Did she actually want to punish me here for Keme's death?

She tugged at Sweet Pea's rope and picked up a rock in her free hand. "We need to make your face look worse. If we fought, I would hit you. Slap you, at least."

I stared at her, wide-eyed. "You … you want to slap me in the face?"

She lifted her chin, and I couldn't read the expression in her hooded brown eyes. "I told you. Numa and Povi think I'm here to confront you." She shook her head. "They think I'm finally going to put you in your place, now that Keme has died. They've been nudging me to do it for years."

Her eyes shone with tears. "Now, do you want to split your own lip, or do I need to do it? We have to get back to camp to mourn Keme."

I shrank back. Sweet Pea watched me curiously.

Inola didn't lunge at me with the rock. Instead, she held it out like an offering. "I'm going to help you—and Awan. I have a plan, and it will work if you both do exactly what I say."

The tension in my stomach relaxed just a little, and I drew in a shaky breath. First she was going to hit me, now she was going to help me and Awan?

Nothing my sister-wife was saying made sense, but I clung to her words all the same.

"I've already spoken to Awan. He knows what to do. He loves you." To my utter shock, there were now tears spilling freely down her cheeks, tracing lines on her face. "Will you do what I say?" She grimaced and looked behind me at the cave opening. "No more talk of running away. No more caves. And no speaking to Awan until it's time. Do you understand?" Her eyes moved to my stomach. "We don't have long."

I didn't understand, at all.

I felt like I was going to throw up. But at the same time, a delicate spark of hope had edged out the tiniest bit of despair.

Could I trust her?

I wasn't sure. But the other alternative was dragging my body back into that godforsaken cave, possibly for the very last time.

I took the rock from her outstretched hand. "Yes."

43. EMMA WILLIS

FILLMORE, UTAH

JULY 1860

I ran headlong through the fig trees, pumping my legs as fast as they would go in the early morning half-dark.

"Kee-eee-ar! Kee-eee-ar!" I cried, flapping my arms and doing my best to mimic the hawks I'd heard screeching overhead.

A flurry of birds that'd been pecking at the half-ripe fruit took off in all directions. I stopped to catch my breath, knowing they'd be back in a few minutes.

My stomach was sour, and my eyes were so gritty from lack of sleep that I could barely see straight, but my heart beat with pride.

I wasn't good at very many things, but I was a good scarecrow. It was the household chore Mama assigned to me. And besides, today was Wednesday. Soon, Peach and Violet would come to find me in the scraggly fig trees or wheatfields, and we'd go to Brother and Sister Robison's house where I could sneak a nap.

"Kee-eee-ar!" I screamed again, launching myself at the birds that returned and were already pecking at the figs. They were relentless, but so was I.

As I started to run, someone echoed the call back to me. "Kee-eee-ar!"

I grinned and flapped my arms harder. That would be Violet, and they were coming to fetch me.

I ran toward the sound. It was hard work tending to the fields and the figs, but there were worse jobs.

If Peach and I were boys, we would've been sent to work in the gristmill or the sawmill with Papa for the summer.

But someone had to mind our wheatfields and the straggling fig trees Papa had planted along the side of the house, in hopes they'd bear a good crop someday. Not to mention keeping watch over Violet, who was still too young to do much of anything.

Unfortunately, this scarecrow job also scared the birds away from eating the grasshoppers that clung to the stalks of grain, nibbling at the ripening kernels with their tiny jaws that kept moving long after the birds gave up and roosted in the evenings.

That was my other duty—to pluck the insects from the stalks, smash them, and pop them into a bucket that I'd use to feed the mama pig.

Papa had given me a "hopper smasher," so I wouldn't have to crush the insects between my fingers. It was a wooden cup he'd carved, along with a round ladle that fit neatly inside the cup. It looked a little like the mortar and pestle Mama used to crush herbs. In went the grasshopper, in went the wooden smasher, and *crunch* went the legs and body and wings.

Thursday through Tuesday, I ran back and forth through the acres of wheatfields all day long, starting before sunup. Sometimes, I bellowed hymns while I ran. Back and forth, back and forth. Even Sundays, that were supposed to be a day of rest, held only a brief break for Sunday school and Sacrament meeting. The birds and the grasshoppers didn't rest, so neither did I.

Each morning before the sun rose, I'd choke down a breakfast of sego roots and cornmeal mush in the dark, then position myself in the center of the wheatfields to work outward in a loop until I reached the fig orchard.

"Emma!" The first rays of light filtered through the inky trees along with the sound of my own name.

Violet let go of Peach's hand and ran toward me like she hadn't seen me in ages. "You're sweaty," she said, giggling.

I shrugged. It was true. My bonnet and dress were always sweaty from running through the fields.

I tossed a last handful of pebbles at the birds in the nearest tree and pinwheeled toward her with my arms flung out wide. "Now you'll be sweaty too!" I cried, laughing as I scooped her up into a hug and she squealed.

The work in our fields was brutal and unrelenting, but I took a certain amount of pride in it, fretting over how many kernels of wheat we'd lose each Wednesday when it was time to make the trek to Brother Robison's house with Peach, and again each Sunday while I fought to stay awake in the pews.

Once, I'd heard Mama brag about how we'd thwarted the birds and grasshoppers out of their share of wheat, on account of my scarecrow and smashing skills. I was determined not to let her down in this one thing, at least.

"Mama said Brother Robison is going to marry Peach tonight," Violet exclaimed.

My mouth dropped open and I looked at Peach, whose brown eyes had gone wide.

"Violet! No," Peach hushed her. "Mama said she thinks he'll most likely *propose* tonight." Her cheeks tinged red at this admission.

My stomach flipped. "Will he?"

She shrugged and started walking, tugging Violet along with her. "He took Papa aside after Sacrament meeting on Sunday and asked for his blessing. Mama thinks he'll come calling tonight."

I wanted to smile and tell her this was happy news. I knew that's what sweet, beautiful, kind sixteen-year-old Peach wanted. But like usual, I couldn't seem to help but wear my insides on my outsides. I could feel my face making a strained, ugly smile that was getting worse by the second.

"You don't like Brother Robison?" Peach asked.

"Do *you* like Brother Robison?" I asked instead of answering, imagining his weathered skin and strange two-toned eyes.

She hesitated just long enough to make my stomach hurt. Then she said, "He's a good man, Emma. Look how he and Sister Robison care for little Amina. He'll be good to me."

But he's old. And he already has two wives, I wanted to say.

I didn't say that, though. I just nodded fast and said, "I'm just tired, that's all. Come on, Violet. I'll race ya!"

44. EMMA WILLIS

FILLMORE, UTAH
JULY 1860

"Your hair looks real nice," I told Peach when she caught up with me and Violet on the long dirt path that would lead us to the Robisons' house.

I felt bad for running ahead. I knew Peach was trying to keep her dress clean on the dusty road. Mama had probably spent extra time fussing over her hair, helping her unwind the rag curls she'd slept in the night before so they wouldn't tangle. Violet and I watched in a sleepy daze as each fresh spiral bounced down the back of Peach's best dress like a ribbon of gold.

It seemed silly to wear the nice dress on a day of chores at the Robisons, but I knew better than to say so.

Even without being there, I knew Mama had gone *ooh* and *ahh* with each curl. I could just hear her saying, *"Vickery Robison will propose today. Yes, I really do believe he will."*

I touched my own frizzy mess of brown cowlicks and wished for the umpteenth time that I had hair like my sisters. When Mama forced my hair into rag curls, they never failed to poof into a wild, tangly mess.

"Thanks, Emma," Peach replied to my compliment. "Do your legs feel better this morning?"

I nodded. They were still sore, but nothing like last night. Last night, my legs had conspired with the nightmares to keep me awake, cramping up and aching like the dickens from running all day in the heat. When Peach woke up to see me thrashing in bed and clutching my calves, she told me we'd sneak some jam from the Robisons' larder. The sugar would help with the cramping. I whispered a thank you and tried not to thrash anymore, but the fierce off and on again cramps kept me awake all night long.

When we got to the Robisons', we found little Amina sitting on the porch waiting for us, like usual.

Her eyes lit up when she saw me, and she leaped off the porch and wrapped her good arm around my waist. I patted her hair and tried not to show how happy this made me. Besides Violet, I knew I could count on Amina to be genuinely happy to see me. I knew it was only because I looked after her and Violet while Peach did chores, but I didn't care. It felt so good to get a greeting like that.

It almost made me wish I was the one who'd be moving into the Robisons' house for good—not Peach.

Almost.

While I played with Violet and Amina on the porch, Peach did the sweeping first like she always did. Then, when the floor was bare and clean of debris, she poked her head out the front door. "Emma, would you please tell the girls a story and help them take a nap?"

My heart swelled up with gratitude whenever she did that. It meant that the best part of the week was here. The part where I could sleep without the nightmares. I'd discovered this one day on a chilly spring morning when I fell asleep from pure exhaustion at the Robisons' house. The just-swept floor behind the stove looked so inviting that I told myself I'd lie down for just a minute. And then little Amina cuddled up next to me, like it was a game, followed by Violet. And the three of us slept for a whole two hours, warm and safe, without a single bad dream.

When Peach saw how happy it made me, she insisted I tuck myself behind the stove for another nap the following week with Violet and Amina. She said it'd keep the little girls out from underfoot.

Amina and Violet were old enough that they didn't really need a nap anymore. Peach did this for me. And I loved her for it.

If Brother and Sister Robison happened to come home to see me asleep on the floor they wouldn't like it. I was meant to be doing chores the same as Peach—not napping. Otherwise, maybe I could have laid down on the bed instead of behind the woodpile and stove. It didn't matter, though. All that mattered was the promise of a couple hours' rest.

I carefully unfolded the quilt from Sister Robison's hope chest and tucked myself into the corner, behind the unlit potbelly stove. "Amina, Violet, do you wanna hear the story about the big old bed?"

Both girls toddled over to me, lured by the promise of a story.

"Oh yes," Violet said.

Amina just nodded, opening her mouth at the same time as Violet, pretending to speak too. It was the only time I'd ever seen her do this.

The girls each tucked themselves under one of my arms, snuggled against me, and popped a thumb in. The gesture warmed my heart for reasons I couldn't explain, and sometimes I was tempted to put my own thumb into my mouth.

Amina's little body tucked so close to mine, on account of her missing right arm, that I could feel her heartbeat.

I closed my eyes and found the beginning of the story. It was the exact opposite of my bad dreams, which made it easy to remember. I hoped that by telling it often enough, maybe someday it would replace the scary version at night. "One day, a little girl named Amina woke up to find out that her bed grew ten sizes overnight."

"Named *Violet!*" Violet pulled her thumb out just long enough to squeak out the words. She protested when I made the story about Amina, but it was Amina who couldn't speak. Who had lost her arm and been sent to a new family, so I did it anyway, giving Violet a gentle pet on the hair and a smile to remind her that I loved her too.

I kept going. "And when she woke up, she squealed from pure joy. Her mama and her papa and everybody she loved was curled up next to her. And not just that, but a whole garden had bloomed on the bedroom floor. The walls and even the ceilings were covered with flowers. It smelled like springtime."

"Were there butterflies?" Violet asked around the thumb in her mouth this time, her head already heavy on my shoulder.

"Yes. All colors. Blue and red and yellow and white."

Amina sighed against me. I could've drifted off to sleep right then, but I wanted to make sure the girls were both asleep first. I heard the front door clunk shut softly and knew it would be Peach, heading into the front yard to dig sego roots until it was time to start on the Robisons' supper.

"There were bunny rabbits hopping all around," I continued. "With their soft pink noses and white whiskers, and grass so soft it felt like velvet. The little girl's mama said, 'Let's skip chores and stay in bed a little longer so we can look at the flowers.'"

I lay my head back on the rough log wall and managed to tuck my cheek into a bit of quilt above Amina's head. "There were sego lilies and daisies and snow in summer and …"

I named every flower I could think of until sleep pulled me under.

* * *

Most Wednesdays, Peach let me sleep as long as I wanted.

That one blissful stretch was never enough to make up for the missed hours at night, but when I awoke to Peach's soft hand on my shoulder in the early afternoon each Wednesday, I felt like a new person. Like what Mama said being baptized felt like, free of sin and fresh as the Virgin River.

Most of the time, Amina and Violet crawled out from under the quilt to leave me sleeping and played on the porch with Amina's rag doll until Peach was finished digging roots.

So when I startled awake with a sleeping Violet and Amina still tucked under each arm, I knew something was wrong.

There were voices just outside the Robisons' front door.

I blinked and tried to listen, but stayed frozen where I was. The girls sighed in their sleep, unaware. The air was still cool inside the shade of the house, and the angle of the sunlight streaming through the tiny window told me it couldn't be much past noon. Who was at the door? A horse's hooves shuffled in the dust. And I could just make out the soprano of Peach's gentle voice.

A terror I couldn't explain sent my heart into a frenzied pounding, and an urge to throw off the quilt and run as fast as I could away from the Robisons' house came over me. Prickles of sweat beaded up under my arms, and I felt like I might die if I stayed put a moment longer.

Stay still. Stop it, I told myself. Peach would send whoever it was on their way. And then I would help her with the rest of the day's chores, like I was supposed to be doing.

The door creaked open. "Emma is just digging roots with Amina and Violet. They'll be home soon, I expect," Peach said loud enough that I could hear. "What a wonderful surprise to see you home early."

The thumping in my chest sped up. Heavy footsteps sounded on the porch.

"Truth be told, I was hoping I might catch you alone," Brother Robison's scratchy bass voice said.

My heart pounded so hard I worried they'd hear it. What was he doing back from the tithing house? He never came home in the middle of the day.

"I wanted to surprise you. I brought a bite of lunch for the two of us," he said awkwardly, answering my silent question.

My stomach rolled.

Violet squirmed in her sleep, hot and sweaty. Amina sighed again. Surely one of them would wake up any moment and holler. The three of us were hidden from view behind the potbelly stove and the stacked firewood beside it, but if Brother Robison came any closer—or if Violet cried out—we were done for.

I cringed closer to the log wall, imagining the willow branch Mama would pick out to whip me if she found out that I'd been sleeping while I was meant to be doing chores. What if Brother Robison blamed Peach—and didn't propose to her after all?

I felt like I was going to throw up. *Please don't find us,* I said to myself.

"What about a picnic?" Peach said abruptly. "It's such a beautiful day outside. And it would be such a shame if Emma and the girls showed up just when we started talking." Her voice was teasing and sweet at the same time. I'd never heard her talk like that.

Yes, go on a picnic, I prayed, grateful for Peach's quick mind. *Please, Heavenly Father, make them go on a picnic.*

"A picnic would be nice," Brother Robison agreed quickly, clearing his throat. He sounded almost nervous to be talking to Peach.

The thud of his boots on the floor came a couple steps closer.

To my horror, Amina suddenly looked up at the sound of her papa's voice.

I caught her gaze and shook my head. *Quiet,* I mouthed.

She nodded without a sound.

I bit down on the inside of my cheek as Brother Robison came a step closer and asked, "How is Emma these days?"

My heart stopped its caterwauling and went very still, like it was listening too. Why was Brother Robison asking after me? There was something pitying in his voice that made me want to stand up and demand to know what he meant by the question. Had Mama and Papa told him about my nightmares? Or about what an unruly, clumsy child I was in my waking hours?

"Emma is well," Peach finally said, finding her voice. It had lost some of the sweetness from a moment earlier.

"Good. Poor wretch," Brother Robison said after a moment.

I could feel Amina looking at me, but I didn't look back. Why had he said that?

As my mind spun, his footsteps moved away from the stove, toward the door. Peach's soft footfalls followed him outside.

The door shut with a quiet *clunk*.

Tears welled in my eyes, taking all the victory out of the fact that he hadn't seen me. Violet mewled and struggled away from the sweaty quilt in the now-quiet house.

Amina stayed where she was, under my arm.

Outside the front door, I could still hear the faint sounds of Peach and Brother Robison talking while they walked away for their picnic.

I stood up with Amina and helped the girls climb over the stacked woodpile, swiping at my cheeks so they wouldn't see me cry. Then I carefully refolded Sister Robison's quilt, brushing off any dirt, and tucked it back into her hope chest.

Violet frowned at me from the floor. She was always grumpy for a few minutes after she woke up. She didn't mean anything by it. But all I could think, looking at her crumpled face framed by wispy gold curls, was that she wore the same look on her face that Mama sometimes did when we locked eyes.

I always knew I was a little less golden than my sisters, on the inside *and* on the outside. But hearing Brother Robison confirm my deepest fears out loud sucked the air out of my lungs and left me numb.

I ran his two words over and over in my mind, in time with the painful way my heart was hammering. *Poor wretch.*

45. EMMA WILLIS

FILLMORE, UTAH
JULY 1860

While Violet, Amina, and I waited for Peach to return from her picnic, we started soaking the Robisons' supper of beans and sego roots. Then, when she still wasn't home, I busied myself with chinking the cabin walls with a half-full pail of sand, red clay, and ashes from the fire.

I'd never done this chore before, but I had watched Peach enough times that I more or less knew what to do. The sticky mass of clay in the bucket was easy enough to spread with my fingers to block out the tiny cracks and pinholes of light that shone between the logs. The job of chinking was never-ending, since the clay mixture weakened over time, crumbling little by little with the change in seasons and the subtle shifting of the log walls.

The little girls weren't any help, but the sound of Violet sitting on the floor with her dolly, singing a tuneless song to Amina, comforted me. Little by little, with each sliver of light I found and blocked out between the stacked log walls, I felt the numb despair recede into the shadows. *Emma is well,* Peach had said in response to Brother Robison's question. Maybe that meant there was hope for me after all.

I was doing well, wasn't I? Mama didn't know I was still having nightmares. And I knew I was a good scarecrow, protecting our fields. If I could just learn to be a little more polished, maybe I could stop being a poor wretch.

I decided that I would ask Peach about it on the walk home. She must know I'd heard Brother Robison. And of anyone, I trusted her to give me a straight answer. She was everything I wanted to be.

When the sound of Brother Robison's and Peach's voices finally floated into earshot, I hurried to tidy up the chinking pail and check on the beans and sego roots soaking in the pot. Then I carried the pot to the stovetop to boil and stood back to look around the cabin. Everything was neat and clean. I'd covered dozens and dozens of tiny cracks in the walls. And supper would be ready for the Robisons in about an hour.

Peach came through the door first, cheeks flushed and her smile bright. She was holding one hand out in front of her, away from her body. Her other hand covered it protectively.

At first, I thought she'd hurt herself somehow. But that didn't make sense with the way she was smiling.

I made my smile as bright as Peach's.

"Go on and show them," Brother Robison said proudly as he came through the door behind her.

Peach nodded and held her hand toward me.

A too-large ring hung limp on her pale, delicate finger. The band was shiny silver and made a sort of twist in the middle. It looked like a little river—or a snake.

My mouth went dry, and my heart set to pounding.

Tell her congratulations, I told myself.

But I stood there like a dead-eyed fish.

Keep smiling. Be happy.

The buckskin horse Brother Robison had tied up outside the house whinnied, announcing the arrival of a wagon and buying me a little time to swallow the lump in my throat. I'd known this would happen, but I felt sad all the same. I didn't want Peach to leave me.

"That'll be Lucy, Kima, and the rest of the family," Brother Robison said, his strange two-toned eyes turning into slits when he smiled. "They'll want to congratulate you," he told Peach, but from the way he said it, we all knew he was trying too hard to make it sound true.

"This is good news, isn't it?" Peach said to me, watching as Brother Robison went into the yard to usher the rest of his family inside the house.

I nodded numbly as Lucy and Kima came through the front door with Adelia, Almon, and Albert in tow.

Almon and Albert were barely younger than Peach. How could she be their mother?

Kima clapped when she saw Peach standing there, holding up her hand with a smile on her face. Lucy did not. Instead, she said, "What a blessing," and her voice was real tight.

Peach blushed and flicked her eyes back to me. "Do you like the ring?" she asked shyly, holding out her hand to me.

Without thinking, I reached out to touch the silver band.

The lump in my throat that I'd managed to swallow came right back up. And before I could even make sense of my feelings—or touch the ring—a little sob escaped my mouth.

Maybe it was what Brother Robison had said earlier that suddenly bubbled up to the surface. Maybe it was just that Peach would be leaving me, but the room full of people suddenly felt far too small.

I'd only just wiped my eyes and started to reach for the ring again, when Brother Robison swooped toward Peach and snatched her hand away from me.

I jumped back, startled. And then, to my horror, the tears started up again. This time, accompanied by full-on sobs.

Brother Robison cleared his throat awkwardly and let go of Peach's hand. "I didn't mean to scare you, Emma. It still needs resizing. Don't want it to fall between the floorboards."

I could hardly hear him over the sound of my sobs. Peach's happy smile had ballooned into a frantic, wide O. "What's wrong, Emma? Oh, Emma, what's wrong?"

Kima and Lucy, as if activated by some kind of mothering switch, hurried to my side as well, patting my arm and telling me everything was all right.

Adelia stared. I wondered if she'd tell everyone in Sunday school about this.

Brother Robison mumbled something about needing to get some work done in the orchard before dark. His sons followed him, clearly eager to leave the scene.

I was so embarrassed I wanted to slip through the cracks in the floorboards myself. Burrow down into the hardscrabble earth and disappear.

Peach wrapped me in a tight hug while my wet cheeks burned with shame. Violet joined in the hug too and started snuffling then set to wailing herself for no reason except that I was doing it. Amina didn't make a sound, but her hand found mine in the chaos, too.

I closed my eyes so I wouldn't see the Robisons staring back at me with a mix of horror and concern.

Poor wretch, they probably all thought.

Maybe Brother Robison was right after all.

* * *

Peach, Violet, and I walked home in silence. Peach took the ring off and tucked it into a little satchel Brother Robison had given her for safekeeping, so it wouldn't fall off before she could show Mama and Papa.

I kept my eyes on the ground, trying not to let any more tears leak out.

I wondered if Sister Robison—either of them—knew the proposal was going to happen this afternoon.

I wondered whether Brother Robison would tell Mama and Papa about my outburst.

I wondered how many weeks I would have left with my sister before she was a married woman.

Weddings were simple affairs for a second, third, or fourth wife. Especially in tiny Fillmore. Brother Robison, Lucy, Kima, and Peach would travel to Salt Lake to be sealed for time and all eternity in the Endowment House as soon as the wheat harvest was over in a couple of months.

My ears still burned with embarrassment over the scene I had caused. Peach had a pained look on her face that made my stomach hurt with anxiety. She didn't deserve this.

Violet ran ahead of us, chasing grasshoppers. Each time one of them spread its wings and flew a few feet out of her grasp, she squealed with delight and chased it again. She was out of earshot.

"I'm sorry I cried," I whispered to Peach.

She reached for my hand and squeezed it. "You're just extra tired, that's all." But her voice sounded funny and too high. She was trying to make me feel better, but even sweet Peach couldn't disagree that I tended to ruin things.

There were chores to be done before Mama and Papa returned home for the day, expecting to see supper on the table. I wouldn't steal the joy from Peach's big announcement again with my tears. So

I swallowed down the question about why Brother Robison had called me a wretch. It would keep until after dinner and chores.

Our house always looked slumped and defeated after we'd spent the afternoon at the Robisons'. I didn't let myself look at the wheatfields or the fig trees down the lane, rustling in the slight breeze. I didn't want to think about how many kernels the hoppers had eaten while I was away today.

Violet and Peach went inside to start supper, but I trudged around back to the pig pen, where Mama Pig was grunting up a storm. Of the twelve babies she'd thrown in April, only six had survived, and Papa had sold them just last month.

The cramped pig pen was a stack of rough logs—a miniature version of the house—and the roof dipped down in the middle from too many heavy snowstorms in winter. But Mama Pig didn't seem to mind. She squealed happily when I pulled out the half-full bucket of hoppers from yesterday. The pulpy mash of wings, legs, and gooey bodies were now clustered with a number of live hoppers feeding on their dead. I shuddered and tipped the bucket into the dirty trough, holding my breath so I didn't breathe in too much of the manure.

"Sorry there's not more today," I told her as I took a step back and watched her munch the hoppers with glee. Her big gray head came up to my chin, but her flanks were skinny and sunken. I could count each of her ribs. "I'll get you lots tomorrow," I promised. If we didn't fatten her up a little by the time cold weather hit, we'd lose her too.

46. LUCY ROBISON

FILLMORE, UTAH

JULY 1860

I nearly screamed for Vick when the four men rode into the yard.

I was hanging the laundry up to dry, pinning up our undergarments like soggy white flags, when I heard the sound of hoofbeats. I turned to see riders and snatched the bulky wet undergarments back to my chest. With the symbols of the holy priesthood I'd sewn into the undergarments as instructed by the prophet, they weren't for prying eyes.

My chest heaved as the front of my dress slowly soaked through.

The men were wearing uniforms.

The Army, my mind screamed, even though I knew the troops were no longer at our Northern border.

Even so, I couldn't help clenching my teeth and imagining myself setting fire to the house and fleeing into the hills.

Stay calm. Cooler heads. Find out what they want, I reminded myself.

The men on horseback were certainly military, but the uniforms they wore told me at a glance that they were gentiles, from the U.S. Army—not our men in the Nauvoo Legion. Instead of patched, pale blue uniforms with missing buttons, these men's coats were dark blue with neat lines of gold brass and collars so crisp I couldn't stop staring at them.

The rider in front, a general, by the looks of the metals on his chest, pulled up his horse and removed his wide-brimmed hat when he approached me. The stern expression on his rugged face relaxed a little as his eyes went to the pile of wet laundry I clutched to my chest.

He offered me a tight smile beneath his neatly trimmed black mustache. "Morning, ma'am. Didn't mean to frighten you."

I didn't speak at first. My eyes moved to the sheathed sabers at their sides.

Why were they here in my yard? The old fears wouldn't let me go.

To drive you into the mountains. To take your home. To set fire to your orchard. To tar and feather your husband.

I gritted my teeth. *No.* Brigham Young had stepped down as governor and signed a treaty with President Buchanan. Utah was not at war with the U.S. government anymore. Soon, our territory might even be recognized as an official state—something we'd fought hard against for so long.

The general rode closer and spoke again. "Sorry to bother you, ma'am. We're looking for Arthur Brunson. Can you point us to his house?"

Bishop Brunson.

I relaxed just a little. They were in the right vicinity, but I felt no need to point them in the right direction. The gentiles were relentless, but like the Prophet Brigham Young said, we'd build the kingdom of God under their noses. And we'd lie for the Lord when we had to.

"Arthur Brunson?" I repeated. Then I scrunched up my nose and pretended to think. "I'm not very good with directions. That way, I think," I said sweetly, pointing toward Corn Creek and feeling a little thrill at misdirecting the polished men carrying swords. Bishop Brunson's house was in the opposite direction, on the other side of the apple orchard.

One of the other riders, an older man with a long salt-and-pepper beard and deep-set eyes, pulled out a piece of paper. "We just came from that direction. Is there a reason you don't want us to find Arthur Brunson, ma'am?"

My stomach clenched. He turned his head to the apple orchard, toward the faint sound of my children's voices. They were helping Vick and Kima thin the fruit that would make the branches snap if we left it until harvest. It would be a bumper crop this year, Vick had said. The one time I could count on seeing him smile.

The general nudged his horse to move a little closer to me. I stiffened and drew the wet laundry tighter. "Any chance you're Mrs. Brunson?" he asked gently. "I think maybe it's best I remind you that we are officers of the United States government, and we're here on official business."

He didn't have to give more of a threat than that. I already knew what officers of the United States government could do.

"Maybe my husband can point you in the right direction," I told them uneasily, feeling a chill from the wet laundry despite the warm day. I wanted Vick beside me so much my hands shook a little.

"What's your husband's name?" the general asked.

"Vickery Robison," I said hesitantly, too afraid to lie again.

The man with the salt-and-pepper beard looked at the list in his hand. My hands shook harder beneath the heavy, dripping clothes. "Good. We have some questions for him, too."

"May I ask what about?"

"About what happened down south of here."

"Down south?" I prodded, not sure what they were even asking.

"The massacre in the Meadow," he said, looking at me suspiciously, like maybe I had information to hide.

I gathered myself up, indignant now. "The Paiutes at Corn Creek can tell you more than my husband or Arthur Brunson. Our men were north in Echo Canyon all that time."

The Army men shared a look among themselves.

"Where can we find your husband, ma'am?" the general asked.

I reluctantly pointed to the thick trees of our orchard.

Without another word, they turned and rode that direction, leaving me standing like a statue.

Their horses moved right across the little gravesite at the edge of the orchard, so close to where Proctor lay buried that the horses must have walked right over his casket.

Maybe they couldn't see the modest headstone. The grass at the edge of the orchard had grown around it so much, and I'd been meaning to clear it away.

I shook myself out of the frozen trance and rehung the dripping, off-white garments as fast as I could. They were meant to protect us from harm—and remind us of the covenants we'd made before God.

The only time we removed them were the few hours it took me to wash and dry them once a week. That meant Vick wasn't wearing his right now—with officers of the United States Army riding through our orchard to find him.

I couldn't warn him in time. The men on horseback would find him quickly, given the noise my children made while they worked.

My fingers trembled so much that I barely got the garments back onto the pins.

Stop it, I told myself. *It's all a fuss for nothing.* They'll move on to speak with the Paiutes soon enough.

Then I sat down in the grass and stared at the orchard, which had gone quiet. My eyes went back to the off-white garments flapping in the breeze and the tiny marks I'd sewn into the material near the knee, the navel, and the chest areas years ago.

The mark of the compass. *Only one path to eternal life.*

The mark of the square. *Exactness and honor.*

The mark of the navel. *Nourishment for body and spirit.*

The mark of the knee. *Every knee will bow to Jesus Christ.*

I'd sewn our holy garments right after the Prophet Joseph revealed the sacred endowment ceremony to us in Nauvoo. When Vick and I received our invitation to the upper story of his red-brick store, we couldn't stop smiling. The temple wasn't quite finished, but the power of God wasn't restrained to physical walls.

Vick and I had followed the prophet's instructions while he showed us the sacred hand gestures and secret words that would one day allow us to enter heaven, together. He told us we were making the same promises and oaths King Solomon had made in his temple, thousands of years ago.

The veil was thin during the ceremony while Vick and I vowed to give our minds, means, and bodies to build the kingdom of God in exchange for the sacred signs and tokens that would admit us into the highest degree of glory as man and wife, sealed for time and all eternity with our children. *All of our children.* Even the two we'd left beneath the frozen ground in Syracuse, New York.

"We'll see our girls again," Vick had whispered in my ear, thinking the same thing. The truth and longing swelled in my heart until it hurt.

Everything we'd endured would be worth it in the end, as long as we kept our covenants.

Repeating after the Prophet Joseph line by line, we'd promised to obey God's commandments and the counsel of his chosen prophet and apostles. To live the law of sacrifice, giving all that we had—or might gain—to the work of the Lord. To remain faithful to the end of our days.

Finally, we'd accepted the penalties for revealing the knowledge we had received, or breaking our promises to God. We drew our thumbs across our throats from ear to ear, symbolizing the penalty.

Should we reveal any of the secrets of the Aaronic priesthood, we agree that our throats be cut from ear to ear and our tongues torn out by their roots.

Heavenly Father's blessings were unfathomably beautiful.

The consequences of disobedience were unfathomably fearsome.

47. EMMA WILLIS

FILLMORE, UTAH

JULY 1860

The sun was just settling on the horizon when I heard Papa's boots hitting our wooden porch.

My heart beat faster. The chores were finished and supper was nearly prepared, but I knew better than to expect smiling faces at the end of a long day in the gristmill and the fields. It was almost the harvest, which meant everyone was keyed up about preserving what was left of the meager yield. Tonight at least, the news of Peach's engagement would put a smile on Mama's face.

Papa came through the door first, his weathered face sunburned in patches where his hat didn't quite shade him, and dark circles of sweat under his arms. His hands always had some new cut or abrasion from his work at the gristmill.

Mama followed behind him, her long thin hair tied back in a bun just above the folded square of fabric that caught the sweat at her neck. Her shoulders were drooped, and her steps slow as she walked inside. I glanced sideways at Peach then hurried to offer her a chair at the table. I could already see her frowning at the apple preserves we'd set out with the biscuits. There was only one jar left until the big harvest down in Fillmore, and I knew she'd been saving them for Papa's birthday.

"We wanted to make a special dinner," Peach said.

This made her sit up a little straighter. She glanced at Papa. Then her bleary eyes brightened and she fixed her gaze on Peach. "And why is that?"

Peach proudly held out her hand with the little silver ring she had carefully placed back on her finger.

261

The sight of it on her hand still made my stomach churn. *Stop it,* I told my insides. *You're being a baby. Be happy for your sister.* This time it worked. I braced myself and kept my smile bright.

"Brother Robison—Vick—proposed today, with a picnic. He came home early from the mission."

Mama clapped her hands with delight, and Papa's weathered face broke into a pleased smile. "I knew it. Didn't I tell you I knew it? He had a little spring in his step this morning when we saw him at the tithing cellar, and I just knew … Well, at least I hoped."

She eyed the apple preserves with new approval. "A special dinner for a special day. You're moving up in the world, my Peach."

Papa nodded. My cheeks hurt from keeping my smile in place. She never said *"my Emma"* like that. I pushed the selfish thought away and sat down next to Violet at the table.

We bowed our heads and folded our arms in prayer. Then Papa offered the blessing, like he did most nights. "Father in Heaven, we bow our heads before Thee with gratitude in our hearts. We thank Thee for thy Prophet Brigham Young. We thank Thee for the food and shelter we are blessed with. We thank Thee for Peach and Brother Robison, and for the blessings that await them through Thy Endowment. We say these things with humble hearts, in the name of Jesus Christ, amen."

"Amen," we all said together when he was finished. My stomach growled for a taste of the apple preserves, but I waited patiently while Mama, Papa, then Peach and Violet took their share. I couldn't keep my eyes off Peach's ring hand as it moved to scoop a helping of beans onto her plate.

I was just about to spoon a dab of preserves onto my plate when Mama suddenly stopped talking and fixed me with a glare. I put the spoon back into the jar, heart beating fast, wondering what I had done to draw her anger.

Her mouth clamped shut, and she stared at my hand, still hovering above the jar of preserves.

"What is it, Mama?" I asked sweetly.

Then I followed her gaze and looked at my hand. I couldn't see anything amiss, at first. It was clean enough. I had washed my hands at the Robisons' house after I finished chinking the walls, and I'd been careful not to get any of the hopper juice on me.

Then I saw it. A lump of clay had snuck onto the edge of my dress sleeve. It had dried there, and part of it had broken off into the half-full jar of apple preserves.

My mouth fell open. I'd ruined the preserves. "I'm sorry," I rushed to say. "I'm sorry. I don't mind, though." I reached the spoon back into the jar, scooped up the crumbling lump of clay and ash scattered on top of the syrupy, golden apples, and plopped it onto my plate.

Before I could eat a bite, Mama reached out and grabbed hold of my wrist.

"I think you've had plenty," she muttered, snatching my plate away from me with her other hand. "The pig needs fat on her bones more than you do, anyway."

48. LUCY ROBISON

FILLMORE, UTAH

JULY 1860

When Adelia and the boys had come spilling out of the orchard with Kima in tow, the children chattered excitedly about the "men in the smart blue uniforms." They were proud the officers wanted to talk to their papa on important business.

Kima looked between the children with wide eyes and stayed silent, along with little Amina. I felt a pang of guilt for directing the soldiers to the Paiutes, but only a small one.

When Vick emerged from the orchard a few minutes later, his eyes found mine. "Might be late to dinner tonight," he said quietly. "Priesthood holders will be gathering at the meeting house."

He didn't say why.

I knew better than to ask.

Still, his eyes gave him away. Whatever was happening, this wasn't a typical meeting. Vick squeezed my hand before he mounted the buckskin. Two tight pumps of his fist.

Careful, careful.

The gesture startled me so much I almost didn't squeeze back. What was happening? Had he meant to give me our signal, or was it an old reflex? It made the hair rise on the back of my neck, like hearing twigs snap behind me at night.

Maybe it was nothing. Maybe it was something. It was impossible to tell without knowing more.

What I did know was I'd been sitting in this dark kitchen after the children went to sleep for so long, my head was nodding to my chest.

At long last, I heard the sound of a horse plodding up the road toward the house.

I sat up straighter, no longer sleepy.

When he didn't come inside right away, I peered out the window.

The buckskin stood saddled by the fence.

Vick, a shadow in the full moon, moved toward the edge of the orchard until I could barely see his dark, lanky figure.

I watched as he stopped at Proctor's grave for a long moment first, shoulders hunched.

He stayed that way for so long, I thought maybe he'd fallen asleep on his feet.

Then, at long last, he trudged toward the house, unsaddled his horse, and came inside.

"I've saved you a plate," I said quietly when his eyes met mine in the doorway.

He ignored me and moved into the living room.

The distance between us felt like the chinks in the cabin, forgotten behind the stove or the bed. So tiny at first, that it was easy to overlook them. The next time you checked behind the bed, they were so big you could fit your hand through the logs, and the extra chill that had been creeping up all winter suddenly made sense.

Vick didn't reply. Just sat at the table in the dim, candle-lit room.

My eyes moved to the plate of cooling food on the table in front of Vick, then up to his face. With the firelight drawing harsh shadows from each wrinkle, he looked older than my own father had before he died back in New York.

Vick wore a cap I'd knit him, even though it was summer. The thinning hair that had covered the top of his head for so long had finally fallen out. And with how much weight he'd lost, he was always cold.

But by now, I knew the faraway, cloudy look in his eyes and the set of his jaw. He wasn't really here with me right now. He was in the place he slipped away to mentally during every quiet moment since he'd come home from Echo Canyon three years ago.

I turned away from the table, bone-weary and ready for bed. I'd tucked Amina into the quilt hours ago, and I was suddenly eager to snuggle her to me.

"Goodnight, Vick," I murmured. I'd long since stopped begging him to tell me what was eating him up. Tonight would be no exception.

But as I shifted to rise from the table, he caught me by the arm so tight I nearly cried out.

He squeezed twice.

Careful, careful.

He studied me for a long moment with tired eyes that shone feverish in the firelight. I couldn't read the expression in them any more than I could decipher the desperate way his fingers still gripped my arm.

"When the children ask, tell them the officers were here about a census," Vick whispered, his face reflecting the glow of the fire in the otherwise dark kitchen.

My breath hitched in my throat, but I didn't say anything in response, desperate for him to keep speaking. Did he want to tell me about the meeting with the priesthood holders? Was there something more? When I peered into his eyes, he turned to face me head on for the first time in so long it made my throat tighten.

His eyes gleamed in the firelight, blinking fast like he was dreaming while awake. Even his dark eye, for once, looked shiny.

As I watched him, I suddenly wondered if I'd been wrong all these years.

Maybe he wasn't wasting away. Maybe he wasn't disappearing little by little, away from me and the children. Maybe he was drowning, like when he was a boy who'd been caught in a river eddy with an undertow when we were children. He was a good swimmer. A strong boy. But the circling current was stronger. All he could do was tread water while it tried to suck him under again and again, getting colder and weaker until his brother found him and reached out a branch. He was so tired of fighting the current that he'd stopped calling for help and was spinning in circles, hoping somebody would find him before the water pulled him under for good.

Instead of shrinking away, I placed my hand on top of Vick's, where his fingers clutched my arm. Then I squeezed twice, sending the signal back.

My voice shook when I spoke. "Vickery Robison, if you don't tell me what happened with those soldiers, I'm going to saddle up the gelding and go ask them myself."

He stared at me in disbelief, and his mouth tipped into a frown. But there was also the barest glimmer of relief in his eyes.

He *wanted* to tell me.

Now that I realized it, I wouldn't stop asking until he did. If I didn't, I was suddenly terrified I'd lose him for good.

I had to draw him back to me tonight, before the house bustled with children—and wives.

"I can't," he rasped. "Bishop Brunson said—"

I gripped his hand tighter. "You cleave unto *me,* not Bishop Brunson. That's what the Bible says. That's what the Book of Mormon says. No more secrets."

At the word *secrets,* he looked away. "I can't tell you. I made an oath. We all did."

"You made an oath not to tell your wife?"

He refused to look at me.

The hairs rose on the back of my neck. I tried again. "Whatever you promised, it can't be more binding than the oaths we took in the temple. We keep our secrets together."

This brought his eyes back to mine, so I kept going, determined not to lose him this time. "We're one in the eyes of God, Vick. Your secrets are my secrets."

I unclasped my hand from his, then replaced the fingers so I held him in the same grip we'd shared in the temple.

I squeezed.

He squeezed back. "The officers want to know what happened in the Meadow," he said, his voice barely a whisper.

I drew in a breath. "I know that much," I admitted. "But you weren't there—"

"I was though," he mumbled.

Then he lay his head on the table and began to sob.

49. EMMA WILLIS

FILLMORE, UTAH

JULY 1860

"Peach, why did Brother Robison call me a wretch?"

The words finally tumbled out of my mouth in the dark bedroom, long after we'd snuffed out the lantern and Violet's telltale sleep-snuffle reached my ears.

When she didn't answer, I thought I'd waited too long to ask. Was Peach asleep already, too?

I wasn't sure I could stand it if she was. My stomach hurt from missing dinner, and the rest of my insides were so twisted up I knew I'd lie awake all night long.

It was just as well. I'd gotten all the sleep I was likely to get earlier that afternoon.

"Peach? Please, if you're awake ..."

I couldn't help it. My voice wobbled on the last word and I was suddenly afraid that I might let loose with a honking, out-of-control sob I couldn't keep back. Just like earlier.

"Peach?" I tried again. "What's wrong with me?"

I sat up in bed. "Peach?" I whispered. The bed she shared with Violet was so close to my small trough bed that Papa made, that I only had to lean over to touch her shoulder.

"Stop," Peach snapped, her voice clear enough that I knew she hadn't been sleeping.

I drew back my hand, stunned. Peach never talked to me like that. She must still be upset about earlier. "I'm sorry about crying today at Brother Robison's. I didn't mean it. I love you."

She was quiet again for so long I couldn't stand it.

"Peach, please. What Brother Robison said—"

"It won't do you any good asking questions like that," Peach whispered back, her voice sounding just like Mama's, except for the slightest tremble to it. "Now let me be."

I lay back in my little bed, not bothering to shift around like I usually did to make the straw in the mattress lay flat instead of poking me through the fabric.

I couldn't make sense of Peach's tone. Was she really that mad at me about how I acted? Hot tears coursed down the sides of my cheeks, trailing into my ears, and all I could do was stare at the ceiling. It felt like I could already see the blood dripping down even though I was wide awake. It was just the tears making a blurry mess of my eyes.

I couldn't even bring myself to pray.

* * *

The dream was different tonight.

It skipped right to the part where Brother Robison became a big, black-winged bird.

Like before, he snatched the ring out of my hand with his talons.

But then something new happened.

He took a few steps away from me, then stepped to the side. That's when I saw he was holding the ring out to Peach. And even more than that, he'd turned back into a regular man—holding little Amina's hand.

He let go of Amina as he reached for Peach. I could hear Mama's voice behind me again. *Try, baby. Try.*

Amina darted away from Brother Robison and ran into my arms. I held onto her so tight, I must've been wrestling the straw mattress. While I clung to Amina, I watched Brother Robison slip the ring onto Peach's finger.

I woke up with my feet on the ground in the dark bedroom. Not screaming, for once.

My hand rested on the shelf above Violet's head, where Peach had set the ring safe and sound in the little bag Brother Robison had given her for safekeeping. I touched the soft velvet material, feeling for the shape of the ring underneath it.

The dream was still so vivid in my head, I felt only the tiniest sliver of guilt when I opened the drawstring.

I looked at my sisters sleeping in bed and felt a wave of loneliness.

Then, before I could wake up any further, I slipped my hand into the bag and slid the cold, too-big band onto my palm.

It was twisted in a pretty shape, and I realized for the first time that it was two bands locked together, not one.

I felt sick and sad and cold and warm all at once when I touched it. At first, I nearly threw the ring to the floor like it was full of hornet stingers.

It wasn't my hand that hurt, though.

It was my heart. And my head.

Blurry memories pressed at my temples like the water in the Virgin River when the dam broke last spring. Wild and dangerous and unstoppable.

Gathering every bit of courage, I ran my finger along the inside band of the ring.

There was a word engraved there, like I just knew there would be. I didn't have to turn on the light to know what it was when I felt the letters.

Beloved.

And that's when I knew why my nightmares wouldn't go away.

Because underneath the nightmares were memories that were even worse.

And suddenly I knew, without a shadow of a doubt, it wasn't Peach's ring.

It wasn't mine, though, either.

THREE YEARS EARLIER

50. NANCY HUFF

MOUNTAIN MEADOWS, UTAH
SEPTEMBER 1857

Mama held my hands so tight it hurt my fingers. I didn't fuss or let go, though.

It felt good to walk through the grass, after sitting still for so long in the trench.

I tried not to think about how my mouth and throat were sticky and dried-up at the same time, because that made me want to cry. All I could think about was water, and how I'd drink and drink when we got out of the Meadow.

"Just a little longer, Nancy," Mama said like she knew what I was thinking.

In front of us were all the other mamas and the older kids who had to walk. Sissy Lou and Mary and William and James were up there somewhere, but I couldn't see them.

Mama kept looking around, trying to spot them.

When the trail in front of us dipped down, I could see the wagon where Uncle Uri was riding with the other hurt people, and the wagon where baby Tri and the little babies were riding, way up front.

All the papas were walking behind us, but not my papa.

I felt jealous about that, but mostly I was thirsty and scared.

There was one military man riding a horse in front of the women and walking children. And another military man riding a horse leading the papas. Both of them had big guns and blue uniforms, and neither of them smiled.

"Will that man shoot us with his gun?" I asked Mama, but she shushed me quick.

I gave her a pout. The past three days had been nothing but gunshots.

"No, he's keeping us safe from the Indians," Mama said. "Just a little longer, and then we'll be all right."

I craned my neck and looked up at the tall, red rock and blue sky, because when I did that my mind stopped thinking about Uncle Uri's torn-up arm and the people with their eyes open and all bloody and not moving in the grass.

I liked staring at the sky, instead of at the mamas and the kids walking in front of us. Some of them had blood on their dresses and shirts. The rest had dirt on their faces and arms that looked a little like blood.

I was so thirsty.

I was so sweaty.

I was so dirty.

The little yucca horse the Indian woman gave me was so full of dust, the black ties on its braided legs were light brown.

I held it tight in one hand and held onto Mama with the other. I felt proud of her, even though we were at the very back of the group. The mean-looking man said she wouldn't be able to keep up with her hurt toes, but she was doing her best.

"We're almost there," I told Mama, same as she told me when my feet got tired and I asked to get in the wagon.

"Mama, do you think—" I wanted to ask if she thought Sissy Lou had any more strawberry jam hidden somewhere. I'd been wanting that jam so bad ever since we had to hide in the trench.

But then everything bad happened all at once.

Right behind us, the military man on the horse screamed one word. "HALT!"

I didn't have time to ask Mama why he yelled that, when we'd only been walking for a little while. Because as soon as he said that word, rifles went off behind him, all at once.

BOOM.

Then, the screaming was everywhere.

I couldn't see Mary or Sissy Lou or James or William anymore, because everybody was running around.

I started screaming, too.

Indians wearing paint all over their bodies had jumped out of the bushes holding clubs and knives and rocks.

One of them, a man with a big stomach, lifted a knife over his head and brought it down on America Dunlap's mama a few feet ahead of us. Red spilled out of her face.

Everywhere I looked, people were making noises like terrified animals.

Men covered in black and red and yellow just kept spilling from the bushes, holding knives and thick clubs. I didn't want to look, but I couldn't make my eyes shut either.

The grass was red now, instead of green.

All the mamas and the children running away tripped over the ones who had already fallen down.

So many of them were covered in red.

"Mama!" I screamed, but she was already pulling me down to the ground, scrambling into the sagebrush.

The sky, then weeds and dirt spun around in front of my face. All I could see through the brush was bodies falling down and red. All I could hear was crying and screaming and more booms.

"Don't look," Mama whisper-cried, turning her head toward me, her voice so upset it scared me even more. There were tears on her cheeks. "Stay quiet. Follow me." Then she started crawling on her hands and knees, belly low to the ground.

I closed my eyes at first, but then the little yucca horse slipped out of my hand.

I popped my eyes open to snatch the horse back. I got hold of it just before Mama tugged me away and pressed it hard into my hand.

I wanted to ask how we'd find Mary, how we'd find Sissy Lou and William and James and Uncle Uri and baby Tri. But the blood and the screaming and the hurting was happening all around us, and I was too scared to do anything but crawl through the grass and trees after Mama.

A few feet away, I saw a man with yellow and black paint smeared across his face lift up a wooden club. I couldn't help but stare, even though I wanted to close my eyes again.

At first, he looked like an Indian with all that paint. But his eyebrows were blond, and so was the hair peeking out from under his hat.

As I scrambled through the brush to follow Mama, the weeds parted just enough for me to see Maryann and Talitha Dunlap,

277

crouched in the grass in front of him. They'd been hiding, just like me and Mama.

My stomach felt sick. I wanted to look away, but I couldn't.

"Please don't hurt us," Maryann said in a tiny voice.

"Please, help us," Talitha begged, holding onto her sister. Both girls were older than me, but younger than Mary. "Nobody saw us but you."

The man with the blond eyebrows who was holding the club grunted. "Unbutton your shirts. Show me those bosoms."

"All right," Maryann was saying in a scared voice. "Come on, Talitha."

I turned away and didn't see what they did next. The sick feeling in my stomach got worse as I crawled faster after Mama.

Tears dripped down my cheeks and thorns stuck in my fingers, but I barely felt them. A little later, I heard MaryAnn, then Talitha, scream so loud I nearly stopped moving forward. Then I heard a wet, thudding sound. And another.

"Don't look, Nancy," Mama whispered, and I tried as hard as I could to make the sound of her voice the only thing in my head.

I realized we were headed for the front of the group, toward the wagons holding the injured and the babies. The last place we'd seen Sissy Lou and Mary and William and James.

Any second, I just knew that one of the painted men was going to leap on top of us and bash our heads with a club like they did everyone else.

When we got to a thicket of brush so dense we had to part the weeds back to see the Meadow, Mama and I peered out into the chaos again.

A little bit ahead, hurt people with bandages on their heads and arms and bodies were spilling out of the closest wagon. Some were limping on one leg while they ran, some were crawling. The red splashing all around looked like puddles from some kind of awful rainstorm that had drowned the people lying in them.

There were so many people. Mamas and papas and children, all tangled together drowning in that red rain.

The Meadow turned into little bits of red and golden light in front of my eyes, and my body felt floaty and heavy at the same time.

No, no, no.

"Uri," Mama breathed.

I saw him right as he tumbled out of the wagon. Before he could duck into the weeds, a painted man with a long knife saw him and screamed something I couldn't understand. The man jumped at Uri, slicing the hands he held in front of his face. Then pushed the knife into his throat.

I bit my tongue so I wouldn't scream and moved my eyes away so I wouldn't see.

That was when I finally saw Mary and Sissy Lou. They were holding onto each other, trying to run back to the papas.

A man with a big rock ran straight for them, his mouth open like he wanted to bite them. He had a big beard that was covered in red and black paint that made him look even scarier.

He wasn't an Indian either, even though he looked like one with all that paint.

When Louisa threw herself over Mary and held out an arm, he brought the rock down on her head.

I knew I was screaming, knew Mary was screaming too from the way her lips made a big O shape, but I couldn't hear any of it anymore.

The man hit Mary next. He hit her and Sissy Lou again and again until there was only red where they once had faces.

My eyes rolled sideways to see William. I closed them right before another painted man holding a knife jumped on top of him.

Mama was shaking. I was shaking. There was nowhere to look, so I closed my eyes.

When I opened them, they landed on the children's wagon. It stood on a rise, overlooking the whole awful scene.

There was a little girl peering through the closed flaps, her mouth in the same terrified O that I knew mine was making.

Baby Tri.

The driver was trying to get the oxen to move, but they'd started bawling and wouldn't budge another step.

"Mama, it's baby Tri," I gasped in a whisper, hoping I was making sounds even if I couldn't hear them.

Mama turned her head just in time to watch with me as baby Tri tipped over the side of the wagon—right as it started to move.

She tumbled down like a rag doll into the weeds, bumping against the big rolling wheel as she fell.

51. NANCY HUFF

MOUNTAIN MEADOWS, UTAH
SEPTEMBER 1857

Where the brush was high enough, Mama and I stood up. Then we ducked low and ran fast, trying to stay down so none of the bad men with the clubs and the knives and the rocks would see us.

I hoped I wasn't screaming, but I still couldn't tell.

Mama reached baby Tri first, at the spot of flattened grass where the wagon carrying the babies had been just a minute earlier.

A few seconds later, so did I.

She was alive. Crying, face red and scrunched up, little fingers on one hand in a fist.

"It's all right, sweet girl," Mama said, but she was crying too, and nothing was all right. The wagon wheel had run over Tri's arm. It hung flopping in the grass, barely clinging to her body by a few strips of skin.

Mama reached for her, then stopped, like she wasn't sure how to pick her up. But with the chaos and killing still happening behind us, there wasn't time to worry about hurting baby Tri more.

She scooped Tri into her arms, took me by the hand again, and then we ran back the way we'd come, to the cover of the sagebrush.

"Here," she said, darting underneath a bushy scrub oak that would hide us. She pulled Tri to her chest, and me under her arm.

Tri couldn't stop crying and screaming. Her voice was so worn out though, it barely made any noise.

"We'll be all right, Tri, I'll take care of you," Mama told her. Then she hugged me hard. "We'll be all right, Nancy," she said into my ear again and again, until my heartbeat calmed just a little. "Shh, Nancy, Nancy. That's my brave girl."

Her face was covered in tears and sweat and dirt but she was my mama, and that was all that mattered.

Baby Tri's screams calmed down to a whimper.

Mama held us close and started to sing, so quiet I could hardly hear. I closed my eyes and listened. I knew that song. I loved that song.

Of all the money e'er I had
I spent it in good company.

She whispered my name, then Tri's, like she meant that the words she was singing were about us.

And of all the harm that e'er I've done
Alas it was to none but me.

And all I've done for want of wit
To memory now I can't recall
So fill to me the parting glass
Good night and joy be with you all

Of all the comrades that e'er I had
They are sorry for my going away
And all the sweethearts that e'er I had
They would wish me one more day to stay

Mama whispered "Nancy," then "Tri," and then, "my girls." I squeezed my eyes shut so hard but the tears leaked out anyway.

But since it has so ordered been
By a time to rise and a time to fall
Come fill to me the parting glass
Good night and joy be with you all
Come fill to me the parting glass
Good night and joy be with you all.

As Mama sang, baby Tri's whimpers went quiet and she tucked her head into Mama's chest and wrapped her one good arm around Mama's neck. I nestled in as close as I could to both of them, even though Mama's chest was turning red from Baby Tri's hurt arm. All I wanted to do was cling onto Mama and cover my eyes and ears.

Now that I could hear again, I wished I couldn't.

All the screams were coming one at a time from the direction we'd escaped, between wet thuds.

"No, please, I'm begging you. We have gold—"

"Stop, please, I'll do anything—"

"No! Not my son—"

Some people from our group weren't saying words at all. Just awful noises like I'd never heard before.

Crack.

The deafening sound rattled back and forth in my head.

Mama's whole body shook.

Her arms let go. Something wet and warm spurted onto my face.

I opened my eyes to see Mama's shoulder—just a few inches from my face. Not a shoulder anymore. A bubbling mess of blood and ripped clothing.

Baby Tri screamed again and flailed hard, her arm that was hanging all wrong whipping toward me.

Mama's face turned frozen as her eyes looked at the bloody mess of her arm that was now as badly injured as Tri's.

Twigs crunched underfoot.

I bit my cheek so hard I tasted blood. Someone was coming. We had to run. But we couldn't run anymore. Mama and Tri were hurt. And there was nowhere to go.

My eyes moved to the wagon Baby Tri had fallen out of. It had stopped just ahead.

I couldn't see any of the children, but I could see the driver. He sat slumped in the wagon seat.

At first I thought he was dead, too.

Then I saw his head in his hands.

His body shook like he was crying.

Mama's body was shaking now too.

Baby Tri had gone quiet again.

I turned to see a man standing above us.

Red and black paint covered his hairy legs. He wore dirty brown pants and a too-big shirt made of cloth that looked like the sacks we stored our potatoes in back home in Arkansas.

He was holding a gun.

The one he'd just used to shoot Mama.

"Please," Mama begged. "Don't hurt my children."

My stomach turned over. He'd already hurt Mama.

The man didn't lift his gun, though.

He took a step closer, staring at Mama.

There were beads of sweat on his painted face.

Mama grabbed hold of my hand and I fingered her ring. The one she let me touch sometimes, feeling for the words on the inside of the band.

Beloved.

"Please, don't hurt my children," Mama was saying about me and Tri. "Please."

I just knew the man wouldn't understand. Or care. He was an Indian. And he'd just shot her right through the shoulder.

Then he leaned his face into the shirt he wore and wiped away the sweat on his forehead.

The red paint smeared onto the fabric. But underneath, there wasn't any of the chestnut brown skin I'd seen when we stopped at Corn Creek or any of the other times we'd run across Indians.

His skin was the same color as mine.

My stomach flipped again so hard I gasped.

One of his eyes was dark, almost black.

His other eye was a wide, pale green.

We stayed staring at each other, frozen while the warm blood dripped down Mama's and baby Tri's arms. The air felt so thick I could barely choke it down.

The man's eyes searched me and baby Tri. He raised his gun at Mama again and gestured to me. "How old is she?"

"Six," Mama said, even though I was almost seven.

I didn't argue.

"That baby should've been in the wagon with the others," the man said, looking at Tri like it was Mama's fault he'd shot her. While he spoke, he turned his face away from us, so all we could see was the dark eye.

More twigs snapped from behind the sage. Plodding hoofbeats.

I looked up to see a clean-shaven man wearing a pale blue uniform. One of the military men who had ridden up to our trench while Captain Alexander's wife held the white flag.

His face looked sweaty and upset, like he was the one hiding in the bloody dirt instead of on top of that horse looking down at us.

"Do your duty, Brother Robison," he said in a soft voice, nodding toward me and Mama. "I'll take the poor wretch to the wagon." He pointed at Tri.

I felt Mama stiffen beside me and make a strangled noise.

The man with two-colored eyes turned so I could see the pale green one. "She's only four," he said, pointing to me, even though Mama had told him I was six, almost seven. "Take them both to the wagon." His voice thick and gruff. It sounded the same way Papa's had when he begged for whiskey right before he died.

"No, Mama," I screamed, terrified to be taken away from her.

"Take care of baby Tri," Mama whispered, hot into my ear. "Hold her hand. Stay together."

I kept hold of Mama's hand, so slippery with blood. I squeezed harder when they pulled me and baby Tri away.

Her ring, the one Papa gave her when they got married, came off into my palm.

I clenched it so tight it cut into my fingers when I heard the scream, then the last boom, from behind me.

52. NANCY HUFF

MOUNTAIN MEADOWS, UTAH

SEPTEMBER 1857

When the wagon started bumping away from the Meadow, my breathing got faster and faster. Where were the men taking us?

I tried to hold baby Tri's hand, like Mama said I should, but she kept screaming and thrashing, even with her arm all broken up.

Her dark hair stuck flat down to her head like she'd just taken a bath. She'd wet her dress, but so had a lot of the kids in the wagon. Everything smelled bad. It was so hot.

Everything felt fuzzy in my head, like what just happened to Mama might be a bad dream.

I told myself that maybe it was. Because I wanted Mama back so bad my stomach felt sick.

Just a bad dream. Just a bad, bad dream, I told myself over and over the same way Mama had when I woke up scared at night. After a while, I realized I was whispering the words out loud and not in my head. It made me feel better, like if I just believed those words enough, I'd make them true. With each whisper, I rolled Mama's ring around the palm of my hand, pretending she'd given it to me to play with for just a little while.

"This is a bad dream," I whispered to baby Tri, but she only cried harder and pulled away from me. I held tight onto the hem of her dress, afraid she might tip over the edge again.

The man driving the wagon talked in a nice voice even though most of the kids were crying and screaming. He had gray hair that covered the top of his head in little bits. He had blue eyes and big, thick eyebrows that moved around when he looked over his shoulder and talked to us. That made me think of Papa.

His top lip puckered at one side a little, like maybe he got hurt there a long time ago.

It made it look as if he was smiling, even when his big eyebrows bunched up and tears rolled down his cheeks.

I decided maybe he *was* Papa. Just for now, because I missed Mama and Mary and Sissy Lou and William and James so much.

Not-Papa told all of us in the wagon that it would be only a little longer. Everything would be all right. Then we'd get some water and some food when we got to the Hamblin ranch.

I didn't know what ranch he was talking about. But anywhere was better than here.

Just a bad dream, I reminded myself as I rolled the ring round and round.

The wagon jolted and Not-Papa made a sweet little whistle to the big old oxen. "Get along now. Steady, steady."

After a while longer, baby Tri finally fell asleep.

A little bit of breeze tickled my hair, feeling good on my face. And as long as I kept on reminding myself that everything would be okay when I woke up from this dream, I felt calm again.

With baby Tri asleep, I slowly scooted next to her and held her good hand like I'd promised Mama.

Then I decided I'd sing her the song Papa used to do with the oxen. Same one Mama sang when Belle and Bright fell down, and when we were hiding together.

I looked at the top of the wagon canvas and sang the only words I could remember, drawing them so they'd last as long as possible even though they sounded funny with my throat all choked up and raw. "And joy be to you all."

"Good girl," I told Tri, even though she was sleeping. "I'll take care of you, Tri."

After a few minutes, I felt her breathing turn slow and heavy. Her little head lay back against mine, and I pretended for a second that I was her mama.

THREE YEARS LATER

53. LUCY ROBISON

FILLMORE, UTAH
JULY 1860

At first, I was afraid Vick wouldn't tell me what had happened in the Meadow.

I was sure he'd push the cold plate of food away, stand up from the kitchen table, and retreat back into the shell of himself and never speak more of it. But when the story finally poured out of him like flood waters, horrifying in its detail, it was me who wanted to get up and walk out.

I didn't.

I had asked, and now, I would listen.

He spewed the whole awful thing, one detail at a time in a voice that was steady and measured as wagon wheels rolling by. If I weren't paying attention to the words he spoke, I might have thought he was talking about the apple orchard. It was like he'd wrung out all the emotion from his voice after he'd cried, and now there was nothing left in it.

I knew Kima and the children, tucked safe in their beds, couldn't hear him. Thankfully, he was speaking too quietly. Besides, they'd been asleep for hours. Unaware of these horrors.

"When we got out of town, Bishop Brunson told us there was a change of plans. We were needed in the south more than we were needed up north," he began.

"A rider met us and led the way to a meadow just past Cedar City. And there were the Lamanites. Chomping at the bit to attack the gentile wagon train. At least, that's what I thought until we got up close. Up close, I could see they weren't Indians at all. They were white men, wearing paint. Some of the men who'd been struck by bullets had their shirts or trousers peeled off, and the paint stopped at the arms or the legs." His voice rose a little here, like he still couldn't believe what he'd seen.

"There were only a handful of real Paiutes left. Just Chief Kanosh and a few other men. The rest had gone back to the village with their dead and injured after they stampeded the cattle. The Paiutes who were left weren't angry—not at the gentiles, anyway. They were angry at Isaac Haight and Colonel Dame and the rest of the leaders. They were scared, saying the Mormon leaders had no power. That we'd lied to them. That the Mormons took most of the cattle. That the wagon train was full of women and children."

I choked back a soft gasp.

Vick bowed his head, not stopping to acknowledge my shock. "Bishop Brunson seemed rattled as I was, but he said to have faith. Wait for further instruction. So we did. We waited until Colonel Dame and President Haight and Brother John D. Lee gathered us up and told us what we were to do. We'd sent a rider to Brigham Young's, but he wasn't back in time."

Brother Haslam.

The hair rose on the back of my neck. I'd never told Vick that I'd given the rider a fresh horse all those years ago. He'd been so unwell, so unlike himself when he returned from the Meadow, that he'd never even commented on the fact that Proctor's mare was gone, replaced by the buckskin.

"President Haight dismissed Kanosh and the last of the Paiutes, saying they'd fallen short of their duty to the Lord. Then he told those of us who remained that the time had come to avenge the blood of the prophets. We were to keep everything that would happen a secret until the day we died. From our wives, our children, our neighbors. Each of us took an oath. To hide what happened in the Meadow, and to blame it on the Paiutes if it ever came to light."

His voice went even quieter. "I made the oath. Then President Haight told us what we were going to do next." He looked up at me with eyes so dull they made me think of Proctor lying in his casket. "I can't stop asking myself if I would have made that oath if he'd told us what we were about to do. I—" His voice cracked. "I fear I would have. God forgive me, I think I would have." He spread his hands flat on the table and dug his nails into the wood. "When some of the men balked, President Haight reminded us he spoke for God. And on this day, he spoke for the God of Vengeance.

"Haight, Dame, Lee, and Higbee rode down to the circled wagons when the gentiles raised a white flag. Told them that the Mormon military was going to lead them to safety. When their captain agreed, the rest of us moved into place."

He looked at me with so much pain in his eyes I wanted to weep. I wanted to comfort him, but I had none to offer. The best I could do was let him continue.

"Those of us who were painted up like Indians hid in the sagebrush at the mouth of the Meadow. While I hid there, I could hear some of the gentile men still arguing with John D. Lee. *'All I wish is for you to surrender your arms and we'll see that you go unhurt,* Lee said. And one of the gentile men kept saying, *'If you give up your arms you are a fool. Don't you be such a god damned fool as that.'*"

I fought the urge to flinch at Vick quoting the man using the Lord's name in vain, and he closed his eyes. "He was right, but the gentiles didn't have any choice. They were out of water. They had to trust us."

He swallowed hard. "A wagon filled with the littlest children—the ones too young to tell what we were about to do—led the way out of the Meadow. Then came the women and older children, about fifty feet behind. Then the men, single file, each with an armed member of the Nauvoo Legion—one who hadn't been painted up—standing by his side."

Vick drew in a shuddering breath. "Colonel Dame told them that if they didn't give up their guns, the Indians would attack." His eyes twitched back and forth like he was dreaming.

I felt like I might vomit. One part of my mind was sure he couldn't be telling the truth. The other part knew he was.

"When everyone was gathered up, we started to lead the surrendered gentiles out of the canyon. All I knew was that I was meant to jump out of the brush and *do my duty*. I just kept repeating that again and again in my head."

His eyes twitched faster, blinking, staring at nothing. "Higbee, who was leading the men, stopped his horse and cried out, *'Halt.'* Then *'Fire.'* And then we were all in hell. Each man escorting a gentile fired his rifle and shot the man dead.

"As the gentile men fell dead to the ground, that's when those of us who'd been painted up to look like Indians jumped out of the brush along the river. Some of us held bowie knives and clubs. Others had rocks. Some of the men screamed like they'd turned wild. The women and children were screaming, begging for their lives until all of them had been bashed over the head or sliced through."

Then my husband looked right in my eyes, and I wanted more than anything to look away. "The sound of the screams. All those women and children. I couldn't do it, but I did do it. I *did* do it," he repeated incredulously. "I helped turn that Meadow red."

I felt my own face tremble and twitch. The sick feeling in my stomach was getting harder and harder to hold inside. Women and children? How? I couldn't find a single word to answer, so I reached for his hand because I needed to anchor myself. His fingers were cold as ice.

"There was ... there was one woman who managed to slip away. Hiding in the bushes with her two daughters. I found them."

Of every horrible thing he'd told me so far, this made my stomach curl so violently into itself, I barely held back the gasp.

"The first little girl was too old, at least six. We ... we were only supposed to save the children who were too young to tell what had happened in the Meadow. The other child ..." He choked on his words. "She'd fallen out of the children's wagon somehow and her arm was hanging on by just a thread. Then ... then Brother Lee rode up and handed me his gun. Said he'd take the baby back to the wagon."

A baby with her arm hanging by a thread. My stomach seized again. *No.*

I waited for Vick to continue. He locked eyes with me, pale green iris wide as the full moon. "I told him the older girl was four, not six. I saved her, Lucy. At least I saved one of them."

"And the baby?" I asked, hardly able to force the words past my lips.

He nodded slowly. "When the men and the last of the women and children were dead, they stripped the bodies, looking for anything valuable. Pulled apart the wagons to get at the gold hidden inside. Took the guns and the ammunition to send up north, to the rest of the Nauvoo Legion. Piled up the clothing and the quilts that hadn't been spoiled. The oxen and horses that hadn't been shot."

He shook his head back and forth, as if he could dislodge the memory. "There were so many bodies. So much blood." He gripped the edge of the table. "Oh, God, Lucy, the blood."

His eyes focused on something behind me, but he continued. "We drove the wagon full of children to the Hamblin Ranch in Cedar City. It took all night to get there. The baby who was missing an arm … she was the only one who didn't cry. Just stared up at me when I wrapped her up in a quilt as best I could to stop the blood." He closed his eyes. "I wanted to tell the children to stop crying for their parents, but I had no right to do it. Not when all of us had just clubbed and stabbed and shot their parents and siblings in front of their eyes."

"And the baby?" I asked again, more forcefully this time. The words tasted like curdled milk in my mouth, thick and sour. But I needed to know.

"Brother Haight—The mayor of Cedar City—sorted the children out," he said, still not answering my question.

"Sorted them out?" I breathed.

"Gave them to families in Iron County, Cedar City, Meadow, and Toquerville who were willing to take them." He swallowed. "He … he paid them with some of what we'd taken from the wagon train. When some of the children refused to be comforted, he said '*Poor wretches. They don't know how lucky they are.*'"

I tried to take this in, but the words knocked around in my mind for a long few seconds. Before I could speak again, Vick opened his eyes and looked at me. "Nobody wanted the little girl with one arm. Said she'd likely not survive. That it'd be hard to explain to their wives. So I said I'd take her. Bishop Brunson amputated the arm and cared for her for a month in Cedar City."

The first tears finally dripped down my cheeks.

Amina.

My Amina.

Not my Amina.

"What were you doing all that time you were supposed to be up north?" I whispered, needing to know but unable to muster any anger for the fact that he'd lied to me. The horror buzzing through my body eclipsed every other feeling. "You were gone for weeks."

Vick drew in a breath. "There would be more and more wagon trains coming up. We couldn't let them … we couldn't let them see the bodies in the Meadow. We tried to bury the bodies, but there were too many. Brother Johnson and I, and a few of the other men, escorted the wagon trains around the Meadow. Told them it was a dangerous spot for Indian attacks. Then, when Little Amina was well enough to travel, we came back home."

"Vick," I whispered. "Oh, Vick." There was nothing else to say.

"When I try to fall asleep at night, I can still see Amina's sister— maybe it was her sister. She was covered up in blood from the wagon ride, smeared all across her face. She wouldn't let her go when I tried to lift her out of the wagon at the Hamblin ranch. The quilt I'd wrapped around her was soaked through with so much blood by then, it was dripping through the wagon floorboards." He shuddered. "When I close my eyes, that's all I can see."

He stared at me, unblinking. "I felt bad we had to separate the girls, but Lucy, the Lord works in mysterious ways. The Willis family ... they adopted the older girl. The one I saved."

I gripped his cold hand harder, afraid to let go. I realized, in some part of my mind, that my fingers had wrapped around his in the same grip we'd shared in the endowment ceremony all those years ago.

"Emma," I whispered. I knew the Willises had adopted a child, right before we'd gotten Amina, but Sister Willis had told me the little girl had come from a sister in Salt Lake.

Vick nodded. He let out a long breath. "The Army men found the bones at the Meadow. They know it's the gentiles we left there. One of the officers was carrying a photo with him. Says the girls have grandparents in Arkansas who think their granddaughters are dead."

My grip on his fingers finally went slack.

Suffer the little children to come unto me. A verse from the Bible drifted through the void in my mind. Matthew 19:14.

Vengeance is mine. I couldn't for the life of me think of the chapter and verse.

Had God really said that, or had I?

I didn't know anymore.

54. KAHPEPUTZ (SALLY)

CORN CREEK, UTAH

JULY 1860

I glanced at Inola across the fire, heart beating in time with the soft drumming that surrounded us, sure that I was about to vomit.

Tonight needed to go as planned, or everything else would fall apart.

Inola ignored me, keeping her eyes on Kanosh as he finished his meal.

My own bowl of food sat untouched in my lap, even though the rabbit stew had been prepared with care for tonight, the celebration of midsummer.

"When the children of the Creator of Men found the apple of wisdom, they reached for it," said Elu, one of the elders, as the drumming quieted. He stood in front of the children, telling the story they'd heard so many times before.

"But what did the children find at the base of the tree? A rattlesnake." Elu shook the staff at his side, which rattled a little. Some of the children made soft "oh" sounds. "Then the white men came. They knocked down the tree and ate the apple."

More murmuring from the children. I'd never been sure what to take from the story myself. Were the white men wise, because they got the apples? Or were they foolish, because they killed the tree that grew them? Were the children of the Creator of Men wrong to be afraid of the rattlesnake? Why hadn't it struck the white men?

I shook my head and cut my eyes to Kanosh once more. The evening was winding down, and mothers were ushering children away from the fire. *Speak,* I begged him silently, for once desperate for him to start blustering about the Mormons and the Meadow.

Earlier that day, a small group of Army men dressed in dark blue uniforms had ridden out to Corn Creek, asking if any Paiutes would speak about what happened in the Meadow.

It wasn't the first time they'd tried to question the Paiutes.

It wouldn't be the last.

Only this time, they claimed they were closing in on making indictments, and arrests. "Over in Fillmore, the Mormons said it was the Paiutes who murdered all those folks in the Meadow," one of the Army men had said, staring at Kanosh. "But we'd like to know where you got the guns. Might be able to avoid hanging if you feel like talking."

Kanosh had turned them away, stone-faced. It was midsummer. And besides, the rumors were untrue.

Now, Kanosh tossed the last of his camas root into the fire and frowned.

I held my breath. Surely, with Keme's recent death and today's visit from the Army men, he couldn't resist the opportunity to say a few words with everyone gathered together. *Speak.*

Elu sat down beside the other elders, and the children moved back to their parents. The fire popped in the silence, sending sparks skyward.

Then, finally, Kanosh spoke. "The Army men are either idiots or they haven't been in Utah very long," he muttered.

I released the breath I'd been holding as quietly as I could as he continued. My heart hammered louder in the silence left by the drums.

"If they keep poking around, they're going to find out what happens when you talk too loud about what happened at the Meadow. I don't care if they are the U.S. Army," Kanosh said to no one in particular. More mothers tugged at their children's hands to lead them away from the fire. This was not a topic for young ones.

I couldn't help but glance at Inola again. Kanosh was doing just what we'd hoped he'd do. The subject had been broached.

The anxious nerves in my stomach fizzed into full-blown nausea, and I wrapped my arms around my middle.

"Not that I'd mind if they strung up Brother Brigham," Kanosh growled, eliciting a few laughs.

Our chief hated Brigham Young. But he knew better than to step on the rattlesnake's tail.

If the Mormon leaders found out that Kanosh or the Paiute men were speaking about what they'd seen in the Meadow, we could expect consequences worse than hanging.

"I made an oath to keep quiet and I'm a man of my word," Kanosh liked to say, even though it was clear he kept silent out of fear, not loyalty.

And that silence had kept the U.S. government in the dark for a very long time. I knew from Awan that the mass graves at the Meadow hadn't even been uncovered until two years after the massacre.

That was what loyalty—and fear—earned a person.

Now, the Army was scrambling to learn the details of what happened. And they were clearly finding few willing to talk.

There was little question that the Mormons had pointed the finger of blame solely at the "Indians," even while they hoarded the lion's share of the gentiles' wagons, cattle, and plunder in their homes. I could see the terror in the gentiles' eyes over the years as a steady stream of wagons passed by Corn Creek.

But so far, there hadn't been any tribes—or chiefs—blamed for the massacre. Just *Indians*.

That was what we got for keeping silent.

"The government really expects us to help them?" Kanosh blustered, his voice rising. "When have they ever helped us? They just keep sending more wagons, more guns. Why don't they investigate what happened at Bear River?" He stood and spat into the fire. "I'll tell you why they don't. Because it was them who killed all those Shoshone women and children."

The men and women gathered near the fire murmured their agreement. My stomach turned again when I thought of the day Awan told me about the hundreds of Shoshone men, women, and children who had been slaughtered in their lodges last year. Kanosh was right about that. There had been no investigation into Bear River. There would be no investigation into Bear River, or any of the other times the Shoshone, the Paiute, the Bannock, the Pahvant, the Lakota, even the Utes had been killed.

"Let the damned Mormons and the damned government sort it out," Kanosh said as if this settled the matter. "They're all liars."

This was his favorite line. The one he always finished with.

I wrapped my hands tighter around my stomach, around the gap in my crinoline dress.

No, every part of me protested. *Walks without sound.*

But the part of me that knew my silence couldn't save me anymore dragged my shaking voice out.

I raised it as loud as it would go.

"But you are a liar, too."

Stunned silence followed, broken only by the crackle of the fire as Kanosh turned to look at me.

No one ever spoke to him like that. Let alone me, who spoke to no one.

I stood up on shaking legs and stepped forward, even though what I really wanted to do was run.

I could feel Awan's eyes on me somewhere in the crowd, and I imagined his warm hand resting on my back, urging, *I'm with you.*

"You lied about the steers being poisoned. You knew that the Paiutes died because of locoweed, *not* poison. Keme and Helaku and all the others died because of you."

Shocked gasps came from those around the fire. Kanosh drew himself up tall, his hand raised like he was going to strike me. "So Brigham Young's little doll can speak?" he mocked, taking a step in my direction. "Sounds like nonsense to me."

I eased back but didn't run. "You say that *I* am Brigham Young's doll? I think it's *you* who are Brigham Young's doll. You're afraid of him and the rest of the white Mormons. You are a coward, afraid to stand up to them. To tell the truth."

With that, Kanosh lunged at me.

I braced, waiting to feel his rough hands on my body. Would he hit me? Push me? I closed my eyes.

Quick as a shadow, Inola stepped forward and grabbed hold of his arm.

He looked at her incredulously. "Have all the women gone mad? What is this?"

Inola released her grasp and lowered her eyes. "Finish your dinner, husband. I will speak with her," she said simply, drawing more murmurs from the crowd as all eyes locked on me.

She pulled a stout club, covered in animal hide, from where it lay beside a wickiup and held it lightly in her hands. More murmurs from the crowd rumbled. The club was used for beating dust out of skins, but that clearly wasn't what Inola had in mind.

Kanosh followed her movements and laughed in surprise. "Well then, maybe you should talk to her."

I shrank back. "No, please," I said, cowering. "I'm sorry. I spoke out of turn. I just think ... I think ..."

"You think nothing." Inola gave me a fierce look. "You *know* nothing, yet you seek to counsel the Chief? My husband?"

Not *our* husband. Numa and Povi, sitting a few feet away, exchanged glances.

"You speak my dead brother's name? You insult my husband?" Inola said, shaking her head in disgust, moving toward me through the firelight.

Out of the corner of my eye, I watched a mother gather her baby onto her lap, rise and slip away into the darkness.

I darted to the left and tried to follow the woman and child, heart pounding in my chest so hard my breath came in gasps. But Inola stepped in front of me, blocking my escape.

Kanosh laughed again.

"You have never belonged here," Inola said in disgust. "And you have never learned your place."

"I'm sorry," I said. "I shouldn't have—"

She leaped forward and grabbed me by the hair. "Be quiet, little doll."

Then she dragged me into the darkness, beyond the fire.

55. NANCY HUFF

FILLMORE, UTAH

JULY 1860

Violet sighed in her sleep and rolled out from under Peach's arm.

I stared down at them, feet rooted to the floor in the middle of the dark bedroom. My whole body was trembling, but I didn't move to get back into bed.

Standing there while everyone slept, I put the ring on my thumb.

I already knew I was never going to take it off. It wasn't Peach's. It was Nancy's.

And Nancy was me.

Why had I forgotten that? Forgotten everything?

My face was warm and wet as I blinked in the quiet room, but it didn't feel like blood on my face anymore.

Just tears. Tears for Mama. For Papa. For Mary. For William. For Uncle Uri. For Sissy Lou. For baby Triphena.

I'd been hearing "Baby, try" in my dreams all this time, but now I knew better.

I now remembered it was "Baby Tri." My cousin. Sissy Lou's baby. I'd called her that. And I'd held her in my arms while the blood soaked through the quilt around us in the wagon.

I felt like the wind knocked out of me so hard that maybe I'd never be able to breathe again. I waited until the choking feeling passed, everything moving in slow motion. The memories flooding my mind were so bad, so awful, I thought I was going to die while they washed over me. It was worse than the nightmares. This was real, and it stung like poison.

Mama. Papa. Mary. William. Uri. Louisa. Baby Tri. Their names spun through my mind.

But as the tears ran down my face, some of that poison seemed to leak out with them. Then a new kind of burning took up in my heart as I remembered the man who sang me songs. *Papa,* I knew now.

And joy be to you all.

I closed my eyes and thought real hard. He had callused hands and a rich, deep voice. And my same blue eyes. And then I saw Mama in my mind. She had soft hands and a gentle voice. Her face was blurry in my memories, but her voice wasn't. She'd recited poems and stories that lived somewhere in my bones, even if I couldn't recall all the words anymore. I knew they'd kept me safe when I was hiding from the men who'd taken her—and the rest of my family—away from me.

She and Papa had my same dark, curly cowlicked hair.

And they loved me. They really, really loved me.

When the memories finally burst through the clouds in my mind, they were clear and bright, like sunshine after a storm. So sharp and detailed, they made the past three years of memories feel like a dream in comparison.

I found myself drawing a little closer to Peach on the side of the bed she shared with Violet.

These two loved me like we were sisters. Sisters who shared blood. But I was certain now that Peach knew we weren't.

I knelt down, put my hand on her arm and leaned next to her ear, so I wouldn't wake Violet. She smelled like sleep and apple preserves. My voice shook a little as I whispered, "Peach? Peach, wake up. Please."

She rose up on one shoulder and rubbed sleep out of her eyes. I couldn't see her face very well in the dark room, but I could tell her brow was furrowed. "Emma, go back to sleep."

My voice wavered, but I forced the words out. "Tell me about when I got here, Peach."

She didn't answer right away. I pictured her blinking in surprise at the question.

I moved my hand into a slice of moonlight coming through the edge of the oilcloth around our window. The ring I now wore around my thumb—the ring Brother Robison had given her—glinted like the blade of a knife.

She drew in a breath and sat up in bed. "What are you doing? That's my ring."

I pulled away from her. "It's my ring. It was my mama's ring." There were still holes in my memory—big ones—but I remembered that ring clear as day now. Like parts of my mind were still foggy, and I was just waiting for those rays of sunlight and memory to breakthrough a little at a time.

Mama loved that ring. Papa gave it to her when they got married.

Peach gasped. Her mouth hung open and I watched the understanding change her face from sleepy and upset to scared. "Your *mama*?"

"I don't know how Brother Robison got it. But I know it was my mama's." I tucked my hands under my arms protectively, locking the ring tight in my grasp.

"Your mama's?" Peach repeated, choking a little. Then she went silent for a few seconds. My heart beat faster. I needed to know what she remembered about how I'd gotten here. Those memories were still locked away. I knew they were there, but I couldn't quite reach them.

"Tell me about the day I got here," I insisted again.

"I'm not supposed to talk about that," she said, her voice barely a whisper.

"I'll wake everybody up right now," I said, feeling braver. "Ask them all myself."

"No. No, they'll be mad," Peach said, reaching out a hand to stop me. Her voice shook. "Mama will get the willow switch."

"She's *not* my mama," I hissed, drawing back, feeling every willow stripe she'd ever given me, every slight she'd ever made about me being wicked, every time she'd made me go to bed without dinner.

I didn't know where the runaway anger was taking me, but I was ready for the ride.

Peach looked back at Violet then got up, grabbed my hand, and pulled me away from the beds and into the tiny closet at the far side of the bedroom. She closed the door behind us.

I couldn't see her face anymore. The sliver of moonlight was gone. But I could hear her snuffling.

After a few minutes she spoke in a voice that didn't sound much like Peach at all. Croaky and shaky and thick with tears. "You got here on my birthday. The day I turned thirteen. Papa told us you were only four years old, but—"

"I wasn't four," I interrupted her. "I was six. Almost seven."

And now I was nine, almost ten years old. Not seven, almost eight. I knew now why I was so much taller than seven-year-old Adelia Robison, so "precocious" as Brother Larsen had said in Sunday school.

I knew it so clearly now. How was it possible I'd hidden all of these memories from myself so completely for the past three years?

Peach stared at me. "Mama said you were a birthday present, but you didn't act like a present. You acted like a wild animal. We ... we tried to give you a bath. You were all dirty ... and bloody."

I grasped around my mind in the raw, burning mess where the nightmares came from. Could I remember that?

The memory flashed, like lightning suddenly making the sky bright. I pictured myself sitting in our old metal wash tub, water pouring down my head while I cried and cried. A hand came past my mouth, trying to bathe me.

I bit it.

Then I threw up, because the blood in my mouth made me think about what had happened to Mama. To Mary and William and Uri and Louisa. To baby Tri, who they'd pulled me away from when the wagon reached the ranch.

They called me Emma. They told me that if I couldn't forget what happened, they'd have to do to me like they did to Mama.

So I had to forget.

Peach was talking again, and I tried to focus on her words. "You kept screaming 'try'," when we got you in the bathtub, even though we were trying to help you. Over and over."

"Tri, not try," I whispered, knowing Peach wouldn't be able to hear the difference. "When ... When did the Robisons adopt Amina?"

Peach drew in a breath. "About a month after you."

The images sloshed. I couldn't grab the right one. They all burned so much.

"Emma?"

"My name is *Nancy,*" I choked out, grabbing hold of the memory burning hottest and refusing to let go even though I knew it would add to the pile of hurt. "And Amina's name is Triphena. She's my cousin."

Peach was sniffling hard again. "How can that be? Mama said you came from Salt Lake. And Amina's mama was dead. Papa and Brother Robison ..."

I stopped listening to what she was saying, even though this was what I'd asked for. Another shifting, molten wall of memory crashed into me with her words.

"He's not my papa," I whispered. Then I sank to the floor of the closet so I wouldn't fall.

Because now I remembered the first time I'd met him and Brother Robison.

56. NANCY HUFF

FILLMORE, UTAH

JULY 1860

I curled onto Peach's lap because there was nowhere else to go in the little closet.

I didn't have any memories of seeing Not-Papa in the Meadow.

But he must have been there.

While Peach hovered above me, stroking my hair, tears dripping down onto my head, I let my tears fall onto her nightgown as my memories found their way through the clouds in my mind.

The first time I saw Not-Papa, it was at the little farm. The place where the man with the bushy eyebrows and the scar on his lip had driven us children.

There were lots of men there. Only men. Some were shouting. Some crying. Some of them were bloody. Some of them were laughing.

Brother Robison was the one who pulled me out of the wagon, away from the other children, away from baby Tri.

Then he handed me to Not-Papa.

There was a thin, half-washed stripe of black paint running along his beard. I saw it when he picked me up in his strong arms, even though I was screaming to stay with Tri.

"She's hurt, honey. Her arm's hurt bad. Bishop Brunson will help her." His voice was so sad. His eyes were so red. His skin looked so raw, like he'd scrubbed and scrubbed.

Then Not-Papa wrapped me in a fresh quilt, set me on the seat beside him in a different wagon, and drove me here, to Fillmore. To Not-Mama and Peach. Violet wasn't born yet.

"Sissie?" Peach was saying. I'd never heard her call me that, only Violet. She didn't know what name to call me anymore.

I didn't answer, just tucked myself tighter into a ball and shook hard.

Maybe I hadn't seen Not-Papa in the Meadow. I had seen Brother Robison, though.

He was the man who'd pulled me and Tri away from Mama, hovering over us like a big black bird, mouth gaping wide.

Then he'd sent us to the wagon with the other littlest children. Keeping us safe from what he was about to do to Mama.

Boom.

The memory of the gunshot tore through my mind. I flinched. A sound came out of my mouth I didn't recognize. Half-crying, half-wailing into Peach's lap.

Peach froze, her hands still on my hair. "Emma . . . Nancy . . . Shh. You're going to wake Mama and Papa."

She drew away from me a little, and I wondered if she was afraid I was going to bite her, like I'd done when I first arrived.

The thought made me sit up, and I suddenly knew as clear as day that I couldn't be in this room, this house, a second longer.

"I love you, Peach," I told her, all the shaking gone from my voice.

I stumbled to my feet and opened the closet door. "I love you, Violet."

Then I put on my shoes without bothering to lace them, and ran into the night.

57. LUCY ROBISON

FILLMORE, UTAH

JULY 1860

I refused to fall asleep after what Vick told me.

I couldn't go back to my bed and lay down next to Amina's little body, knowing what I now knew.

Pieces of Vick's story kept coming back to me unbidden. *Clubs and knives. Women and children. Do your duty. None left to tell. Babies in a wagon. Arm hanging by a thread.*

The second I closed my eyes, I knew I would see the gentile woman I'd seen when I dreamed of my boys picking apples in the orchard beside her children, who sat on Proctor's grave.

Because they were dead, too.

I knew who she was now. The gentile woman that Vick, *my Vick*, had killed. Then scooped her babies into a wagon.

And I suspected I knew what she'd say, when she turned her sad eyes to face me.

How could you exterminate me? My children?

My stomach was sick.

The congealed plate of food I'd tried to serve Vick last night sat untouched on the kitchen table. He'd finally shuffled off to bed, leaving me at the table alone in the dark until the wee hours of the morning.

Before he walked away, he told me that the men from the U.S. Army had moved on toward Cedar City. They already knew some of what happened at the Meadow. After nearly two years, officers had finally found the scattered bones and mass graves. One for the gentile men, who thought they were being escorted to safety. One for the gentile women and children.

Bishop Brunson hadn't told the Army men the truth of what had happened. Neither had Vick.

"Sounds like the work of Indians," was all they'd said, just as they'd sworn to do.

When I heard the sounds of Kima and my children waking in the still-dark house, I walked out into the yard, toward the orchard.

The air smelled sweet with the scent of past-ripe apples and cold dew, but all I felt was sick and numb.

When I reached Proctor's grave, I lay down in the wet grass. Then I closed my eyes, put my arm to my mouth to muffle the sound, and howled.

How could I take Amina in my arms again? How could I work side by side with Vick and the children in the orchard today? How could I keep moving and breathing, knowing what I knew?

I moved my fingers through the grass tangling over Proctor's grave, listening to the children's voices as they did their early morning chores. Every now and then I could feel their eyes on me, sending worried looks my way, probably wondering why I'd been here so long and why their father was still in bed. Why there was no breakfast on the table.

The one voice I didn't hear was Amina's, but I felt her presence, all the same.

No wonder she didn't speak, only whimpered so pitifully it broke my heart when nightmares woke her at night.

I thought of Emma Willis, little Amina's sister who'd been torn from her at the Hamblin ranch, then raised three miles apart until they both forgot their names their mothers had given them, forgot the blood in the Meadow, forgot the horror they must have endured.

I heard the crunch of footsteps and knew one of the children was drawing close, surely wondering what was happening, whether I was sick.

My bleeding heart and rolling stomach told me I was.

I squeezed my eyes shut, knowing the children weren't likely to approach me while I lay by Proctor's graveside.

So there I stayed, unmoving in the predawn dark. After a few minutes, I opened my eyes to stare at the dull green blades poking through the earth, nourished by Proctor's bones.

Had Vick fallen asleep last night? He must have. He'd managed to slumber somehow over the past three years, but now I knew why he'd wasted away like there was cancer in his bones.

I felt some of the same awful, festering burden in the pit of my stomach now, too. If it was even the tiniest portion of what he'd felt for the past three years, I understood why he'd disappeared inside himself the way he had.

Dead men. Dead women. Dead children. All unarmed. And seventeen toddlers and babies, tucked into the homes of the *saints* who'd killed their parents.

One tucked into my home.

My mind kept turning back to Sally, too. What she'd told me that night I rode out to Corn Creek to bless the injured Paiutes.

The wagon train was mostly women and children.

The wagon train hadn't poisoned the steers.

The gentiles weren't to blame for Proctor's death.

I'd never fully been able to push those words from my mind, even though it had been three years.

The Paiute women hadn't been back to my house to bake bread ever since.

Now I understood why.

Vick told me that Kanosh's men were the ones who'd stampeded the gentiles' cattle and tried to raid their wagon train on that very first morning in the Meadow. Apostle Smith, Bishop Haight, General John D. Lee, and the other leaders had given the Paiutes the guns, telling them they'd be protected from harm.

They hadn't been. I remembered seeing their wounded men.

Vick told me that when the Paiutes realized they would be shooting at terrified women and children, they gave the guns back and returned to Corn Creek.

They'd returned to their village mostly empty-handed. The white men had taken the lion's share of the cattle and the plunder in the aftermath.

And as far as I could understand, the Paiutes didn't even know that my husband had joined the other white men in painting their bodies to look like Indians after they withdrew—so they could blame them if the massacre ever came to light.

Sounds like the work of Indians, Vick and Bishop Brunson had told the U.S. Army men.

Bile rose up in my throat and I swallowed it back, pressing my cheek against the flattened grass and feeling certain, for the first time, that my boy would be ashamed of me and his papa.

I imagined Proctor looking down at me from Heaven, eyes filled with tears.

We didn't know! my mind protested weakly. *Your papa was just following his leaders. He didn't have a choice.*

He didn't want to kill anyone.

But no. The dark, dripping doubt in my belly protested. I felt the same questions rise with the bile in my stomach. The questions I'd pushed away the first time Sally said the word *locoweed*. And then again when I saw the hate on the wounded Paiutes' faces while I laid my hands on their heads in blessing.

I closed my eyes and let the sick feeling consume me.

I thought I'd known suffering in my bones.

But thinking of everything Vick had told me was a new kind of agony.

The Army men already knew about the mass graves. More than a hundred broken bodies.

But they didn't know about the tiny bodies that didn't have a grave in the Meadow.

Seventeen children, including the little girl I'd tucked into my bed beside me for the past three years.

The Army men had photos with them. Photos the gentiles' family members had sent over the years, trying to reach someone who could find out what happened to their loved ones who had set out for California. *Find my daughter. Find my son. Tell me what happened to my brother, my granddaughters.*

"Mama?" I looked up to see seven-year-old Adelia taking tentative steps toward me in the predawn light, as if she were afraid she'd startle me.

"It's all right," I croaked, but I couldn't stop my bottom lip from shaking so hard the words came out in a jumbled mess. "I'm not feeling well today, that's all."

Her lips quivered and her brows creased.

I was scaring her.

Tears streamed down my face. I could only imagine the terrified looks on the children's faces in the Meadow.

"Mama, Amina is crying," Adelia said over her shoulder. "She doesn't want me or Papa. I think she wants you."

The soft grass suddenly felt prickly beneath my cheek, and I knew it was time to get up.

I stood, feeling pushed rather than pulled from where Proctor's body curled beneath me. "Go on now, Adelia. Tell her I'll be right there."

She nodded, and seemed to stuff down any fear she had.

I followed her toward the house.

All night, I'd been wondering what I should do with what I'd learned. What responsibility did I have?

And what it came down to was that either Apostle Smith, Bishop Haight, Bishop Brunson, and the others had gotten things wrong, or that God had gotten things wrong when he told them what to do in the Meadow.

Both thoughts were equally terrifying, and I couldn't wrestle my mind into accepting either for long.

All I knew for certain, at this moment, was that seventeen children were suffering for someone's sins. Some of those sins, Vick's. And mine. And when you sinned, you repented, even if it hurt.

58. NANCY HUFF

FILLMORE, UTAH

JULY 1860

For the first time ever, I didn't care about beating the birds to the fields.

I ran through the predawn-dark furrows and between the fig trees that would finally turn a tiny harvest, letting the wheat whip at my bare arms.

Somewhere in the distance, an owl called, *who, who, who?*

Nancy, Nancy, Nancy.

I didn't know where I was going at first, wearing only my nightgown and unlaced shoes. The ones that had been Peach's and were cracking down the soles.

She'd worn them when she was my age. When she was seven. And I was supposed to be four but was really six and a half. When I'd first come to live in Fillmore.

The dirt road dipped and I saw the twice-as-big-as-ours house at the edge of the fields.

The Robisons' place.

I didn't know what time it was, but from the dim gray light above the mountains, morning was close.

Not too early for Brother and Sister Robison and their children to head to work in the orchard. They had their own birds to fight and crops to tend, after all.

But when I got closer, I saw Sister Robison standing at the edge of the orchard.

She was holding baby Tri.

I ducked and crept closer, careful not to make a sound above the noise of my ragged breathing. I crouched behind a stand of sagebrush and watched.

Why was I here?

The only thing I knew was that baby Tri was just a stone's throw away. And that, like the ring on my thumb, she was mine. Her mama had been my aunt Sissy Lou.

I watched as Sister Robison stood there, swaying back and forth, back and forth, holding Triphena, who clung to her neck, tight as anything.

When my breathing and the thudding pulse in my ear calmed, I realized Sister Robison was singing softly.

My stomach twisted again.

Tri's one arm was wrapped around Sister Robison's neck, and her fingers were laced into the long, dark hair that scattered over the woman's shoulders. The sleeve of her nightgown where she was missing an arm had been cut and neatly sewn at the shoulder, so it wouldn't hang down.

The little girl's face was scrunched up like she'd been crying.

She whimpered and buried her face against Sister Robison's shoulder.

I wondered then if the little girl had nightmares like me. Memories locked inside her tiny small body that had been barely one year old in the Meadow. She could hardly say the word "Mama" or "Papa" when it happened.

No wonder she'd never found a reason to speak, all these years.

While I stood there, memories of Sissy Lou and Uncle Uri dripped hot through my veins alongside the tears. But unlike the memories of Brother Robison and Papa and what had happened in the Meadow, these memories warmed as much as they hurt.

Sissy Lou and Uncle Uri had loved me like Mama and Papa had.

They'd loved baby Triphena, too.

And they'd want me to take care of her.

I held my breath to listen to the words Sister Robison was singing.

I wanted to hate her. Wanted to leap from the brush and tell her what I'd seen her husband do to my mama.

I'd never seen Lucy Robison with her hair down before. Standing there in the grass, in the gray dawn light, she didn't look much older than Peach.

Her lips moved and she hefted Triphena higher on her hip, still swaying back and forth, back and forth while I strained to hear the words she sang.

"Roses are red, dilly, dilly
Violets are blue
Because you love me, dilly, dilly
I will love you.
Let the birds sing, dilly, dilly
And the lambs play
We shall be safe, dilly, dilly
Out of harm's way."

I swiped at the tears running down my face, not knowing how to feel anymore.

* * *

As the orchard woke up with birds, I hid myself deeper in the brush and then watched until Adelia and Triphena stood on the porch while the rest of the Robisons prepared for work, then headed toward the irrigation ditch that ran along the west side.

When Brother Robison walked up to Sister Robison, she pulled away from him as if he'd hit her, then said something I couldn't hear.

He drew back, face turned to face me but eyes unseeing.

I studied him in a way I'd never done before.

I thought I'd feel afraid, like I did in my memories. Like I did in my nightmares. But all I felt was sick. His face looked so waxy and gaunt, it reminded me of the skin that formed on warm milk.

He reached out a hand to his wife one more time, then let it fall and hung his head.

I touched the ring on my thumb.

I couldn't understand how this Brother Robison was sad and sweet to Sister Robison and Triphena.

This Brother Robison brought picnic lunches for Peach and sat on the same pew, next to our family at church on Sunday.

I thought of a coyote I'd surprised one morning when I walked through the fig trees in the still-gray light. The wind must've been just right, because I saw her—and her pups—before she saw me. She was letting them wrestle all over her, one biting at her ear, one licking her mouth.

When she saw me, she went from docile to snarling before I could even blink.

People had a little of that in them, too, I decided.

I watched as Sister Robison followed Adelia and Triphena into the house. After a few minutes, she reappeared in the yard, dressed. I thought she was going to follow Brother Robison, Kima, and the older children into the orchard. But to my surprise, she saddled a horse. A few minutes later, she rode away.

I waited until the sound of hoofbeats faded.

Then I stood up from where I'd been hiding and walked to the house, its windows reflecting orange with the first bits of sunlight streaming over the mountains.

Through the window, I could see Adelia inside, maybe trying to coax Amina into eating some mush.

I balled my hands into fists and realized how much I wanted to take a nap behind the pot-bellied stove with Amina, even if it was in Brother Robison's home.

I shivered a little and looked down at myself, remembering that I was still only wearing my boots and nightdress. The adrenaline that kept me coiled all night, heating me, was now fading.

Had Peach already told Mama and Papa—I didn't know what other name to call them—that I'd run?

For now, they probably thought I was out in the fields. Right where I was supposed to be. But tonight, when they came home, what then? Where would I be?

My stomach felt like it might empty out when I asked myself that question.

Where *would* I be then?

Where did I think I was going? What was I supposed to do with the burning sludge of memories choking me?

The momentum that had brought me here was rolling back toward me like a rock on a hill, readying to flatten me.

What did I think I was going to do, walk through the Robisons' door, snatch up Triphena—who had no idea she was my family—and run?

Run where?

I looked to my left at the endless Utah desert beyond the fields. It was miles to the nearest town. I could walk there, but then what? Who would I tell that didn't know Brother Robison, a counselor in the bishopric. Who would I tell who didn't know Brother Willis—the man I'd called Papa only yesterday—at the mill?

Who would I tell that would feel for me—a *gentile*?

Despair made me whimper.

There had been so many Mormon military men in the Meadow. All of them with blood on their hands.

My breath came faster. A sob rose in my throat as I stumbled down the narrow dirt road running along the east side of the orchard.

I ran until I reached the far edge and then stopped.

I was nine years old. I had no plan. I had no family. I had nowhere to go.

59. KAHPEPUTZ (SALLY)

FILLMORE, UTAH

JULY 1860

I stood at the far end of the Robisons' apple orchard, hidden among the trees, and listened in the gray-dawn light.

I never thought I'd come back here.

Especially not with hope making my heart beat so hard I worried it was pounding through the orchard like a drum, pointing back to me.

The smell of sweet fruit made my mouth water, but I didn't dare reach for the apples hanging low on the nearest branches.

There. The soft, rhythmic sound came again. Footsteps.

I hugged my dress around my middle, unable to stop myself from tracing my fingers over the slight bump.

I'd stopped praying a long time ago, but I couldn't help myself.

Please let everything go to plan, I told myself.

Inola had promised me I wouldn't run into the Robisons today. The first harvest was complete, and the remaining apples wouldn't be picked for a few weeks yet. Most of the work to be done now was in preparing the irrigation ditch for the work of watering when the summer heat hit hard.

I tucked myself against the nearest tree and peered through the shady branches.

"Sally?" a quiet voice called out. Then, in Bannock, "Are you there?"

My heart leapt and I stepped from behind the tree to see a young woman holding a satchel, standing a few feet away. Her black hair hung in ringlets to her shoulders, and she wore a starched yellow dress with puff sleeves that looked just like Lucy's.

When she saw me, she waved and hurried closer. She winced when she saw my bruised face and jagged haircut but didn't comment. "Kima," she said, pointing to herself. Then, "I have everything Inola asked me to gather."

She smiled like we shared a secret—which I guess we did—and looked over her shoulder. "I can't stay long. They'll miss me." She pulled a pink gingham dress from her satchel, along with a bonnet, shoes, and stockings.

All of the clothes looked starched and scratchy, and the fabric was ugly and faded but I eagerly took the clothing from her. It would cover me from head to toe, and was far nicer than the torn, bedraggled crinoline dress I'd been wearing for the past three years.

To any casual observer, I'd look just like a Fillmore Mormon woman.

If any of the Mormons or the Paiutes happened to see me walking along the road, they wouldn't see "Sally Indian," and that was all I needed.

"Good luck," Kima told me gently, thrusting the open satchel into my hands. What remained inside was heavy with the necessities I'd need. A thin blanket. Just enough food and water for a three-day walk.

"Thank you," I told her, but she was already gone, running back through the orchard almost before the words were out of my mouth.

I stood where I was for a few seconds, thinking of the stories I'd told Sweet Pea while we walked back and forth to Corn Creek all those days. Stories about me and Awan's imaginary life together.

Maybe, finally, they would come true.

My hands shook while I changed into the clothing and shoved my dingy old dress and moccasins into the satchel, careful to pull the little yucca horse out first.

There were no pockets on this dress, I realized as I buttoned it.

I was about to tuck the horse into the bag when I heard footsteps, fast and light, approaching along the orchard.

I froze where I was, eyes scanning the half-light orchard. Was it one of the Robisons? Maybe Lucy? Had Kima forgotten something?

My mouth dropped open as a little girl, tall and skinny with her dark curly hair wild around her face, ran alongside the orchard on the dirt path and stopped in her tracks. I shrank back and stared at her, confused. She was breathing hard, wearing what looked like nightclothes.

As if she could feel my eyes on her, she whipped her head around and peered through the trees.

I stayed perfectly still in the shadows of the trees.

She didn't see me. But I could see her.

As she rocked from one foot to the other, running her hands along her arms despite the heat, I realized she was just a child. Not more than ten or eleven. When I squinted, I could see that her eyes were red-rimmed and her cheeks were tear-stained.

She slowly spun in my direction, chin tilted skyward and fresh tears dripping down her flushed cheeks.

Then she whimpered a little, and I felt my own mouth drop open ever so slightly as the memory came rushing back like a wave.

It couldn't be her.

I took a step forward, crouching, disbelieving.

It was her.

I remembered those eyes, those curls, that sadness coming off of her in waves.

For a moment, it felt like I'd been dropped back into that clearing in the scrub oak, three years earlier where I found her crying the first time.

She was alive. She was *alive*. How was she alive?

For another few seconds, I didn't move, unsure what to do. I needed to keep moving. What good would come of showing myself?

I could slink away into the middle of the orchard easily enough, hurry down the dirt road on the other side like I was supposed to before daylight broke fully.

Each second I stayed in the Robisons' orchard was a risk that I'd be recognized by someone who remembered "Sally Indian." And if I were recognized, the plan would be ruined.

Especially if this girl told anyone what she'd seen.

But somehow, I knew she wouldn't.

She turned away from the orchard and hung her head, moving east. In a few more seconds, she'd be gone.

She made another sound like she had that first day I'd seen her in the scrub oak three years earlier, only this time she wasn't wailing out loud. She was trying to shove it down, keep quiet.

My heart beat harder, twisting painfully in my chest.

"Nancy," I whispered, so quietly she couldn't hear me. I moved through the grass, through the trees, drawn to the girl. Then loud enough that she startled where she stood, I called her name again. "Nancy."

She stopped and whirled around. Her eyes were wide, desperate, but not afraid. She looked like she was hoping to see someone she recognized.

When I stepped into view from behind the trees, she stopped and took in my stolen pink gingham dress and rough-cut hair peeking from beneath my stolen bonnet. "Who are you?" she whispered in a shaky voice, moving closer to me.

I shook my head, unsure what to tell her.

She studied my face, her brows knitting together and then suddenly parting as she whispered, *"Oh."*

Fresh tears dripped down her cheeks, and she reared back in astonishment. "Oh, I remember you now."

Then she crumpled to the orchard floor so fast, I thought for a moment she'd tripped. Instead, she fell to her knees in a daze, staring at the little yucca horse I held out in my hand.

"They're gone," she choked, eyes on the grass. "They're all gone."

I didn't know how to make sense of the events that had brought her here, of our past, why we were here now in this orchard together like a strange dream.

Part of me wondered if all of this *were* a dream, and maybe I was still back in the Paiute village asleep in my wickiup. So instead of asking questions, I told her the same thing I'd said three years earlier.

"The dead are never really gone," I whispered.

She jerked her head up and shook her head. "No, they're *gone,"* she gasped. "They're gone and I'm here. And I'm all alone." She opened her mouth in a wordless cry, eyes blazing and red.

"You're not alone." I said softly, feeling the truth of it this time.

"But I don't have a mama anymore," she cried, the tears pouring faster. "I need my mama. And my papa. My sister Mary. My ..." She shook her head and bit down on her lip to keep the wails inside.

"They're still with you," I repeated, no longer trying to stop the tears pouring down my own cheeks. "I lost my mama too. And my papa. My home. I didn't know they were still with me, but they were. All this time."

She looked at me and shook her head, disbelieving. "How?"

I swallowed thinking of Awan, of Inola. I touched my hands to my belly, imagining the little flutter of hope inside. "You'll know you found them, because they'll help you find your way back home," I told her, not knowing any other way to say it.

She nodded and went quiet for a few seconds.

"I have a cousin," she whispered finally. "She's my family. But I don't think she remembers."

I took another step toward her, holding out the little yucca horse I'd kept back in my pocket all those years ago.

"For someday when she does," I said as she took it.

60. LUCY ROBISON

FILLMORE, UTAH

JULY 1860

I had been gone longer than I'd planned, following the dusty road outside of Fillmore. My horse seemed inclined to take small steps, and I didn't urge him faster.

Were my children worried?

No. The children would have wandered to the pond to play by now. Surely they'd finished the day's chores and their work at the irrigation ditch.

Vick had likely drifted into the orchard, the one place that seemed to give him some peace.

I already knew I wouldn't tell him what I was about to do. Maybe someday when I had time to sort through all the wrongs and how they began.

Maybe never.

All I knew was that for now, we'd all have our secrets.

I'd rehearsed and rehearsed what I wanted to say to the Army men when I found them, and what I'd tell them if they insisted I give them my name. Or if they recognized me as Vick's wife.

But when I finally saw the dust from their horses and wagons outside Fillmore, all the words left my mind.

"Ma'am," the general said when I stopped my horse within a stone's throw of his horse.

My stomach clenched. Not Sister. "Ma'am." As if I were a gentile.

He looked at me quizzically, like I was familiar to him, but he couldn't remember my name. That made my stomach relax a little. I tucked my chin down to hide the tears that dribbled down my cheeks.

"Ma'am, are you lost?"

Yes, a voice screamed loud in my head, surprising me with its ferocity.

"No," I choked.

Another Army man circled his horse to stand beside the general, and my head felt so dizzy and light that for a second I worried I might topple off my horse.

Like Proctor had that day.

Tell them, Mama, his voice urged, sounding less like a fourteen-year-old boy and more like a man.

I swallowed hard, then opened my mouth that stuck like it was filled with molasses and gasped, "The children."

The rest tumbled out in bits and starts. Not enough to make a full accounting. Not a tenth of what Vick had confessed to me.

But enough.

Just enough for the general to start barking soft orders to the other men when I went silent.

I'd wheeled my horse around before they thought to insist on my name—or Vick's. Before they could see the tears streaming down my cheeks and into my mouth that let out a wordless howl as I finally pushed the horse into a run.

When the dirt road cut south along a rocky rise, I could just make out the first wickiups beyond Corn Creek. There were women washing clothing on a large rock near the creek's edge, while little ones played nearby.

Their laughter, floating toward me on the breeze, sounded just like my children.

That was when I finally stopped the horse and slumped in the saddle.

I couldn't go back to Fillmore. Not until the Army men were gone.

A trail of black smoke rose from the center of camp. A snatch of sound that might have been a wail or a coyote drifted past then faded. I turned the buckskin toward home and looked away from the smoke.

"I'm sorry," I whispered past the tightness in my throat, but even to my own ears it sounded like little more than wind through the grass.

SERMON EXCERPT

"To this day, they have not touched the matter for fear the Mormons would be acquitted from the charge of having any hand in [the massacre], and our enemies would be deprived of a favorite topic to talk about when urging hostility against us. 'The Mountain Meadows Massacre. Only think of the Mountain Meadows Massacre!' is their cry from one end of the land to the other."

— Brigham Young

61. NANCY HUFF

FILLMORE, UTAH

JULY 1860

Peach found me at the edge of the orchard, holding the little horse in one hand and the ring still clutched in the other.

"Sissy," she said, her face red and puffy from crying. She wasn't wearing her nightdress anymore, but she hadn't bothered to comb her hair. She looked wild and unscrubbed and snarly. Like the way I felt most days.

Peach glanced from me to the Robisons' house. "She's theirs," she said, and I knew she meant Triphena.

Then her face bunched up, and I could tell she was about to cry as she took a step closer and put her hand on my arm. "And you're ours. Come home."

So I let Peach lead me by the arm, like a lost lamb.

I didn't unclench my hand. She didn't try to take the ring away from me again.

Not-Mama would, though, when she got back home tonight.

She and Not-Papa were already gone for the day by the time we walked into the dusty yard. Violet was waiting on the porch, her face full of sunshine that clouded over when she saw me. I was supposed to be working. Every day except Wednesdays, I stayed in the fields from sunup to sundown.

"Emma?"

"She's not feeling good, Violet," Peach soothed, like she'd planned out what she was going to say. "We're going to put her to bed so she can rest."

Violet lifted an eyebrow. She was little, but she wasn't stupid. The kind of sick that got you out of chores was the kind of sick that made getting out of bed impossible. "She doesn't look sick."

That was the moment my gut finally let go of the knot it'd been twisting, and I vomited what little I had in my stomach all over the front porch.

Violet scrambled to her feet. "Oh, no. Oh, no, Emma."

"Hush, Violet," Peach snapped, then gently took me by the arm. "It'll be all right," she told me, tucking the quilt around my body as I let her put me to bed.

I nodded, not meeting her eyes. For once, I felt sure I wouldn't have nightmares anymore when I fell asleep. It didn't feel like relief, though. Being awake was the new nightmare, and there was no escape from that.

They're still with you. The words the Indian woman said still echoed in my ears, but I wasn't sure I could believe them.

"I'll bring you some water," Peach began.

"No!" I cut her off. "Just … no." Then I closed my eyes and curled into a ball on the bed. The shaky feeling that had gone away while I ran was back. My teeth chattered, even though I wasn't cold, and my body shuddered like I had a fever, even though I wasn't hot.

The bedroom door clunked shut.

It felt like my skin was too tight and my brain too full. Like if I shook for much longer, I'd burst right through it, spilling my insides out.

I wanted my mama. My *real* mama, alive again. Not the muttering, angry woman who would come back to me tonight.

Terror made me shake even harder as I imagined what she would do when she realized I knew the truth. The man I'd called Papa would disappear into himself, like he'd always done. Barely there. The woman I'd called Mama, on the other hand, would be angry.

I could almost hear the words she'd say. *Ungrateful wretch.*

How could I keep doing my chores, keep calling her Mama? I knew I had to, but the idea of doing any of those everyday things made me want to throw up all over again. I'd always been cowlicked and wild, but I'd tried my best to be a good girl. Tried my best to be sweet and obedient. I didn't want to try anymore. I wanted to bite and kick and scream and run.

But there was nowhere *to* run. Like Peach said, this was my home now. *You're ours.*

I squeezed my eyes shut harder and tried to begin a prayer in my mind, since my teeth were clenched too hard to speak out loud.

Dear Heavenly Father ...

My mind went blank.

All I wanted was my mama.

I reached under the bed and found the second toy horse the Indian woman had given me, tucking it carefully under my arm with the first.

Then I kept my eyes squeezed shut and pretended that the soft pull of the quilt tucked around my shoulders was really arms hugging me tight.

Little by little, my breathing turned slower and my mind went blank.

And then I fell asleep.

And for the first time in my whole life, I had a dream I didn't want to end.

"Mama," I whispered through tears, and she kissed my head in response. I snuggled against her body and breathed in a smell I couldn't identify but I wanted to memorize. I knew without looking that I was tucked behind the Robisons' stove and that Triphena was tucked beneath her other arm.

And I knew without asking that she both was and wasn't the mama I'd lost in the Meadow.

"You're mine, and I love you," she murmured. "Always have. Always will."

And it felt so good to believe her.

* * *

I slept until I heard the sound of hoofbeats in the front yard.

The first thing I felt as I scrambled upright in bed was longing to fall back asleep. To stay tucked in that dream safe and sound.

The second was a burst of fear.

I'd slept all day long. Not-Mama and Not-Papa were home. What would happen now? I leaped to my feet, heart pounding hard again, determined they wouldn't catch me in bed.

Peach was out there, and Violet. I could hear their high, sweet voices but couldn't make out the words, except that they sounded afraid.

My chest seized and I looked around the tiny bedroom like a wild animal, spinning the ring on my thumb around and around.

There was nowhere to run. Nowhere to go. Nowhere to hide.

So I wouldn't.

I balled my hands into fists and clenched my jaw until the fear let go.

Beloved, beloved, beloved.

With those words echoing in my ears, I pushed open the bedroom door, walked through the kitchen, and into the front yard, not bothering to put my boots on.

I wouldn't let them find me cowering. If Not-Mama wanted to lash me, I'd hand her the willow switch and look her dead in the eye. I already hurt as much as a person could hurt.

But I *wasn't* a wretch. And I *wasn't* hers.

Beloved, beloved, beloved.

I took two steps into the front yard and stopped.

There was Peach, there was Violet. But instead of grown-ups I recognized, I saw two men on horseback and one standing on the ground, holding his horse's reins in one hand and some kind of thin, black book in the other.

All three were wearing smart-looking blue uniforms. Everyone turned to look at me.

My face burned hot, and my mind felt foggy and slow. There was a wagon coming up behind the men on horseback—but not one I recognized. As the wagon came into view, I saw another Army man in a blue uniform, with a little girl sitting beside him on the bench seat.

Triphena, holding a little cloth doll, her puffy face streaked with tears.

As the wagon wheels stopped turning, the little girl scrambled down from the seat before the man holding the reins could stop her.

Then she ran to me and hugged my waist. I hugged her back hard, like I'd wanted to do when I stood outside her window that morning. She burrowed into my dress, tiny body shaking.

"I have a present for you," I told her, realizing I was still clutching both toy horses in my hand.

Her eyes brightened for a moment as she took it, then buried her face in my dress again.

The Army man driving the wagon looked flustered, as if Tri wasn't supposed to run away from him, but he didn't go after her. The officer holding his horse by the reins glanced at the other men, then at Peach. After a few seconds, he walked toward me and Triphena.

He was holding something out to me—the thin, black book. He glanced at it one more time then held it out so I could see.

"Oh," I breathed, the only sound I could make.

It wasn't a book after all. It was a delicate photograph in a black velvet case, like one I'd seen hanging on the wall in the Robisons' home. They were the only family in Fillmore who could afford to pay twenty-five cents when the photographer came through.

The thin paper tucked into the velvet case looked so delicate, I didn't want to touch it for fear of hurting it. But I couldn't keep my fingers from hovering over the top.

The Army man didn't try to stop me.

In the photograph was a family.

My family.

In the middle, sitting on some kind of bench, was Papa. Taller than any of us by a head. Curly, dark hair and pale eyes that seemed to look right through into my soul. Mary leaned against him on one side, William on the other. James stood behind him, one hand resting on Papa's shoulder.

My eyes moved to Mama, her dark hair curled around her ears in thick, graceful ribbons. And on her lap was a little girl, frowning in concentration, wrapped up in a frozen hug.

The little girl looked just like Triphena.

It wasn't Triphena though, it was me.

Nancy.

A new memory leaped through the fog. Only this time, it didn't burn.

I remembered sitting for that photo. We'd had to stay perfectly still for what felt like forever—sixty seconds, the camera man counted. Papa told me I'd done a very good job, and I knew I had. If I'd had to sit on the bench by myself, I would have wiggled. But I could relax against Mama's chest, and I knew she'd keep both of us still.

337

Before I could say a thing, the officer handed me another slim velvet case.

Another photograph.

A tall man with a thick, fluffy beard, a bald head, and a smart black vest. He stood with his arm on the shoulder of a seated woman. At first, I didn't know him. Then my eyes flicked to the woman, the tilt of her nose and the rise of her cheeks familiar to me before I could remember the word I'd called her. It hovered in the back of my mind then whispered through.

Nana.

She was my grandmother. And the man was my grandfather. These were Papa's parents. The ones we'd left behind when we packed up our wagon in Arkansas. I couldn't pull a single memory to the surface of what their voices sounded like or what kind of grandparents they'd been, but I knew they'd loved me, sure as anything.

"Do you know those people?" the Army man was saying. I blinked and looked up at him. His voice was gentle, but his face was as stern and unsmiling as the people in the photographs.

"Yes," I managed. "That's my mama and my papa and Mary and William and James." I pointed out each person in the first photograph, then looked at the second.

Triphena lifted her head from my dress for the first time to look, too.

Her eyes went wide as she studied the photograph of my family. "Papa?" she whispered haltingly, her tiny hand pointing out the man who wasn't her papa but was the spitting image of Uncle Uri.

Peach drew in a sharp breath. It was the first time any of us had heard the little girl speak.

I swallowed hard. "Yes, your papa looked just like that."

Triphena looked directly at me, her eyes wide as saucers.

I pointed to my own chest. "Nancy," I told her, knowing the word she was searching for.

"Nancy," she said, like my name had been just waiting for her to find it.

I burst into tears all over again and hugged her tight, because I didn't know what else in the world to do.

62. KAHPEPUTZ (SALLY)

MOUNT TIMPANOGUS, UTAH
JULY 1860

The sun had gone down hours earlier, but I stayed right where I was, at the big rocky ledge that, if followed, led up to jagged peaks that looked like a sleeping woman lying on her side.

Yes, this was the place I was meant to wait, I reassured myself for the thousandth time.

Before Inola had sent me on my way to the Robisons' orchard, she'd told me the story of jagged-looking peaks above the thin waterfall that dribbled down their side in the summer heat.

I would know the place when I found it, if I kept walking for three days. And my story would be different from the woman the weeping waterfall had been named for.

Uconogos was a Native woman whose forbidden love had died trying to meet her at the top of the mountain. In despair, she'd thrown herself off the tall peaks. Inola said her tears still dripped down the mountain, on and on, making this canyon waterfall.

When I found Uconogos's tears, I was supposed to wait on the ledge where the seldom-used, hardscrabble road leading into the mountains ended.

"You will wait with Uconogos. But you will not join her, no matter what," Inola had told me firmly, lacing her fingers gently around me and pulling me close, her lips brushing my cheek that was still sore from when I'd brought the rock against it.

At a glance, I looked like a dusty Mormon woman in my pink dress and bonnet.

On closer inspection, I looked like a bruised melon. Face and arms battered just enough that Numa and Povi had started to look at

339

me with the slightest hint of pity. They—and Kanosh—were quick to notice that Inola and I had fallen out when we returned from the caves the day Keme died.

Nobody did anything to stop the way she began to seemingly torment me, of course. It was Inola's right as first wife, and Keme's grieving sister. Over the past month, I had come back from collecting water with a growing number of suspicious bruises and cuts.

I would make a point of shrinking back from Inola whenever we crossed paths in the village.

Kanosh had laughed when he came into our wickiup to find her tipping nettles onto my bed one night.

It wasn't pleasant. Not on the outside. But on the inside, my body hummed with sparks like an approaching storm.

And then, the night I insulted Kanosh, Inola had taken me to Corn Creek for the last time.

No one in camp followed us.

Inola took a knife to my hair until it was cut short and ragged all around. Then we dragged a sharp rock across my arms, letting the blood flow to the ground until she stopped it with a strip from my dress.

We'd strewn pieces of my hair all over the dried purple flowers still peeking through the cattails at Corn Creek, matted and scattered along with some of my torn clothing, blood and some entrails from the rabbits I'd had hidden in the pitch baskets.

Afterward, Inola had walked back to camp without me, blood on her hands, to let the others know of my fate. A puma, she'd say. Of course, everyone would know Inola had done it.

What they wouldn't know, if all went to plan, was that she'd sent me off with a brief embrace before I ran for Lucy Robison's orchard as fast as I could go in the darkness to meet Kima the following morning.

And a little girl I'd thought was dead.

Before I escaped, I learned that the Army men had told Kanosh that there would be an inquiry about the murdered gentiles in the Meadow by something called Congress. And that the new governor of Utah, Alfred Cummings, was willing to offer asylum to anyone who wanted to leave Utah Territory with protection. Especially those who were willing to speak about what happened at Mountain Meadows.

Inola had been sure she'd be able to convince the Paiutes to send someone to reveal the secrets we'd kept for almost three years. Secretly, of course. At the fort in Wyoming, where the Army men would be returning.

Awan would volunteer to go.

And Inola, as his mother—and the chief's wife—would give him permission.

Kanosh would try to stop him. But others—including Elu—would support Awan's decision.

Inola told me that most of the Paiute men were still haunted by what had happened in the Meadow. Haunted by the faces of the terrified women and children they'd seen peering above the trench their men had dug for protection. They'd been horrified then about what the Mormons were about to do. And they were still horrified now. Especially now that they wondered what it had all been for.

Would Awan succeed? Would he find me, on his way to Wyoming? Would our plan work?

I closed my eyes and listened to the slow drip of water down the side of the darkening canyon.

I hadn't seen another soul in three days. I was out of food, out of supplies. I was tired all the way to my bones, and not nearly warm enough even with the threadbare blanket.

I held my breath as fast footsteps, too light to be human, whispered through the trees behind me.

My heart pounded hard and I whipped around. I could handle the calculated bruises and insults, the nettles in my bed, the whispers and the stares as I fell further into my role as pariah. But tears sprang to my eyes when I thought about what would happen if this plan didn't work.

What if I stayed here in the trees all night long, shivering in the dark, feet blistered from walking so many miles in too-small shoes on dirt roads?

What if morning arrived and I was still alone?

I wrapped my hands tighter around my stomach. *Point me home,* I prayed silently to everyone I had ever loved and lost.

"Awan?" I whispered, pretending I could hear hoofbeats but knowing it was just the sound of my own heartbeat thudding.

More snapping twigs. More rustling.

I reached for the knife in the satchel Kima had given me, terrified at the thought that I might have to use it. I wouldn't be a match for a puma or a pack of coyotes.

"Kahpe!"

The sound of my own name—my real name—came from within the dark, skinny pines.

The branches parted. And there he was—not on the paint mare like I'd expected, but on foot, running fast toward me.

Awan.

"I'm sorry it took me so long to find you, I had to leave the mare when the ground got too rocky, I was so worried—"

He stopped talking and took me into his arms, burying his face against my short, uneven hair.

Even feeling his heartbeat against mine, I still couldn't believe it. That he'd really leave his home, his family, everything he'd known, to be here in the middle of the wilderness. But the way he held onto me told me that, in time, I would.

The tears ran down my face hot and fast, the waterfall Inola had warned me not to become.

I didn't know where we'd spend our lives. That notion was still as murky as the night that surrounded us. In my heart, I wondered if, after Wyoming, maybe we might search for the Bannock and my true family whose faces I couldn't remember anymore but whose memories filled my belly with a longing for home.

Was my mother still out there? My father? My brothers and sisters?

I curled my fingers into Awan's shirt and breathed him in, feeling safe for the first time in so long.

In a few weeks, Awan would send word to his mother that he had arrived at the Army fort in Wyoming, to tell the officers everything he knew about what had happened in the Meadow. A few weeks after that, he'd send word that he had fallen in love with a Bannock girl named Kahpeputz and would not be returning home.

No one would question him.

No one else knew my name.

63. NANCY HUFF

BENTONVILLE, ARKANSAS

SEPTEMBER 1860

The Army men gave me a chance to say goodbye to Not-Mama and Not-Papa in Fillmore, but I told them no. I didn't want to.

I cried when I hugged Peach for the last time though, and Violet.

I cried when Kima Robison came bursting into the yard and ran after the wagon, calling for Amina, begging the men to bring her back. Triphena wailed too, and as I held her tight against me I thought about how both ends of the time we spent in Fillmore were spent rocking in a wagon full of hurt.

There were other children who traveled with us, in more wagons driven by other Army men. Seventeen, in all. The oldest was thirteen, a little girl with bright red hair and a scar on her cheek that I knew better than to ask about. The youngest was the same age as Tri, barely more than a toddler.

For the most part, we kept to ourselves, tucked into our own places in the wagon, wondering what would become of us. The Army men said they were taking us back to our families, in Arkansas. What was left of our families, at least. Everyone had an aunt or a grandmother waiting there. They'd been trying to find out what happened to us and our mamas and papas and brothers and sisters for nearly three years. They'd sent their precious photographs with the Army, knowing they might never get them back.

At first, everybody thought us kids were dead.

But when the Army men started looking at the mass graves in the Meadow, they realized that the bodies didn't line up with Captain Alexander's list of travelers. Some were missing. Seventeen children's bodies, to be exact.

We were a surprise, tucked away into Utah Mormon families, scattered from Cedar City to Salt Lake.

The Army men said the newspapers were talking about all of us. That there were people waiting to scoop us up when we arrived.

Some of the children looked afraid when they said this. Others couldn't stop crying, no matter how many miles we traveled. I felt a nervous kind of hope fluttering in my chest at the idea of being scooped up into arms that wanted me so much they'd been trying to find me for years.

It took a long time to get back to Arkansas, and while we went, I told Tri every single thing I could remember about her mama and papa and my mama and papa and everyone else who loved us before the awful thing happened.

Some of it I made up, since I couldn't remember. Every time Tri —who let me call her Tri without a fuss—asked me for "another story," I couldn't help myself but tell one. It felt like a little miracle that she'd said anything at all.

Some of the memories really did come back, and those were the ones that made the long trip pass in a blur.

"We called your mama Sissy Lou," I told Tri. "She hardly let anybody else carry you except Mary. And then she fussed so much with your bonnet, worried you'd get sun in your eyes, that Mary always had to give you back before long.

"Our papas were strong. They could take the big heavy yoke off the wagon like it was nothing. My papa, your uncle, would sing them a song and they'd close their big old eyes and stand there calm and quiet. We liked the song, too."

Tri sighed against me like some part of her remembered, even though I knew she couldn't. "Sing it."

The words whispered around my mind like leaves in the wind.

"And joy be to you all," I sang softly over and over.

* * *

The Army men seemed to delight in spoiling us, preparing stews and biscuits for dinner that made my mouth water every time we stopped for the night. Once, after a rider appeared in camp, they gave us red lollipops after dinner.

I got the feeling the men were as uneasy as us children, at first. These stiff, uniformed men with their shiny brass buttons and wide-brimmed hats. But as the miles went by, they seemed to take it as their own personal goal to draw smiles from even the most tearful children.

And by the time we pulled into Bentonville, I saw some of those big men wipe their eyes just like us kids.

There was a group of people gathered to meet the wagons, standing outside a red-brick store with glass windows.

There in the streets were men and women wearing clothing I'd never seen back in Fillmore. Fancy dresses of all different colors, shaped like bells. Men in smart jackets that almost looked like the Army men's uniforms, but longer. Some of the women wore delicate shawls over their shoulders.

To my surprise, Triphena didn't shrink against me. Instead, she joined me and a couple of the other kids in gawking out the side of the wagon flaps as it rolled to a stop.

My eyes scanned the crowd that was beginning to rush toward us. People were talking excitedly. Some were crying. My heart beat faster.

I'd learned that me and Tri's grandparents were named Eliza and William Huff.

My eyes landed on a tall, thin woman with salt-and-pepper curls peeking out from her hat. She stood next to a man with a bald head and a fluffy white beard. She gripped his arm harder, and her mouth puckered in a way that I knew she was about to cry.

"Nancy." Her mouth formed the word, even though I couldn't hear her yet.

Then, "Tri."

She reached out a hand to the woman and man standing beside her, not taking her eyes off me.

The commotion on the street turned into a dull roar that quieted when I moved my gaze to the people standing beside her. There were an elderly man and woman who looked so much like Mama it made my teeth hurt.

The Army men hadn't said anything about Mama's parents. Just Papa's. But there they were, all four of my grandparents, like memories brought to life.

We stared at each other for a long time, and I could read in their eyes that they were seeing ghosts in me and Tri, too.

Then all four of them rushed forward, jostling through the crowd to scoop us up and hold us tight.

AFTERWORD

I was a Mormon girl for most of my life. My immediate and extended family are a stronghold of devout members of The Church of Jesus Christ of Latter-Day Saints (the preferred name for the religious organization). I grew up singing songs about pioneer children crossing the plains with handcarts. I learned about the heartbreaking stories of Haun's Mill and Winter Quarters, where violent mobs killed and harmed Mormons for their religious and political beliefs. I read *The Book of Mormon*, attended Brigham Young University, married in the temple, and served as a Relief Society President.

I was a believer, through and through. So were my ancestors— several of whom inspired main characters in this novel. Lucrecia (Lucy) Robison and Joseph Robison Jr. (who I renamed Vick to avoid confusion with the other key Joseph in this story) are my great, great, great grandparents. The Robisons helped settle Fillmore, Utah, and their apple orchards still grow there today. Proctor Hancock Robison was my great, great, great uncle.

Lucy was a devout woman who did her best to live a life of faith. She and Joseph were so eager to be baptized into the LDS faith that they cut a hole through the ice in the Oswego River. Soon after, Lucy and her family traveled west to Utah to escape religious persecution. From all accounts, she struggled there, saying, *"If these rocky mountains were made of gold I would gladly give them all for old New York state . . . it is only because of my testimony of the gospel that I came here and that I remain here."*

Lucy's grandson Albert's account of the wagon train headed for Mountain Meadows states this: *"A vivious [sic] company of travellers [sic] moved southward through Utah enroute to California. Among them were some vindictive Missouri Mobsters, and in their hatred of the Mormons, they left poison in some of the springs or water-holes where they camped . . . Among the animals that died from poison was a cow ... Cowhides were too valuable to*

347

waste at that time, and the fourteen-year-old boy, Proctor, was sent to skin the cow. While he was engaged in this job, his face itched, and without thinking he scratched it with his stained fingers. The mischief was done; neither his mother nor any medical skill could counteract the deadly effects of what those murderous people had put in the water. He was struck down in the bloom of youth. " There is no mention of what happened next.

While it's true that Proctor's death near Corn Creek fueled false rumors about the gentile wagon train poisoning the creek and steers, his parents did not, to my knowledge, participate in the massacre itself or adopt surviving children. That said, many of the men who participated in the killing remain anonymous. Church leaders and citizens of Utah Territory worked diligently to hide all knowledge of the massacre, and most men who participated kept their oaths to blame the massacre on Native people and hide the events from anyone, including their wives.

In 2011, the LDS Church exhumed Proctor Robison's body in an effort to investigate longstanding rumors that his death was caused by poison left by the California-bound wagon train. While the soil samples proved inconclusive given the amount of time that had passed since his death, historians theorize that "cattle anthrax" (an infectious disease in cattle that can cause violent death in humans) or toxic levels of locoweed consumed by the cattle were the likely causes of his death—not poison.

I thought I knew the story of Mountain Meadows before I started writing this book. The tragedy came up from time to time as a side note in the history of Utah pioneers. For most of my life, I had a vague idea that some Native Americans—and maybe a couple of wayward Mormons—had ambushed a wagon train and killed a number of settlers.

I was deeply wrong.

The LDS Church did not acknowledge responsibility or officially apologize for what happened at Mountain Meadows until 2007. The LDS Church has purchased the land where the Mountain Meadows Massacre took place and maintains a memorial there.

The topic of Mountain Meadows is still taboo, and many leaders and members still perpetuate false narratives about Native people planning and executing the attack, or the Arkansas wagon train provoking the attack by poisoning a creek and ultimately killing Proctor Robison.

It's worth noting that the state of Missouri did not officially rescind—or apologize for—the governor's Mormon Extermination Order—until 1976.

I have spent the past several years researching and reading every credible source I can find about the events that took place at Mountain Meadows (about an hour south of Cedar City, Utah) in 1857. If you are interested in learning more about the Mountain Meadows Massacre, I strongly recommend *Blood of the Prophets* by Will Bagley; *Vengeance Is Mine* by Barbara Jones Brown and Richard E. Turley Jr.; *Massacre at Mountain Meadows* by Glen M. Leonard, Richard E. Turley Jr., and Ronald W. Walker; and *The Mountain Meadows Massacre* by Juanita Brooks.

The vast majority of the names, events, places, quotes, and people in this book are historically accurate and based on careful research. Some characters (like Kanosh and the Robisons) are composites, who represent the experiences of several real people. The story itself is so captivating and outrageous that, if anything, I had to resist the urge to tone down certain events for the sake of believability. Any choices I made to deviate from real chronology, names, events, or details were made for the sake of condensing this story into a cohesive narrative. Whenever possible, I made every effort to stay true to real events.

The term "Paiute" is another notable composite. While there is evidence that Southern Paiutes did agree to help raid wagon trains' cattle at Mormon leaders' urging, it is extremely difficult to parse out which individuals might have played a role in the massacre. Because of local government and church leaders' decision to scapegoat Native people, rumors and blatantly false narratives persist to this day. Historians essentially agree on one thing: The attack was overwhelmingly planned, perpetrated, and covered up by white Mormons in Utah Territory.

Sally's character is based on Sally Young Kanosh, whose given name was Kahpeputz. She was kidnapped from her village when she was seven years old and sold to Brigham Young's fourth wife Clara as an indentured servant. She was later "gifted" to the real Chief Kanosh at Corn Creek near Fillmore as a plural wife. Chief Kanosh was baptized as a Latter-day Saint and, along with many Native

349

leaders, met with Brigham Young regularly. It's unknown what became of Kahpeputz, but there's some speculation she may have been killed by another of Kanosh's wives.

Preserving and sharing Sally's story was particularly important to me in writing this book. The story of the Mountain Meadows Massacre is a painful subject for descendants everywhere, but particularly for Native people in Utah who suffered and were scapegoated for this crime for generations. Rumors STILL persist among Latter-day Saints that the Mountain Meadows Massacre was an "all-Indian massacre." This blame, coupled with the fact that the United States government unapologetically massacred thousands of Native people in the spirit of "manifest destiny", is horrifying and heartbreaking. I'm grateful to early readers with Native heritage who were willing to read this difficult material and help me stay true to Kahpeputz's story and culture.

It feels important to note that because Brigham Young was the registered "Indian Agent" of Utah Territory, he had access to funds that were supposed to be used in preserving relationships with Native people and providing safe passage for wagons headed west. Instead, Brigham Young used these funds and his position of power to manipulate Native people into aligning with the Mormon church against the government. To Young and religious leaders at the time, this fulfilled the prophecy in *The Book of Mormon* that *"If the Gentiles do not repent,"* the so-called "Lamanites" would *"cut off"* their enemies.

There is a great deal of documented evidence that, when the U.S. government moved to remove Brigham Young as governor, he authorized and encouraged cattle raids, in an effort to illustrate just how dangerous passage through Utah could become if he were removed as governor. A letter from Daniel Wells with instructions from Brigham Young to militia leaders stated, *"Instruct the Indians that our enemies are also their enemies ... [the Native people] must be our friends and stick to us, for if our enemies kill us off, they will surely be cut off by the same parties."*

Historians generally agree that what happened at Mountain Meadows was intended to be another large cattle raid that then escalated to violence.

Katrina's character is based on Saleta Huff, widow of Peter Huff, who died in the Mountain Meadows massacre. Her daughter, Nancy Saphrona Huff, survived. She was adopted by the Willis family in the aftermath. She said of the massacre, *"The Mormons got all the plunder. I saw many of the things afterward. John Willis had in his family, bed clothes, clothing, and many other things. When I claimed the things, they told me I was a liar and tried to make me believe it was the Indians that killed and plundered our people, but I knew better."*

Seventeen children, the oldest just six and the youngest infants, survived the massacre. They were chosen based on their age, being *"too young to tell tales."* These survivors were taken to the home of Rachel and Jacob Hamblin, who lived near the Meadow. While the fifty or sixty men who had carried out the massacre returned to hide what they had done, bury bodies, and redirect the approaching Duke wagon train, Rachel Hamblin cared for the children that long night. She later described that horrifying scene, *"In the darkness of night ... most of them with their parents' blood still wet upon their clothes, and all of them shrieking with terror and grief and anguish."*

While seventeen children survived the massacre, many others did not. In a Sacrament meeting service held immediately after the massacre, Lee spoke at the pulpit, bragging that he had killed a father and child with a single bullet—when the father refused to give up his baby.

In the weeks and months after the massacre, Church leaders worked diligently to deter anyone who might reveal what had happened at the Meadow, encouraging members to keep silent. Isaac Haight delivered a sermon in which he told everyone to *"Join the [k]no[w] nothings, to mind our own business and hold our tongues."* Other sermons encouraged church members to *"Know nothing that will injure our brethren in righteousness."*

The surviving children were scattered among homes across Southern Utah. Many, into homes of the men who had murdered their families in front of their eyes. Most were rebaptized, given new names, and told to forget what they had seen at the Meadow.

When the United States Army emancipated the children and returned them to their relatives in Arkansas, some of the families actually attempted to bill the US government for the food and shelter they had provided the children after the massacre.

The true scope of what had happened at Mountain Meadows didn't come to light until twenty years after the event took place. Federal authorities indicted twelve men for the Mountain Meadows

Massacre, including Colonel William Dame, Isaac C. Haight, and Philip Klingensmith. All held significant positions of leadership and responsibility within the church. Both Dame and Haight were stake presidents. Klingensmith was a bishop. Several of these men went into hiding with the help of church members and evaded arrest. At one point, the United States government posted a reward of $5,000 (more than $120,000 in today's money) for the capture of key massacre participants.

Only one man was ever indicted, tried, and convicted for his role in the massacre: John D. Lee.

Lee was executed by firing squad in 1877. In an unusual move, officers escorted Lee back to the Meadow, where he was killed in the very spot he had helped carry out the massacre of so many innocent lives. While Lee never denied his own guilt, he was vocal in his claims that he was a scapegoat meant to draw attention away from higher ranking leaders. His last words before he was executed in the Meadow were, *"I have been sacrificed in a cowardly, dastardly manner."*

While it's difficult to know who bore the most responsibility in the massacre, it's clear to me (and the firsthand accounts and narratives that are deemed credible by historians) that John D. Lee was a scapegoat for the many Mormon leaders who were involved. Particularly Apostle George A. Smith, Stake President Isaac C. Haight, Commanding Officer William Dame, John Higbee, and of course Brigham Young, whose response of *"The Indians, we expect, will do as they please,"* when asked for guidance about the ongoing siege in the Meadow, speaks volumes. While there is great debate about how much Brigham Young knew about the massacre, his violent teachings about "Blood Atonement," thundering sermons about rising against the United States with the "Lamanites," and efforts to stonewall investigations about the massacre are troubling, to say the least.

Years after the attack at Mountain Meadows, the U.S. Army marked the massacre site with a crudely constructed memorial to the dead that read, VENGEANCE IS MINE, AND I SHALL REPAY. When Brigham Young visited the massacre site years on a subsequent occasion, he ordered the memorial to be torn down and stated, *"Vengeance is mine, and I have taken a little."*

As for the lay members of the Mormon church who participated in the massacre, I found their stories both horrifying and incredibly sad. Some arrived on scene at the unfolding siege, summoned by their church leaders to bury bodies from an "Indian attack." When they arrived at the Meadow carrying shovels, they were then instructed to *"do their duty."*

There is only one account of a man who refused to participate. He was chained to a wagon wheel while the massacre commenced. John Higbee, who was instructed to shout "Halt!" as the code word for the killing to begin, initially failed to give the command at the decided time. He waited nearly a quarter of a mile past the agreed-upon ambush spot before finally giving the order. Historians suspect that the sight of so many women and children, grateful to be "rescued" right in front of him, was the understandable cause of his hesitation.

Many massacre participants were tormented until the day they died. On his deathbed, perpetrator Nephi Johnson, screamed *"Blood, blood, blood!"* When George Armstrong Hicks (who did not participate in the massacre) wrote to Brigham Young in 1867 (twelve years after the massacre) protesting that John D. Lee was still delivering sermons and being approved to marry additional wives, Brigham Young replied that the massacre was, *"None of [his] business ... that anyone reading [Hicks'] letter to [Brigham Young] would conclude that [Hicks] had taken part in the massacre, and if so he would advise [Hicks] to take a dose of rope around [his] neck."*

There's no way to deny that some strange things occurred while writing this book. Particularly when I became discouraged or overwhelmed by the weight of trying to craft a compelling, cohesive narrative that stayed true to the very real people who lived these events—many of whom have been relegated to a side note in history or forgotten altogether. Saleta Huff (Katrina in this story) was thirty-eight years old when she died in Mountain Meadows—the same age I was when I began writing this novel. That was part of the reason I chose her as a protagonist.

In the first sources I read about Saleta's family, she was misidentified as *"Saladia Huff, who had a son named William, two other unknown children, and a surviving daughter named Nancy."* I chose names for her unknown children in my notes for the sake of placeholders—Mary and James—then continued with my research. When I returned to dig deeper into Saladia's story, I found an updated source that named her correctly as Saleta Huff—and revealed the names of her unknown children: Mary and James. While these were common names at the time (which is why I chose them!) it felt less like a coincidence and more like a nudge to keep going.

That same day, I got a text notification from my bank, alerting me of a suspicious charge on my debit card—originating in Benton, Arkansas. Saleta's hometown. When I called my bank to learn more and cancel my card, the woman on the phone was confused. She could see that the text notification had been sent to my phone about the suspicious purchase, but there was no pending charge on my account. When I pressed her as to whether there would be a record of the charge if it had been attempted and then withdrawn, she insisted there would be. I asked her to check for this record. She put me on hold, then returned a few minutes later, baffled to find that no such record existed. She had no explanation for why the text had been sent.

Again and again, I had the distinct sensation of someone—maybe several someones—standing over my shoulder while I wrote. And as I wrote, I learned again and again that the America of the 1800s wasn't nearly as different from modern society as I'd always believed. The setting and the era was distinct, but the people were the same. Uncomfortably so.

During my research, I quickly learned that this was never going to be a story about angels and devils, villains and heroes. Those ugly, starkly drawn lines of us-versus-them are at the heart of this tragedy. And yet so is the will to survive, the drive to protect those we love even at great personal cost, and the strength to persist against seemingly impossible odds.

In the end, that is what I will choose to remember most about what happened at Mountain Meadows. The ones who chose humanity. The ones who chose love.

Even if it was the last choice they made.

— Noelle W. Ihli

P.S. If you'd like to hear the soundtrack for *None Left to Tell* (the songs that played in my head while I wrote this book) you can find it by scanning the QR code below:

LIST OF VICTIMS IN THE MOUNTAIN MEADOWS MASSACRE, BY FAMILY

Thank you to the Mountain Meadows Monument Foundation and Dr. Burr Fancher for their work in compiling this list.

Captain Alexander Fancher Family
- Alexander, 45
- Eliza, 32
- Hampton, 19
- William, 17
- Mary, 15
- Thomas, 14
- Martha, 10
- Margaret, 8
- Sarah, 8

John Twitty Baker Family
- John Twitty Baker, 52
- Abel Baker, 19

George W. Baker Family
- George, 27
- Minerva, 25
- Mary Lovina, 7
- Melissa Beller, 14
- David Beller, 12

Jesse Dunlap, Jr. Family
- Jesse, 39
- Mary, 39
- Ellender, 18

- Nancy, 16
- James, 14
- Lucinda, 12
- Susannah, 12
- Margerette, 11
- Mary Ann, 9

Lorenzo Dow Dunlap Family
- Lorenzo, 42
- Nancy, 42
- Thomas, 17
- John, 16
- Mary Ann, 13
- Talithia Emaline, 11
- Nancy, 9
- America Jane, 7

Milum & Newt Jones Family
- John Milum, 32
- Eloah Angeline, 27
- Newton, 23

Peter Huff Family
- Peter (died prior to massacre)
- Saleta, 38
- John, 14
- William, 13
- Mary, 11,
- James, 8

Charles & Joel Mitchell Family
- Charles, 25
- Sarah, 21
- Joel, 23
- Baby John

Allen Deshazo Family
- Allen Deshazo, 22

Pleasant Tackett Family
- Pleasant, 25
- Armilda

William Cameron Family
- William, 51
- Martha, 51
- Tillman, 24
- Isom, 18
- Henry, 16
- James, 14
- Martha, 11
- Larkin, 8
- Niece Nancy, 12

Cynthia Tackitt Family
- Cynthia, 49
- William, 23
- Marion, 20
- Sebron, 18
- Matilda, 16
- James, 14
- Jones, 12

Josiah Miller Family
- Josiah, 30
- Matilda, 26
- James, 9

Milum Rush Family
- Milum Rush, 28

Drovers and Bullwhackers
These young, single men were charged with caring for and driving the cattle.

- Alf Smith, age unknown
- George Basham, age unknown
- John Beach, 21

- Silas Edwards, age unknown
- Tom Farmer, age unknown
- John Prewit, 20
- William Prewit, 18
- James Matthew Fancher, 25
- Robert Fancher, 19
- Lawson A. McEntire, 21
- Poteet Brothers, ages unknown
- Charlie Stallcup, 25
- Richard Wilson, 27
- William Wood, 26
- Solomon Wood, 20

Surviving Children
- Elizabeth Baker, 5
- Sallie Baker, 3
- William Baker, 1
- Rebecca Dunlap, 6
- Louisa Dunlap, 4
- Sarah Dunlap, 1
- Prudence Dunlap, 5
- Georgiana Dunlap, 2
- Kit Carson Fancher, 5
- Triphenia Fancher, 2
- Felix Marion Jones, 2
- Nancy Huff, 4
- Milam Tackett, 4
- William Tackett, 2
- John Calvin Miller, 6
- Mary Miller, 4
- William T. Miller, 1

ACKNOWLEDGMENTS

Writing and researching this book has been a deeply emotional experience. I'm so grateful to everyone who has walked this path with me, offering their time, insights, perspective, and unique skills.

To Steph Nelson, Anna Gamel, Faith M. Gardner, Brett Mitchell Kent, Dan Blewitt, Nikki Hunter, Chelsea Robarge Fife, Lisa Butterworth, Jacob Robarts, Lisa Hunter, Caleb Stephens, and Jeanne Allen—thank you from the bottom of my heart. Your feedback was instrumental in shaping this novel. Each of you brought unique perspectives that helped me dig deeper into the characters, the story, and the emotions underpinning the novel. I'm profoundly lucky to have had your thoughts and encouragement along the way.

To Deborah J Ledford, who took this manuscript and elevated it so skillfully—thank you. Your keen eye and unique perspective as both a talented author of psychological suspense and a woman of indigenous heritage, brought so much clarity and polish to the story. I'm so appreciative of your dedication, kindness, and care in helping me refine this book.

A special thank you to Sarah Clark, who lent her expertise as a cultural consultant. Sarah, your guidance ensured that this story was shaped with the respect and authenticity it deserves. Your knowledge and sensitivity were invaluable, and I am so thankful for your input.

To Patti Geesey, thank you for your skilled proofreading. Your sharp eye caught those little things that slipped through the cracks, ensuring that this story was as clean and cohesive as possible.

And last, but not least, to Nate Ihli who listened to me exclaim at every other sentence in the different historical reference books I carried around with me for so many months, and believed in this project before I'd written a single word.

This novel wouldn't be what it is without all of you. Thank you for believing in this story—and in me. I'm endlessly grateful for your support and for the roles each of you played in bringing this book to life.

ABOUT THE AUTHOR

Noelle lives in Idaho with her husband, two sons, and two cats. When she's not plotting her next thriller, she's scaring herself with true-crime documentaries or going for a trail ride in the foothills (with her trusty pepper spray).

None Left to Tell is Noelle's sixth thriller-suspense novel. You can find her on Instagram @noelleihliauthor

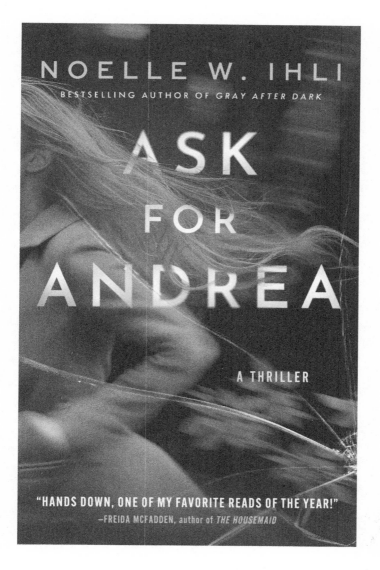

NOELLE W. IHLI

BESTSELLING AUTHOR OF *GRAY AFTER DARK*

ASK
FOR
ANDREA

A THRILLER

"HANDS DOWN, ONE OF MY FAVORITE READS OF THE YEAR!"
—FREIDA MCFADDEN, author of *THE HOUSEMAID*

1. MEGHAN

1 YEAR BEFORE

Despite the crushing weight of him, my brain screamed at me to run.

Run, it demanded as he grunted and pulled the scarf—my scarf —tighter around my neck.

Instead I lay frozen, like a mouse under a cat's paw, until the vise of pressure and pain suddenly released.

He looked at me for a few seconds as he got to his feet, his mouth turned down in disgust. He was breathing hard. His pale face hovered above me in the darkness, the distinctive mole on his cheek a stark punctuation mark.

He let the limp, pink-and-green scarf fall to the ground beside me.

Run, my brain roared again. *RUN!*

I still didn't move. I didn't even blink.

He turned toward the car he'd precariously parked on the shoulder of the rutted dirt road.

I could only imagine what he'd left in the trunk. But if I didn't move, I knew I'd find out.

So that's when I finally ran, bolting into the shadows of the pines that beckoned with hiding places, if not safety.

I scrambled down a steep embankment toward a dry stream bed, pushing myself faster and willing myself not to fall, no longer even conscious of the pain in my throat.

I wasn't sure where I was going. All I knew was that I needed to put as much distance as I could between myself and the spotless blue Kia Sorento. And more importantly, I needed to get away from the soft-spoken, fine-as-hell man who drove it: *The needle,* I'd called him when I told Sharesa about our upcoming date. As in, the needle in a deep haystack of bachelors on the MatchStrike app: divorced dads with kids, complicated custody agreements, and cringey gym-bathroom selfies.

Jimmy was different. With his dark amber eyes, a close-shaved beard along his angular jawline and a hard-part haircut, he was a dead ringer for Chris Hemsworth.

When I showed Sharesa his photo, she'd actually squealed.

I, on the other hand, had kept my expectations in check. I wasn't new to the online dating scene. I'd taken an Uber to Gracie's Spot in Salt Lake after my shift and braced to meet Chris Hemsworth's creepy cousin. I even texted Sharesa on my way. *Call me in an hour with an out?* I could see the text bubbles appear immediately after I hit send. *Whatever, you know you're thirsty.* I rolled my eyes. More bubbles. ... *I'll call <3.*

We talked in the back booth of Gracie's until last call at eleven. I texted Sharesa from the bathroom that there was no need to rescue me after all. She'd replied immediately, like always: *Thirrrrrsty.*

As I washed my hands, a paper sign taped to the bathroom mirror caught my attention. "On a date that isn't going well? Do you feel unsafe or just a little uneasy? Ask for Andrea at the bar. We'll make sure you get home safe." I smiled as I dried my hands, grateful I didn't need to ask. Not tonight. Not with him.

I stopped looking at the sign and studied myself in the mirror. I'd taken extra time with my hair, which I usually let fall in a blunt line across my shoulders. Earlier, I had coaxed it into waves that looked like spun gold in the restaurant lighting. I reapplied some of the deep pink lipstick that had become my signature accessory over the years and pressed my lips together, wondering if he'd kiss me later.

I had two beers over the course of the evening. Not enough to get me drunk or anything. Just enough to take the edge off my nerves. Because he did not in fact look like Chris Hemsworth's creepy cousin. He was thoughtful and funny. Even the large mole on his cheek somehow made him all the more attractive.

He drank ginger ale. It didn't faze me. I lived in Utah, after all.

The last thing I remember was feeling a little bit too warm. And really, really happy. The syrup-colored lights blazing in the trendy sputnik chandeliers suddenly had these little auras surrounding them. So when he suggested that I let him drive me home instead of waiting for an Uber in the cold, I didn't even hesitate.

The car had those crinkly paper covers on the seats, like it had just been cleaned.

That's the last thing I remember. Until I woke up with his hands—and my scarf—around my neck. The warm lights of Gracie's were gone, replaced with the bite of pine needles and dirt under my hair and the swirling dark of the freezing night air.

For a few seconds, I couldn't understand what was happening. I couldn't scream. I couldn't move. I couldn't even tell where I was. All I knew was that everything hurt.

The memory of our date crashed through the haze when I saw his eyes glinting above me. They weren't warm or even amber-colored anymore like they had been in the booth at Gracie's. These eyes were cold. Wide. And full of rage.

I thought about the sign in the bathroom at Gracie's. *Ask for Andrea.*

Andrea couldn't help me now. No one could.

I moved faster than I'd ever moved in my life, the pounding in my head and my chest and the crushing pressure of the scarf forgotten.

I didn't care where I was going. All that mattered was putting as much distance between us as possible, even if it meant running headlong into the looming woods.

I thought I heard someone call out as I dove down the rocky slope of the shallow stream bed. It sounded like a woman.

I ignored it and kept running.

He didn't follow me.

He didn't need to.

Because when I finally stopped running, I realized to my amazement that I wasn't out of breath.

Just as quickly, the amazement turned to horror.

I wasn't breathing hard because I wasn't breathing at all.